GW00322592

John Dunning

Booked To Die

A Mystery Introducing Cliff Janeway

POCKET BOOKS
New York London Toronto Sydney

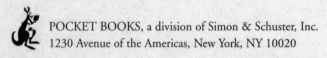 POCKET BOOKS, a division of Simon & Schuster, Inc.
1230 Avenue of the Americas, New York, NY 10020

ISBN: 0731813014

First Pocket Books trade paperback edition February 2005

10   9   8   7   6   5   4   3   2   1

POCKET and colophon are registered trademarks
of Simon & Schuster, Inc.

Printed and bound in Australia by Griffin Press

© istockphoto.com/rasmus rasmussen
© Kurhan. Image from BigStockPhoto.com
Cover Design: Sarah Barron

For information regarding special discounts for bulk purchases, please
contact Simon & Schuster Special Sales at 1-800-456-6798 or
business@simonandschuster.com.

Books by John Dunning

FICTION

"The Bookman" Novels
Booked to Die
The Bookman's Wake
The Bookman's Promise
The Sign of the Book

OTHER FICTION

Two O'Clock, Eastern Wartime
Deadline
Denver
Looking for Ginger North
The Holland Suggestions

NONFICTION

On the Air: The Encyclopedia of Old-Time Radio
Tune in Yesterday

IT'S ALL IN THE BOOKS . . .

National bestselling author

JOHN DUNNING

is

"A master yarn-spinner whose prose is so mesmerizing that you hate to come to the end of the tale."
—*Chicago Sun-Times*

and his thrillers are

"Mad, fantastical, and darkly original."
—*Kirkus Reviews*

BOOKED TO DIE

Winner of the Nero Wolfe Award

"No one . . . can fail to be delighted by the sort of folkloric advice Janeway carries with him."
—Boston Sunday Globe

"Fascinating. . . . Assured and muscular prose."
—San Francisco Chronicle

"Very credible. . . . An involved tale that satisfies the mystery reader's wants."
—United Press International

"Memorable. . . . Compelling. . . . Vividly realistic . . . fascinating and utterly convincing. . . . A suspenseful, well-crafted mystery."
—Mystery Scene

"A perfect mystery. It's intelligently written, the action is bafflingly logical; the reader learns something, and it's got a sucker punch of a finale."
—St. Petersburg Times (FL)

"Crisp, direct prose and pitch-perfect dialogue enhance this meticulously detailed page-turner."
—Publishers Weekly (starred review)

"An intriguing peek inside the antiquarian book business. . . . Book lovers will be fascinated."
—Houston Chronicle

THE BOOKMAN'S WAKE

A *New York Times* Notable Book of the Year

THE BOOKMAN'S PROMISE

"A thorough delight. . . . No crime writer has ever written more knowledgeably or more entertainingly about the world of rare books than John Dunning. . . . Impeccably plotted, with characters who spring to life and bits of arcana about Burton and the rare-book trade."

—Otto Penzler, *The New York Sun*

"A guaranteed high-five moment for suspense lovers. . . . As usual, Dunning throws out intriguing tidbits on book collecting. You will surely be inspired to buy one great, hellacious, killer book: Dunning's next novel."

—*Miami Herald*

"Bookman devotees should be overjoyed."

—*The Denver Post*

"Dunning and Janeway can't be beat."

—*The Clarion-Ledger* (Jackson, MS)

Also Available from Simon & Schuster Audio

"The combination of Burton the adventurer-author and Janeway the cop-bookseller is a match made in crime-fiction heaven."

—*Booklist*

"Endlessly inventive, exhilarating, and literate. Quite a knockout punch."

—*Kirkus Reviews*

Booked TO Die

Bobby the bookscout was killed at midnight on June 13, 1986. This was the first strange fact, leading to the question, *What was he doing out that late at night?* To Bobby, midnight was the witching hour and Friday the thirteenth was a day to be spent in bed. He was found in an alley under one of those pulldown iron ladders that give access to a fire escape—another odd thing. In life, Bobby would never walk under a ladder, so it would seem ironic to some people in the Denver book trade when they heard in the morning that he had died there.

You should know something about bookscouts and the world they go around in. This is an age when almost everyone scouts for books. Doctors and lawyers with six-figure incomes prowl the thrift stores and garage sales, hoping to pick up a treasure for pennies on the dollar. But the real bookscout, the pro, has changed very little in the last thirty years. He's a guy who can't make it in the real world. He operates out of the trunk of a car, if he's lucky enough to have a car, out of a knapsack or a bike bag if he isn't. He's an outcast, a fighter, or a man who's been driven out of every other line of work. He can be quiet and humble or aggressive and intimidating. Some are renegades and, yes, there are a few psychos. The one thing the best of them have in common is an eye for books. It's almost spooky, a pessimistic book dealer once said—the nearest thing you can think of to prove the existence of God. How these guys, largely uneducated, many unread, gravitate toward books and inevitably choose the good ones is a prime mystery of human nature.

They get their stock in any dusty corner where books are sold cheap, ten cents to a buck. If they're lucky they'll find $100 worth on any given day, for which an honest book dealer will pay them $30 or $40. They stand their own expenses and may come out of the day $30 to the good. They live for the prospect of the One Good Book, something that'll bring $200 or more. This happens very seldom, but it happens. It happened to Bobby Westfall more often than to all the others put together.

In one seventy-two-hour period, the story goes, Bobby turned up the following startling inventory: *Mr. President,* the story of the Truman administration, normally a $6 book unless it's signed by Truman, which this was, under an interesting page-long inscription, also in Truman's hand—call it $800 easy; *The Recognitions,* the great cornerstone of modern fiction (or the great unreadable novel, take your pick) by William Gaddis, also inscribed, $400 retail; *The Magus,* John Fowles's strange and irresistible book of wonder, first British edition in a flawless jacket, $300; and *Terry's Texas Rangers,* a thin little book of ninety-odd pages that happens to be a mighty big piece of Texas history, $750. Total retail for the weekend, $2,000 to $2,500; Bobby's wholesale cut, $900, a once-in-a-lifetime series of strikes that people in the Denver book trade still talk about.

If it was that easy, everybody'd be doing it. Usually Bobby Westfall led a bleak, lonely life. He took in cats, never could stand to pass up a homeless kitty. Sometimes he slept in unwashed clothes, and on days when pickings weren't so good, he didn't eat. He spent his $900 quickly and was soon back to basics. He had a ragged appearance and a chronic cough. There were days when he hurt inside: his eyes would go wide and he'd clutch himself, a sudden pain streaking across his insides like a comet tearing up the summer sky. He was thirty-four years old, already an old man at an age when life should just begin.

He didn't drive. He packed his books from place to place on his back, looking for a score and a dealer who'd treat him right. Some of the stores were miles apart, and often you'd see Bobby trudging up East Colfax Avenue, his knees buckling under the weight. His turf was the Goodwill store on Colfax and Havana, the DAV thrift shop on Montview Boulevard, and the dim-lit antique stores along South Broadway, where people think they know books. Heaven to Bobby the Bookscout was finding a sucker who thought he knew more than he knew, a furniture peddler or a dealer in glass who also thought he knew books. On South Broadway, in that particular mindset, the equation goes like this: old + bulk = value. An antique dealer would slap $50 on a worthless etiquette book from the 1880s and let a true $150 collectible like Anne Tyler's *Celestial Navigation* go for a quarter. When that happened, Bobby Westfall would be there with his quarter in hand, with a poker face and a high heart. He'd eat very well tonight.

Like all bookscouts, Bobby could be a pain in the ass. He was a born-again Christian: he'd tell you about Christ all day long if you'd stand still and listen. There was gossip that he'd been into dope years ago, that he'd done some hard time. People said that's where he found the Lord, doing five-to-ten at Canon City. None of that mattered now. He was a piece of the Denver book world, part of the landscape, and the trade was a little poorer for his death.

He had been bludgeoned, battered into the bookscout's hereafter by a heavy metal object. According to the coroner, Bobby had felt no pain: he never knew what hit him. The body was found facedown in the alley, about three blocks from the old *Denver Post*. A cat was curled up at his feet, as if waiting for Bobby to wake up and take her home.

This is the story of a dead man, how he got that way, and what happened to some other people because of his death.

He was a gentle man, quiet, a human mystery.

He had no relatives, no next of kin to notify. He had no close friends, but no enemies either.

His cats would miss him.

No one could think of a reason why anyone would kill Bobby. Who would murder a harmless man like that?

I'll tell you why. Then I'll tell you who.

Book 1

1

The phone rang. It was 2:30 A.M.

Normally I am a light sleeper, but that night I was down among the dead. I had just finished a thirteen-hour shift, my fourth day running of heavy overtime, and I hadn't been sleeping well until tonight. A guy named Jackie Newton was haunting my dreams. He was my enemy and I thought that someday I would probably have to kill him. When the bell went off, I was dreaming about Jackie Newton and our final showdown. For some reason—logic is never the strong point of a dream like that—Jackie and I were in the hallway at East High School. The bell brought the kids out for the change of classes; Jackie started shooting and the kids began to drop, and that bell kept ringing as if it couldn't stop.

In the bed beside me, Carol stirred.

"Oh, Cliff," she groaned. "Would somebody please get that goddamn telephone?"

I groped for the night table, felt the phone, and knocked the damn thing to the floor. From some distant galaxy I could hear the midget voice of Neal Hennessey, saying,

"Cliff? . . . Cliff? . . . Hey, Clifford!" I reached along the black floor and found the phone, but it was still many seconds later before Hennessey took on his bearlike image in my mind.

"Looks like we got another one," Hennessey said without preamble.

I struggled to sit up, trying to get used to the idea that Jackie Newton hadn't shot me after all.

"Hey, Cliffie . . . you alive yet?"

"Yeah, Neal, sure. First time I been sound asleep in a week."

He didn't apologize; he just waited.

"Where you at?" I said.

"Alley off Fifteenth, just up from the *Denver Post.* This one looks an awful lot like the others."

"Give me about half an hour."

"We'll be here."

I sat for another minute, then I got up and went into the bathroom. I turned on the light and looked in the mirror and got the first terrifying look at myself in the cold hard light of the new day. You're getting old, Janeway, I thought. Old Andrew Wyeth could make a masterpiece out of a face like that. Call it *Clifford Liberty Janeway at thirty-six, with no blemish eliminated and no character line unexplored.*

I splashed cold water on my face: it had a great deal less character after that. To finally answer Hennessey, yes, I was almost alive again. The vision of Jackie Newton rose up before me and my hand went automatically to the white splash of scar tissue just under my right shoulder. A bank robber had shot me there five years ago. I knew Jackie Newton would give a lot to put in another one, about three inches to the left and an inch or so down.

Man with an old bullet wound, by Wyeth: an atypical work, definitely not your garden-variety Helga picture.

When I came out of the bathroom Carol was up. She had boiled water and had a cup of instant coffee steaming on my nightstand.

"What now?" she said.

As I struggled into my clothes, I told her it looked like another derelict murder. She sighed loudly and sat on the bed.

She was lovely even in a semistupor. She had long auburn hair and could probably double for Helga in a pinch. No one but Wyeth would know.

"Would you like me to come with you?"

I gave a little laugh, blowing the steam from my coffee.

"Call it moral support," she said. "Just for the ride down and back. Nobody needs to see me. I could stay in the car."

"Somebody would see you, all right, and then the tongues would start. It'd be all over the department by tomorrow."

"You know something? I don't even care."

"I care. What we do in our own time is nobody's business."

I went to the closet and opened it. Our clothes hung there side by side—the blue uniform Carol had worn on yesterday's shift; my dark sport coat; our guns, which had become as much a part of the wardrobe as pants, shirts, ties, badges. I never went anywhere without mine, not even to the corner store. I had had a long career for a guy thirty-six: I'd made my share of enemies, and Jackie Newton was only the latest.

I put the gun on under my coat. I didn't wear a tie, wasn't about to at that time of night. I was off duty and I'd just been roused from a sound sleep; I wasn't running for city council, and I hated neckties.

John Dunning

"I know you've been saying that for a long time now, that stuff about privacy," Carol said dreamily. "But I think the real reason is, if people know about me, I make you vulnerable."

I didn't want to get into it. It was just too early for a philosophical discourse. There was something in what Carol said, but something in what I said too. I've never liked office gossip, and I didn't want people talking about her and me.

But Carol had been looking at it from another angle lately. We had been seeing each other, in the polite vernacular, for a year now, and she was starting to want something more permanent. Maybe bringing our arrangement into the public eye would show me how little there was to worry about. People did it all the time. For most of them the world didn't come to an end. Occasionally something good came out of it.

So she thought.

"I'm going back to bed," she said. "Wake me when you come in. Maybe I'll have a nice surprise for you."

She lay back and closed her eyes. Her hair made a spectacular sunburst on the pillow. I sat for a while longer, sipping my coffee. There wasn't any hurry: a crime lab can take three hours at the scene. I'd leave in five minutes and still be well within the half hour I'd promised Hennessey. The trouble is, when I have dead time—even five minutes unfilled in the middle of the night—I begin to think. I think about Carol and me and all the days to come. I think about the job and all the burned-out gone-forever days behind us. I think about quitting and I wonder what I'd do. I think about being tied to someone and anchoring those ties with children.

Carol would not be a bad one to do that with. She's

pretty and bright, and maybe this is what love is. She's good company: her interests broaden almost every day. She reads three books to my one, and I read a lot. We talk far into the night. She still doesn't understand the first edition game: Hemingway, she says, reads just as well in a two-bit paperback as he does in a $500 first printing. I can still hear myself lecturing her the first time she said that. Only a fool would read a first edition. Simply having such a book makes life in general and Hemingway in particular go better when you do break out the reading copies. I listened to myself and thought, This woman must think I'm a government-inspected horse's ass. Then I showed her my Faulkners, one with a signature, and I saw her shiver with an almost sexual pleasure as she touched the paper where he'd signed it. Faulkner was her most recent god, and I had managed to put together a small but respectable collection of his first editions. You've got to read this stuff, she said to me when she was a month deep in his work. How can you collect the man without ever reading what he's written? In fact, I had read him, years ago: I never could get the viewpoints straight in *The Sound and the Fury,* but I had sense enough at sixteen to know that the problem wasn't with Faulkner but with me. I was trying to work up the courage to tackle him again: if I began to collect him, I reasoned, I'd have to read him sooner or later. Carol shook her head. Look at it this way, I said, the Faulkners have appreciated about twenty percent in the three years I've owned them. That she understood.

My apartment looked like an adjunct of the Denver Public Library. There were wall-to-wall books in every room. Carol had never asked the Big Dumb Question that people always ask when they come into a place like this: *Jeez, d'ya read all these?* She browsed, fascinated. The books have a loose logic to their shelving: mysteries in the bed-room; novels out here; art books, notably by the Wyeths, on the far wall. There's no discrimination—they are all first editions—and when people try to go highbrow on me, I love reminding them that my as-new copy of Raymond Chandler's *Lady in the Lake* is worth a cool $1,000 today, more than a bale of books by most of the critically acclaimed and already forgotten so-called masters of the art-and-beauty school. There's nothing wrong with writing detective stories if you do it well enough.

I've been collecting books for a long time. Once I killed two men in the same day, and this room had an almost immediate healing effect.

I've missed my calling, I thought. But now was probably years too late to be thinking about it.

Time to go.

"Cliff?"

Her eyes were still closed, but she was not quite asleep.

"I'm leaving now," I said.

"You going out to see Jackie Newton?"

"If this is what it looks like, you better believe it."

"Have Neal watch your flank. And both of you be careful."

I went over and kissed her on the temple. Two minutes later I was in my car, gliding through the cool Denver night.

2

I crossed the police line and walked into the alley. The body was about thirty yards in. Strobe lights had been set up and pictures taken. The lights were still on for the benefit of the sketcher, and the narrow canyon was ablaze. The sketcher stood at the edge of things, working with a pencil and clipboard while two assistants checked measurements with a tape. The coroner had arrived only a short time before me, but an assistant coroner had been there for more than an hour. The two men stood over the body talking. I didn't interrupt: just hung back and watched. Hennessey appeared out of the gloom with two cups of coffee. I took mine and he filled me in on what little he knew. Police had responded to an anonymous call at 1:32 A.M.: report of a dead man, which checked out affirmative. Officers arrived at 1:37: homicide detectives had been sent over and the crime lab summoned. Then, because the case strongly resembled a series of such apparently random derelict murders, Hennessey had been called. Hennessey was my partner, and he called me. We had been working that chain of cases for two years; if this one fit the pattern, it would become ours.

There had been no one to interview at the scene. The caller, who was described by the dispatcher as a white-sounding male, probably under fifty, had hung up when asked for his name. Later we'd want to listen to a tape of that conversation, but I didn't have much hope for it. Chances were we'd never find the guy because, chances were, he was just someone who had stumbled over the body and didn't want to get involved.

The scene itself wasn't a good bet for evidence. The alley was narrow and paved. On one side was an old department store; on the other, an old hotel. The walls of the hotel were red brick, worn smooth by many years. The department store had a fake marble facade, which continued into the alley to just about the place where the body lay. Orange powder had been dusted on both sides, and it looked like they'd come up with some prints. In all probability they'd turn out to be everyone but the mayor of Denver and the guy we wanted.

That was all we had. That was all we ever had. The first murdered bum had been found in an alley much like this one two years and two months ago, April 1984. His head had been kicked in. There had been three more that year and two the next, all the same general method of operation: a helluva beating, then death. The guy's hatred for street people, winos, and the homeless seemed compulsive. Hennessey thought he might be a skinhead, one of those jerks with a brownshirt mentality and an irresistible need to take out society's lower elements. I thought his motives were simpler. He was a sadist: he didn't care who he killed, as long as he got his little shot of violence when he needed it. Street people were easy marks, so he did street people. If you murder women and children, society will try to track you down, but the best effort society gives the killer of a bum is a quick shuffle. Time is fleeting and manpower limited: we do what we can, and sometimes a killer gets away because we can't do enough.

It turned out Neal and I were both right. The guy we'd fingered for all these jobs was Jackie Newton, ex-con, refugee from the coast, a real sweetheart in anybody's book. Jackie wasn't a skinhead but he might as well have been: his mind worked the same way. We now knew all about his sadistic streak. Jackie hated everybody who didn't think, act, and look just like him. He particularly hated people whose personal, racial, or intellectual characteristics could be summed up in one cruel gutteral word. Queers, freaks, spics, shines, gooks, dopes—Jackie hated them all, twenty-four hours a day. And let us not forget cops. Pigs. Jackie was a product of the sixties, and pigs were the group he hated most of all.

The feeling was absolutely mutual on my part. There's something in the book, I know, about a cop keeping his feelings out of his work. If detection is a science, which I believe, it should probably be done with unfettered intellect, but God damn it, I wanted Jackie Newton dead or locked away forever. Don't tell me it shouldn't be personal: we were way beyond that little phase of drawing room etiquette, Jackie and I. I had been working on him two years and was no closer to putting him away than I was when I first heard his name, almost three years ago.

He had blown into town, broke, in 1983. Today he was involved in two $30 million shopping center deals and owned property all over the city. There are guys who have a streak of genius for generating money, and Jackie, I will admit grudgingly, was one of them. He owned an estate in undeveloped Jefferson County, where he lived alone and liked it, and reportedly he was connected to what passes in Denver for the mob. This alone brought him to our attention before we learned that he murdered drunks for a hobby. It was a strange case that way: we knew who the killer was before the first victim was killed. A cop in Santa Monica told us not to be surprised by a sudden rise in derelict deaths. This had happened in California and in Newark, where Jackie lived fifteen years ago. We knew before the fact what Newark knew, what Santa Monica knew, and we still couldn't stop it and we couldn't prove it once it had started. It had almost seemed too pat, and we went through a phase of exploring other ideas—the skinhead, the unknown sadist—before we learned, without a doubt, that Jackie was our boy.

In the killing of Harold Brubaker, we'd had a witness. Jesus, you never saw such a beating, our boy had said: this guy has sledgehammers in his fists and what he does with his feet . . . it's like something inhuman. The witness was a highly credible young man who had watched from a dark doorway less than ten feet away: a kid working overtime who had stepped out for a smoke and seen it all. It was like Providence was suddenly in our corner. A light had come on and Jackie had looked straight up at it. The kid had seen him clearly, not a doubt in the world. I had the son of a bitch where I wanted him at last. I brought Jackie in and ran him through a lineup. The kid had no trouble picking him out: he was a first-rate witness all the way. I did everything according to Hoyle and the Miranda ruling: the last thing I wanted was for the bastard to slide on tainted evidence or technical bullshit. We threw a protective shield around the witness, for Jackie had friends in slimy places, but what can I say? Things happen . . . court dates get postponed, his attorneys drag it out, weeks become months, and in all that time there's bound to be a breach. They got to our boy, and when they were done he had no heart for testifying against anybody. They never put a hand on him, but they sure made him see things their way. He stammered in court, he hesitated, he wasn't sure . . . and the case against Jackie Newton went down the drain.

Jackie had been quiet since then: we had scared him with Harold Brubaker and he had been lying low. Now he was starting up again, and I'd bet there'd be another one before long. Success breeds success. There's nothing worse than a cunning killer who strikes down people he doesn't know, for no reason other than a blood lust.

3

I waited until the coroner was finished, then I moved in for a look at the body. They had turned him over, and he lay on the pavement with his arms crossed gently over his chest. He looked like he might get up and walk away. His eyes were closed and he had the unwashed, unshaved look they all had. But there was something different about this one, something vaguely familiar, as if I had known him once, long ago.

"What can you tell us, Georgie?" I said.

The coroner, a spectacled man in his fifties, spoke while his assistant looked on.

"It's a lot like the others, but there are some significant differences. As you can see, the victim is a guttersnipe, body not well nourished, white male, probably mid-thirties, five foot seven inches, hundred fifty, sixty pounds. Murder weapon was a heavy blunt instrument, a pipe wrench or a crescent wrench or some steel tool would be my guess. The victim was hit twice in the center of the rear

18

cranium, once for business and once for good measure. There was no doubt in the mind of the killer what the objective was. I think the first one did it—we'll know more in the morning. Time of death was within the last three hours."

"Call came in about one-thirty," Hennessey said.

"He had probably been dead a little over an hour then," the coroner said.

I looked at the face of the dead man and again felt that disquieting rumble deep in my brain.

"There's some evidence he was killed somewhere else, then dumped here," the coroner said.

"That's new," Hennessey said.

"What evidence?" I asked.

"I think there's a good deal of blood unaccounted for," the coroner said. "Again, we'll know more in the morning, but let's say I'm about eighty percent sure. That pipe really opened his head up. A wound like that will bleed like a geyser, but this one didn't, or, if it did, where's the blood? This little puddle's just leakage, as if the heart had stopped some time prior to his being put here. I think that's what happened. Somebody did this man in somewhere else, then dropped him here."

"Any signs of a beating?"

The coroner gave me a look. "You don't consider this a beating?"

"I mean injuries to other parts of the body . . . indications that he was beaten severely before he was killed."

"Nothing so far. Looks like he was hit twice and that's that."

I shook my head. "I've seen this guy somewhere. I can't make him."

Hennessey asked the coroner if they had a name. The

coroner looked at his notes and said, "The deceased had no driver's license. There was a fragment of a social security card. Most of the number had worn away, but we were able to get a name. Robert B. Westfall."

The name clicked. "Yeah, I know him," I said. "He's a bookscout."

"A what?"

"A guy that hunts for books. That's where I've seen him, selling books in the neighborhood stores."

"I always heard you were the intellectual type, Janeway," the coroner said.

"Is that what you hear?" I said dryly.

"It's a small world, my friend, and the night has a thousand eyes."

"You've been observed reading books again, Clifford," Hennessey said. "I guess I'm the man of action on this team."

I turned my attention back to the corpse. The coroner hung over my shoulder like a scarecrow. I was trying to place the guy, to remember where and when I had last seen him.

"In the bookstores they call him Bobby the Bookscout," I said. "He was pretty good, from what I hear."

"How does a bum get to be good at something like that?" the coroner asked.

"They're not bums in the usual sense. Most of 'em work like hell, don't drink, and stay out of trouble."

"What about the ones that don't like to work, do drink, and don't stay out of trouble?" Hennessey said.

"I guess there are some of those."

"I don't know much about this kinda stuff," Hennessey said. "You tell me, Cliff. Could one of these boys find something, say a book, since that's what they look for, that's so valuable another one might kill him for it? And where does that leave us with Jackie Newton?"

"I'll let you boys hash that out," the coroner said. "Call me tomorrow."

"Thanks, George."

We stood for a moment after the coroner had left. Hennessey's questions kept running through my mind. I felt a pang of disappointment that Jackie Newton might slide on this one for the plain and simple reason that he hadn't done it.

"Cliff?"

"Yeah, Neal. Just give me a minute."

I watched them cover the body and take it away. The sketcher had left and the lab men were packing up: the sad saga of Bobby the Bookscout was just about over. All that was left was the hunt for his killer.

"We sure can't rule out the possibility of Jackie," I said.

Hennessey didn't say anything.

"Let's go see the son of a bitch," I said.

"I'll call Jeffco."

As peace officers, we were empowered to investigate and arrest anywhere in the state of Colorado. Usual procedure when you went out of your jurisdiction was to take an officer from that district along, in case something happened. Thirty minutes later we had arrived at the Jefferson County Sheriff's Department, where Officer Ben Nasses was waiting for us. Officer Nasses was young and articulate, one of the new breed. He was also very black. Jackie Newton would love him.

Jackie lived in an expensive villa a few miles south of the town of Morrison. He wasn't quite in the mountains, but the house was perched at the top of a bluff where you could see most of Denver and the front range south, halfway to Colorado Springs. We pulled into the driveway. The house was dark, with no sign of life. I had a sinking feeling that we'd find Jackie Newton asleep, that he'd been asleep all night. I had the feeling, not for the first time, that I'd never be able to make him on anything.

But Jackie wasn't home. Nasses rang the bell three times and knocked, but no one came. "What now?" he said. I told him we would wait, if he had nothing better to do, and he said that was fine. "I'd like for us not to be visible when he comes home," I said, and Hennessey went to move the car on down the street. By the time Neal came back, Nasses and I had moved off the step and onto a gravel walkway that skirted the house. Hennessey was nervous. "I don't think we want to mess around here, Cliff," he said. He had been my partner for a long time; he knew all about my impatience with oppressive procedure, and he also knew how much I wanted to put Jackie away. Don't be stupid— that's what Neal was saying. But I was very much aware of the rules of evidence. I had never had a case thrown out because I was weak in court, and Hennessey knew that too. Sometimes you play by the book, sometimes you had to take a chance.

"I'm going to take a look in the garage," I said.

Hennessey whimpered but stayed with me. I moved around the house. "You boys're crazy," Nasses called. He wasn't going anywhere. Hennessey tugged at me in the dark. "Cliff, the kid's right. This makes no sense. Even if you find something you won't be able to use it. Let's get out of here."

"If I find something, I'll find a way to use it."

"The bastard's liable to come rolling in here any minute."

"Then let's do it quick."

The garage was locked but that was no problem: I had it open in less than half a minute. There were two vehicles inside, a Caddy and a Jeep four-wheel. There was an empty space for the third car, the one Jackie Newton was now driving.

I felt the hood of each car, then went through the glove compartments. There was just the usual junk—papers, ownership, registration. John Randolph Newton was listed as the owner of both vehicles, but I knew that. I knew where and when he had bought them, that he'd bought the Jeep on time, paid it off in six months, and paid cash for the Cadillac. I knew the salesmen who had dealt with him. *A real laid-back guy,* one salesman had said, *a pussycat.* Money wasn't anything to a guy like Jackie: he had made, lost, and made again three times over more money than those boys would see in their whole lives. That's one thing you could say for Jackie Newton: he was free with his money, and salesmen loved him.

There was an unpaid ticket on the seat of the Caddy. I took down the information. Jackie had been tagged for speeding—fifty-five in a twenty-five, a four-pointer. This was good news: the last time I'd looked at his record he had had nine points against his license. Jackie liked to drive fast, and it was costing him. I knew he hadn't paid the ticket because of the points: he'd have his lawyer go in and plead it down, try to get two points knocked off in the city attorney's office before it ever got to a judge. A word from me in the ear of the city attorney might not be out of order. Anything that hassled Jackie Newton was a good use of my time. From little things big things grow. Get Jackie's license suspended and I knew he'd drive anyway. Then I could bust him for something bigger. Al Capone never got indicted for murder, just tax evasion, but it was enough.

I put everything back the way it was. Hennessey was standing at the door, the man of action watching for headlights. I looked along the shelves. There were paint cans,

23

tools, boxes of screws, all meticulously in their places. Jackie Newton was a neat man: the compulsively neat killer.

"Cliff," Hennessey said. His voice fluttered in his throat.

"All right," I said. "There's nothing here."

I turned off the lights and locked the door. We started across the yard but a vision brought me up short. I thought I saw a body hanging from a tree. It was one of those sights that makes you wonder if your eyes are getting old. "Look at that," I said, but Hennessey still didn't see. I took out a penlight and cut across the lawn, and slowly the thing came into focus. It was a dog, the Doberman, hung by the neck like some western desperado. "It's Bruno," I said numbly. Again I realized what an obsession Jackie Newton and I had become to each other: I knew everything about the guy, even the name of his dog. Supposedly, Jackie had loved the dog: the only thing Jackie Newton had ever been said to love. This was what happened if he loved you: you didn't ever want to give him cause to hate you, as I had.

"Looks like somebody's got it in for Jackie," Hennessey said.

"I don't think so, Neal. I think he did it himself."

I was playing my light around the barbecue grill, which had been turned over and spilled. There was a half-eaten steak in the grass, many hours old. The steak had been chewed as if by an animal. Beside it were two upset plates. "I'll tell you what happened here," I said, "you tell me how it sounds. Jackie had been entertaining somebody— probably a woman since there were just the two of 'em. Something happened to take him away for a minute . . . maybe the phone had rung . . . but something made him go inside. When he came back, the dog had turned over the grill and eaten one of the steaks and was starting on the other. Jackie went into a rage. We've seen him in action, we know how he can be. He strung the poor bastard up with the clothesline. Then he did what he always does when he gets like that. Took his fastest car, the Lamborghini, and went out for a drive. That's where he's been tonight, out in the country driving at a hundred and fifty miles an hour."

"You could make me buy that," Hennessey said.

"Then I'll tell you what else he did. He couldn't get rid of it, the rage just wouldn't go away. Nothing worked. He hated killing that dog, hated himself for doing it, so he went downtown and killed the bookscout. Somebody he didn't know or care about . . . just an outlet for all that murderous energy. That's why the bookscout wasn't beaten before he was killed: that's why he was different from all the others. Jackie didn't do this one for pleasure, he did it because he needed to."

"I don't know about that part," Hennessey said.

"What's the matter with it?" I snapped.

"For one thing, you want it too much. You want it to fit, Cliff. I know where you're coming from with Jackie Newton, you'd pin the goddamn Kennedy assassination on Jackie if you thought you could make it stick."

"It does fit," I said impatiently. "It fits, Neal."

Hennessey didn't say any more, which was probably a good thing. We didn't touch the dog except to confirm that it had been dead for some time. It was very stiff. Its eyes were open. If a dog's face can show feelings, this one showed shock, sadness, and, finally, disbelief. Its front paws had been clawing the air and had finally come to rest, frozen there, in a posture much like a man in prayer. I had to fight an impulse to cut it down. Hennessey was right: we had no warrant, no authority, no right to be here. This was very bad police work. The dog didn't exist for us, even assuming that it might be relevant to our case, until we established some proper groundwork.

We had pushed luck about as far as it can go. We went around to the front of the house, where Officer Nasses again told us his opinion, no offense intended, that we were out of our minds. I still wanted to be here when Jackie came rolling in: I wanted to see what time it was, how he looked, what his car looked like. I wanted to see as much as possible of what he did, what the state of his mind was. I put Hennessey and Nasses out front, in the trees across the road, and I went around to watch the back. This could be a very long wait. Jackie might be in Wyoming by now: that's the kind of state a Lamborghini was made for, empty roads and wide-open spaces and cops who didn't care how fast you went. He might be gone for a week.

So I'd wait. If the wait got too long, I'd let Hennessey and Nasses go in, but I would stay. Jackie Newton was turning me into an eccentric. I had a disturbing vision of myself waiting here for days, then weeks, into the changing seasons, my beard coming in, my clothes becoming tattered and worn, Hennessey bringing me food and water once a day. I was like Fred Dobbs in *The Treasure of the Sierra Madre:* I had started out a sane and decent man and slowly the obsession had turned me crazy. I looked at my watch: the sky was getting light in the east. Sanity came with the dawn. I'd give him till eight o'clock, nine at the latest, then I'd go in and catch him later. Hennessey was right again: I had nothing on Jackie. It didn't fit, the pattern was broken. For once, Jackie Newton wasn't my man.

I snuffed that thought fast. One of my problems was beginning to resolve itself. In another twenty minutes it would be daylight: then, I thought, we could see the dog from the road. That would make it legitimate discovery, as long as Jackie didn't find out that we'd been here earlier. I wasn't going to tell him. Hennessey wasn't. Nasses was the unknown factor. I gave up the idea of confronting Jackie as he stepped from his car. I decided to do it by the book from here on out. I would join the boys in the bushes across the road. When Jackie did come home, we'd go get the car and pull up in front and ring his doorbell, as proper as Emily Post.

Let the fun begin, I thought.

4

We waited almost another hour before Jackie
came home. We heard him first—the squeal of the tires,
the angry, impatient growl of the engine. "Helluva way to
treat a car like that," Hennessey said. The Lamborghini
roared past in a swirl of dust. It made the turn and went
behind the house and into the garage. Jackie came out,
looking as he had the first time I'd seen him, like some plastic hero from Muscle Beach. He was a serious bodybuilder:
his arms looked like a pair of legs, his chest like a fifty-
gallon drum. He had grown himself a mustache and he
needed a haircut. The image was formidable, a guy you
don't mess with. He stopped for a moment and looked at
the dog, and the anger began again. "Get out of that car!"
he shouted, and the woman peeped meekly through the
open garage door. "Come on, come on!" Jackie said. She
was none too happy about it: I could see that even from
where we crouched in the bushes. Jackie grabbed her by the
scruff of the neck and pushed her toward the house. They
disappeared inside.

We waited. Nothing happened.

"Looks like the ball's in our court," Hennessey said.

"Yeah. Let's go see the son of a bitch."

We walked down the road to the car; then we drove back and turned into Jackie Newton's drive, three officers of the law, proper to the bone. We stepped out and started up the walk. You could see the dog even from there, swinging grotesquely from the tree.

"Jesus, look at that," Nasses said. "You boys see that last night?"

"See what?" I said.

Nasses gave a dry laugh. "Play it that way, then. I'll help if I can."

"Translate it for us, Nasses."

"Don't ask me to lie to cover your ass. I won't volunteer anything, but don't ask me to lie."

"Ring the doorbell," I said.

I had my badge pinned to my belt, like some cop on a TV show. I was pumped up: I always was when I was about to face Jackie. I heard him coming. The door opened and he filled the space.

"Mr. Newton?" Nasses said.

Jackie had seen me right off. He looked straight through Nasses and locked eyes with me. He probably didn't even notice yet that Nasses was black.

"I'm Officer Nasses, Jeffco Sheriff's Department. These gentlemen are from the Denver police. They'd like to ask you a few questions."

His eyes cut to my badge. Nasses had taken a little involuntary step to one side. There was nothing between Jackie Newton and me but two feet of violent air.

"Hello, Jackie," I said.

"What the fuck do you want, Janeway?"

"You must be having trouble with your ears. The man just told you, I want to ask you a few questions."

"You arresting me for something?"

"Maybe."

"Go fuck yourself. Bust me right now or come back with a warrant."

"How do you know I don't have a warrant?"

"If you did you'd use it. Go away, you're wasting my time."

He started to close the door. I stepped past Nasses and put my foot in it. I started reading him his rights, thinking maybe it would throw him off, buy me a minute. At least if he slipped and said something, we'd be protected.

He listened, uncertain.

"Where were you last night?" I said.

"I drove out on the plains. I was gone all night and, yeah, I had company. I got an alibi for any goddamn thing you want to dream up about last night."

"Where's your alibi, Newton? I want to see him."

"Her, flatfoot, her . . . my alibi's a girl."

"Bring her down."

"Come back with a warrant."

Again he tried to close the door. Again I put my foot in it.

"I told you, Newton, you've got the right to remain silent. That doesn't mean you can keep me from a witness. Now bring the girl down here or I'll have your ass in jail for obstruction of justice."

It was a bluff and I figured Jackie would know it. He didn't know it, not for sure. He went and got the girl, who actually was a woman in her late twenties.

He had slapped her at least three times: there were that many distinct welts on her face. In another day she'd look like she'd been face-first through a gauntlet.

"Would you step outside, miss?"

She did. She was blond, and might've been pretty in a glassy kind of way. She wasn't pretty now.

"What's your name?"

"You haven't got to tell him one fucking thing," Jackie Newton said. There was an implication in his voice that she'd better not.

"What's your name, miss?"

"Barbara."

"Do you need help?"

She looked confused, scared.

"We can take you out of here if you want to go," I said.

"She doesn't want to go anywhere with you, cop," Jackie Newton said.

"Miss?" I tried for eye contact, but I couldn't get a rise out of her. "Did this jerk beat you up?"

"She ran into a door," Jackie Newton said.

"You'd better get that door fixed, Newton. Looks like she ran into it three or four times."

"She ran into a goddamn door, okay? You want to make something out of that?"

"Miss," I said, "do you want to go with us?"

"I don't know," she said shakily.

"We could go over to the car and talk it over. Come on, let's do that."

"She's going nowhere with you, cop."

"Don't pay any attention to that," I said. "If you want to go, you go. Fatso's got nothing to say about it."

I knew that would get to him. He balled up his fists and said, "I'll show you fat, motherfucker. Take off your badge and I'll beat your fuckin' head in."

I gave him a bitter, pathetic smile, the kind you'd give a talking worm. I kept looking at him the whole time I was

31

talking to her. "I want you to be very sure, miss, what your options are. It's all up to you. If this jerk beat you up, you can file charges against him. He can do some good time for that. Maybe when he gets out he won't feel so frisky."

"I've had about enough of this shit," Jackie Newton said.

"I don't think so, Newton. You and me, we've got a long way to go with each other."

"You wanna go now, Janeway? You wanna go now, huh? What do you say, cop, just you and me, bare hands, an old-fashioned fight to the finish."

"I see you've been reading comic books again, Jackie. I wish I could accommodate you, I really do. You could show me how you beat up women and murder dogs. Or murder bums on the street."

"Is that what this is about? Are you still trying to stick me with that?"

"I'm going to stick you with it, pal. You watch me."

"Why don't you fight me, Janeway? Just pick the place and time."

"I wish I could. We don't do things that way."

"That don't surprise me. Now if you're all through, I'm going in."

I had been working my way slowly around, putting more distance between Newton and the woman. Now I put an arm out and moved her completely aside.

"Barbara," I said. "Why don't you come on with us?"

"All right."

"I wouldn't do that," Jackie Newton said.

"You wouldn't do anything unless it was stupid or mean," I said. I got my hand on her shoulder and guided her away from the house. We got her to the car and inside, and there she broke down in a fit of sobbing. Her whole body trembled. I took off my coat and covered her shoulders, but it was a long time before she was ready to tell us about it.

We let Nasses off in Jeffco and were coming down Sixth Avenue toward Denver when I started to get her story. Hennessey was driving and Barbara was huddled against the shotgun door. I was in the back, leaning over the seat. I started with the little things. Her last name was Crowell. She lived in a Capitol Hill walk-up near Eleventh and Pearl. She worked for one of the companies that did business with Jackie Newton. Yesterday was the first time she had seen him . . . socially. She was flattered that he had asked her: he was rich and some people found him attractive. No one had warned her what he was really like.

It had happened pretty much as I had figured. Jackie's idea of a date was apparent soon after they arrived at his house. He had a waterbed the size of a football field, with a hot tub, mirrors, the whole nine yards. That hadn't bothered her much: she wasn't entirely indisposed to going down with a guy the first time out, if she liked him. If a guy knew how to treat a girl, what was the harm in it? But then the dog ate the steaks and Jackie went crazy. You wouldn't believe how strong he was. That was a big dog, and he'd pulled it up over that limb like it weighed nothing. She had tried to stop him: she hated cruelty, she just couldn't stand there and watch that animal kick its life out. She had tried to cut the rope and Jackie slugged her. He was strong, all right, no mistake about it. With one punch he knocked her senseless.

The next fifteen hours were a nightmare. When she opened her eyes she was in the car. They were on the interstate heading east out of Denver. He drove the same way he did everything, always one inch from the brink of insanity.

He kept his foot jammed on the floorboards—Jesus, you couldn't imagine a car could go that fast. Later he'd gone off the freeway into a narrow country road. Once they'd stopped in the middle of nowhere. She didn't seem to want to go into that, but I had started to taste blood and there was no way I was going to let her drop it.

"Barbara," I said softly. "Did he rape you?"

She shook her head.

"Because if he did, you know, we can give him a lot of grief."

"I didn't struggle."

"You don't have to struggle for it to be rape."

She took a deep shivery breath. I gave her a handkerchief and she dabbed her eyes.

"Barbara," I said.

"I just want to forget about it."

"I can see that you do, and I understand that. But if you don't do something he'll just do it again."

"Not to me."

We didn't say anything more for a minute. Hennessey drove smoothly into the city, turning north on Santa Fe. From there we could go easily to her place or to Denver General.

"We need to go to the hospital," I said. "Get you examined, get a doctor involved. You can make up your mind what to do later, but we need to get this done now."

"I want to forget it. I want to go home."

I sighed tiredly. "Jackie wins again."

"He'd win anyway. They'd let him off, and then where would I be?"

I couldn't argue with her. The way I had taken her out of there, without a warrant or probable cause, might give a judge fits. We could make the probable cause argument to some judges and win, based on what we had seen from our stakeout across the road. But there was another kind of judge who always held a cop's nuts to the ground, who'd view everything said and done after I'd stuck my foot in the door as tainted evidence. It was the luck of the draw.

We pulled up at her place on Pearl Street. She didn't want us to come in, but I had a few more questions. I wanted to hear all of it, everything they'd been doing since yesterday afternoon. Nothing much to tell, she said: he just drove like a maniac and she huddled in the car and expected death every minute. Once he had run over a flock of chickens. If there was anything on the road, a squirrel, chipmunk, any living thing, he'd swerve and crush it.

That car, though, was something else. That car was amazing.

She had been with Jackie Newton without a break since 3:00 P.M. yesterday. They had gone halfway across Kansas before he'd turned and come back.

She knew nothing about a dead man in an alley.

5

Sometimes when I get going, I can work thirty hours without a break. This is tough on my partner, especially a guy like Hennessey, who needs his beauty rest. Neal went home to catch up on lost sleep and I went running. I used to be a marathon man in college. I can still do thirty miles, but it's harder and I'm slower now. I'm not bad for my age and I go through a lot of pain to keep it that way. I run two, three times a week, and every year I run in the Bolder Boulder and finish respectably. I don't try to beat the world anymore: if I can just hold up my little part in it, that's enough. When I was young I had thoughts of a career in the ring, but the cops won my heart, and my mind and balls soon followed. You've got to be realistic, as people keep telling me. It's a long way from the Golden Gloves to any kind of fighting career, and I had seen enough of the fight game to know it wasn't for me. While I was at it, I was pretty good. I had people comparing me to Marciano. I was light for a heavyweight, just over one ninety, but so was Marciano. I was fast and tough: no one had ever been able to knock me down. It was said that I could hit like a mule and take any punch ever thrown. I liked it when they said that.

This is all by way of saying that I'd've been delighted to take on Jackie Newton some dark night. He had me by four inches in height, at least that much in reach, and thirty pounds that would never be called excess baggage. On paper he should whip my ass. But that's what they said about Jess Willard when he ran into another of my old heroes, Jack Dempsey. Dempsey put that lardbucket flat on the floor, and when it was over Willard's corner was screaming about plaster of paris and everything but the Rock of Gibraltar being in Dempsey's gloves. It ain't the size of the dog in the fight, is it? And I had a feeling that, under all that bullshit, Jackie Newton didn't have much heart.

The one sure thing was that I'd never find out. It got tiresome, always having to play by the rules while the other guy did his mugging and raping under a cloak of protections and rights. I jogged out Sixth Avenue, past expensive homes along the parkway. Somewhere, somehow, I was missing something: I didn't know what. I had stepped off the treadmill way back when and didn't know how to get on again. I was molded by a conservative father; I had rejected him and everything he stood for. I'd fought in the last stages of Vietnam, returned a fiery liberal, and slowly, over the past decade, I had watched those values trickle away as well. Today I'm a mess of contradictory political views. I believe in human rights: I liked Jimmy Carter for that reason alone, though I later came to believe that he had sold out his own cause in the game of pure politics. I think the Miranda ruling has generally been good, though the public will never know what a pain it can be to work

John Dunning

with. I believe in due process, but enough is enough: I'm a fan of a just and swift execution where vicious killers are concerned. It's just ridiculous to keep a guy like Ted Bundy on death row for ten years. I don't believe it when psychologists tell me the death penalty doesn't deter—take a look at kidnapping statistics in the 1930s, when it was made a capital crime after the murder of the Lindbergh baby, before you start to argue with me. I think justice started collapsing under its own weight when they let shrinks into the courtroom. The plain fact is, for some murderers, I just don't care whether they were incapable of reason, were whipped as children for wetting the bed, or had a mother who bayed at the moon. Gacy, Bundy, Manson, Speck—you'll never make me believe the world is a better place with that quartet alive and kicking. I hate abortion, but I'd never pass a law telling a woman she couldn't have one. I believe in the ERA, find it hard to understand why two hundred years after the Bill of Rights we're still arguing about rights for half our people. I like black people, some of them a lot. I supported busing when it was necessary and would again, but there's something about affirmative action that leaves me cold. You can't take away one man's rights and give them to another, even in a good cause.

I was burned out, and never more than today. My police career had been solid, some said brilliant, but I was on a long slide to nowhere, a treadmill to oblivion, as Fred Allen called it. These are the days that try men's souls. I wanted to fight Jackie Newton with a broken bottle and a tire iron, and society, decency, and my own good sense said, *You can't do that.* There was something about gun law that was immensely appealing: it really cut through the crap and got to the heart of things. Barbaric? Maybe. But I'll tell you this: watching a guy kill people and not being

38

able to do a damn thing about it, that's no bowl of cherries either.

My apartment, as always, was the great healer. I stripped off my sweats, turned on a light, and sat surrounded by treasures. I looked for a while at an old *AB:* my fascination in the life of the bookman was almost as acute as my interest in books, and I had been a faithful subscriber to the bookseller's trade journal for almost five years. I thumbed through Wyeth's Helga pictures, lingering on that lovely scene in the barn. Carol Pfeiffer, of course, had long gone: she had been gone when I had come in earlier and changed for my run. I took a cold shower and dressed slowly, planning my day. Barbara Crowell's statement seemed to alibi Jackie Newton nicely, which meant I had to start from scratch. It never occurred to me to call Hennessey, or to check downtown and see if we'd been assigned to the case. Hennessey would just be turning over for his second forty winks, and downtown they'd know we were on it. They knew all about my work habits.

I drove out Sixth to Colorado Boulevard, went north to Colfax, then east to the bookstores. This was my turf: I was as much at home along Book Row as I was in the world of hookers and pimps that surrounded it. Colfax is a strange street. It used to be known as the longest street in the world: people with more imagination than I have used to say, in the days before interstate highways, that it ran from Kansas City to the Great Salt Lake. Its actual length is about twenty miles, beginning on the plains east of Denver and dwindling away in the mountains to the west. Just about every foot of it is commercial space. About twenty years ago, urban renewal came in and ripped out old Larimer Street, and the whores and bums who lived there landed on Broadway south and Colfax east. Lots of whoring goes on on East Colfax Avenue. It starts at the statehouse, where they know how to do it without ever getting in a bed, and works its way through the porno shops between Broadway and Colorado Boulevard. From Colorado east, for about thirty or forty blocks, the street goes respectable in a chain of mom-and-pop businesses of every imaginable type. Here you'll find produce stands, garages, video rentals, fortune-tellers, antique dealers, 7-Elevens, liquor stores, and, of course, Book Row.

More than ten years ago, an old-time book dealer and his wife hung their shingle on an East Colfax hole-in-the-wall. Those people are gone now—the old man died and the wife lives in another state. Their store has passed along to a succession of younger bookmen: it has spawned other bookstores until, today, the area has become known as Book Row. This is the honey-draws-flies concept of bookselling: put two bookstores in one block, the theory goes, and business doubles for everybody. It seems to work: the stores have all stabilized where business was lean for one before. As a book collector, I did Book Row at least twice a month. A couple of the dealers knew me well enough to call me at home if something came in with my name on it; the others knew me too, though some of them were a little shy about calling a cop. Book dealers are like everyone else: they come in all sizes and shapes and have the same hangups that you see in a squad room or on an assembly line. If you picture a wizened academic with thick spectacles, forget it. Once they get in the business, they have little time to read. They are usually a cut or two smarter than the average Joe. I've never met a stupid book dealer who was able to make it pay. Some of them, though, are definitely crazy. There are a few horse's asses, a few sow's ears, but today's bookseller is just as likely to be an ex-hippie ex-boozer ex-junkie streetfighter like Ruby Seals.

I liked Ruby: I admired the old bastard for his savvy and grit. He had pulled himself out of the gutter the hard way, cold turkey and alone. He was a bottle-a-day drunk and he'd kicked that; he had been on cocaine and later heroin and had kicked that. He had been busted for possession, beginning in the days when, in Colorado, you could get two years for having a leaf of grass in your car. Ruby had served a year on that bust, another year for speed, and two years of a seven-year rap for heroin. By then the laws had been liberalized or he might still be languishing at Canon City. I had known him all this time because I was into books, and Ruby, when he was straight, was one of the keenest book dealers in town. A lot of what I knew I had learned watching Ruby work. "I'll tell you something, Dr. J," he had said to me long ago. "Learn books and you'll never go hungry. You can walk into any town with more than two bookstores and in two hours you're in business."

You did it the same way the scouts did, only on a higher level. While the scouts looked for $2 books that could be turned for $10, you looked for the $100 piece that would fetch a McKinley. You bought from guys who didn't know and sold to guys who did. If nobody in town knew, you wholesaled to people on the coast. You worked the *AB* when you could afford the price of it; you put a little bankroll together and before you knew it, you had three or four thousand books. Ruby had done this more times than he could remember.

Seals & Neff was the last store on the block, but I went there first. It was in their store, about a month ago, that I had last seen Bobby Westfall. I vaguely remembered it now: Bobby had come in to sell something, and there had been a dispute over how much and in what manner Ruby would pay for it. I hadn't paid much attention then: I was wavering on the price of a nice little Steinbeck item. There wasn't much to the argument anyway, as I remembered it: Bobby didn't want to take a check and Ruby didn't have the cash, so Bobby had left with the book. But that was the last time I had seen him and it seemed like a good starting place.

Ruby and his partner, Emery Neff, were sorting books from a new buy when I came in: they were hunkered over with their asses facing the door and didn't see me for a moment. The stuff looked pretty good: lots of fine modern firsts, some detective novels, a Faulkner or two. My eye caught the dark blue jacket of *Intruder in the Dust.* Carol's birthday was coming up: maybe I'd buy it for her, see how she liked it when she actually owned a book like that. A $100 bill flitted through my mind. That's what the book was worth, though I expected a good deal of preamble before we got to that point. I didn't like haggling. I wasn't one of those cheapskates always trying to pry a book away from a dealer for half its value, but I didn't want to pay twice retail either. I knew how Seals & Neff operated. They tended to go high with stuff they'd just bought. That sometimes worked with pigeons and sucker books. But then the rent would come due or the sheriff would call for the sales tax, many months delinquent, and they'd scramble around, wholesaling their best books for pennies on the dollar in a mad effort to keep from being thrown out or padlocked.

Ruby was dressed in his usual country club attire: jeans, a sweatshirt, and sandals. He wore a heavy black beard that was streaked with gray. His partner was neater. Emery Neff had blond hair and a mustache. Taken together, they were a strange pair of boys. Ruby was gritty, down-to-earth, real; Neff put on airs, oozed arrogance, and, until you passed muster, seemed aloof and cold. Ruby could sell birth control to a nun; Neff seemed reluctant to sell you a book, even at high retail. Neff wasn't quite a horse's ass, but he was close: I guess it was his deep well of knowledge that saved him. He really was a remarkable bookman, and I seemed to like him in spite of himself.

They still hadn't seen me: they were engrossed in the hypnotic, totally absorbing business of the bookman—sorting and pricing. I had seen the ritual before and had always found it interesting. Ruby would pick up a book and fondle it lovingly, then they'd bat the price back and forth and finally they'd settle on something, which Neff would write in light pencil on the flyleaf. They were just getting to the Faulkner when I leaned over their backs.

"Buck and a half," Neff said.

"Too high," Ruby said.

"It's a perfect copy, Ruby. I mean, look at the goddamn thing, it's like it was published yesterday, for Christ's sake."

"You never see this for more than a bill."

"You never see a copy like this either."

"Go ahead, if you want the son of a bitch to grow mold over there on the shelf."

"Buck and a quarter, then. That's rock-friggin'-bottom."

Neff penciled in the price. I cleared my throat and got their attention.

"Well, Dr. Janeway, I do believe," Ruby said, brightening. "We just got in some stuff for you."

"So I see. The masters of overcharge are already at work."

Neff gave me a pained look, as if the mere discussion of money was a blow to one's dignity.

"Always a deal for you, Dr. J," Ruby said, and Neff's pained look drifted his way.

I put the Faulkner out of my mind for the moment. I never could split my concentration effectively.

"I want to ask you boys a few questions."

"Jesus, Mr. Janeway," Neff said seriously. "This sounds official. Let me guess what it is. Somebody knocked off the sheriff and right away you thought of us."

I gave him a mirthless little smile. "When was the last time you saw Bobby Westfall?"

"Jeez, I don't know," Ruby said. "He ain't been coming around much."

"What's he done, rob a bank?" Neff said.

"See if you can pin it down for me," I said.

"Well," Ruby said, "he come in here maybe two weeks ago. Ain't that right, Em? About two weeks ago."

"About that," Neff said. "What's it about?"

"I told you, I'm trying to pin him down," I said. "Did he have something to sell when he came in?"

"Just a few turds," Ruby said. "Nuthin' I wanted."

"Bob was on a losing streak," Neff said. "He hadn't found much all month long."

"He was bitchin' up a storm about it," Ruby said. "Bobby never bitches much, but I guess he needed the money and for once in his life he couldn't find any books."

"You have any idea what he needed the money for?"

"Hell, Dr. J, I just buy books from these bastards, I don't go home and sleep with 'em."

"They always need money," Neff said.

"Who doesn't?" Ruby said. "But bookscouts . . . yeah, Em's right. Those guys're always scraping like hell just to get two nickels to rub against each other. But I'm not telling you anything you don't already know."

"When was the last time Bobby had a big strike?"

"Oh, Jeez," Ruby said, shaking his head.

"What do you call big?" Neff said.

"I don't know, Neff," I said. "What do *you* call big?"

"Big to him might be this Faulkner you're looking at. We'd give him thirty, forty bucks for that. Nothing to sneeze at if you got it for a quarter."

"Bigger than that," I said.

Ruby's eyes went into mock astonishment. "You mean like maybe he found *Tamerlane* in the Goodwill? Something like that, Dr. J?"

"Something like that."

"You're kidding."

They had stopped grinning now and were hanging on my next words. I let them wait, and finally Neff stepped into the breach.

"That's been done. Remember the guy who found *Tamerlane* in a bookstore for fifteen dollars a few years ago? Do you know what the odds are of that happening, anywhere in the world, twice in a lifetime?"

"I'm not talking about *Tamerlane*," I said. "Just maybe something like it."

They both looked at me.

"What's going on, Dr. J?"

"Somebody beat Bobby's brains out last night."

"Holy Christ," Ruby said.

"Killed him, you mean," Neff said numbly.

I nodded.

"Now who the hell would do that?" Ruby said.

"That's what I'm trying to find out. Let's go back to what I asked you. When was the last time Bobby had a big strike?"

"Oh, hell, I can't remember," Ruby said. "Jesus, Dr. J, this's terrible."

"You're asking us when Bob might've had something somebody would kill him for," Neff said.

"Let's make like I'm asking you that."

"Hell, never," Ruby said.

Neff nodded immediately. "Even that big score he made a few years back, when he found all four of those big books in one weekend . . . I mean, that's the biggest score any of them ever make, and all four of those books don't add up to more than two grand. Who'd kill a guy for that?"

"Some people, maybe," I said.

"Nobody I know," Ruby said. "Goddamn, this's terrible. I can't get over it."

"Let's say he had something worth two or three thousand," I said. "That's a lot of money to guys on the street."

"It's a lot of money to *me*," Ruby said.

"But to a guy who lives like they live, it's more money than you'll ever see again in one place."

"You think that's what happened . . . Bobby found something and some other bookscout took it away from him?"

"I don't think anything," I said. "I'm trying to find out something and put it together with what I know. It's unlikely Bobby found anything worth a real fortune. You said so yourself. Pieces like *Tamerlane* don't just drop off trees into somebody's lap. The reason they're worth a quarter of a million dollars is because there are no copies out there to be found. A guy would have a better chance of winning the Irish Sweepstakes, right?"

"I'd give him a better chance," Ruby said.

"And yet it happens."

"In movies it happens."

"Once in a while it really happens."

"I'd sure hate to chase that down," Ruby said. "Talk about a needle in a goddamn haystack."

"On the other hand, if Bobby found something worth a few thousand, you'd have to ask yourself a different set of questions. Anybody might kill for a quarter of a million, but who'd kill for three grand?"

"Three grand wouldn't begin to solve my problems," Ruby said. "Hell, I owe the sheriff more than that."

"But it's a lot of money to a bookscout," I said.

"I see what you're saying."

"So," I said, "who did Bobby go around with?"

"Well, there's Peter. I've seen the two of 'em walking together, that's all. Doesn't mean they were fast and tight. Other than that, old Bob ran alone. I've never seen him with anybody else."

"Who's Peter?"

"I can't remember his last name. You remember it, Em?" Neff shook his head.

"Just called him Peter the Bookscout, just like Bobby. Hell, half those boys never had a name, or don't want you to know it if they do."

"Does Peter come by often?"

"He was in here yesterday," Neff said.

"Comes in three or four times a month," Ruby said.

"When did you see Bobby and Peter together?"

"Oh, maybe a year ago," Ruby said. "They were going up to Boulder together, to a book sale. Bobby didn't drive, so he was hitching a ride with Peter."

"What do you mean Bobby didn't drive?" Neff said. "I've seen him drive. Don't you remember that old car he had?"

"That was a long time ago, pardner," Ruby said. "The cops busted him for no valid license, no insurance. He cracked up the car and ain't had one since. I know damn well he didn't have a license."

"I think you're wrong about that," Neff said.

"There was no driver's license found on the body," I said.

Neff shrugged. "Then I guess you're right."

"I know I'm right," Ruby said.

"Why would one bookscout drive another one up to a sale?" I said. "It sounds like cutting your own throat to me."

"That's what makes me think maybe they were friends," Ruby said. "At least as much as those guys get to be friends."

I made a note in my book. "Any idea where I can find this Peter?"

"The only time I see him is when he comes by," Ruby said.

"If he comes by again, tell him I want to see him."

"Sure, Dr. J. You bet."

I looked through my notes. There are many reasons why people get murdered, but 99 percent fall into four broad motive categories: love, hate, greed, insanity. I had looked at two of these.

"Did Bobby have any girlfriends?" I said.

"Not that I ever saw," Ruby said.

"He ever talk about women he knew, or might have known in the past?"

They shook their heads.

"Anybody you boys can think of who'd want to see Bobby dead?"

"Oh no," Neff said.

"He was the easiest of 'em all to deal with," Ruby said.

"Who'd he sell most of his books to?"

"Us, as much as anybody," Neff said.

"Not so much anymore, though," Ruby said.

"Why not?"

Neff gave a little shrug. "We've been going through some lean times, Mr. Janeway. We've had a few setbacks."

"Oh, let's call a spade a bloody fucking shovel," Ruby said. "We bounced a few checks on him. That's no big deal, people do it all the time. We always made it good. But these bookscouts hate to take a check anyway. They go all the way down to the bank and the check's no good. I know where they're coming from. I understand why they get pissed off."

"Then why do you do it?"

"You mean write a hot check? You know that, Dr. J, I know you do. It's book fever. You've got it just like I have. You see a book you want, you do what you have to do to get it. My intentions are honorable, it's my performance that lags a little."

"Where else did he go to sell his stuff?"

"Might be any one of a dozen places. You know the scene, Dr. J: hell, there's thirty bookstores in Denver. Probably half of 'em pay well enough for bookscouts to be able to deal with 'em. Not many places will pay forty percent across the board, but some do. You could narrow it down that way, I guess. Start with the boys up the street, see if they know anything."

I thought for a minute. Then I said, "Do either of you know where Bobby lived?"

"I do," Ruby said. "I drove him home a couple of times."

"You think you could show me where it's at?"

"Sure. You want to go now?"

"In an hour. I want to talk to the boys up the street first."

"I'll be here whenever you say. You better let me sell you

this Faulkner before you leave. It's the world's best copy and it won't last long."

"How much?"

"For you . . . Today? . . . Ninety-five bucks."

Neff groaned as I reached for my checkbook. "Oh, what the hell," he said. "I get tired of selling Faulkner anyway."

6

I walked up the street carrying Mr. William Faulkner under my arm. The next store along the row was Book Heaven, owned by Jerry Harkness.

Denver is a young man's book town. In the old days there were only two dealers of note: Fred Rosenstock and Harley Bishop. Those boys died and the book trade fractured into twenty or thirty pieces. The new breed came in and the books changed as well. In Rosenstock's day you could still find documents signed by Abraham Lincoln or the framers of the Constitution. The trouble was, you couldn't get much for them. Forty years later, those papers and books are worth small fortunes but can't be found. What can be found, and sold for good money, is modern lit. We live in a day when first editions by Stephen King outsell Mark Twain firsts ten to one, and at the same price. You explain it: I can't. Maybe people today really do have more money than brains. Or maybe there's something in the King craze that's going over my head. I read *Misery* not long ago and thought it was a helluva book. I'd put it right

51

up with *The Collector* as an example of the horror of abduction, and that's a heavy compliment since I consider Fowles one of the greatest living novelists. Then I read *Christine* and it was like the book had been written by a different guy. A bigger crock has never been put between two covers. What the hell do I know? I sure can't explain it when a book like *Salem's Lot* goes from $10 to almost $1,000 in ten years. That's half again what a near-perfect *Grapes of Wrath* will bring, if you need a point of reference. You can buy five copies of Hemingway's *Old Man and the Sea* for that, or six copies of Thomas Wolfe's *Of Time and the River*. You can buy first editions signed by Rudyard Kipling or Jack London for less money. So the business has changed, no question about it, and the people in it have changed as well. The old guard is dead: long live the new guard. But I can still remember old Harley Bishop, in the year before he died, stubbornly selling King firsts at half the original cover price. The big leap in King books hadn't yet happened, but even then *The Shining* was a $100 book. Bishop sold me a copy for $4. When I told him he should ask more, he gave me a furrowed look and said, "I don't believe in Steffan King."

Jerry Harkness most definitely did believe in Steffan King. He specialized in King and his followers—Dean Koontz, Clive Barker, et al., the little Kinglets. Behind every big ship you'll find a dozen little ships atrailing. Most of their plots make absolutely no sense, but again, they stand tall where it really matters in today's world, at the damn cash register. There's something seriously wrong with a society when its best-selling writer of all time is Janet Dailey. Don't ask me to prove it: it's just something I know. I don't mind a good scare story once in a while, but Jesus Christ, the junk that goes down! The stupidity of some of these plots that sell in the billions is the scariest thing about them. *The Exorcist* is a truly scary book because it only asks you to believe one thing—that Satan does exist. There are no talking dogs or curses lingering from antiquity: there's no literary sleight of hand, no metaphorical bullshit. Accept the guy's premise (and who can totally deny it?) and he's got you where you live. All it takes after that is talent. The trouble today (do I begin to sound like Mel Brooks's two-thousand-year-old man when I get on one of these soap boxes?) is that show biz is often mistaken for talent. Get to the end, though, and ask yourself what it all meant, what was it all about? The answer's usually nothing. Relieve the author from the obligation to make sense, and what's there to be afraid of?

I have come to the conclusion that the people who buy these books don't care much about books at all. You will seldom see a King guy or a Koontz guy browsing in a bookstore. I've been in Ruby's store and watched the action myself. A guy opens the door. He doesn't even come inside. He stands on the street with his head sticking in and asks his three questions. Got any King? Got any Koontz? Got any Barker? If the answer's no, he's gone. Ruby points him up the street, to Jerry Harkness, and later learns that the guy dropped two grand with Jerry. Unbelievable! What else can you say but absolute around-the-bend insanity? "All a guy needs to make it in this business," Ruby says, "is an unlimited amount of Stephen King."

Jerry Harkness had started in the book business as a teenager. He had worked for Harley Bishop and had learned the ropes, but had gone on to do things his own way. He knew his market and his people. His shop contained many items of general interest, but it was his horror, fantasy, and sword and sorcery sections that drew people from all over the country. Harkness had the only copy I've ever seen of the signed, very limited edition of King's *Firestarter,* a $3,000 piece.

Twenty years have passed since Harkness worked for old Harley Bishop. He must have been young then, full of dreams of this—his own business. I looked in the window and wondered, not for the first time, how the reality matched the dream. I might like it myself, if I wasn't a cop, if I hadn't been born a cop. Where's the truth in that, I wondered: was I really born to wade through guts and mop up blood every Saturday night? Suddenly I had the strangest feeling of my life, almost what they call déjà vu in the superspook trade. *I have been here before. I have walked these paths and done these things.* I've missed my calling, I thought for the second time in ten hours. I've been a book dealer before, I'm a book dealer now, I already know more about books than ninety percent of the bozos in the trade. I've always thought I might be a book dealer someday, maybe when I retire. I had begun to put some things in storage for that distant day. Maybe it ain't so distant, I thought for the first time ever: maybe I'll just chuck all this crap and do it. I had already made one incredible buy, an act of good judgment that I'd be hard-pressed to duplicate. Almost fifteen years ago, I stumbled across John Nichols's *Milagro Beanfield War* on a B. Dalton's remainder table for ninety-nine cents. I read the book in a weekend and loved it, and I went all over town, to every Dalton's I could find, buying them up. They were all unmarked first editions. At the end of that week I had seventy-five copies. I was twenty-two years old when I did that. I've run into Nichols a few times over the years and he's always been happy to sign books. I had gotten about half of them signed. The book now goes for $150, probably $200 with a signature. I had at least $12,000 worth of books sitting in storage for my $75 investment. Maybe the time had come to do something with it.

Jerry Harkness was long and lean and still fighting the good fight against middle age. He perched on a stool behind his counter and watched me all the way past his front window and through the front door. He had been reading a Clive Barker paperback when I came along, and he put it aside for the customary greeting as I came in. I went straight to the counter and got to the point.

"When was the last time you saw Bobby Westfall?"

"You mean the bookscout? I don't see him, unless he's got something for me. He knows I don't buy stock from scouts. They want too much for the run-of-the-mill stuff. He comes in if he's got a King or a Burroughs, or maybe an early Gene Wolfe. He knows I'll pay him more than anybody if it's something good in my field."

"So you see him what . . . once a month?"

"If that. I did see him about two weeks ago. I think he was up the street trying to sell Ruby Seals some books. I don't know, he didn't bother showing 'em to me."

"Did he seem any different than he usually did?"

"I don't know how he usually seemed. These bookscouts are almost nonentities after you've seen 'em around awhile. I don't think about things like how they usually are. But since you asked me, I guess he seemed the same as ever."

"Which was what?"

"Quiet. Almost mousy. He just walked around looking at my stuff. That's how they learn, you know . . . look at the books on the shelves and see how they're priced. None of 'em ever have any reference books, they can't afford that, so they have to keep it all up here." He tapped himself on the head. "What's the matter? Bobby get himself in trouble?"

"Bobby got himself dead."

Harkness opened his mouth and it hung there for a moment.

"Did you ever talk to him?" I said.

"As a matter of fact, we passed a few words that day in the store."

"About what?"

"Usual run of stuff. How bad business is, on both his end and mine. This is the slow time of the year. I'm used to it. In the early summer, right after tax time, you'll go whole days without seeing more than ten people. Then a dealer will come through and drop five hundred, and in the end the figures balance out okay. But bookscouts have it tough. Books have been drying up. Even Goodwill is putting horrendous prices on their books lately. God, I wonder who'd kill Bobby."

I looked at him strangely. He got my drift and shrugged. "You're a homicide cop; I put two and two together and assumed he'd been murdered."

I nodded.

"I don't know what I can tell you. Bobby was singing the blues about those stupid asses at Goodwill. People are just plain greedy: they don't want to leave anything for anybody else, they don't want the next guy to make even a dime. Goodwill's trying to play bookstore again. They're a thrift store, for God's sake, and they put everything out at bookstore prices. They've got some clerk there who can't find her ass with both hands, and she's gonna figure out what a book's really worth. Right. Of course they get it all wrong. They go on weight and glitz. They'll put out some useless novel about two lesbians fighting for control of their dead aunt's cosmetics company for five dollars. Then they'll let a King first go for fifty cents."

"How does that hurt the bookscout?"

"It's the stock he makes his bread and butter on. You don't find Kings every day. What the bookscouts used to be able to do is grab up a handful of these glitzy titles for a buck apiece and double or triple their money in one of the big general bookstores. They can't do that anymore. Goodwill goes through this silliness once every three or four years. Somebody in the front office gets a wild hair up his ass and they start marking everything through the roof. After a while they learn they can't sell the damn things and they go back to the old prices. But while they're at it, guys like Bobby really hurt."

"So this is the gist of what Bobby was complaining about?"

"That's what he said to me."

"Did he give you any indication that he might've made a recent score?"

"Are you kidding? The way he was talking, he didn't have bus fare back downtown."

"Maybe he found something and hadn't had a chance to sell it yet."

"I doubt that. I don't think he had a prayer of seeing any money in the immediate future. He was just too down, too pissed off at the world."

"Who else did he do business with?"

"Almost everybody. You're gonna have to go to every bookstore in Denver if you want to touch all of Bobby's bases."

"But they have their favorite guys they sell to, isn't that right?"

"Sure. They all do that. They'll find a dealer who pays 'em well and they'll stick with that guy for a while. Then something happens—either they get pissed off or the dealer does—and they go somewhere else. But it's never perfect and eventually they come back. It's a vicious circle. When a book doesn't sell to anybody reputable, they wind up giving it away for pennies to jerks like the one two doors down."

"You mean Clyde Fix?"

"What an idiot. I wish we could get that junkman off the block."

"Can you think of anybody else Bobby might've sold to regularly?"

"I think he was in with Roland Goddard. Don't tell Goddard I sent you, though. He used to be my partner."

"I didn't know that."

"Oh, yeah. But don't bring it up. We don't get along now."

"How come?"

"You don't really want to get into that. It's ancient history."

"Humor me a little."

"When we were kids we both worked for Harley Bishop. Then we moved on to the Book Emporium, you remember, that big place that used to be on Fifteenth, across from Public Service? They closed it up and Goddard and I bought out the stock and used it to start our first store together. It didn't work out, that's all. We've got different aims in life, different tastes. At the bottom of it, we just didn't like each other. Sometimes you've got to go into business with somebody to find out how little you like each other. So we flipped a coin to see who would buy the other out. Goddard won. Or lost, depending on how you look at it."

"That's a pretty classy shop he's got."

"Yeah, but so what? Everything in life has a trade-off. He's got a great shop and a super location in Cherry Creek, probably makes two hundred grand a year. But the overhead's got to be unreal. Me, I was out of the business for a couple of years after the big coin flip, but I'm back again. I've got what I want."

"Can you think of anybody else I should see?"

"As a matter of fact, yeah. Go talk to Rita McKinley."

"Who's that?"

He raised his eyebrow. "You're a bookman in this town and you've never heard of Rita McKinley?"

"I guess I never did."

"Well, Officer Janeway, you've got a treat in store for you."

"Who's Rita McKinley?"

"She's got a closed shop in Evergreen. Appointment only, that kind of place. Operates out of her house."

"What's she got to do with Bobby?"

"I don't know, except when he was here he dropped a piece of paper with her name on it."

"You still got it?"

"Sure. I've been waiting for him to come in again so I could give it back to him." He reached into the cash drawer and took out a small sheet of notepaper. In pencil, someone had written the name and a phone number.

I looked at Harkness. "You ever met the lady?"

"She was in here once, a year or two ago. A real looker, young and pretty and sharp as a new brass tack. She knows books, brother. She knows as much as I do, and I'm talking about books in my field. You know what she did? Bought two copies of *Interview with the Vampire* out of here for fifty bucks apiece. That's what the son of a bitch was going for then. Now it's three hundred, and it's gonna go to five, I'll betcha. I'd love to have one of those babies back; hell, I'd pay her four times what she paid me. It's not often that somebody teaches me a lesson in my own field, but Rita

McKinley did it. A real cool customer. And I got the feeling talking to her that she knows every field like that. And she can't be much over thirty."

"How long has she been up there?"

"A few years, I guess. I've never seen her place. She's goddamned intimidating if you want to know the truth. You don't just call her up because you're out for a drive some Sunday and you want to scout her shelves. At least I don't."

"How does she sell her books?"

"She's got clients who come in from out of town. Does mail order. And deals in very expensive stuff."

I wrote her name down.

"It doesn't sound logical, does it?" I said. "Her and Bobby?"

Harkness shrugged. "That's all I can tell you."

I believed him for the moment, and left.

There were two more dealers on Book Row. One was a specialist in collectible paperbacks, who kept odd hours. His store was closed. Near the end of the block was a junk shop called A-1 Books, owned by Clyde Fix. I had never dealt with Fix, for two reasons: I have never seen a book in his store that I wanted, and his hatred for cops was well known and documented. He and Jackie Newton might make a great pair that way, but that was the only way. While Jackie was carving out land deals, Clyde Fix was struggling to stay alive. Where Jackie had brains, Clyde Fix had only animal cunning. It was a safe bet that Clyde Fix had never heard of a Lamborghini: he clattered around town in a red '62 Ford that always seemed two miles from the scrap heap. He was in his forties, with thinning hair and a gaunt, consumptive profile. He had owned bookstores all over Denver in the last fifteen years, all of them dumps like this one. Ruby had known him for years. Before he had discovered books, Ruby said, Clyde Fix had been a seller of graveyard plots; before that, he had sold shoes. With books, he had found a way of keeping body and soul together without having to punch a time clock. There are lots of customers for cheap books, and a junkman in almost any kind of junk will usually make a living.

He had a deceptive manner: he could ooze charm and in the same moment turn on you like a snake. People who had never seen his bad side thought of him as a nice man; the rest of us knew better. Fix had been busted half a dozen times for disturbing the peace, and Traffic had pulled him in a few times for speeding. He always argued with the cop. He was his own worst enemy. Once, I knew, he had talked himself from a simple taillight violation to creating a disturbance and ultimately resisting arrest. Cops have a lot of discretion in things like that.

My interview was a short one. Fix was hostile, as I knew he would be, and he wouldn't give me much. He didn't seem to know or care that Bobby Westfall was dead. "Why should I worry over that fool? That's just one less fool out there working my territory."

"Where's your territory?" I asked.

"Wherever the hell I say it is."

I knew that mentality well. Beat me to a book and you're my enemy for life. Turn over all your best books to me. Sell that to me for ten cents on the dollar, and don't give me any damn guff about it either. Fix would intimidate if he could, cheat if he could do that. He'd buy a $1,000 book for a quarter, then laugh all year at the sucker who'd sold it to him.

It occurred to me suddenly that there was a lot of latent anger in the Denver book world. I could easily see

Clyde Fix bashing Bobby's head in. But with Fix it wouldn't be calculated: more likely it would be a spur-of-the-moment thing, in broad daylight with fifteen witnesses looking on. They had had one run-in last year: the story had gone through the trade like a shot and quickly taken on the characteristics of an urban legend. I remembered it now and could almost see it: Bobby and Fix at the Goodwill store, both spotting a treasure nestled among the junk. James Crumley's *One to Count Cadence,* a $100 book then, two or three times that now. The mutual lunge, the struggle, the tumble into a counter of glassware, Fix coming up with the book, whirling and knocking a little old lady flat. The cops arrived, but Fix and Bobby were gone. So was the book.

I hassled him for a while: it was good for my constitution. Where were you last night, Fix? Anybody there with you? Can you prove where you were between ten o'clock and midnight? You didn't like Bobby much . . . did you kill him?

Pleasantries like that help get me through a dull day. If only I had something to do with my hands.

I moseyed back up the street. It was a quiet day on Book Row. At Seals & Neff a few customers had come and gone and the day was quickly settling into its inevitable, uneventful course. There was a young woman in the store, who had brought in a bag of books. Bookscouts, like dealers, come in all sizes, colors, and sexes. This one was a cut above the others I had seen, at least in the category of looks, but it was clear from what was being said that she had more than a smattering of ignorance when it came to books.

Neff was explaining to her why her as-new copy of Faulkner's *The Reivers* wasn't a first edition. "But it says first edition," she protested. "Right here on the copyright page . . . look. First edition. How much clearer can it be than that? Random House always states first edition, right? You told me that yourself the last time I was in here. Now I've got a first edition and you're telling me it isn't a first edition. I don't know what to believe."

"Believe this, honey," Neff said. "I don't need the grief. If you think I'm trying to steal your book . . ."

"I didn't say that. I'm not accusing you, I just want to know."

"It's a Book-of-the-Month Club first," Neff said, enunciating each word with chilly distinction. "It's printed from the same plates as the first, or maybe the same sheets are even used; that's why it says first edition. But the binding is different, there's no price on the jacket, and the book has a blind stamp on the back board."

"What's a blind stamp?"

"A little dent, pressed right into the cloth. Look, I'll show you. You see that little stamp? That means it's a book club book. Whenever you see that, it came from a book club, even if it's written 'I'm a first edition' in Christ's own blood inside. Okay?"

She sighed. "I'll never learn this stuff. How much is it worth?"

"This book? Five bucks tops. There are eight million copies of this in the naked city."

"I *paid* more than that for it. Didn't I come in here last week and ask you what it was worth? You said fifty dollars. That's why I went and bought it."

"We're talking about two different animals. You asked me a question, I answered you. How was I supposed to know you couldn't tell one from the other?"

"I paid seven-fifty," she said sadly.

"You got rooked."

"Damn shit," she said.

"You tell her, Mr. Janeway," Neff said. "Lady, this guy is a Denver cop. Would a cop lie to you? He's a cop and he's also a damn good bookman. Show him the book."

She handed it to me. I looked at it and told her Neff was right. It was a $5 book and you had to pray mighty hard to ever get the five.

"Let me see your badge," she said. "You don't look like a cop to me."

I showed her my badge. She sagged in final defeat.

"It's a tough world, hon," Neff said.

"Don't give me that. I see some of the characters who sell you books. They don't look like any Einsteins to me. If they can do it, I know I can. I've got as much brains as they have."

"I'm sure that's true. The difference between you and them is that they've already made their mistakes."

"Seven dollars and fifty cents, shot to hell," she said. "Bet you won't even give me two for it."

"I can pick those things up in thrift stores all day long for fifty cents."

"Aw, give her the money," Ruby said, coming out from the back room. "We'll subsidize this mistake. Just don't make any more, and bring us all your good books first. Give her the seven-fifty, Em."

"No wonder we're going broke," Neff said.

"This'll pay big dividends down the road, I can feel it in my bones," Ruby said. "What's your name, lady?"

"Millie Farmer."

"Here—here's your money back. I'm taking a two-buck loss, that is if I ever sell the son of a bitch. Bring me a good book next time."

"I will," she said determinedly. "By God, you watch me."

"It's easy," Ruby said. "Like taking candy from a baby. When you see a box of books, don't take any bad ones and don't leave any good ones. That's all there is to it."

I had been taking all this in as a spectator. Now, at the end of it, I couldn't help shaking my head and asking her one question.

"Why would you want to be a bookscout?"

"I'm a teacher," she said. "Would you like to try to make it on what they pay you to teach third grade in this town? I need the extra money."

"All right," Neff said. "Stick around, I'll show you some ropes. It doesn't look like much else is gonna happen today."

"Ruby," I said, "I'm ready to go to Bobby's place if you are."

We picked up my car and headed down Seventeenth Avenue toward Capitol Hill. Ruby talked as we drove, a seemingly endless chain of stories about Bobby Westfall and his adventures in the book trade. Ruby knew all the scuttlebutt. "I can't believe the little bastard's dead," he said at one point. I told him he could believe it. "I sure hope you get the son of a bitch that did it, Dr. J," he said. I told him I would, but you never know about that. You just never know.

Bobby lived in one of those old tenements on Ogden Street. It was a garret, up three long flights of stairs. We stopped at the manager's on the ground floor. I showed him my badge and told him the news. He was shocked. The manager was about fifty: he wore a sweatshirt and had a dark, unhealthy look. His name was Marty Zimmers. I told him we'd need to see the apartment and he got his spare key. At the top of the stairs, I said, "I don't want you boys to touch anything. In fact, I think I'm gonna ask you to wait out here."

I opened the door and the cats came running. I went in alone.

It was a small place, one room with a kitchenette and a tiny bathroom. It was a maze of books, a veritable cave of books. There were books piled from the floor to the ceiling, books stacked around the hideaway bed he'd slept in, books on the toilet, on the kitchen counter. I could see at a glance it was mostly crap, the kind of things a bookscout buys on a wing and a prayer, because it's cheap, because he has a hunch that never pays off, because he makes mistakes. Millie Farmer ought to be here now, and see what it's really like, I thought. There were later printings and books without jackets and books with vast, unfixable problems. Later I'd have to go through every piece in this room on the off chance that, if Bobby had found something, it might still be here. For now the main job was to get the area secured.

"This the only key?" I called out into the hall.

Marty Zimmers stuck his head in. "Well, he had one."

"This is the only spare, though."

"That's it."

I gave the place one quick look-see before going down to call the lab. The only things that stood out were the cats and a cheap little notepad that he had used for a telephone book. I picked up the notebook carefully and thumbed through it. Everybody was in it, all the book dealers in Denver by name and address. For some he had home numbers. Ruby and Neff were there, both home numbers and the store. On the back page of the book he had scrawled "Rita McKinley," and a telephone exchange that I recognized as Evergreen, in the mountains. I checked it against the number on the paper that Bobby had dropped in Jerry Harkness's bookstore. The numbers were different. I copied the new number in my notebook and left Bobby's book on the rickety little table beside the bed.

In the manager's office I made my calls. The first was the new Rita McKinley number. It rang once and was answered by a machine. The cool female voice said, "You've reached 670-2665. No one's here now. Leave a message and I'll get back to you soon." The phone beeped. I didn't leave a message.

I tried the other number. A cutoff recording came on and said that the call could not be completed as dialed.

I called downtown. Hennessey had come in. I told him I was at Bobby's place and I gave him the address. "We'll need a crew over here to comb through things. You come supervise, will you? Tell them to leave the books for me. I want to go out and talk to some more book dealers."

"Will do. You had a couple of calls while you've been out. One of them might be important. Barbara Crowell."

"When did that come in?"

"Time on the message said one-fifteen. Just a few minutes ago."

"Did she say anything?"

"The dispatcher wrote 'urgent' on it, underlined in red. Said the woman sounded scared to death. But she wouldn't talk to anybody else."

"What's her number?"

He read it to me. I hung up and dialed it. Another goddamn answering machine.

"Hi, this's Barbara. I can't come to the phone right now, but . . ."

I slammed the phone down. I had a very dark vision suddenly. Jackie Newton walked over my grave.

"Ruby, I want you to stay here and keep Mr. Zimmers

company. I'm leaving you the key, so you can give it to Hennessey when he comes. I don't want either one of you guys to go into that apartment. You understand what I'm saying?"

"I think I do, Dr. J."

"You boys need to vouch for each other that nobody's been up there between the time I left and when the cops came. Okay?"

"Sure. What're you gonna do?"

"I've got to be somewhere, right now."

Five minutes later I pulled up at Barbara Crowell's place on Pearl Street. The Lamborghini was parked out front.

7

The house where Barbara lived had two apartments on each floor. I parked in the loading zone behind Jackie Newton's car, got out, went inside, and started up the stairs. The place seemed like a mausoleum, still and deathly quiet. The steps creaked as I moved up, but that was the only sound until I got to the second floor and heard the radio. It was soft rock music, trickling faintly from above. I knew it was her radio playing—the apartment across the way was vacant. I took a grip on my gun and started up to the top. The radio came closer but still there were no voices. At her door I stopped and listened. Nothing. It was one of those *oh-hell* bad times in a cop's life. You want I should maybe knock on her door? Not this boy. I'd walk in and catch him in *flagrante delicto*, my only witness the terrified victim. Can't you just see it? *No, Your Honor. I didn't invite him in.* That's me she's talking about now, not Jackie Newton: we know from past experience what she'd say about a guy who could make her heart stop just by saying boo. *I asked Mr. Newton over to*

69

make up a quarrel we'd had. . . . I certainly didn't expect or want Detective Janeway to come walking into my bedroom. . . .

Why couldn't she scream? Throw something against the wall? I'd take any help I could get, any way I could get it.

But there was only profound stillness and the refrain from *A Lover's Concerto* on the other side of the door.

Ah, fuck it. I turned the knob. It was unlocked. I pushed it just a crack, enough to see into the front room. The radio got suddenly louder and that was all. I could see it blaring away on a table across the room. I pushed the door a little wider and I could see through to the kitchen. Still nothing. Nothing. No . . . living . . . thing. The bedroom door across the room was closed. Here I come, ready or not. I pushed the door wide and stepped in, the gun pointing my way like a beacon. I saw that the wood had been shattered where she'd had a chain lock fastened. That had stopped him for all of twenty seconds. I took four long steps to the bedroom door and listened again. It wasn't going to happen, was it? They just weren't going to invite me to their little party. I stood on the verge of big trouble, a brilliant, silly line from James Jones running through my head. *They can kill you but they can't eat you.* I had news for Mr. Jones, whatever corner of Eternity he'd gone to. They could kill you, yes, and they could eat you too.

I opened the door. They weren't there.

They weren't anywhere.

The bed had been neatly made up, not a ripple showing on the pink-and-white spread.

I looked in the closet and found nothing I could call unreasonable. I looked in the bathroom. Finally I went into the kitchen and began to see what had happened. There was a door that opened onto an outside landing, and a wooden staircase that ran down the rear of the apartment house to a small parking lot. The door had been slammed open with such force that the glass was broken. I walked back into the main room, the gun still in my hand. The scenario was becoming fairly clear. The curtains were drawn back: the Lamborghini was parked directly below. Barbara had looked out this front window and had seen Jackie Newton down in the street. She had called me: when I wasn't there, she had hung up. The recorder had activated automatically, and here we were. She had panicked when she heard him coming up the stairs. She took the only way out—down the back way. The lock had bought her a few seconds, then he came through the door and went down after her. That's where they were now, playing a game of chase on the streets.

Probable cause had dropped in my lap like a plum. I had never been in here—that was my story before God, Mother, and the state of Colorado. I had come up on a response to a phone call. I had come to her door and knocked: when no one answered, I had gone away. If I happened to spot them in the course of cruising the neighborhood, if it looked to my casual eye like Barbara Crowell was being unlawfully pursued . . . well, events could take care of themselves.

I didn't think it would be hard to find them. Barbara had run without any money, it seemed—her handbag was still on the table beside the radio. She wouldn't be jumping into any buses or cabs, and I didn't think she'd be flagging any cops, either. There was too much fear in her: it was an old story to me, I had seen it so many times. As for Jackie Newton, he was out there in hog heaven. This was the kind of game he loved: the cat-and-mouse, the heading-off, the dodging up alleys and down side streets. Playing with people, working on their fear.

I went downstairs and opened my trunk. In the toolbox I

found a rubber hammer and a punch. I flattened one of Jackie's tires and the Lamborghini sagged back on its haunch, hissing.

I drove in a widening circle, coming back to Pearl Street every few minutes to check on the Lamborghini. It took me twenty minutes to find them. I came upon Jackie on East Eighth Avenue, a few blocks from the governor's mansion. He was standing under a tree like a predator, watching. I drove on by. He didn't see me: like the leopard, his attention was fixed on the prey, on the place where the prey was hiding. I couldn't see it at first: all I knew was that she was there somewhere. I circled the block, parked the car, and got out. I walked to the corner and got behind a tree of my own. That's the way we did it for half an hour: Barbara hiding in a place unknown, Jackie watching her, me watching Jackie.

It was all a lot of fun till it started to rain.

I went back to the car and pulled into a vacant lot that had a clear view up Eighth. Jackie hadn't moved. He looked almost like a statue, every muscle chiseled in infinity. The rain fell. From a slight drizzle it had become a summer storm, water swirling in the street in the wind. It didn't seem to bother Jackie: he watched with an intensity that was almost scary, as if to watch all week, all year, wouldn't worry him a bit. Only once in that hour did he look up the street. But I was in an unmarked car, settled back with only my eyes above the dash, and he turned away none the wiser.

Rainstorms in Denver are often fast and furious. This one was over in forty minutes, becoming what had started it, a drizzle. I saw Barbara come out of a flower shop and look around nervously. Was he there? Of course. When someone scares you that bad, he's always there.

She had to do something, even if it was wrong. She

walked to the corner, looked around again, and started up the block to the north.

Jackie leaped into action. He ran straight toward me, then doubled up the next block toward East Ninth Avenue. He was going to cut her off, try to get close enough to grab a wrist before she knew he was there. I started the car, drove up Eighth and hung a right. Barbara Crowell was half a block ahead, walking briskly. But she kept stopping and looking back, not trusting the evidence of her eyes that he was gone. Once she stood for half a minute, giving him plenty of time to get in place on Ninth. I had pulled to the curb about forty yards behind her, opposite side of the street. When she started up again, so did I.

I could see him now, a shadow behind a tree on Ninth near the corner. I don't think I knew what I was going to do until that moment. She had reached the corner and looked both ways. He was now no more than ten yards away and could have caught her easy. But no . . . he was waiting for the big shock when he could grab her after she thought she'd made it. He wanted to see the fright, the heartbreak on her face. She had stopped on Ninth to look around, and I got out of the car and gave her the high five sign.

I had my finger to my mouth, the universal gesture for quiet. I came up beside her and took her arm. With my other hand I got out my gun. I turned her east on Ninth, a course that would carry us right past the tree where he hid. She started to speak: I shushed her with a low hiss. The tree loomed up, then we were by it and Jackie leaped out. This all happened in less than five seconds. Jackie made a grab for my arm, still thinking it was Barbara he was grabbing. I said, "Hello, sweetheart," and jammed him in the ribs with the gun. I saw him start to swing and I brought the

73

gun up and let him taste the barrel, hard. It knocked him down and split both lips. He rolled over in the grass and got to his feet. He stood like a panther ready to spring and I stood there waiting for him.

Then nothing happened. He didn't say a word: his eyes said it all. You are dead, Janeway, his eyes said, you are one dead cop. He had me quaking like Mount Saint Helens. With his eyes, Jackie said, I don't know when, I don't know how, but I am gonna bury you. With my mouth, I said, "I told you before, Newton, you better fix that door." He didn't think that was funny. He turned his evil eye on Barbara. She couldn't look at him: her skin had gone white with goose bumps. I stepped in front of her and locked eyes with Jackie for what seemed like forever. He turned and walked away first. He was going up the hill toward her place, where his car was parked.

"Come on," I said. "We'll go a different way."

Again she had been taken by a fit of shivering. I draped my coat over her shoulders. "I'm gonna have to start charging you rent for this coat," I said. It didn't cheer her up. We cut up alleys and went in the back way to her place. I sat her on the couch and put on a pot of water for instant coffee. While it was coming to a boil I went to the window and looked down where Jackie Newton had discovered his flat tire. I saw him throw his jack halfway across the street, then flip off a passing driver who had blown his horn. He was a bad son of a bitch, Jackie. All that remained to be seen was how bad.

8

I got the coffee down from a cupboard. I found her liquor cabinet and stirred in a generous shot of brandy. She sipped it, then sat staring at the oval rug under her feet. I went to the window to check on Jackie's progress. He was still in the stage of initial disgust and hadn't done much yet. I should've punched two out, or maybe all four, I thought.

"How you feeling now?" I asked without turning away from Jackie.

Numbly, she said, "Why is this happening?"

"You're letting it happen."

I turned in time to see the anger in her eyes. But she didn't say anything.

"You've got to play his game by his rules," I said. "He's like a bully in a schoolyard. Either you stand up to him or he kills you, piece by piece, day by day."

Her voice trembled, from anger, fear, or both. "How the fuck do I stand up to *that?*" she shouted.

"Start showing him you mean what you say."

She shivered, drawing my coat tight around her neck. "A week ago I'd never heard of the goddamn man. Now he's got control of my life."

"Take it back."

"You keep saying that. I'm sick of it. It's easy for you to say."

"I didn't say it was easy. But it may be your only choice."

"Then tell me, please, what exactly do you want me to do?"

"Show some guts, Barbara. Maybe it'll get you killed, but how do you know this won't?"

I got her some more coffee. She had gulped the cup and it seemed to be doing her some good. Her shivers had subsided and in another minute she let my coat hang loose on her shoulders.

"For starters," I said, "if he ever touches you again, get the cops involved. Don't just hang up because I'm not there. I'm a homicide cop; you don't need me here unless he kills you. There are other cops who handle this kind of stuff. I'll give you some names; I'll grease the skids downtown so you'll get priority treatment. In other words, I'll do what I can."

She shook her head.

"Look, you had a start on him this morning, then you let him get away. He raped you. What you should've done right then was go to the hospital. Swear out a warrant. Let him cool his heels in jail for a few hours. Take him to Denver District Court. Take him all the way. If you get one of those lemon-suckers on the bench, he gets off. But at least he knows you're ready to play hardball."

"Which means I go to the morgue next time."

"Or maybe there won't be a next time. I've got a theory about our friend Jackie. If you show a white flag, he'll tear you to pieces. Jackie takes no prisoners: he loves to take on people who won't fight back. If you do fight, he'll give you a hard look before he comes back again."

"I think you're wrong. I think he takes it very personally when you fight. I think he's going to kill you for what you did to him today."

"I'm not gonna argue with you. I didn't become a cop because of my grades in psych. You asked me what to do and I told you. Rack his ass if he blinks at you twice. Get yourself a restraining order and then the cops can bust him if he doesn't leave you alone. That's the first step."

"And the last. Oh, Christ, you can't protect me."

"We can try. We can do the best we can do."

"Then what? You can't take me by the hand and walk me to work. You can't sleep with me. . . ."

We looked at each other. She said, "What if you do the best you can do and it still isn't good enough? What do I do then, challenge him to a duel? Quit my job and leave my friends and start over in another state?"

"I got no guarantees, ma'am. All I can do is tell you this—I'm on your side and so is the police department. We got a guy out there who thinks he's one tough cowboy. Our job is to show him he isn't. There are many ways of doing this, and some of them you don't need to know about."

She took a deep breath. "It's really bad between you two, isn't it?"

I gave her my sour little smile in return.

I told her I'd be back in a minute. I had looked out the window and seen that Jackie Newton was now hard at work on his flat tire. I didn't want him to leave without saying good-bye.

I went down and sat on the coping and watched him work.

Jackie was into his silent act. It was supposed to be intimidating, and I guess it was. He knew I was there: I could tell by the way he breathed. He had scraped his hand and blood had oozed out between his knuckles.

I started a running line of chatter, thinking it would annoy him.

"I sure wouldn't leave a car like that on the street," I said pleasantly. "You never know when you'll come back and find a door kicked in."

He grunted over his lugs. I heard them squeak as he jerked on the lug wrench.

"There're gangs around who do stuff like that," I said. "Just bash up expensive automobiles."

His lugs squeaked.

"Scumbags," I said. "Everywhere you go."

Squeak.

"It's getting so you can't do anything without running into some scumbucket who wants to take away a piece of your life."

Squeak.

"Take the lady who lives here," I said. "There's a certain asshole I know who won't leave her alone. Tries to screw around with her head, make her wish she'd never been born. What do you think of a man who'd do something like that?"

Squeak-squeak.

"Some man, huh?"

Squeak.

"Tighten those things too tight and you'll have a helluva time getting them off again."

There was a sharp clang as he threw the lug wrench down on the street.

"Never know when you'll have another flat."

He came around and let the car's weight jiggle down off the jack. Then he stood up tall and gave me a look. His face was a mess: blood had dripped onto his fine white shirt and his hair for once was tousled. He threw the tire and jack into the car and made ready to go.

"When this guy comes back again, he's gonna pay a heavy price," I said. "A real heavy price."

He pulled up the door and stood there for a minute. I thought he might say something then but he didn't. He ducked his head and got in his car, and I stood up and backed away under the shadows of the front porch. You never knew when a guy might have a piece hidden in the car, and if something serious started I wanted some cover.

But he drove away. Calmly. Like a man of reason. He didn't even peel rubber.

A real scary guy, Jackie. A bad son of a bitch.

I knew an old man once who swore he saw a sailor beat the hell out of Gene Tunney in a barroom brawl. Tunney was at his peak then, the heavyweight champion of the world. Titles don't mean much when you're getting your lunch eaten.

The meanest son of a bitch in the world can only be the meanest while he's at his absolute peak and the other guy hasn't quite come up to his. Say a month on the long end, a few minutes on the short.

I know guys who could make Jackie Newton wish his mamma had never set eyes on his daddy. I grew up with one of them. Vincent Marranzino wrote the book on tough guys. I haven't seen Vince in a long time: his life and mine have taken different paths and we both understand that. But Vince still owes me one—a certain fight with knives in a north Denver backlot when we were sixteen. I had taken

79

his side against a pack of wolves and the two of us had kicked ass against great odds. Guys like Vince never forget something like that: they have a streak of loyalty that goes to bedrock.

A simple phone call was all it would take. Before morning, Jackie Newton's anatomy would be rearranged.

Tempting, isn't it?

A nice hole card, if the system couldn't be made to work.

This was what I had meant when I told Barbara that there were things in life she'd be better off not knowing. The genie was out of the bottle, just a phone call away.

But of course I wouldn't do it. Like Brutus, I am an honorable man.

9

I spent another futile hour with Barbara Crowell. There's no way to talk common sense to someone who's that scared, so there wasn't much else to do but wait for the locksmith to come fix her door. While I waited, I made some calls on the Bobby Westfall case. I called Bobby's apartment and talked to Hennessey. Our boys had been there for an hour and weren't finding much. They had lifted some prints, probably the victim's, and had arranged for the pound to come pick up the cats. They had sent Ruby Seals back to his bookstore in a police car. It didn't look like the apartment was going to give us much. There were still piles of books to go through, but that would take a bookman's eye—my job, and I'd be at it far into the night.

I tried Rita McKinley: same answering machine, same message.

I sat with the telephone book opened to "Book Dealers, Used and Rare," and I went through the stores in my mind. Some eliminated themselves from my priority list—junk shops, paperback exchanges, dealers in comic books: these

I'd get to, eventually, if something didn't pan out higher up. I called Roland Goddard in Cherry Creek and told him I wanted to see him tomorrow about the murder of Bobby Westfall. There was no use pussyfooting around anymore. The book world is amazingly tight, and even now the word of Bobby's death would be racing from one store to another. By tomorrow it would be all over town.

I called three or four other dealers who might have bought books from Bobby. All of them had. I told them I'd want to see them, and would try to stop in in the next couple of days.

This was going to be a long haul.

I tried calling Carol, to tell her I'd be late tonight. She was out on the streets and I didn't want to leave a message. The only world tighter than the world of books is the world of cops.

The locksmith had fixed Barbara's back door and was installing a deadbolt in the front. Nobody was coming through that door once that baby was put in, the locksmith said. I wasn't too sure of that, but I didn't say anything.

I went back to Bobby's place. The boys were gone, all but Hennessey. We sat and talked the case out, as it stood to now. It didn't stand anywhere. We had nothing: we were shooting in the dark. We might be dealing with something totally outside Bobby's book-dealing activity, and in that case it might never be solved.

Hennessey had talked to the coroner, and the guesswork of last night had been confirmed. Bobby was killed somewhere else, then dumped in the alley. Time of death was sometime between eleven o'clock and midnight. This told us nothing, as we had been going on that assumption anyway. "Let's forget about it till morning," Hennessey said. "Come on home with me, we're having a big pot roast tonight." I took a rain check: I wanted to get started on Bobby's things, and I knew that I wouldn't stop till the last scrap of paper had been sifted to the watermark. This is just the way I work. It made Hennessey feel guilty, but that's life. "I should stay here and help you, Cliff," he said. "I'd probably just get in your way. I don't know from Shinola about this stuff." I agreed and told him to go home. It was getting dark outside. I hadn't eaten in more than twelve hours, so I asked Marty Zimmers to call Domino's and have a deep pan pizza and a bucket of swill sent over. Then I got to work.

It was a long, thankless job. You wouldn't believe the crap that accumulates in a bookscout's den. Book after book came down from the pile and went into another pile that I had labeled "Junk" in my mind. I thumbed each piece carefully, I went page by page to make sure a $50,000 pamphlet wasn't hidden inside a $2 book. It wasn't. There were some real heartbreakers—a fine little Faulkner poem, original 1932 issue, paper wraps, a $250 piece that Bobby could've sold to me on the spot except that someone had lost his supper on the title page . . . an early Steinbeck, nice, except that somebody had ripped out the title page . . . Robert Frost's first book, inscribed by Frost on the half title, very quaint except that a kid had been at the book with crayons. There were so many books eaten by mold that I had to wash my hands after handling them. My pizza came and I washed my hands again. I went munching and sorting my way into the early night. At nine-thirty I seemed to be about half through. I went downstairs and called Carol, told her I'd be another two or three hours, and said she'd better not wait up.

I chugged my swill, burped, and went back to it.

I was resigned by then to coming up zero. I took a break

at ten-thirty and let my eyes skim over the books as a lot.
If there was anything worthwhile in that mess, I sure
couldn't see it. I started on the books in the toilet. Nothing.
I was mucking it out pretty good now. There were a few
papers in the closet and some books in the kitchenette. No
great secrets were hidden there that I could see. Nothing
the Russians would kill for: nothing anybody would kill
for. Slowly the one natural motive—that Bobby had found
something valuable—was dwindling before my eyes. Of
course, the killer might've taken it away with him: I was
going on the slim, bare hope that he had killed Bobby and
had failed to find what he had killed for. But I was beginning to believe it was something as simple, and insane, as
an old grudge, or a sudden fight between rivals.

Then I found the good books.

There were two stacks of them in the cupboard in the
kitchenette. They stood like sentinels, acting as bookends
for the Cheerios and the Rice Chex. The first thing I
noticed was the quality. There were some very good pieces,
some real honeys. I took them into the living room and sat
with them, browsing. There were fifteen titles, and I made
a list, adding my own idea of what they were worth.

Gardner, Erle Stanley. Case of Dangerous Dowager. $200.
Finney, Jack. Time & Again. $150.
Uris, Leon. Battle Cry. $150.
Kennedy, William. The Ink Truck. $200–250.
McMurtry, Larry. Last Picture Show. $200.
Heinlein, Robert A. Glory Road. $250.
Cain, James M. Postman. A biggie—maybe a grand.
Bellow, Saul. Augie March. Buck and a quarter.
Jackson, Shirley. The Lottery. $150.
Bradbury, Ray. Illustrated Man. $200.

Miller, Henry. Books in My Life. $100.
Isherwood, Christopher. Berlin Stories, signed by C. I.
   $150.
Irving, John. 150-Pound Marriage. $200.
Bloch, Robert. Psycho. $200.
Rawlings, Marjorie. The Yearling. $150.

I did a quick tally. Call it three grand retail and put me down as momentarily confused. When we last saw Bobby Westfall, through the eyes of Jerry Harkness, Ruby Seals, et cetera, he was broke, pissed off, and without hope. Books had been drying up: Harkness doubted that Bobby even had bus fare back downtown. That was two weeks ago, and now I had discovered a stash of books, extremely wholesalable at a thousand dollars. There was simply no way for this stack to have been scouted in two weeks, probably not in two years. I looked at it again. No way, I thought. Even a titan of bookscouts couldn't've done it piecemeal. So where did they come from and what did it mean? Here were the possibilities that initially occurred to me.

Bobby had come upon them as a lot, sometime within the past ten days, and had stolen them from some ignorant soul for pennies.

He had literally stolen them.

He had been hoarding them for a long time.

It was possible, I guessed, though not likely, that he had been hoarding books. There are people like that, guys who pigeonhole things for a specific reason and then have the willpower—no matter how bad the times are—never to touch the stash. Say Bobby had been building this pile for three or four years. When he found a book he particularly liked, it went into the Good Pile marked NFS, not for sale. Sometimes he had to sell books that he'd like to've put there, but once a book actually went in the cupboard he never, ever took it out again.

That made sense, didn't it?

I looked at the books again, singly and as a group. Hoarding was possible, but thievery was likely. Bobby had shafted someone; then that someone had found out what the books were really worth and had come after Bobby with a crescent wrench. Maybe, maybe. I stared at the books and let my mind play with them. Common denominators, I thought. For one thing, they were all modern lit. They were all easily disposable—any bookstore worth the name would buy any or all at forty percent. I revised my estimate of condition upward. These were uniformly pristine. There wasn't a tear anywhere: even on the Cain and Gardner and Rawlings, the three oldest, the jackets were fresh and bright and had minimal sun fading to the spines. Three grand might actually be very low retail for stuff this nice: books don't come along every day in this condition. So Bobby had a standard, if I wanted to go back to the hoarding theory, and that was another common denominator. Nothing went in here unless it was damn near perfect. One hundred retail seemed to be the cutoff point on the low end. There was a healthy mix of mainstream and genre fiction, but you had to keep going back to one sure thing: the books were all desirable, all eminently salable.

Now I began to examine them page by page. Tucked into a back page of *The Last Picture Show*, I found the sheath of notes.

They were figures, chicken scratches, columns of multiplication like a kid might have to do for homework. There were lots of figures on four separate sheets. The sheets were small, the kind you might tear off of a memo pad. At the top of each was a printed name: Rita McKinley. She had signed each with scribbled initials. One had some writing at the bottom. It said: "These are the good ones. Not much gold, I'm afraid, for all the mining. R. M." I took the papers, handling them carefully, and dropped them into an envelope. Then I put the books back in the cupboard, closed the door on them, and turned off the kitchen light. I felt an almost physical pain leaving them there.

Good thing I'm an honest cop.

I drank the last of my swill, and that pretty well threw a wrap on it.

I picked up Bobby's little address book and put it in my pocket along with the Rita McKinley notes. I turned off the light in the bathroom and felt the first wave of weariness wash over my aging bones.

Then I heard a noise, a creaking sound, like a man trying to be quiet.

I waited. It came again, then died and went away.

I listened.

Rats, maybe?

Rats with two legs.

I took out my gun and eased up to the door. I put my head against it and in a minute I heard it again. Someone had come up the steps and was standing just outside in the hallway.

I leveled the gun and ripped open the door.

He let out a yell and cringed back against the stairwell.

"Jesus Christ, Dr. J! God Almighty, don't shoot me!"

I sighed and put the gun away. "Ruby, what the hell are you doing here?"

He held up his hand and with the other hand clutched his heart. "Jesus, you scared me out of ten years' growth.

You better let me come in and take a leak before I lose it right here in the hall."

"Not in here you don't. What the hell are you doing here?"

"I came up to see if I could help."

I looked at him.

"Swear to God, Dr. J. I was over to some friends, shootin' the shit and listenin' to some old Dylan records. We just broke up. I drove by and saw the light on and I figured it was you. Thought you might be able to use a hand, you know, from somebody who's been around the Cape and knows his books."

"You know better than that. Look, I appreciate the thought, but you can't come in here. I thought I made that clear this afternoon."

"Yeah, but the cops've already gone through the place. What do I know about po-lice procedure? I just thought a question might pop up that you couldn't pin down for yourself. The last thing I want to do is get in the way. I want you to catch the prick that did this, that's all I want."

"All right, Ruby. I'm sorry I scared you."

"Took ten years off my goddamn life is all."

"Just stay away from here. Don't even think of stopping here again. If I need any help, I'll come to you."

"That's all I want, just to help out. You know how tricky this stuff can be, trying to figure out what's what in books. I know you're pretty good, Dr. J, but a real bookman could maybe help you knock some time off the clock."

"All right," I said. "I'll call you if I need you."

"You think it'd be okay if I took a leak? I got a sudden urgent need, Dr. J, and that's no lie."

"I'll have to watch you."

"Hey, I ain't proud."

I walked him through to the bathroom. I lifted the lid on the toilet and stood back in the doorway while he did his business. His eyes ran down the book titles on the back of the toilet, a natural bookseller's habit.

"Some crap," he said.

"Yeah."

He zipped up his pants and flushed the toilet. "Thanks, Dr. J."

We walked back to the door. Suddenly, I said, "What do you know about Rita McKinley?"

"The ice lady?"

"Is that what you call her?"

"That's what everybody calls her. Once every year or so she makes a sweep through all the Denver stores. Drops a ton of dough. Buys anything unusual but cherry-picks like hell. She's got the best eye I've ever seen. Won't touch a book with a bumped corner, no matter how much it's got going for it. She won't take anything that's got even a little problem, but doesn't mind paying top money for those perfect pieces."

"And that, I guess, is why she's called the ice lady."

"That's part of it. The other part is that people in the trade think she's got a cold shoulder. She don't stand over the counter engaging in mindless bullshit. She don't seem to be interested in shoptalk at all."

"How do you like her?"

"Man, I love her. I wish she'd come twice a week; maybe then I could get out of the poorhouse. She's not bad-looking, either. Brightens up the joint while she's in there."

"How come I never heard of her before today?"

"Beats me. Maybe 'cause she don't do retail."

"How long's she been here?"

"In Denver? I don't know, a few years I guess."

"Where'd she come from?"

"Back east, I think. Hell, I don't know. I don't exactly ask her this stuff when she comes in."

"When was she in last?"

"It's been a while . . . maybe a year? Longer than usual. I remember that last time because we had some great stuff for her. She dropped six grand in our place alone. Man, what I could do with six grand now."

"What else do you know about her?"

"Not a damn thing, really. Is she mixed up in this?"

"That's what I'm trying to find out."

"It don't make much sense to me. I mean, Bobby Westfall and Rita McKinley? It just don't play in Peoria."

I had said the same thing a few hours before. But the human comedy makes some strange whistle-stops on the way to Peoria.

I kept looking at him, encouraging him.

"Look, Dr. J . . . almost anything you hear about Rita McKinley is gonna be rumors. Nobody knows her well enough to talk about her. That doesn't stop 'em from talking anyway, though. Sure, I hear some shit. You can't help but pick up stuff in this business, but I hate to spread trash about people when I really don't know. You see what I'm saying?"

"Ruby, I've got a dead man and no suspects. You see what I'm saying?"

He sighed. "Some people think she's a gold digger."

"What people?"

"Who the hell knows where something like that starts? One day you just start hearing it. If you hear it enough, you might even start believing it."

I looked at him.

He shuffled and said, "For one thing, she didn't always have money. Didn't always have books. She's got a lot of both now. I know plenty of rich book dealers, but very few who started with no money. It's hard to work your way up in this business without a bankroll to start with. There are damn few ways, inside the law, to get that much money and that many good books in that short a time . . . divine intervention excluded."

"Where do people think she got 'em?"

"Oh, everybody knows where she got 'em. There wasn't any mystery about that—it was all wrapped up in a big *AB* spread a few years ago. What nobody knows is the circumstances of that deal. That's what the mystery is. What I remember about it is this. She had been dating a book collector. She moved in with him. He died, and when he went he left her everything . . . books, estate, money . . . the whole works."

"Was this man old?"

"I don't think so."

"Do you know anything about when and where he died?"

He shook his head. "I can't remember. You could write to the *AB,* I'm sure they'd send you the article. There was another piece about Rita McKinley when she moved her stuff here and opened her business. I remember reading it. It wasn't much of a piece, just a little one-column job saying she had come here and was open for business . . . about three, four years ago. The guy's name escapes me just now . . . I ought to remember it; he was a good enough collector that the *AB* devoted two pages to his death."

"Did the article say how he died?"

"Sure. That's the part that keeps the tongues wagging. He killed himself."

10

Ruby's visit to Bobby Westfall's apartment bothered me, and on second thought I decided to take the good books along with me when I left. Carol was sitting by the bed reading Faulkner when I came in. I put Bobby's books on the floor and pushed the bag containing her birthday present behind the stack.

"Hi," she said. "What's that you've got there?"

"Just some stuff for the evidence room. I didn't want to leave it in that empty apartment."

She came over and looked. "These are valuable?"

"Yeah, but this is all of it. The rest is like total junk." I looked at my watch: it was one-fifteen. "What're you still doing up?"

"Couldn't sleep. What's your excuse?"

"Liftin' that barge. Totin' that bale . . . payin' my debt to the company store."

"So how was your day?"

"Ducky."

"Did I ever tell you, Clifford, that the thing I love best

92

about you is your communications skill? Did you go out to see Newton?"

"Uh-huh."

She sighed and rolled her eyes. *"And?"*

"He's gonna be my date at the policeman's ball."

"Wonderful. You girls will look great together."

"Look, I'm sorry. I'd really rather talk about the cockroach problem some other time. Right now I'm gonna grab a shower and mount a major assault with heavy artillery on your body."

Later, in bed, she lay in the crook of my arm. She was a great lover, good for what ailed me after a twenty-four-hour shift. Now, I thought, I could sleep. But again I found myself thinking about us, our situation, permanence, and me. I was in the middle of a vast sea change. I wondered what she would think of me if I suddenly wasn't a cop anymore. She had been a tomboy: being a cop was all she'd ever wanted. She had never mentioned children: we had simply never talked of it. In my mind I could hear her saying, I've got to tell you, Cliff, I don't want kids—I'm just not cut out for the motherhood bit. I could see her staring in disbelief when I told her I'd rather be a bookman, I think, than a cop, and not thirty years from now. Maybe she wouldn't do any of those things. She had been in the department long enough now—almost eight years—to be building up her own case of burnout. Maybe she was getting ready to hear what I was thinking but was still not inclined to talk about it.

"What're you thinking?" she said.

"Think I'm gonna turn in my badge and become a book dealer," I said.

But I said this in a safe, singsong voice, the same tone you use when you say you're going to the policeman's ball with Jackie Newton. She couldn't do much with it but laugh.

Only she didn't laugh. She just lay there in my arm and we didn't speak again for a long time.

It was the telephone that finally broke the spell.

"God Almighty," I said wearily. "If that's Hennessey I'll kill the bastard."

"I'll get it," she said, reaching over me. "I'll tell him you've died and the funeral's the day after tomorrow."

She picked up the phone. I heard her say hello and then there was a long silence. Without saying another word, she hung up.

"What's that all about?"

"A guy trying to sell me a water softener."

"At two o'clock in the morning?"

She didn't say anything.

"What's going on?" I said.

"I seem to've got myself a heavy breather. That's why I couldn't sleep. It started about eight o'clock and he's been calling back every hour or two."

"Does he say anything?"

"He whispered once."

"What'd he say?"

"The usual stuff. Cunt, bitch, whore. Some other stuff."

"Did he say anything personal . . . anything to indicate that he might know who you are?"

"Why would he know who I am? Those kinds of calls are mostly random, you know that."

"I don't think this one is."

She sat up and turned on the light.

"What happened out there today?"

I told her about my day with Jackie. I could see it wasn't convincing her that Jackie had taken up telephone harassment for revenge.

"I'm taking the phone off," she said. "If you don't get some sleep you'll be a zombie tomorrow."

The phone rang.

"Let it go," she said. "He'll get tired of it and hang up."

But I picked it up. Didn't say anything, just listened. He was there, listening too. This went on for almost a minute. Then I said, "You having fun, Newton?"

He hung up.

"It's Newton," I said. "He hung up when I called him by name."

"That doesn't mean anything."

"All right, then, I can smell the son of a bitch, okay?"

"Okay, Cliff. I'm sure not going to argue about it at two o'clock in the morning."

"Listen," I said sometime later. "Jackie and me, we shift-ed gears out there today. There never was any love lost between us, you know that. But it's different now, it's on a whole new plain."

She had propped herself up on one arm, a silhouette against the window.

"He'll do whatever he can to get at me. I don't think it matters to him that I'm a cop, or that you are. I don't think anything matters. It's him and me."

"Hatfields and McCoys."

"Yeah. It's gotten that deep. I may've given Barbara Crowell some very bad advice today."

"Cliff, you need a vacation."

"I need to get something on that weasel. That's the only vacation I need. To get him good and make it stick."

"You're a classic type A, you'll die before you're forty. You need to go and lie on a beach and listen to tropical breezes blowing through luscious palm trees."

"And go crazy with boredom. That's not what I need."

"I'd go along too . . . try to keep you from getting too bored."

More long minutes passed.

"I'll do whatever I can," Carol said.

"As a matter of fact, there is something you can do."

"Just tell me."

"Get the hell out of here."

"Oh, Cliff, that's not going to help anything."

"I've been thinking about it all day, ever since I gave Jackie the thirty-eight-caliber lollipop. Newton doesn't know who you are. All he knows is, he called my place and a woman answered. Nobody knows about us. We've taken a lot of trouble to keep what's ours private."

She took a deep, long-suffering breath.

"Well? Will you do it?"

"Of course I'll do it," she said. "But God damn it, don't ask me to like it."

I patted her rump. "Good girl."

"You sexist bastard."

We laughed. At that moment I came as close to asking her the big question as I ever would.

It was a long time before we got to sleep. When I did sleep, I slept soundly, untroubled by dreams. In the morning we got her things together and I carried them down the back way and put them in her car. I watched the street for ten minutes before I let her come down and drive away.

She rolled down her window. "I'm not afraid, you know."

"I know you're not," I said. "But I am."

11

I called Rita McKinley and got the same recording. This time I left a message, telling her who I was and that I needed to speak with her on official business regarding a homicide investigation. I left both numbers, home and office.

I called the *AB* in New Jersey. Also known as *Bookman's Weekly*, the *AB* is the trade journal of the antiquarian book world. Each week it lists hundreds of books, sought and for sale by dealers everywhere. Thus can a total recluse operate effectively in the book business without ever seeing another human being: he buys and sells through the *AB*. In addition to the listings, which take up most of the magazine, there are a few articles each week on doings in the trade—obits, career profiles, book fair reports. Sometime during the past few years, I explained to the editor, a piece or pieces were run on Rita McKinley. He was a wise gentleman who knew his business, and he knew right away who McKinley was and about when the stories had run. He promised copies in the next mail.

I went to see Roland Goddard, in Cherry Creek. This is a neighborhood of high-class and expensive shops in east Denver. Nestled in the center of things was Roland Goddard's Acushnet Rare Book Emporium. Goddard had a cool, austere manner, almost like Emery Neff only somehow different. You could break through with Neff, if you were patient enough and gave a damn: with Goddard, you never could. He had an icy, slightly superior attitude about books and his knowledge of them, and he could intimidate a customer or a bookscout before the first word was said. If he had friends, they were not in the book business: no one I had ever spoken to knew Goddard personally.

It would be hard to imagine two guys less alike than Goddard and Harkness. At least with Ruby Seals and Emery Neff, their differences seemed to complement each other: Harkness and Goddard were ill-suited for partnership in almost every way. It's hard sometimes to look back over twenty years and know why the boys we were then did things so much at odds with the attitudes and philosophies of the men we had become. Goddard was fastidious: Harkness tended to be sloppy. Goddard disdained everything about the book business that Harkness found interesting. Oh, he'd sell you a Stephen King— whatever else you could say about Roland Goddard, he was a helluva bookman and he knew where the money came from—but you might leave his store feeling faintly like a moron.

Goddard dealt primarily in Truly Important Books— incunabula, sixteenth-century poetry, illuminated manuscripts, fine leather stuff. He had some great things. Even the name of his store simmered in tradition. *Acushnet* was the whaler Melville served on in the 1840s. I liked his store and I loved his stock, though I never did much business there. When I marry one of the Rockefellers, Goddard will have a big payday, most of it from me.

Acushnet was one of only three bookstores in Denver that could afford full-time help. The man who worked there was Julian Lambert, a good bookman in his own right. Lambert bought and sold as freely as his boss did: Ruby, in fact, had told me once that bookscouts preferred dealing with Goddard because he paid them more. Goddard wasn't in when I arrived, but I busied myself looking through the stock until I saw him come in through a back entrance. The morning rush had waned: he and Lambert sat behind the counter cataloging. I knew that Goddard issued catalogs a few times a year, though no one in Denver ever saw one. He had the best reference library in the state, but played it close to the vest when it came to sharing information.

Goddard and Lambert were surprised when I introduced myself. I knew they had seen me around—we had spoken a few times in passing—but until this moment they had not put my face together with the Detective Janeway who had called on the phone and asked to see them. I got right down to cases. When was the last time they had seen Bobby Westfall? The same questions, the same answers, with Goddard doing most of the talking. It had been almost two weeks since Bobby had been in. He had come in one day just about the time he was last seen on Book Row. "He had a couple of books he was trying to sell me," Goddard said, "but they weren't the kind of things I use." I told him I had heard through the grapevine that he had been dealing with Bobby rather heavily. He frowned and said, "That must be Jerry Harkness talking, and as usual he doesn't know what he's talking about. Westfall made one very lucky find about a year ago and I bought all the books he had on that particular day. I wouldn't make any more out of it than that. He had some books and I bought them."

"What were the books?"

"Oz books. Westfall stumbled over them in a garage sale. Thirty-two Oz books for a dollar apiece. Most of the time when you see those they're in poor condition. These were very fine, beautiful copies."

"Were they firsts?"

"Only a few were. None of the Frank Baum titles were, but there were a couple of Ruth Plumley Thompson firsts and the one Jack Snow. The main thing about them was the condition. Half of them still had dust jackets. All the color plates were fresh and unscuffed, even the plates on the covers."

"You got any of 'em left?"

"Oh no. They didn't last the month."

"Nice little strike for both of you, then. What did you pay him?"

He looked offended and tried not to answer.

"I'd really like to know that," I insisted.

"I prefer keeping my finances private."

"You'd have every right to, if the man hadn't been murdered."

He hedged. "I don't remember exactly."

"Did you pay him in cash?"

"Not for something that big."

"Then you wrote a check. Which means you've got a record of it."

His eyes narrowed. "Do I have to talk to you about this?"

I didn't say anything.

"It's just that I don't want people knowing my business.

Most of the time I pay more money per book than anyone in town. But you never want people knowing exactly what you're doing."

"This is a homicide investigation," I said. "I'm not gonna take out a billboard and plaster it with evidence."

"I just don't see how a transaction that we did a year ago can have anything to do with evidence. But if you promise me you'll keep it private, I'll tell you. I gave him seven hundred."

"You have the cancelled check?"

"At home, yes. I can produce it if necessary."

"I'll let you know. How did the books price out?"

"I'm not sure exactly. Julian?"

"Twenty-two hundred dollars," Lambert said.

"So you paid him a little less than one-third," I said.

"Which was fair, under the circumstances," Goddard said. "He had thirty-two dollars in it."

"Which shouldn't matter. That is very salable stuff."

"Yes it is."

"All right," I said with a little sigh. "You're right, it probably doesn't matter anyway, but if it does I'll ask you for that check. Now you say he was in here a couple of weeks ago. What happened?"

"Like I told you, he had a couple of books. One was a good book, but the condition wasn't there."

"So you bought nothing from him?"

"That's right."

"And that's the last time you saw him."

"That's the last time I saw him."

Something unfinished hung in the air. It took me a moment to realize what it was. Lambert, who had been busily engaged writing book descriptions on index cards, had looked up and caught his boss's eye.

"That is right, isn't it, Julian?"

"He did come in once since then," Lambert said. "You weren't here, and it was a busy morning, like today. He was only here for a few minutes. It was unusual because he didn't do anything. He didn't look at any of our books and he didn't have anything to sell."

"When was this?" Goddard said.

"Recent. No more than a week." Lambert closed his eyes and went into deep thought. "I think it may've been Thursday."

"What went on?" I said.

"Nothing. He just came in to see Roland. He said he had a deal cooking and he wanted to see Roland."

"Was that his exact language?"

"Just like that," Lambert said. "He had a big deal cooking and he wanted to see if Roland was interested."

Roland was far more annoyed than interested. "Why didn't you tell me about this?" he said.

"I was busy that morning; I didn't have time to talk to the man. Then I just forgot about it. I didn't think it was anything that would set the world on fire. You know how these guys are. Everything's important. Everything's a big deal."

"It's not like you to forget something like that," Goddard said.

"I should etch it in stone every time one of these characters opens his mouth? I was busy. I was running the bookstore. I assumed if it was important he'd be back. Then I forgot about it."

"If you guys don't mind," I said, "I'd like to get back to my questions. You can grumble at each other all day after I'm gone." I flipped a page in my notebook. "Have either of you got any idea what Bobby would be doing with Rita McKinley?"

Goddard just stared. Lambert laughed out loud.

"Who told you that?" Goddard said.

"Everybody."

"Well, it's the first time I've heard it."

I looked at Lambert. "How about you?"

His laugh had been cut off in the middle of a ha-ha, and his face had begun to turn red. He had busied himself with a book and was pretending to be somewhere else. That's a sure sign with a guy like Lambert that he knows something more—something he'd rather not tell.

"Don't fall all over yourself answering the question," I said. "It's just that a man has been murdered, and I'm supposed to make some kind of effort to find out who did it."

He looked up defiantly. "All right, I just this minute remembered. When he walked out that day, he was kind of angry. He had been waiting for Roland for more than an hour, and I finally said I didn't know how much longer it would be. That's the day you went to get license plates for your new car," he said to Goddard. "How can you ever tell in advance how long that's going to take?"

"I was there three hours," Goddard said.

"That would make it . . . what?" I said. "You thought it was Thursday."

"It was Thursday," Goddard said.

The day before the murder.

"So what happened?" I said, looking at Lambert.

"Suddenly Westfall gets impatient. He stalks over to the door like he's going to leave. But before he does, he turns and says to me, 'I guess Rita McKinley would be more interested in what I have to sell.' And he stomped out."

Goddard shook his head. "This just gets worse all the time. How could you forget something like that?"

"I told you," Lambert said. "The store was a madhouse

that day. I can't buy, sell, and be a secretary all at once."

"Let's get back on the point," I said. "Did Bobby say, or even hint, what he might have to sell?"

"No, and like I told you, he wasn't carrying anything with him."

"Did he say anything else?"

"No," Lambert said.

We looked at each other for a moment.

"You've got to remember one thing," Lambert said. "You've got to consider the source. How many times have these guys come in thinking they've found a thousand-dollar book and it turns out to be nothing? I don't consider it my first line of business to keep up with people like Westfall. Especially when we're doing seven hundred in real business in the space of an hour."

"All right, forget it," Goddard said.

But it wasn't over yet. "What can you boys tell me about Rita McKinley?" I said.

"I can't tell you a thing," Goddard said. "I never met the lady, wouldn't know her if I saw her on the street."

"You're aware of her reputation, though?"

"I know she has some good books. That's what I've heard. But I don't scout the other dealers. I don't do business that way."

I looked at Lambert. Again he had gone red around the ears. He'd be a terrible witness in court, if he had anything to hide.

"It's a good thing you didn't kill Bobby, Lambert," I said. "All a cop would have to do is ask you."

He looked up shakily. "I went up there once," he said.

Then, after a long pause, he said to Goddard, "I didn't say anything to you because I knew you wouldn't like it."

Goddard didn't like it. The temperature in the room dropped another five degrees.

"I wanted to see her stock, that's all," Lambert said. "There's been so much talk, and I wanted to see what she had."

"I hope you didn't represent yourself as a buyer for this store," Goddard said.

"I didn't have to. She knew exactly who I was. She knows everybody."

"When did you go up there?" I asked.

"Last fall, before Thanksgiving."

"Could you show me how to get there . . . draw me a map?"

"Sure. It's not that hard to find. You'll need more than a map, though. There's a high fence all around her place, and nobody gets in without calling ahead. You have to call and leave a message."

"Is she pretty good about calling back?"

"She called me back. I heard from her within a couple of hours."

"What was she like?"

"All business."

"But she gave you no trouble about coming up?"

"Why wouldn't she have me up? She's in the business to sell books."

"I just heard that she doesn't exactly roll out the red carpet."

"You won't hear that from me. She's a real lady," Lambert said, his face reddening. "She's got perfect manners and I'll tell you this. She knows her stuff. I was damned impressed."

"Obviously," Goddard said.

"What did you think of her stuff?" I asked.

"Absolutely incredible. I've never seen books like that. She's got a *This Side of Paradise,* signed by Fitzgerald, with

H. L. Mencken's bookplate and a personal note from Fitzgerald practically begging Mencken for a review. The book is in a bright, fresh jacket with no flaws. She's got a whole wall of detective stuff—prime, wonderful books. Have you ever seen perfect copies of Ross Macdonald's first three books, or the first American edition of *Mysterious Affair at Styles?* She's got a *Gone With the Wind* signed by Margaret Mitchell, Clark Gable, and Vivien Leigh. Gable wrote a little note under his name that said, 'And now, my dear, everyone will give a damn.' There's so much great stuff, you don't know where to start."

Goddard grunted.

"Here's another thing," Lambert said. "You remember that old rumor about Hemingway and Wolfe signing each other's books?"

It was a rumor I had never heard, so I asked him to fill me in.

"Sometime in the thirties, a woman in Indiana was supposed to have sent a package of Hemingway and Wolfe books to Max Perkins, begging for signatures. The books sat around in Perkins's office for months. Then one night Hemingway and Wolfe were both there and Perkins remembered the books and got them signed. But both of them were three sheets to the wind and Hemingway thought it would be a great joke if they signed all the wrong books. He sat down and wrote a long drunken inscription in *Look Homeward, Angel,* and signed Wolfe's name. Wolfe did the same with *A Farewell to Arms.* They started trying to outdo each other. Wolfe's inscription in *Green Hills of Africa* fills up the front endpapers and ends up on the back board."

"Thomas Wolfe never could write a short sentence if a long one would do just as well," Goddard said sourly.

"But the point is," Lambert said unnecessarily, for by then even I knew what the point was, "McKinley has all those books, with the handwriting authenticated beyond any question. She seems to look for unusual associations, offbeat signatures, and pristine condition. Hey, she's got a *Grapes* with a drunken Steinbeck inscription and a doodle of a guy, drawn by Steinbeck, who has a penis six feet long. I mean, a guy would fall on his face from the force of gravity if he had a schmuck like that. Under the picture, Steinbeck wrote, '*Tom Joad on the road.*' All I can say is, I've looked at a lot of books, but I've never seen a collection quite like that."

I had some more questions, mostly insignificant, which they answered in terms that were generally inconsequential. Then I had Lambert draw me a map to Rita McKinley's house and I left them to their unfolding squabble. I called headquarters and talked to Hennessey. Rita McKinley had not yet returned my call. I gave Hennessey the names of additional book dealers to check out, and twenty minutes later I was in the foothills, heading for Evergreen.

It was pretty much as Lambert had said, a waste of time. She lived near the top of a dirt road that snaked up the mountainside. You went through Evergreen, a bustling little mountain town about thirty minutes from Denver; then, eight or ten miles out of town, doubled back onto a road that was clearly marked PRIVATE. There were half a dozen places up there, McKinley's being at the far end. She had the entire mountaintop to herself. Her privacy was protected, just as Lambert had said, by a locked gate and a fence ten feet high. I wondered about covenants: I didn't know you could build a fence like that anymore, but there it was. I looked through the chain links and followed the fence through the woods, until it became clear that I was

John Dunning

simply circling the mountaintop and the fence went the distance. At one point the trees thinned out and I could see her house, the glass glistening two hundred yards above my head. I called up through the break—cupped my hands to my mouth and shouted her name—but no one came.

I talked to people on the way down: stopped at each of the houses and asked about the mystery woman at the top. She remained that, a faceless enigma. No one knew her. She never stopped to chat. All people saw as they passed on the road was a figure, obviously female, in a car. One man had put together a Christmas party last year for all the neighbors on the mountain. Everyone had come but Rita McKinley, who had sent regrets.

In Evergreen, I called her number again and got the recording. I left her a stiff message, telling her I wanted to see her right away. But I had a hunch that I wasn't going to hear from the lady, that I'd have to track her to earth and pin her down. I had another hunch, that that might prove to be heavy work.

12

For all my alleged expertise, it was Hennessey
who got the first break in the case. While I was spinning
my wheels in the mountains, Neal had hit the streets and
talked to more book dealers. He had come to a store on
East Sixth Avenue where Bobby had sometimes been seen.
The owner was a man in his forties named Sean Buckley.
He had a good eye for books and he sold them cheap. His
store was dark and was sometimes mistaken for a junk
palace, but Buckley was no Clyde Fix. He knew exactly
what he was doing. His books were priced intentionally
low, sometimes drastically low. People talk when they find
bargains like that, and Buckley's store was always crowded
with eager treasure hunters.

It was not a place for a claustrophobic: it was dusty,
shabby, disorganized; books were piled on the floor and
shoved into every nook. Buckley was a pleasant man, easy-
going, shy, well liked, highly intelligent. I had spent a rainy
afternoon a year ago talking with Buckley about politics,
police work, and the intricacies of the book trade. He had

just sold a $250 *Naked and the Dead* to another dealer for $85, knowing full well but not caring much what the price guides said the book was "worth." The other dealer might eventually get that high-end money, but it wasn't easy. Norman Mailer has lost a lot of luster since 1948. People don't care much anymore, so let the other guy take the chance. If it worked, more power to him. The book had cost Buckley eight-five cents at a flea market. Buckley was the best example I had ever seen of the "keep the stock moving" school of bookselling.

I had put him fairly low on my list of people to see. Bookscouts didn't do much business there: they don't like to sell to a low retail man because the margin just wasn't good enough. But Bobby had come in about a week ago with his pockets stuffed with cash. He had flashed a wad bigger than a man's fist, and no small bills either. It looked like all hundreds from what Buckley could see: it must've been several thousand dollars at least. After much prodding, Hennessey had pinned Buckley down to a date. Last Tuesday it was, three days before the murder.

There was another thing. Bobby had been dressed to the hilt, three-piece suit and tie, hair and beard trimmed and combed, shoes shined. It had taken Buckley some time to recognize him. He had come to the store at quarter to five, just before closing. Buckley had been on the phone and hadn't paid much attention at first. Bobby just moved back into the store and started browsing the stacks. As time passed, Buckley began getting restless. He was a man who ran by the clock—he opened and closed on time and seldom stayed open late for anyone. At five-fifteen, Buckley began turning off the lights. At last he walked back and said, in a soft, apologetic voice, "I need to close now."

Bobby looked up and grinned. Buckley had to take a

few steps back, so great was his surprise. No one had ever seen Bobby the Bookscout in a coat and tie.

"My gosh, Bobby," Buckley said. "Where you going, to a funeral?"

"Yeah," Bobby said. "Tonight I'm burying my old life."

You could see right away how much he was enjoying it, Buckley said. There was always a tendency in these street people to strut when they got a little money—delusions of grandeur, you know. "Tonight I'm making the biggest deal of my life," Bobby said expansively.

That wouldn't be much of a deal, Buckley thought, but he was too much of a gentleman to say it.

"I'm not gonna be a bookscout anymore, Buckley," Bobby said. "Not gonna be anybody's doormat."

"What are you gonna do?" Buckley said.

Bobby grinned, a sly that's-for-me-to-know look crossing his face. "You'll see soon enough. I'll tell you this much. After tonight I'll be a book dealer, same as you guys. That's all I ever needed, just a stake."

That's when he pulled the money out, just for effect.

"Well," Buckley said, "looks like you got it."

"This is just pocket money. I'll be shopping here a lot from now on, Buckley. It kills me to see you selling books for a quarter on the dollar and I can't buy them myself. That's all gonna change."

"Well," Buckley said, "whatever's happening tonight, I wish you luck."

"Don't need luck; just need to be there at seven o'clock. This is the biggest deal Denver's ever seen, and nobody even knows about it."

"Good luck anyway."

This was the gist of the conversation between Bobby and Buckley, as Buckley told it to Hennessey.

• • •

"So," Hennessey said, "what's it mean?"

"Exactly," I said.

"Looks like a motive anyway."

"You mean simple robbery?"

"Sure. The guy flashes a wad like that one time too many. There's plenty of people who'll kill you for a roll like that . . . especially out on the street where this guy worked."

"That might make sense if it had happened the same night," I said. "But he was going somewhere just to spend that money. He was due there in two hours: all he was doing in Buckley's was killing time. That's why he didn't buy any books there—he didn't have any money to spend."

"You mean the big wad was spoken for."

"To the last dime. In real life, Bobby was still broke."

"What's it mean, then?" Hennessey said again.

"Let's think about it. Where'd he get the clothes, for one thing? I went through his place, you know, and I didn't see anything that looked like a necktie or a three-piece suit."

"You were looking for books. I've seen you lose track of time when you're looking at books."

"Maybe. I'll go back and look again, but if there's a coat and tie anywhere in that apartment I'll eat your shorts."

"Whether there is or whether there ain't," Hennessey said, "the question still remains, what does it mean?"

"It means Bobby had a coat and tie for one night only. It means he either borrowed or rented it. It doesn't sound like a rental—not formal enough. Buckley didn't say he showed up in a tux, did he?"

Hennessey gave a little laugh. "Suit and tie is what he said."

"I think we'd better ask Buckley how well the clothes fit. I think he borrowed that coat and tie, from someone who was just about his size."

"Could be anybody," Hennessey said. "He was pretty average."

"It didn't have to be a perfect fit for one night. My guess is he got the coat and tie from the same guy who gave him the money. And I think he was as broke as ever two hours after Buckley saw him. Three days later he was in Goddard's store trying to sell something. Lambert says he didn't have anything with him, but maybe it was something small. The fact was, he didn't have that money anymore. He had given that to someone on Tuesday night, and they didn't have to kill him for it. I think the fact that he wasn't killed till Friday night rules out robbery as a motive."

"It might've still been robbery," Hennessey said. "Maybe not for money. Maybe whoever did it took what Bobby *got* for the money."

"That makes it robbery of a different kind, though, doesn't it? Not your garden-variety thug. The average thug would walk right past fifty thousand dollars' worth of books to lift twenty bucks from the cash register. This would've been somebody with a fairly sophisticated span of knowledge. And a damn cold motive for what he was doing."

"Well," Hennessey said, "there are guys like that."

"There are a lot of guys like that."

"I'll tell you how it looks to me. Somebody pays Bobby to do a job. Say he was taking delivery of some literary masterpiece. At this point we don't know how Bobby got involved—we don't know why whoever hired him couldn't've taken delivery himself instead of hiring a bookscout to do it for him. Maybe that part of it isn't important. The bookscout gets hired, then does a double cross and keeps the merchandise. It takes the client three days to track him down."

"Maybe," I said.

"How small can something like that be?"

I looked at him, not understanding the question.

"Bobby had several thousand dollars on him the night he went to Buckley's," Hennessey said. "Presumably he was going to buy something at a wholesale price."

"Okay, I'm with you so far."

"What's the retail valuation on something you'd pay up to five grand for?"

"Hell, Neal, it could be anywhere from ten to twenty-five thousand dollars."

"Could it be more than that?"

"If it gets to be much more than that, it stops being wholesale and starts being fraud. Most honorable book dealers figure 25 to 40 percent as a fair wholesale price. Twenty would be rock-bottom. But for a big-money piece, sometimes you have to go higher than forty percent. If you fall into a piece that's worth a quarter mil, you might have to put up three-quarters, maybe even eighty percent. That's still a lot of change for the book dealer."

"If he can sell it."

"On that level he can always sell it. The easiest thing in the world to sell is a truly rare book. The biggest problem would be getting the money to buy it."

I still didn't see where his mind was going. Hennessey tends to plod in his thinking—that's why we were a good team. I tend to leapfrog, and sometimes it takes a guy with a more fundamental approach to rein me in and make me see what's been in front of my face all along.

This time he didn't seem to know where he was going. He was groping, trying to find a handle.

"You said something a minute ago," he said. "That most honorable dealers figure such-and-such. How honorable do these guys tend to be?"

"As a group, they're just like everybody else. There are some old gentlemen straight out of the last century. Fewer of those every day. There are egomaniacs . . . more of those every day. There are shysters, a few scumbags, a nut or two. There are some guys who'll take your pants off if you don't know anything. But I think as a group they have a pretty good standard of ethics. They'll vary right up and down the scale."

Hennessey nodded.

"Neal, I still don't see what you're getting at."

He blinked and brought himself back to his premise. "Robbery. Bobby bought something and somebody brained him and took it away from him. That idea works, Cliff, if it was something small enough for him to carry it around with him. I think this is going to be a very stupid question, but does it sound feasible for something that small to cost so much money?"

"Hell yes. Why would you think otherwise?"

"It just seems like, for five g's, you ought to get something more than a booklet."

I told him the *Tamerlane* story—how some guy had found one in a bookstore for fifteen bucks and sold it at auction for two hundred grand.

"I hate to say it, but I don't know what *Tamerlane* is."

"Poe's first book. Just a booklet, like you said, but some of the most expensive stuff in the world is very small. Broadsides, pamphlets, papers . . ."

"Stuff you could put in a pocket."

"Sure. That's the first thing a dealer or a bookscout has to learn. Always look at the little stuff."

"So it's not far-fetched to think that the bookscout might have been carrying something that somebody would kill him for."

"Not at all. Just imagine that somebody had found a little piece of scroll signed by Jesus Christ. A silly example—I don't know who the hell they'd get to authenticate it—but for the sake of argument, okay? How much do you think something like that would be worth?"

"I get your point. And I guess that's what I've been trying to pin down ... a motive for robbery. Something so tiny he could carry it in his pocket, but worth big bucks. That's what he was sent to buy, and somebody killed him and took it away from him."

"If that's true, it points back to the book trade. It wasn't a sudden fight or an old enemy. The answer is in the money. Where did the money go, where did it come from? If we can follow the money, we'll know a lot more than we know now."

"There's one more thing we could check," Hennessey said. "How about the religion angle?"

I saw it suddenly, what Neal had been pushing around in his head all day.

"They say our boy was religious," Hennessey said. "Found the Lord in prison a few years ago. That means he went to church somewhere. That means he had a life outside the book business. Maybe friends on a whole different level. Maybe a minister he'd confide in. You only see one side of him when you see him in a bookstore."

I sat up straight in my chair. "How the hell could I miss something like that?"

"You're too busy looking at the books," Hennessey said.

13

The body of Bobby Westfall lay unclaimed in the morgue: if there was a church in Bobby's life, it had not yet made its presence known. No one had stepped forward and offered Bobby a Decent Christian Burial. The coroner had done more for Bobby in death than most people had in life: his office had spent many man-hours on a long and fruitless search for next of kin. They had found a rumor of a sister living in Salt Lake City, but that had not checked out. Bobby had told people that his mother was dead and he never knew his father. He had mentioned Pennsylvania to several people, but that had not checked out. At seventeen, he had once said, he had been in the army: medical discharge, flat feet. Amazingly, that had not checked out. The army had no record of a Robert Westfall in its service at the time and place that Bobby would have been there. This was important, the coroner said, because if military service could be established Bobby would qualify for burial at Fort Logan. They still had a few leads to check: sometimes a body had to be kept on ice for weeks, until everything

117

petered out. Lacking everything—church, service, next of
kin—Bobby would go to an unmarked pauper's grave at
Riverside, and have the earth plowed over him by a bull-
dozer.

In the morning, I went back to the bookstore beat and
Hennessey began checking churches around the neighborhood where Bobby lived. I visited some new stores and
went back to the old ones with new questions. Did Bobby
ever mention what church he attended? Did he ever mention any names of ministers or people he knew outside the
book world? I talked to Ruby Seals, Emery Neff, Jerry
Harkness, and Sean Buckley. I went back to Cherry Creek
and talked to Roland Goddard and Julian Lambert. It was
a wasted morning. Even two bookscouts in Ruby's store
didn't know much about Bobby. One of them had seen
him a few times with the scout called Peter, but no one
knew where Peter lived or what his last name was. I wrote
down some stuff in my notebook, but I had a feeling that
none of it meant anything.

Meanwhile, Hennessey found the church before noon.
We thought it likely that Bobby would go to church in his
own neighborhood. He didn't have a car, and probably
wouldn't want to spend Sundays doing what he did every
other day of the week—walking or riding a bus. We looked
closely at churches that would appeal to born-again types
rather than older establishment religions. Ruby remembered that Bobby had once referred to Catholicism dis-
paragingly—"not a true faith," he had called it—so he
wouldn't like the Episcopal church any better. He probably
wasn't a Lutheran, and anything from the outer limits, such
as Unitarianism, was unlikely. No, Bobby was probably
caught up in some evangelical splinter group formed by a
diploma mill preacher with a slick tongue and a ready sup-

ply of hellfire. It was easy: Hennessey found the church on the fifth try. It was one of those little chapels off University Boulevard, the Universal Church of God, it called itself. The preacher recognized Bobby's picture at once. Yes, Bob was a regular: he seldom missed a Sunday and usually came to Bible studies on Wednesday nights as well. He always came with a fellow named Jefferson or Johnson, good friend of his. They were always together. Hennessey asked if they had come last Wednesday. As a matter of fact they had, the preacher said. Suddenly Jefferson or Johnson became the last known man, except Julian Lambert, to have seen Bobby Westfall alive.

The preacher got the man's name from the church registry. Jarvis Jackson lived on Gaylord Street, just a few blocks away. The preacher didn't know either Jackson or Bobby well. They kept to themselves and were quiet and reflective in church. The preacher looked a lot like those birds you see on TV Sunday mornings: sharp and cunning, and dressed in an expensive tailored suit. Hennessey didn't like him much.

"What does the church do about burying its members?" Hennessey asked.

"That all depends," the preacher said.

"On what?"

"On whether they've made arrangements."

"In other words, on whether they've got any money."

"Money runs the world, Mr. Hennessey."

"It looks like old Bob's headed for a potter's field funeral, unless somebody stands the tab," Hennessey said.

The preacher cocked his head and tried to look sympathetic.

Riverside loomed a little larger for dear old Bob.

• • •

We met at Ruby's bookstore and went to talk to Jarvis Jackson together. Jackson lived in the south half of a shabby little duplex. He lived alone except for half a dozen cats. The cats, he explained, were what first drew him and Bob together. The place smelled strongly of sour milk and well-used kitty litter. There was a case of books in the front room and I gravitated toward them and let my eye run over the titles while Hennessey and Jackson went through the preliminaries. There wasn't anything in the bookcase— some condensed books and other assorted junk. The bottom shelf was well stained with cat piss, the books all fused together. I would've cried if there'd been a Faulkner first in there.

Jackson and Bobby had met a year ago at the church. They had sat on a bench after the service and talked cats. After that riveting conversation, Jackson had invited Bobby home for some lemonade and lunch. They had soon become friends. Jackson thought of himself as Bobby's best friend. He was fifteen years older, but age doesn't matter when the chemistry's right. They liked the same things, shared the same philosophy. They liked the Lord, books, and the smell of cat poop, in approximately that order. They never ran out of things to talk about. Twice a week they would meet in a café on East Seventeenth and eat together. They discussed the Lord and the Lord's work. Bobby had an idea that the Lord had something in mind for him. It was probably a surprise, I thought, when he found out what it was. Bobby had always wanted to do missionary work, but he'd spent all his life putting out brushfires. Jackson had heard of Bob's death only this morning, when he'd read about it in the paper.

"When did you see him last?" I said.

"Wednesday night. He always came by here. We'd eat

something, then walk over to church. Neither of us drove. We always walked together."

"Did you talk about anything?"

"We discussed the Lord's work over dinner."

"Anything other than that?"

"Not then, no."

"Some other time, then?"

"After church we came back here and talked some more. Bob didn't seem to want to go home. Me, I'm retired . . . I don't mind staying up late to talk things over."

"What did you talk about that night?"

"He said he'd done a big book deal. But it wasn't working out like he'd thought."

"When had he done this?"

"The night before. He had been up all night."

"Did he tell you what the deal was?"

"Not exactly. He did say it involved a lot of money. But it wasn't working out."

"What did you mean by that?"

"He didn't go into any details. Just said things never seemed to work out right for him, somehow it just never went right. He couldn't understand why the Lord always wanted him to fail. The only thing he could figure out was that the Lord was still angry from the things he'd done as a young man. That's why he wanted to talk to me—he needed reassurance that the Lord is good, not vengeful, that the Lord doesn't always work in ways we can understand. He doesn't do things for our convenience or personal glory. There's a bigger purpose to His acts. We all need to be reminded of that on occasion."

"Yes sir."

"So I listened and we talked. It seemed to help him to talk about it. I think he was trying to make up his mind."

"About what, sir?"

"What to do about it. He was angry. I think he was even angry at the Lord until we talked about it. I think I got him to focus that anger where it really belonged."

"Where's that, Mr. Jackson?"

"At himself. At his failings and weaknesses."

"Or maybe at someone else?"

He shrugged. "I didn't tell him to do that. It would never be any advice of mine that one man should hate another."

"Did he say he hated somebody?"

"He was angry. He felt he'd been lied to and cheated. And I think he was trying to make up his mind what to do about it."

"But he never mentioned any names?"

He shook his head.

"Maybe a name you've half forgotten."

He looked at me blankly.

"Did he give you any idea where he'd gotten the money for the deal?"

"I assume someone gave it to him. I know he didn't have any money of his own."

"Did he say anything that might indicate where the deal was done?"

"No . . . nothing."

I looked at Hennessey. He gave a frown and turned his palms up.

"I'm sorry I'm such a dead end," Jackson said. "I want to help if I can. It's an awful thing, what happened to Bob. I want to help, but it was his business and I just didn't pry. All I know is that he worked all night on it. He borrowed a coat and tie from me . . . he wanted to make a good impression . . . said it was to be the first day of his new life.

He was sorry later that he hadn't gone in his old clothes. There was too much work for him to be dressed like that. He brought the suit back in pretty bad shape."

"Could we see that suit?"

"It's right back here in the closet."

He went into a back room and returned a moment later with the coat and tie. The pants hung loosely under the coat. It had a vest, as Buckley had said, and it looked worn and limp in the light of day.

"He was sorry he had taken it," Jackson said again. "It's pretty well ruined, as you can see. He apologized and said he'd buy me a new one if he ever got enough money together. Bob was like that. He never thought ahead. He wanted to dress up and see what it felt like, and he never gave a thought to the work he had to do."

"Then there were a lot of books?"

"Oh, yes . . . that much I do know. It took him all night to move them."

I went through the coat pockets, then the vest. In the pants I found two receipts from a 7-Eleven store.

"Are these your receipts?" I asked.

Jackson looked at them and shook his head. "Must be something he left in there."

I showed them to Hennessey. "No telling which store," Neal said. "Must be hundreds of 'em in Denver."

Suddenly Jackson said, "It was on Madison Street. I remember it now, he went in that store late that night. He was hungry, he hadn't had anything to eat in almost two days. He had been working about four hours and was feeling faint. He went out on the upper porch for some air. He saw the sign, 7-Eleven, about half a block away. It was the only place open that time of night. It was unusual that way—usually they don't put those places in residential areas like that, but there it was . . . like the Lord had sent it just for him. He had two dollars in his pocket. So he walked up and got a soft drink and a Hostess cake."

I asked for his phone book. There was only one 7-Eleven on Madison Street. It was in the 1200s, only a few blocks away.

We found the house without much trouble after that. It was half a block north of the 7-Eleven, on the opposite side of the street. It was the only house in the block with an upper porch. The doors were open and there were people inside, pricing stuff for an estate sale. There were signs announcing that the sale would be this coming weekend. Inside were bookshelves. There were bookshelves in every room, all of them empty.

14

"Where're your books?" I said from the open doorway.

The man looked up. "We don't open till Saturday."

"I'm just wondering where all your books went."

"Come back Saturday and I'll tell you."

A smartass, I thought. I walked into the room and Hennessey came in behind me. I flashed my tin and said, "How about telling me now."

He looked at the badge, unimpressed. "So you work for me. Big deal. Am I supposed to hyperventilate and lose control of my body functions because you can't find a real job?"

"Look, pal, I'm not trying to impress you. I'm asking for your cooperation on a murder case."

"Oh yeah? Who's been killed?"

"How about letting me ask the questions."

I knew it was a bad start. I meet a lot of characters like him, cop-haters from the word *go,* and I never handle them well.

"You can ask all you want," he said. "There's nothing that says I have to talk to you."

125

"Are you sure of that?"

"I should be. I'm a lawyer."

Wonderful. So far I was batting a thousand.

"I don't owe you bastards one goddamn thing," he said. "I got a ticket coming over here this morning."

Now the woman looked up. She was in her mid-thirties, five to ten years younger than the man. Pretty she'd be, in a cool dress, relaxing by a pool: pretty in the bitchy way of a young Bette Davis, mean and intelligent and all the more interesting because of that. Now she was dirty and hot, doing a job that must seem endless—cataloging and sifting and finally putting a price tag on each of the hundreds of items of a man's life.

"You have just made the acquaintance of Valentine Fletcher Ballard," she said. "Charming, isn't it?"

I didn't know what to make of the two of them, didn't know if they were playing it for laughs or if I had come in in the middle of something. The look he gave her seemed to say that they weren't playing anything.

"You'd think the goddamn mayor of this goddamn city would have better things for the goddamn cops to do than sit in a speed trap with goddamn radar guns harassing the hell out of honest citizens," he said.

"Don't even try to talk to him," the woman said. "You can't talk to a fool."

The guy went right on as if she hadn't said a word. "Have you seen what they did on Montview? *Lowered* the goddamn speed limit all of a sudden to thirty miles an hour. It's four lanes in there, for Christ's sake, it ought to be fifty. You think the mayor gives a rat's ass about safety? Don't make me laugh. They bring ten cops in on fucking overtime just to write tickets and generate revenue. When you get your cost-of-living raise this year, copper, remember whose pocket it came out of and how you got it."

I hate the term *copper*, but I couldn't argue much. I've never liked the city's use of cops that way. If you have to bring a cop in on overtime, let him do the legwork on a murder case or chase down a rapist. Let him walk the streets in a high-crime area, where his presence might mean something. Don't put him in the bushes with a radar gun on a street that's been deliberately under-posted. Don't make sneaks out of cops. The guy was right, people don't like that, and that's how cop-haters are born.

"Goddamn pirates," he said. "You fuckers are no better than pickpockets."

All I could do was try to lighten it up. "Hey, I'm doing my part," I said. "I'm looking for a killer."

"So I'll ask you again," the guy said. "Who's been killed?"

"The guy you sold these books to."

He blinked. The woman stood up and looked at me.

"You want to talk to me now?" I said. "Maybe we can get off on a better footing. I'm Detective Janeway. This is Detective Hennessey."

The guy finally said, "I'm Val Ballard."

He made no attempt to introduce the woman: wouldn't even acknowledge her presence. I thought it was strange that neither had spoken directly to the other, but maybe that was just my imagination.

It wasn't. She said, "I'm Judith Ballard Davis. The klutz you've been talking to likes to pretend he's my brother. Don't blame me for that."

He ignored her fairly effectively: all she got for her trouble was a look of slight annoyance. I was beginning to see a pattern emerging in the hostility. He ignored her: she heaped insults upon him, but only through another person.

I said, to anyone who wanted to answer it, "Whose house is this?"

They both began talking at once. Neither showed any willingness to yield, and the words tumbled over themselves in indecipherable disorder.

"Let's try that again," I said. "Eeeny meeny miney mo." Mo came down on her. That was a mistake, for Ballard began immediately to sulk, and in a moment he went back to his work. I'd have to warm him up, if you could call it that, all over again.

"The house belongs . . . belonged . . . to my uncle. Stanley Ballard."

"And he died, right?"

"He died," she said.

"When did he die?"

"Last month. Early May."

"What'd he die of?"

"Old age . . . cancer . . . I don't know." She didn't seem to care much. "When you're that old, everything breaks down at once."

"How old was he?"

"Eighty, I guess . . . I'm not sure."

"He was your father's brother?"

"Older brother. There was almost twenty years between them."

"Where's your father?"

"Dead. Killed in an auto accident a long time ago."

"What about your mother?"

"They're all dead. If you're looking for all the living Ballards, I'm it."

I looked at him. "What about you?"

"I told you what my name is."

Something was slipping past me. "Are you two brother and sister or what?" I said.

Neither wanted to answer that.

"Come on, people, what's the story? Do you inherit the old man's estate?"

"Lock, stock, and barrel," she said.

"Both of you?"

She gave a loud sigh. At last she said, "Yes, God damn it, both of us."

"All right," I said pleasantly. "That wasn't so hard, was it? You inherit the house and all the contents equally, right?"

"What's this got to do with anything?" Ballard said. "Whose business is it, anyway, what I inherit and what I do with it?"

"I have to watch every goddamn penny," Judith said to no one. "If he gets a chance, he'll screw my eyes out."

"Gee, but it's nice to see people get along so well," I said. "Have you two always been so lovey?"

"I hate his guts," she said. "No secret about that, mister. The only thing I'm living for is to get this house sold and the money split so I won't ever have to see his stupid face again."

"When you decide you want to talk to me, I'll be in the other room," Ballard said, and left.

"Son of a bitch," Judith said before he was quite out of the room.

I had this insane urge to laugh. She knew it, and did laugh.

"We're some dog and pony show. Is that what you're thinking?"

"Yeah," I said. "What's with you two?"

"Just bad blood. It's always been there. It's got nothing

to do with anything, and I'd just as soon not talk about it."

"How do you manage to work together if you don't even speak?"

"With great difficulty. What can I tell you?"

"What happened to the books?"

"We sold them. You know that."

"You split the money?"

"You better believe it."

"Did you know the guy you sold them to?"

"Never saw him before. We were in here working and he just showed up. Walked in on us just like you did. Said he heard we had some books and wondered if we wanted to make a deal for them."

"Did he say where he'd heard about it?"

"No, and I didn't ask. The man had cash money, that's all I care about."

"Did you go through the books before you sold them?"

"What do I care about a bunch of old books? Besides, I told you we were in a hurry to sell them. I don't want to stay around *him* any longer than I have to."

"So neither of you looked at the books, or had a book dealer look at them, before you sold them?"

"Look," she said shortly. "There weren't any old books in there, okay? It was just run-of-the-mill crap. Anybody with half a brain could see that."

She was angry now. The thought of blowing an opportunity will sometimes do that to people. She said, "Everybody knows books have to be old. Everybody knows that."

I shook my head.

"What do you know about it?"

"Not much. A little."

"What could a cop know about books? Don't come in

here and tell me what I should've done. You see those book-shelves? They were all full. There are more like this in every room. He had the basement laid out like a fucking library. Do you have any idea how many books were in this house? I haven't got enough to do, now I've got to go through all this crap looking for a few lousy books that might be valuable?"

I shrugged.

"Besides," she said, "Stan did that."

"Did what?"

"He had a book dealer come do an appraisal. It was three, four years ago, when he first got the cancer. He had an appraisal done and it was there with his papers when he died."

"Do you remember the name of the appraiser?"

"I don't have enough to do without remembering names?"

"I'll need to see that appraisal." I made it a demand, not a request. "Do you have a copy?"

"You better believe it. I've got a copy of everything. With a son of a bitch like him around, I'd better have a copy."

Ballard, in the next room, had heard this, and he came in fuming.

"If you want to talk to me, talk," he said. "I've got things to do today."

I shifted easily from her to him.

"Did you look at the books?"

"Hell no. There wasn't anything there worth the trouble. Read my lips and believe it, there was nothing there. This joker wanted them, I say let him *have* the damn things. I told him he could have my half."

"Is that the way you sold 'em?"

"I sold him my half," Ballard said. He still refused to admit that his sister shared the same planet.

"He came here and took all the books," Judith said. "Is that what you want to know, Detective? The little man came and took *all* the frigging books, okay? He gave me some money and the rest went . . ." She jerked her thumb at her brother, who stiffened as if he'd just been slapped.

"Let's talk for a minute about the man who came and took the books. You say he just showed up one night?"

"We were in here just like we are now. I looked up and he was standing in the doorway. I thought he was full of shit." She lit a cigarette and blew smoke. "He was wearing this cheap suit that didn't fit and strutting around like one of the Rockefellers. He came in the night we started and said he wanted to buy the books."

"Who the hell is telling this?" Ballard shouted. He made sure he talked to me, not her. "God damn it, are you talking to me or what?"

"Oh, I don't care," I said wearily.

"I said the only way I'd sell the damn books before the sale started was all in one fell swoop. I didn't want any damn picking and choosing, you see what I'm saying? Get 'em all out of here, that's what I wanted."

"What did he say to that?"

He gave a sweep of his hand. "They're gone, ain't they?"

"I'm not asking you the question, Mr. Ballard, to belabor the obvious. I want to know what the man said when you told him he'd have to buy all the books. Did he act like he wanted to do that or not?"

"He didn't act any way. He just said put a price on 'em."

"And what price did you put on them?"

"In a sale I thought they'd be worth a buck or two apiece. For a guy to take 'em all, I told him I'd knock something off of that."

"Could we maybe get to what the final price was?"

"He gave me two thousand dollars. What he did with the other two thousand's none of my business."

I looked at Judith, who managed to look quite sexy smoking. "Did you get the other two thousand, Mrs. Davis?" I asked in my best long-suffering voice.

"You better believe it."

Ballard took me on a tour of the house. Judith followed at a distance, as if she didn't trust him long out of her sight. I tried to imagine what long-ago rift had ripped them so deeply and permanently apart. I tried to imagine them locked away in here for days on end, divvying up the old man's loot without speaking. The picture defied me. Only greed could motivate them, greed and hate and the all-powerful ego motive to come out on top.

The basement was impressive, but then, I could see what it had been with all the books in it. It was lined with bookcases, against the walls and in rows, library-style, in the center of the room. I did some quick arithmetic and figured that the shelves here and upstairs might hold as many as nine thousand books.

"The old man really loved his books," I said with admiration.

"Some guys like sex," Judith said from the doorway. "Stan liked books."

"So you sold the books for forty, fifty cents apiece?"

"I wasn't gonna quibble," Ballard said. "The guy came back with two grand. Two grand is two grand, and I wanted the crap out of here."

I took a picture of Bobby Westfall out of my notebook. "Is this the guy?"

"That's him," Ballard said. "That a dead picture?"

I nodded and showed it to her. She nodded and looked away.

"Who do you think killed him?" she said.

"We'll see," I said.

We talked some more, and it all boiled down to this:

They had struck a deal and Bobby had come one night last week and stripped the house of everything that remotely resembled a book. He had worn that same silly suit for the heavy work. They didn't know anything else about him—where he'd come from, where he'd gone—the only record of the transaction was the receipt that Ballard had written out (copy to her, and you'd better believe it) to keep it straight and legal. Bobby had signed it with an undecipherable scrawl and left his copy on the table. All he wanted was to get the books and get on the road.

He had come for the books in a huge truck, a U-Haul rental. Now we were getting somewhere. Ruby had said that Bobby had no driver's license: that meant someone else had to have rented the truck. I was hungry for a new name to be thrown into the hopper: I was eager to begin sweating that unseen accomplice. I felt we were one name away from breaking it, and I wanted that name and I wanted it now.

But Bobby had come to Madison Street alone. If someone else had rented the truck, why not ask that buddy to give a hand with the heavy lifting? The obvious answer was that Bobby wanted no one to know what he had really bought from Stanley Ballard's estate. He had insisted on loading the books himself, which was fine with the two heirs, who had no intention of helping anyway. Bobby had brought hundreds of cardboard boxes and had spent all night packing and loading the books. Ballard and his sister kept after their own work and before they knew it the night slipped away. Bobby loaded the last of the books as dawn broke in the east.

• • •

During all of this, Hennessey had not said a word. This is the kind of cop Neal is: he melts into the woodwork; he listens, he looks, he adds two and two, then stares at the number four to see if there's any broken type. I didn't notice when he'd stepped away: I found him on the front porch talking with a neighbor.

"Cliff, this is Mr. Greenwald. He and Mr. Ballard were friends for fifty years."

We stood on Ballard's front porch and Greenwald stood on his, and we talked easily across the hedge. Ballard was already living here when Greenwald moved in in 1937. They had a great mutual passion—books. In a very different way, they reminded me of Bobby Westfall and Jarvis Jackson—two lonely guys held together by honest affection and one or two deep common denominators. Ballard was an old bachelor: Greenwald's wife had died in 1975, and the two men took their dinners together at a place they liked, a few blocks away.

Greenwald was a leathery old man, bald with white fringe hair and a white mustache. I could see his books through the window. They had belonged to the book clubs together, Greenwald said: every month they'd get half a dozen books, read them and discuss them. They weren't collectors in the real sense, though both had accumulated a lot of titles over fifty years. It was a comfort, Greenwald said, to see a copy of a book you loved on the shelf. It didn't have to be a fine expensive edition. This was how they both felt: books were meant to be read, not hoarded. Both of them gave a lot of books away—to nursing homes, library sales, and other worthy charities. "What's the use of having a book that's too good to read?" he said. "Half the fun is giving the books away."

I could see his point, though I hadn't agreed with it for

years. "Did Mr. Ballard ever have anything that might be called valuable?"

Greenwald looked away and shrugged his shoulders. "I can't imagine. We didn't do it for that reason."

"Still, sometimes people pick up things, sometimes by accident."

Greenwald shrugged again.

"Did Mr. Ballard ever go to estate sales or junk stores looking for books? Maybe he found something that way."

"Never, and I can tell you that with absolute certainty. He wasn't a book hunter, he was a book buyer. He never went to used bookstores. He bought them when they were new and read them all. He was in the Book-of-the-Month for as long as I knew him, maybe longer. I think he started soon after the clubs came in, in the early thirties. You can check on that—he kept all his records from the clubs, all the way back to when he started."

"Really?"

"Oh, yes. He kept all the flyers and bulletins . . . I know you'll find them there in his den, in that big filing cabinet. He used to keep the club flyers and write his notes in the margins. He'd never write in a book, of course, but he'd mark up those advance flyers they sent every month, little notes to himself—which books to buy, which ones to keep, which to give away. I do the same thing, but it's a habit I picked up from him. I've only been doing it about twenty years. His files go back much further."

"May I come over, sir, and see your books?"

"Certainly."

We walked across and went into Greenwald's house. It was like a branch library: row upon row, bookcase after bookcase, all cheap editions of great books. The two old men had fine taste. Anyone could see that.

"We had a lot to talk about, Stan and I. We had been around the world together many times, without ever leaving this block, if you know what I mean."

"I sure do," I said. "It's a wonderful hobby."

"Oh, it is. It's harder today, though. You can't find the good books, like you once could. People don't read anymore, or when they do read they read things that couldn't have been published in the old days. I don't know: my days are all in the past. Everyone I knew is dead, and no one is writing anything worth reading. This is a different world from when I was a boy. I can't read the stuff they publish today, can you?"

"Some of it," I said. "Every once in a while it still happens, Mr. Greenwald. I don't know how it happens, or why, but it still does. Sometimes a great book not only gets published but read, by one helluva lot of people."

"Stan would've liked you," Greenwald said. "He liked everybody who read and appreciated good things. He was an old gentleman, I'll tell you that. Not like those two next door, squabbling with their silly silent feud over every last dime. Stan's turning over in his grave this very minute. Money never came first with Stan. Honor, trust, friendship, those were the qualities he believed in. A great old man. His like will not come this way again."

We went back to Ballard's house. I told Judith I would have to see her uncle's files. The two of them followed us into the den and watched while I went through a great old filing cabinet. It was all there as Greenwald had promised—the entire record of Stan Ballard's love affair with the Book-of-the-Month Club: receipts, billing statements, flyers so annotated and footnoted that I groaned at the thought of wading through it. But Ballard came from a generation that was taught penmanship: his writing was small but precise and, in the final analysis, beautiful. It looked to me like the old man had kept the economy of Camp Hill, Pennsylvania, going strong since March 1931. He had bought the main selection and six other titles that month. The average price was around a dollar: not much in today's world of the $20 novel, but in 1931 there were men working a sixty-hour week for less money than Stan Ballard was spending per month on books.

"What did your uncle do for a living?" I asked.

"He was a stockbroker," Judith said.

"He got into the book club in 1931. That couldn't've been much of a year for stockbrokers, but he seemed to have plenty of money to spend on books . . . even in the Depression."

"He inherited money," Judith said. "I don't know how much; he sure didn't leave much cash in his estate. He probably spent it *all* on books. It didn't matter how the times were, he always had money for that."

I thumbed through the papers. "I'll have to take these files."

They didn't like that. They were on guard now, full of new suspicion. I could almost hear the wheels turning in their heads. Maybe the old man had kept his cash hidden somewhere. Maybe there was a big, juicy stack of thousand-dollar bills tucked into the book file—book money unspent.

"I don't think you should just walk out of here with that stuff," Ballard said.

"I can get a court order if I have to, and I think you know that," I said. "Why don't we make it easy on ourselves?"

"What is this stuff?" Judith said. "Is there anything in there worth any money?"

"I'd be amazed if there was. You can look for yourself

while we pack it up. I'll give you a receipt and after this is over you'll get it all back."

"*Who'll* get it back?" Ballard said.

"Whoever the hell wants it."

We started packing the files. I could see it was going to take some time, because Ballard and Judith wanted to examine each file microscopically as we went.

"This could take all night," I said. "Let's try to cut to the chase. Where's the original copy of that appraisal he had done?"

"The executor has it," Judith said. "A lawyer named Walter Dreyfuss. I think he and Stan were soldiers together in the Revolutionary War."

"One of us ought to go see him," I said to Hennessey.

"I'll go. I'll have to take a cab."

"Good. If you hurry you might make it before his office closes. I'll call and tell him you're coming."

It was dark before I was finished at Ballard's. We packed all the contents of Stanley Ballard's filing cabinet into six big cardboard boxes and I loaded them into my car. Neither Ballard nor Judith offered to help. I thanked them and left them to their awful job. I hope I never hate anyone the way they hate each other, I thought as I drove downtown to fetch Hennessey. Then I thought of Jackie Newton, and the world was a darker place again.

Hennessey was waiting for me on Seventeenth Street. Under his arm he had a single folder, which contained Stanley Ballard's will and a copy of the appraisal. He had made no attempt to read the will—Walter Dreyfuss had given him a verbal summary—but he had looked the book appraisal over.

"What's it say?"

"Book club fiction, almost without exception. Worthless."

"Who did the appraisal?"

"That dame up in Evergreen. Rita McKinley."

I grunted.

"So where does this leave us?" Hennessey said.

"Right back where we started. It was something small, and Bobby had to buy the whole damn library to get it; something so tiny you could carry it in your pocket, but so potent it makes the hair stand up on my neck just thinking about it."

"How're we gonna find it?"

"I'm gonna dig. I'm gonna comb through every piece of paper in this state if I have to."

I dropped Hennessey at Ruby's store, where he had parked his car, and I started back to my apartment for what I thought would be another long night's work.

Then something happened that changed my life for all time.

15

I was full of nervous energy: I wanted something to break that would engage me fully and keep me going through the night. I had two possibilities, either of which ought to do it. I took the Ballard files up to my place, but when I started to work I decided to run down the U-Haul lead.

There are almost fifty places in Denver that rent U-Hauls. A lot of gas stations are subagents and rent them out of their back yards. I sat at the phone with a Yellow Pages and began to work. I did it the same way we had found the church, beginning at Bobby's place and working in a widening circle between there and Madison Street. This is what police work is all about: your trigger finger always gets more action on the telephone than in any gunplay. I hummed "Body and Soul" between calls, trying to get a hint of the way Coleman Hawkins used to play it. "Dah-dah de dah-dah dumm." It didn't work. Nothing worked. I gave them Bobby's name on the insane chance that someone somewhere might've had soup for brains and rented a

$25,000 truck to a guy with no driver's license. You never can tell. Lacking a file on Westfall, they would have to look through all their receipts for the night of June 10. I waited through interminable delays. Most of the little places had no extra help—the guy who rented the U-Hauls was the guy who pumped your gas. Customers came and went while I dangled on the phone. One place took almost thirty minutes, and it turned out that they hadn't rented any trucks on the night in question.

The truck outlets themselves were, if anything, slower than the corner gas stations. Those places are all on computer now. This is supposed to make finding information faster and easier, but in real life it doesn't turn out that way. Have you noticed how much longer you have to wait in bank lines, and at Target and Sears stores, since the computer came in? I hate computers, though I know that without them police work would be like toiling in a medieval zoo. After three hours of being told that the computer was down, that there were no such rentals, that they'd have to check and call me back, I was ready to adjourn to my favorite beanery. I couldn't raise Carol, but when I'm that hungry I don't mind eating alone.

Before I could get out of there, the phone rang.

It was Barbara Crowell. Her voice was quaking, terrified.

"Janeway! My God, I can't believe you finally got off that phone!"

"Hello, Barbara," I said without enthusiasm.

"Can you come over here?"

"What's the matter?"

"It's . . . him."

"Ah," I said.

"I know he's out there."

"Out where?"

"Somewhere outside. I saw him."

"When did you see him?"

She breathed at me for fifteen seconds. Then she said, "I think I'm losing my mind. I see him everywhere. I don't know what to do. Everywhere I look I see his face. Then I look again and he's gone. Then he's there again. I hear a sudden noise and I freak out. I'm afraid of the dark. The telephone rings and I jump out of my skin. I answer it and there's no one there. I know it's him. All of a sudden I'm afraid of the goddamn dark. I've never been afraid of anything and now I see shadows everywhere."

"All right, calm down. I'll be over in a few minutes."

I parked a block away from her place and walked over. I came up carefully, keeping in shadow. For a long time I stood across the street and watched her apartment, and nothing happened. Her light was a steady beacon at the top. I walked down the street and around the corner and came up from the back. There was no one around: I could see quite clearly. I skirted the house and went in through the front, and I stood in the dark hall and watched the street. It was quiet: people were settling in for the night.

I climbed the three flights to the top and knocked on her door.

"Who's there?"

"It's me."

She clawed at the locks and ripped the door open.

"Jesus, what took you so long?"

"I wanted to walk around and look the place over."

"Did you see him?"

"Barbara, there's nobody there."

She closed her eyes and collapsed against me. I held her with one arm and closed the door with the other. Eventually I got her to the sofa and sat her down. Then I went through it all again, the same routine we'd done before: the coffee, the calming words, the lecture. She looked like a little girl, ready to explode in tears. I couldn't help being angry and sorry for her at the same time.

"Jackie doesn't need to torture you, honey," I said. "You do a good enough job on yourself."

"I know I saw him this morning. That's what set me off."

"Where did you see him?"

"I was on my way to work. I had stopped at a red light and he pulled up beside me. I could sense him there looking at me."

"What do you mean you could sense him? What does that mean?"

"I couldn't look at him."

"It might've been the man in the moon sitting there for all we know."

"It was him. I saw his car. There couldn't be another car like that, so don't tell me I'm imagining it. When the light turned green he pulled out ahead of me and turned the corner. I couldn't be mistaken about that car."

I left her alone for a while. I turned down the lights and went to the window and looked down in the empty street.

"While you're scaring yourself to death, Jackie's probably home watching TV," I said. Or breaking in a new dog, I thought.

"He's not home," she said. "He's out there somewhere."

I didn't say anything. There didn't seem to be anything to say.

"Call him up if you think he's home," she said.

I looked at her.

"Go ahead, call him and see. You're not afraid of him; call him and see if he's home. If he is, I won't bother you anymore."

"All right."

I didn't need to look up the number: I had known it for more than a year. I dialed it and waited. No one answered.

"I guess you're right," I said. "Looks like Jackie's hiding out there in the bushes, just waiting for you to show your face."

She shivered and the goose bumps started.

"I guess you can go hide in the bedroom," I said. "Tremble in the dark for the rest of your life."

She cried at that. She cried a good deal. I didn't want to hurt her, but I didn't know how to push her off the dime. What was worse, I wasn't sure anymore what Jackie was capable of, or what I wanted Barbara Crowell to do about him.

"God, I hate having you hate me," she said at one point.

"If I hated you I wouldn't be here. I told you before, this isn't my line of work. I should be well fed and home by now, settling in for a long night's work."

I kept looking down in the street. Softly, I said, "Jackie's probably working somewhere. Trying to figure out a new way to rip somebody off. Maybe he has a date tonight. Maybe he'll like her better than you. Maybe you'll get lucky and it'll be her problem."

"You bastard!" she cried.

"Yeah, I know. It's the company I keep. Pogo was right. We have met the enemy and it is us."

"I don't know what you're talking about half the time."

"It doesn't matter. You got anything to eat here?"

"I could fix you some bacon and eggs."

"Jesus, that sounds marvelous."

We ate. The coffee and the food warmed her up. I tried to get away from that judgmental tone I had taken with her, and after a while we were able to converse in a more or less normal way, the way men and women have always done. I even managed to make her laugh. When that was over, she said, "What do people call you . . . friends, I mean."

"Cliff usually does it."

She turned it over in her mind. "That's a good man's name. Can I call you that?"

"Sure, if you want to."

Suddenly she said, "Will you stay with me tonight?"

I was off duty. I didn't have anything better to do. The murderer of an unknown bookscout could wait till tomorrow.

"Sure," I said.

She was surprised. "Do you mean it?"

"Yeah, I'll stay," I said.

She looked at the bedroom, then at me. Clearly, she didn't know how to read me.

"It'll be all right if you want to . . . you know . . . if you don't hate me too much."

"I'm not staying here tonight for a shackjob, Barbara. I'll make you an even trade-off. I'll get you through the night, then you've got to do something for me."

The look of frightened warmth faded, till only the fright was left.

"I know what you want. The only thing you ever cared about was putting him away. You'll do anything for that, won't you?"

My silence was like a nolo plea.

"I can't do it," she said.

"Then I'm leaving."

I started toward the door.

"Wait!" she cried.

I stopped and turned.

"Please wait . . . please. Look, I'll try, okay?"

"You've got to do better than that."

"Help me, Cliff . . . please don't leave."

"I'm trying to help you. I don't know what the answer is. I may only end up getting you killed . . . I don't know. I know you can't go on the way you are. So tomorrow morning, accompanied by me, you will drive out to the Jeffco DA's office. You will swear out charges of kidnapping, assault and battery. I don't know, it's probably too late for the rape charge, but we'll tell him about it and let the DA decide. Then we come back to Denver and find us a judge and get you a restraining order. If the son of a bitch comes near you after that, you will call a number I will give you and we will come and bust his ass. If you won't meet me that far, there's not much I can do."

She didn't say anything. I said, "We just keep going over the same ground. It won't get any easier. One way or another, you've got to face it."

"Don't tell me what I've got to face. You won't be here, you won't have to face it. Why should you care? You just want one thing; you don't care what happens to me."

"That's not true."

"It is true. You hate him so much you'd use me to get him. At least be honest enough to admit that. Who was it that took me out of his place? If you'd left me alone I'd probably be fine now. He'd've done what he wanted and that would be the end of it. But you had to take me. You had to put me between you, and now you tell me there's nothing you can do. Go on, get out of here."

I couldn't go after that. I still didn't know what to say to her.

"I don't understand you two," she said. "How do two men come to hate each other that much?"

"I don't know. It's not covered in the police manual."

"It's called human nature," she said. "I guess they don't have writers for that."

Here's how it happened. I put Barbara to bed and settled down on her sofa. I watched TV till my brain went limp, then I turned it off and lay quiet with my own thoughts. At 2:30 I heard a car door slam. I went to the window and looked out. Jackie was across the street, looking up at me. I knew he couldn't see me with the light out, so I stood still and watched him. Poor Barbara, what a mess she's in, I thought. He really is crazy, I thought—here he comes now, across the street, into the dark places under the window, up the stairs. In another moment I could hear his footsteps. I had maybe twenty seconds to decide what to do. Whatever I decided, there wouldn't be any logic to it. None of this made any sense: it never does when you're dealing with a Jackie Newton. I will kill him, I thought: when he comes through that door I'll blow his brains out and take all the heat tomorrow. This was a rational, cold decision: in that twenty seconds all the consequences raced through my head. I saw it with crystal clarity: all the flak that would trickle down from City Hall to the cop on the beat. All over town tomorrow, guys in blue would be asking one question: *What the hell was Janeway doing there at that time of night?* Did I set Jackie up? Did I goad him, then execute him with no more thought than a gangster gives his enemy? Everyone knew I hated the man: even Barbara knew it, and she barely knew me. All this flashed through me with the power of instinctive knowledge, something as simple as your own name, something you don't have to ponder or weigh. Give me some time and I could describe every memo and phone call, everything they'd be saying tomorrow from the mayor to the manager of safety, and from there to the chief of police. Give me time, I thought.

Then Jackie came to the door, and my time was up.

I eased back into the bedroom and woke Barbara. "Don't make a sound," I said. "Just get up and put on a robe. Jackie's here."

I had to put my hand over her mouth to keep her from screaming. Luckily, I had anticipated that.

I got her up, though it wasn't easy. She had gone rigid with fear. I pushed her into the closet and closed the door. Then I got in her bed and pulled the covers up to the top of my head. I'm as crazy as she is, I thought: I'm as nuts as Jackie. Is this police procedure? Is this the way you catch a guy? All I can say is, it felt right. I took out my gun and held it like a hot water bottle, tight against my heart. I savored the surprise Jackie had coming: I could hardly keep from laughing.

Nothing from then on seemed real.

I heard him kick the door in. It's amazing how quiet that can be when it's done in one swift blow. The unbreakable deadbolt ripped through the wood like so much cardboard and he was coming fast. He crossed the room in four giant strides and came into the bedroom. He jerked back the covers and even then I didn't know whether to kill him. I came up with the blanket, the gun leading the way. "Kiss me, sugar," I said, and I cracked steel against his head. He went down like I'd shot him, and before he could move I had the light on and the gun cocked against his head.

I had him facedown on the floor beside the bed, the gun jamming him behind the ear. One move and Barbara Crowell would have Jackie Newton's brains for a throw rug. He knew it too: the blow had dazed him but he was coming out of it now. He kept trying to look back at my gun.

John Dunning

He was bleeding out of the left eyebrow where I had opened his head to the bone. I kept him there, kissing the floor for another minute while I patted him down. He wasn't carrying anything, the arrogant bastard. I backed off slowly. "Just stay where you are, Newton. Don't even think about getting up."

When I was ready, I told him to get up. "Get against that wall," I said, "face-first." He didn't say a word, just let his eyes rake me over like before. I was terrified so it must've worked. "Turn around," I said again. I shoved him against the wall and jerked his hands behind him. Then I got the cuffs and shackled him. I made it tight; I didn't care much about chafing him. I called Barbara out of the closet but she wouldn't come. I called her again, louder.

"Just stand there, punk," I said. "Keep your face to that wall and you might make it downtown in one piece."

I went to the closet and opened it. Barbara was sitting with her hands over her eyes. I took her by the arm, but she looked to be in shock. I told her it was okay, she could come out now, but she didn't seem to believe it.

"Come on," I said. "You've got to get dressed and go downtown with us."

She didn't seem to understand simple English. She couldn't look at Jackie, who had turned slightly so he could see her. Jackie knew what intimidation was: he knew what a hold he had over her. I kicked him in the ass, hard enough to break a bone, and he turned slowly back to the wall. Blood was everywhere, on the wall, on the floor, and all over Jackie.

"Get dressed," I said to Barbara.

She didn't move. I went to her closet and took out a blouse and a pair of jeans. "Go in the bathroom and put

150

these on," I said. When I looked in her face, I saw a picture of fear and despair so absolute it was heartbreaking. "C'mon, Barb," I said, as gently as I could. "Get dressed, hon, we've got work to do." She shook her head and dropped the clothes on the floor. I picked them up and guided her to the bathroom. I left the door open a crack, and every so often I peeped in and tried to talk her into her clothes. Put on the jeans, Barbara. That's good. Now the blouse. Real fine.

Suddenly she found her voice. "Tell him to go away," she said through the door. "I don't want him here."

When she came out of the bathroom, I took her under my arm and gave her a big hug. It only got the tears started again. She began to tremble and whimper and I didn't know what to do with her.

Jackie began to laugh.

I knew how to stop that. I whipped him around and cocked the gun and rammed it in his mouth. "Laugh now, asshole," I said. He didn't seem inclined to. I held him like that for a full minute, my eyes burning into his: I let him see my hand tremble, my finger waver on the trigger. "I may kill you yet, Newton," I said. "Just give me an excuse, just any at all, and they'll be picking pieces of your head out of that wall for a month. You got me, pardner?"

Jackie got me. I turned him to the wall and tried to work on Barbara. She had begun talking again, dangerous, mindless drivel in monologue, nonstop. "I think we could just let him go," she said. "Just make him promise not to come back if we let him go this time." The same thought came up, over and over, in different words. Let him go. Turn him loose. Get him out of here. Do this and Jackie, I guess out of gratitude, would leave her alone in the future. Bullshit, I said. She talked over my one-word argument as if I weren't there. "Bullshit, Barbara," I said, louder. This was not looking good: she'd make the worst kind of witness, assuming I could get her downtown to sign the papers in the first place. I don't know what else I expected: the fact was that, for the first time in my career, I hadn't thought far enough ahead to deal with even the most obvious problem. The victim was going to let Jackie walk: I had to've known that, so why was it making me so angry? I was almost beside myself with rage.

"Bullshit!" I shouted, loud enough to wake the block.

Barbara just stared at the floor and said she was sure he'd leave her alone if we let him go this time.

And Jackie was laughing again. He wasn't, really, but I could hear him anyway.

Something frightening happened inside me. Sometimes it happens to an old cop when one asshole too many has been patted on the head and turned back on the streets— you want to go out and take care of a few of them yourself, the fast and easy way. A few cops had done it: maybe I would too. I grabbed Barbara by the scruff of her worthless neck and pushed her to the front door. Jackie I handled a good deal rougher. I pushed them down the dark stairs and into the deserted street. Barbara was still muttering about turning him loose. I told her to shut up and walk, and a moment later we reached my car.

I opened the trunk and got a roll of electrical tape out of my toolbox. I fished a handkerchief out of Jackie's pocket and told Barbara to bind up his wound with that. I didn't want his crappy blood all over my car. But Barbara wouldn't touch him, so I wrapped the tape myself, right over his hair. Then I pushed his head down and forced him into the front seat. Barbara said she didn't understand why we couldn't just let him go, if he'd just promise not to come back. I told her to get in back. I got behind the wheel and started the car. I made Newton roll over with his head against the door. Then I drove up to Speer Boulevard and turned north.

We weren't going downtown, that much was certain. Jackie didn't say anything, but there was a feeling of tension in the car, of an act yet to come. He had misread me all the way: I had seen the fear in his eyes when I stood him up with the gun in his mouth, and he waited now for a telltale sign. You assume when you're dealing with a cop that everything gets played according to Hoyle. It doesn't always happen that way. Cops roll with the tide like everyone else. The good ones don't let the tide swamp them and so far I had been one of the good ones. But tonight I hadn't even read Jackie Newton his rights.

I hit the interstate, heading north, then east. Now they were both quiet, waiting to see what I was going to do. I didn't know either. I was driven by long frustration and the dim outline of a foolish idea. As a cop I had only two choices—let Jackie go or take him downtown and try to make a good case out of bad evidence—and I was quickly pushing myself to a third choice that, as a cop, wasn't mine to make. Procedure was out the window, but as I drove that mattered less and less. All I can do now, as I look back on it, is plead temporary insanity. It works for the assholes, why not for me? Answer—I'm supposed to be better than that. I'm supposed to know what the law says. I knew this much: there comes a point when a cop stops breaking procedure and starts breaking the law. An arrest becomes an abduction, and blame shifts easily, almost casually, from his shoulders to mine. Go far enough and you might as well go all the way.

The city limit slipped past us and so, in my mind, did that fine line.

Ahead lay five hundred miles of open prairie. We were

playing on Jackie's court now, with his rule book. That didn't seem to please him much. I didn't blame him; it wouldn't've pleased me either, in his place. I understood suddenly that this was a solitary thing between Jackie and myself: Barbara had no place in it; she was simply the instrument that had pushed us over the limit. I'm not thinking clearly, I thought—should've left her home. But by then we were fifteen miles out of town.

I pulled off the road. The morning was still very dark. I bumped along a dirt trail until I came to the river. There I told them to get out of the car.

Jackie found his voice. "What do you think you're doing, Janeway?" His big bad silent act was finished. He was trying to sound tough but it wasn't working: his voice was thick with worry. "What the hell do you think you're doing?" he said. Barbara said, "What are you gonna do, Janeway?" as if she hadn't heard the question just being asked. There was no fear in her now, just wonderment. They had both glimpsed the shadow of my foolish idea.

"I think I'll kill him for you, Barbara," I said. "Would you like that?"

She didn't say no. Again I told them to get out. Jackie was convinced: he turned to me and his mouth moved in the dashboard light as if to form a word, but nothing came out. He looked a lot like Barbara had looked back at the apartment. I guess real fear is the same all over.

We got out. A streak of light had appeared in the east and we began to see each other not as dim shapes but as people, faces, types. The thug, the brittle beauty, and me. What type was I? What type was I?

I gave Barbara my keys. "Here. Take the car and get out of here. Park in your spot behind the house. Lock it up. I've got an extra set of keys. . . . I'll come by for it later."

She looked reluctant, suddenly unwilling to leave. "What are you gonna do?"

"Don't worry about me."

"How will you get back?"

"Barbara," I said, anger rising in my voice, "get out of here, right now."

She got in the car and drove away. Jackie Newton and I stood alone on the empty prairie and looked at each other.

I pushed him down toward the river. He was trying to talk again—"Listen, Janeway," he said—but I told him to keep walking and shut up. We came to a little grove of trees. Daylight was coming fast: I could see the fear working at him. I took off my coat. Jackie Newton watched every move I made. I folded my coat and put it on the ground. "What are you doing?" he said, his voice suddenly shrill. I was taking off my gun, unstrapping the holster from under my arm. I draped it over a low-hanging branch. "Head down that way," I said, pushing Newton along a path by the river. We went about thirty yards. He turned and his eyes went past me, to the gun hanging from the tree. It dropped like a piece of deadly black fruit.

He began to grin as he realized that I wasn't going to shoot him.

Slowly, he understood.

I had circled him a couple of times. The last time, I came in close and unlocked the cuffs.

All that stood between Jackie Newton and the gun was me.

"Okay, tough guy," I said. "There's the gun. Why don't you go get it?"

He took a deep breath. The old arrogance came rippling back. He flexed his hands, rubbing the circulation into his chafed wrists. He threw the handcuffs to the ground and stood up tall.

"That's the biggest mistake you ever made," he said.

I walked up through the trees, alone. I had come with a question and was going home with an answer.

What type was I?

You're a killer, Janeway. Oh, what a killer you are. I knew what Kong felt like after the big tyrannosaurus fight, how the soul of David must've soared when he cut down Goliath. I felt the joy of victorious underdogs everywhere. It was a crummy fight, if I have to hang a label on it. Jackie hit me with everything he had: when I didn't go down, that was the end of it. His little chicken heart crumbled and broke into a thousand pieces. I ducked under his next punch and pounded his guts on the inside. He exploded in a hurricane of bad breath. I came up fast and got him on the button. He tottered and I punched him again and he went down. He sat on his ass in the dirt and I knew he wanted to quit but he couldn't. I let him get up in his own time and I moved in and let him hit me. I started to talk to him. *Fuck you, Jackie, I thought you had some balls.* I punched his stomach into great swollen slabs of meat, then went upstairs, for his eyes and chin. He toppled and went down. He rolled in the dirt and I waited for him to get up. Three more times he got up, just enough to salvage some pride and get his face caved in. I punched him with both hands, butted him with my head, and put him down for the count.

Hallelujah, brother. I had no illusions about what this would cost me, and it felt great.

I looked back once. He was still lying in the dirt. I thought he had a broken nose and two or three cracked ribs. I had the skin peeled off my knuckles and a mouse under one eye. It didn't hurt a bit.

A killer. God, I shoulda stayed in the ring.

The thug, the beaut, the killer.

Me.

I was finished as a cop. I strapped my gun on and threw my coat over my shoulder.

Soon I was on the highway, heading west. The morning rush hour was getting started and there was a steady flow of traffic into Denver.

I walked for a while, not wanting company.

My police career was over. I didn't need a mystic to tell me that. A line kept running through my head, that famous speech of Lou Gehrig's when he was losing not only the job he loved but also his life. *Today I consider myself the luckiest man on the face of the earth.*

For the first time in years, I knew where I was going.

I flagged a state cop, showed him my badge, and let him drive me home.

16

Ruby Seals and Emery Neff were working late, still pricing books from their big score.

They hadn't been listening to the radio. The newspaper accounts were still twelve hours away, but the TV and radio guys already had it.

I wanted to buy something I couldn't begin to afford.

"What's the best piece of fiction in the store?" I asked.

Ruby showed me a *Catcher in the Rye,* crisp, lovely in its first-state jacket. I stared into the impenetrable eyes of J. D. Salinger and bought it.

Four hundred dollars, a steal.

"What else've you got?"

Ruby looked at Neff and Neff looked back at Ruby. They cleared their throats and went to work.

"Got some King, but I know you don't care about that," Neff said.

"Which ones?"

"*Carrie, The Stand,* and that book of stories . . . ah, *Night Shift.*"

"I'll buy 'em if you want to wholesale 'em," I said.

"We'd consider that," said Ruby, his face a wall of dignity. "Yes sir, I believe we would. We bought these right, didn't we, Em? I think we could do a little wholesaling and still come out on top."

I gave a little laugh. "I'll bet you could."

"Screwed a little old lady out of her life savings, kicked her shins and took her books away," Ruby said.

"Now I don't feel so bad, offering you three-fifty for the three of 'em."

"We'll take it," Ruby said in a heartbeat.

"Not so goddamn fast," Neff said. "Ruby, these books don't just walk in here every day."

"Do I need to remind you again that the Greeks are at the gate?" Ruby said. "That's not a wooden horse they're knocking with, that's a battering ram. And that's not Helen of fucking Troy I hear calling my name."

Neff just stared.

"Sold to American," Ruby said. "Now, Dr. J, since you're in such a buying mood, take a look at these." He pushed a *Lie Down in Darkness* at me, the most beautiful copy I've ever seen of the only salable Styron. There was an *Out of Africa* in the same condition, and a great copy of Pynchon's *V.*

"God damn it, you're wholesaling the heart of this goddamn collection," Neff said.

"There'll be another collection, but not if we don't get the sheriff paid. This gentleman is gonna help us get well again."

"Oh, we're never gonna get well," Neff groaned.

"That's because you guys've got too many bad habits," I said.

"Yeah," Ruby said, "we like to eat."

I took the Styron, the Dinesen, the Pynchon. I took the Kings, too, and wrote them a check for $1,000.

"Don't it feel great to buy good books?" Ruby said.

"Yeah," I said, and it did.

"So when are you opening your place?" Neff said suddenly.

"Why the hell would I do that? Maybe I'll stake somebody, just to get my hand in."

"You want to stake somebody, stake us," Ruby said. "We are, after all, the most knowledgeable sons of bitches we know. Besides, I know where there's twenty thousand good books just waiting to be picked up for pin money."

"What kind of pin money?"

"Twenty-five grand. You might even get 'em for a buck a book, cash money."

Twenty thousand dollars was just about all I had in savings. Such a coincidence.

"Why don't you tell me where those books are, Ruby? You know, for old time's sake."

Ruby grinned through his beard and waved at me with his most prominent finger.

Neff, from on high, said, "The books are in a very safe place, Mr. Janeway. They'll be there when we've got the means to go get them."

"Maybe they will, maybe they won't," I said. "Who knows when somebody else will come along with twenty grand?"

"Not . . . very . . . likely." Neff peered through his glasses at a cracked hinge he was gluing, then smiled at me without much humor.

"Not where these books are hidden," Ruby said. "You couldn't root out these babies if you had the Lost Dutchman himself to lead you there."

"Must be in Arizona," I said. "You know . . . Lost Dutchman . . . Arizona?"

"Dammit, Ruby, don't screw around with this," Neff said. "This man is a detective, for Christ's sake."

But Ruby was enjoying the game. "Arizona's a big state."

"With not much going on in the empty spaces," I said. "There can't be many places to hide twenty thousand books in the Petrified Forest, so we must be talking about . . . ah, Phoenix."

Ruby chuckled.

"Tucson," I said, watching his eyes. "Tucson, Phoenix . . . or Flagstaff."

"Guess," Ruby said.

"Tucson."

Neff sighed with disgust.

"Your eyes moved when I said Tucson," I said. "Just a little, but it was enough."

"They're sittin' in a Tucson warehouse where they've been the last twenty years. There's nothing startling in there, just new blood; fresh faces that people in Denver haven't seen over and over for the past hundred years. Damn good stockers that you'd price in the seven-to-ten-buck range. Biography, history, some scholarly religion, some anthropology. I've known about 'em since the day they were put in there and never had the money to do anything about it. If you can spring those books, Dr. J, more power to you."

"I think I'll quit this business and take up something easy, like rolling queers in the park," Neff said.

"Em, it just don't make any difference. You see us *ever* having twenty grand? Why shouldn't somebody make use of those books, and why shouldn't it be a good guy we both like? I hate to see good books sit. And I think Dr. J would treat us right. Hell, I know an honest cop when I see one."

John Dunning

Neff's mind was shifting to that place where Ruby's had already gone. "I suppose we could release any claim we'd have on first dibs," he said, "for a finder's fee."

"What would you want?" I asked. "Assuming I'd be interested and the books could be sprung."

"Oh, I think a thousand dollars would be fair."

Ruby brightened suddenly. "I got a great idea. You go down there, Dr. J, and take me with you. Let me do all the talking. This is a weird bird that's got these books and you gotta stroke him. I'll get those books for fifteen grand, sixteen tops. You give me a two-grand finder's fee and let me pull out fifty books. You get out for eighteen and I get a new lease on life."

"Until next month," Neff said with a sigh.

"And what do I do with twenty thousand books?" I said, knowing the answer so thoroughly it seemed I'd always known it.

"I don't think I have to tell you that," Ruby said.

"We've seen it coming, Mr. Janeway," Neff said. "We know all the signs. You're hooked, you just don't know it yet."

"We've got a bet going, if you want to know the truth," Ruby said. "Em's betting you'll go this year. Me, I think you'll spend your whole life dreaming about it. A guy'd have to be crazy to give up your job—good money, prestige, interesting work, ten years already on the greasepole. And you're gonna give up that for this?"

"Ruby jests, of course," Neff said. "This is God's own occupation and he knows it. What would you rather be, Rubes, a bookseller or a cop?"

"Rather be a stinkin' garbage man if it put a beefsteak on my table tonight."

"Every day is like a treasure hunt," Neff said. "You never

162

know what might walk through that door five minutes from now."

"Most likely it'll be shit," Ruby said. "Neff don't tell you about that side of it—the jackoffs that come through your front door every day and grab off a piece of your life."

"Are you talking about our beloved customers?" Neff said.

"My beloved ass. I'll tell you what a customer is, my friend. That's a guy who comes in here and knows what he's doing. He knows as well as I do what the damn book's worth, so I don't have to waste my time justifying the seven lousy bucks I'm asking for it. If you don't have a book he wants, he goes on about his business: he don't stand in your face for two damn hours telling you about it—how his grandma read it to him when he was five years old, over and over till they were both brain dead. On the other hand, there are the jackoffs. You got any idea how many jackoffs you see in the book business on a given day, Dr. J?"

"This man is trying to win a bet, that's all there is to it," Neff said. "Trust me: he wouldn't be caught dead doing anything else."

The door opened suddenly and a ragged man in jeans came in.

"Hiya, Peter," Ruby said.

"You buyin' books?"

"Does a cat have an ass? You ever known me when I wasn't buying?"

The bookscout opened his bag. I knew enough about bookstore etiquette to move away while they did their business. Their voices dropped to a dim hum. I heard Neff say, "Where'd you get this book?" Then the bookscout said something, then they were all talking at once, the scout lost in the flanking din between Seals and

Neff. It turned angry. Ruby cursed and walked away. Neff continued to negotiate with the scout, who quietly stood his ground. "It don't matter where it came from," the bookscout said. "I didn't steal it, but I don't have to tell you my sources either." Ruby came back to where I stood, shook his head, rolled his eyes, turned, and walked back into battle. The fray went on for some time. At last it was quiet, but I could still hear them breathing up there.

"Dr. J?"

I came up from the shadows.

"Wanna buy a book?"

"I just bought a bunch of books, Ruby."

"Wholesale, man. All of a sudden Peter here don't trust our check."

"I need the cash," Peter said stubbornly.

"The hell with it," Ruby said. "You guys are all alike. I'm tired of the bunch of you. Maybe this gentleman will buy your book for cash money."

I looked. The book on the counter was a fine American first of Golding's *Lord of the Flies.*

I wasn't sure what to pay for it. But when I looked up, Ruby had moved behind Peter and was holding up two fingers, pointing with his other hand to the ceiling. The signal seemed to mean two hundred, high retail. I had two bills in my wallet, a hundred and a ten. Peter took the hundred gratefully.

When he had gone, Ruby said, "You paid him too much. You don't want to go over forty percent when it's a wholesale deal. Eighty bucks you shoulda paid. You're still thinking like a customer. You gotta be mean and lean if you're gonna make it in the book biz."

Neff's hand trembled as he picked up the book. "On

the other hand," he said in a dull voice, "this is such a nice copy, I think I'd mark it three."

"Two seventy-five, that's the perfect price for it," Ruby said.

I looked at the book, and at the seven others I had bought. "There sure are a lot of good books showing up all of a sudden."

"It goes like that," Neff said. "You get a run, then it peters out. When that happens, you can't find a goddamn Dr. Atkins diet book."

"Millie Farmer found the Kings," Ruby said. "She's gonna be a good bookscout yet. I told you we'd get our seven bucks back."

I nudged the Golding. "This one's yours. Your store, your book, I'll take your check, if you want it for a hundred."

Ruby had already started reaching for the checkbook. Neff said, "Can't do it."

"The hell we can't."

Neff reached across the counter and snatched the checkbook away. Ruby bristled and for a moment I thought a fight was coming. The moment passed and Ruby laughed it off, though his face was still flushed with anger.

"Everybody in this business is crazy, Mr. Janeway," Neff said. "That probably includes me. But I'm not so crazy that I'll let my partner write a hot check to a cop. You keep the book."

"I'll tear up my check," I offered. "Write you one for a hundred less."

Neff sighed. "We need every dime of that check, Mr. Janeway."

"I just remembered something," Ruby said. "I just plain

forgot about it in the heat of battle. That's Peter the Book-scout . . . you wanted to talk to him about Bobby, remember? If you hurry, maybe you can catch him before he gets to the bus stop."

We went outside, but Peter was gone.

I guess we all had a lot on our minds that day.

"When he comes back, tell him to call Hennessey," I said. I packed my books carefully in a small box and again opened the door.

"I'm not on that case anymore," I said.

17

The press was ugly. You could avoid radio and TV, but those newspaper headlines, when they came, were everywhere.

I had made the decision to go light on myself. I would read each paper once, to know what I was up against: then I'd forget it.

The *Denver Post* was simple and sweet: COP CHARGED WITH BRUTALITY, it said. Beneath that, in a smaller headline: HANDCUFFED AND BEATEN, JEFFCO MAN ALLEGES.

The *Rocky Mountain News* wanted me shot at sunrise: COP'S BADGE DEMANDED IN WAKE OF BRUTAL ATTACK was what *News* readers read over their morning coffee. Nice objective slant.

I had made top headlines in both daily rags.

They were, as usual, about ten hours behind the tubes. The later developments, I knew, would help keep the story on the front pages for another day.

I had been summoned to Internal Affairs to give my statement on the charges of John Randolph Newton. I told

167

it to two steely cops I barely knew, and they took it down without comment and asked only a couple of questions at the end.

It all sounded silly and unjustified a day later. I must seem like a character out of a 1945 movie: a cop with an Alan Ladd complex. And that was according to *my* version, which was supposed to make me look good. Jackie's version was another story. In that, I had beaten him with his hands cuffed behind him. He had the scars for evidence—the chafed wrists, the broken nose, the hamburger face. And he had a witness, Ms. Barbara Crowell, who was prepared to back up his version in court.

Let no one doubt that this was going to court. Even as I gave my statement to Internal Affairs, Jackie and his lawyer—a tough New Yorker named Rudy Levin—were still in the building raising hell.

Boone Steed, chief of detectives, was not happy. Boone was a tough cop who knew the ropes. He told me what to expect, what I already knew. Jackie would sue. He would sue us all, but it was me he really wanted. He would break me if he could. The department would do what it could for me, but I had acted illegally and that gave our insurance a loophole. I might end up having to mount my own defense, at my own expense. Goddamn lawyers and insurance companies, Steed said. I could run up a $20,000 legal tab in no time. And the weights of the system were all on Newton's side: they were always on the side of the guy with the dough. Newton would drag me over every bump in the courts: he'd stall and prolong it so that he could drain my account of its last dime.

I was called to Steed's office again at the end of the day. I had been suspended with pay pending the outcome of the investigation by Internal Affairs.

That night I went out to Ruby's and dropped another grand on books.

I bought wholesale, and I bought well.

By the time the second-day stories appeared I was hardened to it: COP SUSPENDED, they both said. There was a picture of Jackie, looking like the sole survivor of Nagasaki. There I was, too, plastered next to him, one mean-looking bastard. They had used my old mug shot, my killer pose. You'd never know from just a look which of these two guys is the real hood, I thought. Take a look and guess.

I didn't get much comfort from my friends. I talked to Hennessey and that was okay—Neal never changes: he reminds me of a Saint Bernard dog, always there with a keg of cheer at exactly the right moment. Others in the department weren't so hot. Somebody leaked the gory details of my long feud with Jackie, and the papers picked that up and ran with it. It looked like I had had a long vendetta against the guy, without a helluva lot in the proof department. All the times I had picked Jackie up were examined and dissected. It didn't look good.

Finally there was Carol. We talked several times over the next few days and nothing came of it. She wanted to come over but somehow it didn't happen. There was a coolness now, a distance between us. I thought I knew how that was going to turn out too.

18

In the middle of the third day, my phone rang.

"Dr. Janeway, I presume."

"You got me."

"Rubio here. That's quite a beating you took in the papers this morning."

"You should see the other guy."

"I did, my friend. His nose looked like one of my legs flopping down between his eyes. But look, I didn't call just to be sociable. I've got three questions for you. Ready?"

"Shoot."

"Number one. You want to make a fast two bills on that Golding item?"

The book happened to be on the table before me. I looked at it and thought. *No, hell no, I'll never see another one this nice.*

Ruby, catching my drift, said, "If you're gonna deal books, Dr. J, you can't fall in love with the bastards."

"Sure," I said, and my rite of passage began.

"Number two," Ruby said. "Will you let me make a little money on it?"

"That seems fair."

"All the right answers so far. Now for the big one. You ready to take the plunge?"

"I might be."

"I thought you might after I read the papers. A lot of things started coming clear after that."

"What've you got in mind?"

"Tell you when I see you. Meet me at the store in an hour, and bring the book."

The client was a man in his fifties who had been looking for the Golding for a year. "Pickiest bastard you ever saw," Ruby said. "He'll pay top dollar, but it really has to be the world's nicest copy." He had seen and rejected half a dozen copies, Ruby said, and was primed for this one. Ruby had warned him that the tariff would be four hundred dollars.

The guy bought it without a whimper. He paid with a check to Seals & Neff and left a happy man.

I felt strangely elated, inexplicably confident. In that moment, every book I had was for sale.

"Mr. Janeway, it looks like you're a book dealer after all," Emery Neff said. "All you need now is a place to hang your shingle and the guts to take the leap."

"Which brings us back to that third question," Ruby said. "The place on the far corner has been empty about six months. It used to be a Greek restaurant and nobody thinks of it any other way. But man-oh-man, what a great bookstore that'd be. Plenty of room, lots of atmosphere—I'd rent it myself if I had the money and wasn't tied in here with a five-million-year lease."

I walked up the street and looked in the window.

It was one of those old places with alcoves and side rooms

and high ceilings. The house had been built, I guessed, around 1910: a residence long ago, before East Colfax had hardened and become Hustler's Avenue. When the hustlers had moved in, the place had gone commercial: the porch had been stripped away and bricked up; a storefront had been added and grates put over the windows. The last tenants had not been kind: there was grime on the walls and grit on the floor; the ceiling sagged and the carpet, where it existed, was a nest for all the rats and bugs of east Denver. But if you could see past the dirt to what it could be, none of that mattered.

I copied the number from the sign in the window, went back to Ruby's and called the man. He wanted $800 a month and a two-year lease: he would maintain the outside and I'd take care of the inside. The place was 2,500 square feet, which included two rooms in the basement. I told him I was interested, and we agreed to meet later in the afternoon and talk some more.

"If I do it we'll be in competition," I said to Ruby.

"That never scared me any."

"Do it and in a year this block will be known from coast to coast," Neff said.

"Believe that, Dr. J," Ruby said. "Believe it. Have faith. Know that the good guys always win."

"I've been a cop too long to buy into that, Ruby."

"Believe this, then," he said, holding the check between two fingers.

"He made the check out to us," Neff said. "If you'll allow us fifty for selling it, I'll write you our check for three-fifty and we're square."

"Things must be looking up," I said cheerfully. "You're writing checks again."

"Cash it fast, Dr. J," Ruby said. "There's still a little left over from your check the other day. I'm goin' down to the bank and put this in right away. But you cash that check real fast."

19

I met the guy and signed the lease. Then I quit the department.

I called in and told Steed. We talked for ten minutes. Most of what he said could be wrapped up in a couple of short sentences.

You've been a damn good cop, Janeway: don't throw it all away because of a stupid mistake. Fight the bastards.

I didn't have the heart for that fight anymore. I went home and put it in writing.

It swept through the department like wildfire. My phone started ringing and didn't stop for three days.

20

I wanted to build it myself. I wanted to feel it going up around me. I had no sense of urgency: I hadn't touched my savings yet, and what I'd get in mustering-out pay, back vacation, and my refund from the retirement pool would more than keep me going. I bought lumber, paint, and carpet. There was a bank less than a block away, perfect for a book fund checking account. Bookscouts, who hated checks, could cash them on the spot. I knew I'd need a name and I didn't want the obvious: Clifford L. Janeway, Books. I wanted something soft and literary, not cute. I settled on Twice Told Books, and I called a sign man and told him what I wanted.

I knew it would take at least a month to get it ready. The first night I spent getting rid of the old carpet, a rotten job. Ruby came by and pitched in, unasked. He had been a carpenter in the old days, long before books, before booze and dope had jerked him screaming through life's most ragged porthole. He wasn't fast anymore but he was good. We walked through the store and he pointed out things and made suggestions, and he said he'd be back now and then with his tools to help. I slipped him a double sawbuck. He said he wasn't doing it for money and I knew that, but he was too broke to refuse. He came two or three times that first week. Our evenings settled into a routine. I had pizza brought in and we worked till ten. We talked and laughed and I felt the first faint stirrings of a new camaraderie.

In the second week the book editor of the *Denver Post* called. He wanted to do a story on the cop-becomes-bookman motif. I wasn't thrilled at the idea, since the papers were still gorging themselves on my resignation under fire, as they called it, but I knew I'd need all the help I could get. The piece ran in the Sunday supplement. The headline said, HE SWAPPED HIS BADGE FOR A BOOK-STORE. The picture of me looked almost human. "Look at that," I said to the empty store. "I ain't such a bad guy after all." The article was okay, too. There were a few disparaging remarks from unnamed sources within the department: there was a brief recap about the two guys I had killed, and a couple of lines about Jackie Newton. All this I could've done without. But there was a quote from Ruby, too. Ruby Seals, longtime Denver antiquarian book dealer whose store is half a block east of Janeway's new establishment, said, quote, Janeway is the best bookman I've ever seen outside the trade; I know he's been thinking of this move for years, and he'll do extremely well. He has an eye for books that will carry him to the very top of his new profession. Unquote. "Aw damn, did you really say that?" I asked incredulously. He gave me his scholar's profile and farted loudly. "I think what I said was, he ain't bad for an old flatfoot. Jeez, that shrimp curry does it every time."

• • •

I never saw Emery Neff at all that week. "Neff don't like to sweat," Ruby said with a laugh. He told me he and Neff had become partners a few years ago after an on-and-off ten-year acquaintance. "Man, we thought we'd grab the book business by the ass," Ruby said. "Neff knows everything about early books. He knows seventeenth-century English poetry like I know the whorehouses of Saint Louis, Missouri. Neff's an expert on magic and ventriloquism. He used to perform and give shows but he don't do that anymore. Too much hassle, not enough pay. He had one of the best collections of magic books in this state, but like everything else he sold the high spots and the rest just trickled away. Me, I know illustrated books, American lit, and off-beat stuff. I like books about strikes, headbusters, radical politics. I got a real feel for what can be milked out of a good book that nobody's ever heard of. Both of us have good juice in all the other fields. Turn the two of us loose in a store that hasn't been picked in a while and it's tantamount to rape. We're damn good bookmen, Dr. J: between us, we thought we'd have all the bases covered. The problem is . . . well, you know what the problem is. You said it yourself. We got too many bad habits, especially together. We see a book we've got to have and we pay too much. Then we've got to wholesale for less than we paid to cover the rent. You can't keep doin' that, but we can't seem to stop. Books're like dope, and me and Neff seem to feed off of each other's worst habits. We egg each other on."

"Then why don't you split?"

He shrugged. "For one thing, we really like each other. I've still got the feeling we could be the most dynamic duo since Batman and Robin if we could just get our shit together. And we'd damn near have to declare bankruptcy and start all over again if we split. I'm too old for that. So we keep after it, day after day, trying to keep from losing too much ground, looking for the big score."

"Big scores don't come along every day, Ruby."

"Tell me about it. They do happen, though. They happen when you least expect 'em. But I'm beginning to believe what Neff's always said, the big score always happens to the guy who isn't looking for it."

We were at the end of another night. I was packing the tools and putting things away.

"And then there's the problem of gettin' old," Ruby said. "I can't do this forever, I can't keep hauling books all my life. Frankly, I don't care if I never see another ten-dollar book. I want to do expensive stuff, like Rita McKinley. But almost everybody I know who does that has money to begin with. The rest of us just break our backs and get old."

"You sure find your perspectives changing."

"Ain't that the damn truth. Everybody gets old in different ways. Me, I'm just slowing down. Neff's becoming a recluse. His uncle died a year or so ago and left him a scruffy broken-down ranch in Longmont. He lives up there on weekends now, and you know what? . . . He won't even give me his goddamn phone number. He's like Greta Garbo, he vants to be alone. He says if the store burns down he don't want to know about it anyway, and he doesn't want to be bothered for anything less. But I'll tell you a secret, Dr. J, if you don't tell anybody you heard it from me. I think he's gettin' in that Millie Farmer's pants. She let something slip last week about the ranch, so I know she's been up there. She thinks Neff's the most brilliant bastard she's ever met. Hard to believe, considering she's also met me."

• • •

I was still at least two weeks from opening, but already the books were piling up. Bookscouts were coming by at all hours, tapping on the glass, offering their wares. People were curious and that was good. Neighbors looked in and some gave me a thumbs-up gesture as they walked away.

I knew I would open with good stock, but it wouldn't begin to fill the place up. I had to decide about the books in Arizona. Ruby waved his hand, a gesture of dismissal. "I'll tell you something, Dr. J, and I'll tell you this in good faith because you and me, we're becoming friends, I hope. You don't need that stuff. I would really give my left nut for that finder's fee, but if I were you I'd build this mother from the ground up. That's how you learn, that's how you keep deadwood off your shelves. Trust me. You'll be up to your ass in books before you know it. As soon as people find out you're paying real money, you won't know where all the damn books came from."

We had barely begun work that night when the girl arrived. It was still midsummer and the door was open to catch the early-evening breeze. I looked up and she was standing in the doorway, looking about seventeen in her spring-green dress. She had long coppery hair and when she spoke her voice had Scotland stamped all over it.

"Is this the bookstore? The new one the paper wrote about?"

"You've found us," I said. "You're a little early, though. I haven't put out the Shakespeare folios or the Gutenbergs yet, and we won't open for another week or two. What can I do for you?"

"I'm looking for a job. I'm honest and I work hard, I'm pleasant to be around and I like books."

"You're hired," Ruby said from across the room.

"Pay no attention to this street rat," I said. "I'm the boss."

"I knew that from your picture. I did think when he spoke up so forcefully that perhaps he's the power behind the throne."

"Hire this kid, Dr. J," Ruby said. "In addition to all the obvious stuff, she sounds smart."

"I am smart. I've got a brain like a whip. Ask me something."

"What's your name?"

"That's too easy. Ask me something bookish."

"What's the point on *The Sun Also Rises?*" Ruby said. "Every bookman knows that."

"What's a point?"

We laughed.

"You can't expect me to know something I never learned. But tell me once and I'll never forget it. Oh, I forgot to mention one other thing. I work cheap."

"Hire this woman, Dr. J, before the word gets out," Ruby said.

"Don't pressure the man, I can see he's thinking it over. Why don't you make yourself useful and tell me what a point is."

"Three p's in 'stopped,' page 181," Ruby said. "That's a point."

"In other words, the first edition has a mistake and the later ones don't. Now that I know that, I'm a valued employee."

"How old are you?" I asked.

"What difference does that make?"

"I'd like to know I'm not aiding and abetting a runaway."

"For goodness sakes! I'm twenty-six."

"In a pig's eye."

"I am twenty-six. What are you looking at, don't you

John Dunning

believe me? That's another of my virtues—I never lie. My judgment's good, I'll always give you a sound opinion, and I'm compulsively punctual. What more do you want for the pittance you're paying me?"

We looked at each other.

"I have a great sense of humor," she said.

"You don't look a day over fifteen," I said.

"I'm twenty-six. When I come back tomorrow, I'll bring you something to prove it."

"We won't be open tomorrow. I won't be ready for a couple of weeks."

"I know that. I'm coming in to help you paint and stuff."

"Look, miss, I haven't even opened the door yet. I don't know if I can afford an employee."

Ruby cleared his throat. "May I interject, Dr. J?"

"I haven't found a way to stop you yet."

"A word to the wise is all. You don't want to shackle your legs to the front counter. You don't want to be an in-shop bookman. You want to keep yourself free for the hunt."

"Exactly," the girl said.

"You need to be out in the world. Meet people. Make house calls."

"House calls are important," the girl said.

Our eyes met. Hers were hazel, lovely with that tinge of innocence.

"If you're twenty-six, I'm Whistler's mother," I said.

"I'm nineteen. Everything else I've told you so far's the truth, except that I do fib sometimes when I have to. I'm hungry and tired and I desperately need a job. I need it bad enough to lie, or to fight for it if I have to. I'll come back tomorrow in my grubbys if you'll let me do something— no charge, just a bite to eat during the day. I'm wonderful with a paintbrush. I could save you a lot of time staining those shelves."

I started to speak. She cried out: "Don't say no, please! Please, please, *please* don't say anything before you at least see what I can do! Just have something for me tomorrow; in a week you'll wonder what you ever did without me. I promise . . . I promise . . . I really do."

She backed out the way she had come and hustled off down the street.

"Well," I said. "What do you make of that?"

"I told you what I think," Ruby said. "She's a Grade-A sweetie, right off the last boat from Glasgow. She's just what this place needs, the pièce de résistance. She might even be two pieces."

We went back to work. After a while Ruby said, "Remember what Neff told you about the book business, Dr. J? Honey draws flies. Truer words were never said, and it works on more levels than one."

"She never even told us her name," I said. "Five'll get you ten she'll never come back."

But there was something relentless about her, something that didn't give up, something I liked. She was sitting on the sidewalk in the morning when I got there; she was wearing an old gingham dress that had seen better times.

"You're late," she lectured. "I've been here since eight. Here, I brought you a plant for the front window."

She handed me a tin can in which grew a pathetic little weed.

"It's a symbol," she said. "It starts out little and insignificant, almost nonexistent like your business. Both will get strong together."

"If this thing dies, I guess I can give up and close the doors."

"It won't die, Mr. Janeway. I won't let it."

I opened the door and we went inside. The early-morning rays from the sun came through the plate glass, making everything hazy and new. The place smelled like fresh sawdust, tangy and wonderful.

"Are you gonna tell me your name or is that some deep secret you're keeping?"

"Elspeth Pride." Her hand disappeared into mine. "What friends I've had have called me Pinky, for my hair. You may call me Miss Pride."

I laughed.

"I believe in keeping things professional," she said. "Don't you?"

"Absolutely."

"Let's get to work."

She started in one of the back rooms, staining while I worked the shelving up front. In a while the smell of the stain mingled with the sawdust and made a new smell, pleasant but strong. I propped open the front door. The sound of the saw buzzed along the street: people stopped and looked in and some of them asked questions. I've never been good at idle chatter, but these were potential customers and I was now a businessman. I didn't get as much done as I might have, but Miss Pride worked steadily through the morning and never took a break. At noon I went back to ask if she'd like some lunch. She had done two-thirds of the room and her work was excellent.

I went to a fast-food joint and brought back some sandwiches. We ate together in the front room. She was very hungry, and it didn't take long and she didn't say much. Personal questions were put on a back burner. Now there was just the job: the work finished and the work yet to come. She was relentless. When she spoke it was to make suggestions about color schemes and decorating and what the walls would need. "Are you going to do art as well as books?" she asked. When I told her I believed in learning one difficult trade at a time, she said, "Then you'll need a picture for that wall, not for sale, for show." The interest she took was personal and real, and by midafternoon I found her promise coming true: I was beginning to wonder what I'd have done without her.

At three o'clock I looked up and Peter was standing in the door. "I got a box of sports books, Dr. J." They had all taken to calling me that, taking their cue from Ruby. I went through his books and bought about half. I bought with confidence and paid fair money. I knew what I wanted and nothing else qualified. I would buy no book that had a problem: no water stains, no ink underlined. I set a standard that still holds: if one page of a book is underlined, that's the same as underlining on every page; if the leather on one volume of a fine set is chipped, the whole set is flawed. I would have only pristine copies of very good books. I would do only books of permanent value, not the trendy cotton-candy junk that's so prevalent today. I paid Peter out of my pocket and reminded him that Hennessey still wanted to see him about Bobby Westfall's death. "I don't know nuthin' about that," he said, and went on his way.

When I turned back to my work, Miss Pride was standing there. "I'm not sluffing off, you know. I wanted to see how you bought these things. I'm going to be your buyer someday, so you might say this is my first lesson. Why did you buy these and not something else? Why pass up the Jane Fonda book? I thought that was an enormous seller."

I sat beside her on the floor and went through them

John Dunning

book by book. Some of it Ruby had told me. *Baseball books are all wonderful, Dr. J. Football books are a waste of paper. For some reason baseball fans read and football fans drink beer and raise hell. Basketball sucks and hockey can be slow. But always buy golf books, any damn golf book that comes through the door will sell. Buy anything on horses or auto racing. Buy billiards and chess, the older the better, but don't ever buy a bowling book.* On my own, I added this: a good biography on Jackie Robinson is worth ten books on Joe Namath. Robinson's story had conflict and drama and racial tension, not to mention baseball. It would still be interesting a hundred years from now.

And as for the *Jane Fonda Workout Book,* phooie! There are two distinct kinds of book people, best-seller people and the others. Sometimes they cross over, but usually a best-seller like Jane Fonda or Dr. Atkins lives and dies on the best-seller list. Every single person who wants one gets it while it's hot: six months later you can't give them away.

We worked on toward evening. I could see she was getting tired, but I was just coming into my second wind. Every so often she'd come out and stretch, then go back in for another hour. She asked if Mr. Seals was planning on coming tonight. I said I didn't know: Mr. Seals came and went according to his own whim. That night Mr. Seals did not come. At eight o'clock I told her to go home: I'd stay and putter around a little more. She said she'd stay and putter with me. We ate a late supper, delivered, and I pushed on to eleven o'clock. I could've gone another three hours, but it's no fun working with a zombie. She was making a heroic effort, however, for a dead person.

"Come on," I said, "I'll drive you home."

"You don't have to."

"I know I don't have to. But it's midnight and you've

184

worked hard and this is East Colfax Avenue. Get your stuff and let's go."

"Well the fact is, Mr. Janeway, you're embarrassing me. I have no home. There's no place to drive me to."

"Then where are you staying?"

"At the moment I'm, um, between things."

"What the hell are you doing, sleeping in the park?"

"I hadn't quite decided yet, for tonight." She went into the back room and fetched the little valise she's been carrying. "The fact is, I just got to Denver an hour before I turned up on your doorstep. I got here with five dollars and spent half of that in the Laundromat. That's how I found out about you—there was an old newspaper there from Sunday. Fate, Mr. Janeway."

"Well, Miss Pride, tonight you sleep in a good bed." I reached for my wallet.

"No you don't, I'm not taking any money for this. I told you—"

"Pardon my French, Miss Pride, but bullshit."

"I want a job, sir, not day wages."

"Day wages would look pretty good to me right now if I had two bucks in my pocket. Besides, nobody works for me free, not now or ever. So take the money"—I shoved $60 in her hand—"and we'll go find you a motel."

"I will take it, then, but only if you agree that it's a loan against wages."

"Don't push me, Miss Pride. You've been real good today; don't try to back me into a corner at the last minute. Now let's button it up and get out of here."

It had been a good day. We had gone from strangers to those first halting steps into friendship. We had sat on the floor and broken bread together, which is a fairly intimate thing: we had talked about books and points, and about hope. What we didn't know about each other would fill its own book: what we did know was a simple broadside. I sure liked what I did know. I liked her. She brought out something I had never felt before, an unexpected sensation of paternity. I felt suddenly responsible for her welfare.

The motel we found was a few blocks from the store: she'd be able to walk back and forth easily. I gave her a key so she wouldn't have to wait on the sidewalk in the morning, and I went into the motel and paid her up for a week.

The next day was a copy of the first: we worked, we ate, we said little. Bookscouts came to sell their wares, and Miss Pride stood and watched over my shoulder. In the evening Ruby joined us and we worked till ten. I paid them both and Miss Pride did not argue. Ruby never argued when money was coming his way.

The three of us got along fine. The place was shaping up. "Lookin' booky, Dr. J," Ruby said. It felt solid, good; it felt great. We talked and laughed, especially at dinnertime, and I paid the tariff and was glad I had these people around me.

Miss Pride was from Edinburgh, "Auld Reekie," she called it. In natural conversation she spoke a Scotch dialect that was all but indecipherable: I was *so* glad she had learned English as well. Her story—what she chose to share of it—might have been one of those Horatio Alger tearjerkers of the 1890s. She was an orphan, desperately poor in her own land. America had always been her big dream. She was here on a one-year work visa, which, she hoped, could be extended. She had been here six months, mostly in New York, but the last three weeks on the road. New York had disappointed her: her sponsor had died suddenly, leaving her to cope in the tough Big Apple. But Denver felt right. She felt good about Denver. Denver was where her version of the American dream was to begin.

Ruby draped himself in a drop cloth and stood with his paintbrush pointing up. "Send us your tired, your wretched, your bookscouts," he said, and we got a good laugh out of that.

We finished up one night ten days later. The place looked like new; it looked truly marvelous. Miss Pride went over it with a vacuum while Ruby packed his tools for the last time. I just walked from room to room, unable to remember when I'd last felt such peace and satisfaction.

Now came the books. I emptied out my apartment and brought in everything from storage. Ruby was astounded at what I had. "I'm tellin' you right now, Dr. J, this fiction section is gonna be the most important one in the West. Good God, look at the *Milagros!* I can't believe it. John Nichols hasn't got this many." I told him I thought I'd make a pyramid of *Milagros* in the glass case, but he shook his head. You put these out one at a time, he said: in a rare book section, you never put more than one copy out, it would undercut the illusion of scarcity. You wanted that feeling of urgency to always be a customer's companion, the notion that he must act now, *today,* else it be gone forever. The three of us sat up all night pricing. Miss Pride priced the common stock using the standard ratio: she'd look it up in *Books in Print,* and if ours was a perfect copy she priced it half of the in-print tariff. Ruby and I priced the collectibles, arguing incessantly about high retail and low, scarcity, demand, and, always, condition. "Remember, Ruby, I don't want to be high," I would say, and Ruby would look at me with great disgust. "You still haven't learned anything," he would say. "You still don't know that it's easier to sell a good book high than low. Dammit, people like to think that

187

what they're buying is worthwhile. Price it too low and it
looks like you don't value your own stuff." He would hold
a book against his head and close his eyes as if the book
could speak. When it spoke to him, he would make his
pronouncement. "Seventy-five bucks," he'd say, and I
would argue, and he'd throw up his hands. "Seventy-five
dollars, Dr. J, you can't *sell* the son of a bitch for less than
that. Do you want to look like a fool?"

And so it went, till well after dawn. The night had
passed in a wink and suddenly it was over. "It's always that
way when you're lookin' at books," Ruby said. "An hour
goes by in a minute: you don't know where the hell the
time went. It's like making love to a woman . . . the most
hypnotic business a man can do."

Then they were gone. Ruby went home for a few hours'
sleep and Miss Pride went to her room. I walked through
the store and only then did it hit me—what I had taken on,
what I'd left behind, how drastically my life had changed in
only one month. I took a deep breath. The place smelled of
paint fumes and sawdust. It smelled like a new car, though
the actual odor was nothing like that. It was real, it was
alive, and it was mine. It was sweet and exciting. I had a
sense of proprietorship, of direction. I had a lifetime of
work ahead of me, and it was very good.

21

That was all some time ago.

We had a sensational opening week. I sold two signed *Milagros* the first day, and did almost $1,000 before the day was out. The three Stephen Kings flew out the door on the second day. By the end of the week I had taken in $3,000. I started a beard, shaved it, started it again and shaved it. I never, ever, wore a necktie. People said I was in danger of becoming a bohemian.

Jackie Newton sued me for $10 million. It looked like something that would drag on for years. I had a lawyer who was also a friend, and he said not to worry, we'd work it out.

I didn't worry. I had one or two regrets: occasionally I dreamed about Bobby Westfall and his unknown killer, but I told myself I was out of the worrying business forever.

Today it seems as if my years as a cop were all part of another lifetime. I never hear sirens in my sleep, and even a report of a gunfight in progress between police and drug dealers leaves me strangely detached. I've gone to a few funerals since I quit the department, but as time goes by I'm treated more and more like an outsider. I still run. I keep in good shape because it makes good sense. I keep my gun because that makes good sense too, but I've got a permit now, just like any other law-abiding citizen.

I see a few old friends a few times a year. I never see Carol. I hear she's living with a sergeant over on the west side. Hennessey's the same old buffalo. We sit and drink beer and talk about old cases, old times.

I get the feeling he doesn't try as hard these days. He never did talk to Peter. He never found Rita McKinley. The U-Haul lead fizzled and went out.

The cops weren't about to solve the Westfall case. As it turned out, I had to do that.

Book 2

22

My days settled into a glorious routine. I was up at seven; I ate breakfast in a café a few blocks from my apartment, I read the paper, had my coffee, and was on the streets by nine. I left the opening of the store to Miss Pride. She had her own apartment now, still within walking distance; she was there faithfully by nine-thirty, leaving me free for, as Ruby put it, the hunt. From the beginning I was amazed by the stuff I found. In the old days I had gone into thrift stores and junk shops occasionally and never found anything. From the moment I became a book dealer, good things began to happen. Suddenly there were real books on the shelves of those dust palaces where there'd been only dogs before. I know two things now that I didn't know then. Then I had been looking with a much narrower eye, seeking out titles in my area of interest only. Now I bought a medical book on eye surgery, a fat doorstop with color plates, circa 1903, that I never would've touched in olden times. It cost me $1: I lowballed it to an out-of-town medical specialist for $100. I bought a two-volume set on farming from the early 1800s, very technical, for $10; I think $125 would be very reasonable for it in a store. The second thing I learned is that books are seldom found on a hit-or-miss basis. The hunt is not a random process. I had to be where the books were, and I had to be there all the time. A good book placed in the open for a small price could be expected to last only hours, maybe minutes—then a bookscout would come along and pick it off. I tried to be there first, and I was, a fair number of times. I drifted across town and sucked them up like a vacuum.

I bought extensively and well in my chosen field, first edition lit and detective fiction. I read the trades and saw trends coming. I got on the Sue Grafton bandwagon, though I don't care much for her stuff, at just the right time. Her first book, *A Is for Alibi*, has been going crazy in the used book world, appreciating at around a hundred percent a year until now people are asking $300 to $400 for a fine first. Grafton is breezy and readable, entertaining but never challenging. Her father, C. W. Grafton, once wrote one of the cleverest, most gripping novels in the literature. His book, *Beyond a Reasonable Doubt*, is by most accounts a cornerstone, but if I want to sell it I have to do it on *her* popularity. I put one away for a more enlightened time. I discovered Thomas Harris when people were still selling *Black Sunday* for $6.50. His *Red Dragon* put me on the floor, even if he did make a sophomoric break-and-enter mistake with a glass cutter in the early going. You can't break into a house that way, you might as well use a hammer and knock the glass out, but writers and the movies keep the myth going anyway. *Gimme my glass cutter, doc. I'll just cut a little hole in this here glass case and pluck the Hope diamond out.* Uh-huh. Try it sometime. Somehow it didn't matter. *Red Dragon* was such a good book that Harris could've fed me the untreated discharge from the Metro Denver Sewer Plant and I'd've been standing there like little Ollie Twist with my gruel-bucket in my hand, begging for more. *More? You want MORE!* Even then he was putting the polish on that big riveting pisser of a book, *Silence of the Lambs,* simply the best thriller I've read in five years. I thought of old Mr. Greenwald all the time I was reading it and I wondered if he'd like it. It proves, I think, the point I was trying to make that day, that wonderful things can come from anywhere, even the best-seller list. Thomas Harris. All he is is a talent of the first rank. I hope the bastard lives forever, but in case he doesn't, I've been squirreling him away. Collectors are starting to find him now: in recent catalogs I see that *Black Sunday* is inching toward the $100 mark, and I've got six perfect copies hidden in a safe place.

Janeway's Rule of the Discriminating Bookscout was born. Buy what you like, what you read. Trust your judgment. Have faith. The good guys, like Melville, might die and be forgotten with the rest, but they always come back.

I was practicing what Maugham has called the contemplative life. At night I read some of the books I'd found. I read things I had never imagined or heard of, and I listened to good music, mostly jazz, and studied incessantly the catalogs of other dealers. I learned quickly and never forgot a book I had handled. This is how the game is played: you've got to be part businessman, part lucky, part clairvoyant. The guy with the best crystal ball makes the most money. The guy in the right place at the right time. The guy with the most energy, the best moves, the right karma.

I had been here before: I knew things that hadn't yet happened. I was home at last, in the work I'd been born for.

I had been in business three months when I was pulled back suddenly into that old world. It started a few days before Halloween. I had two visitors in the store: Jackie Newton and Rita McKinley.

23

I had come to the store late that day after a tough round of fruitless bookscouting. The days were getting shorter: we were off daylight saving time and darkness had fallen by five o'clock, the time we normally close for the night. Usually I tried to get in by four—Colfax is a rough street and I didn't like leaving Miss Pride to close up alone—but that day I had scouted Boulder and had run later than expected. It was almost five when I pulled up in front of the place and parked. I saw Miss Pride, alone in the front room, adding up the day's receipts. When I came in she rolled her eyes toward the back rooms, and when I came closer she held up the calculator to show me what she'd done that day. The total was $1,425, my best day ever. I gave a little whistle. "Couple of high rollers," she said. "They're still here, in back."

She showed me the receipts. They had bought John Stephens' *Incidents of Travel in the Yucatán,* a very nice 1843 first edition in the original boards, and the expensive Louise Saunders-Maxfield Parrish *Knave of Hearts,* which I had bought from a catalog only last month. The tariff for the two items came to almost $1,200.

"Just an average day if it wasn't for them," I said.

"They are definitely strange ducks, Mr. Janeway," she said, keeping her voice down. "But when they spend this kind of money, who's going to quarrel?"

"Strange how?" I asked.

"Well, they came in here about three-thirty. The one did all the talking. He asked for you right off. When I told him you weren't in, he asked when you'd be back. I said probably before five. He asked to see the best books in the house. I showed him the Stephens and the Parrish. He said, I'll take these, just like that. Paid with hundred-dollar bills." She cocked the cash drawer open slightly, so I could see the wad of money. "Then he wouldn't take any change. He gave me twelve hundred-dollar bills and said keep the change. I told him it was against policy, we didn't accept tips, but he went on as if he hadn't heard me. I thought he was going to leave but he didn't. He walked all around the store. Like I said, he's in the back room now."

I shrugged. "No accounting for people, Miss Pride. I'll take his money."

"I thought you would."

I sat where she had been sitting and started looking through the other sales. "You can take off now if you want."

"Oh, I'll hang around a bit. Mr. Harkness is coming by in a few minutes to take me to dinner."

I sat up straight. "Jerry Harkness?"

"Something wrong with that?"

I went back to my bookkeeping. Far be it from me to tell her who she could see. But yes, dammit, now that she mentioned it, there was something a little wrong. She was a sweet young girl and Jerry Harkness was a relatively old man.

Honey draws flies, remember? And yeah, I was a little ruffled and I didn't like it much. Hell, *I* was too old for her, and Harkness had me by a good eight years. I had gone around the horn to keep my relationship with Pinky Pride on a purely professional level, and she was going out with Jerry Harkness.

"Mr. Janeway? Is something wrong?"

"It's your business, Miss Pride. He just seems to be a bit old, that's all I was thinking."

"Funny I never thought of him that way. But you're right, he's got to be almost as old as you are."

I stared at the ceiling.

"I'm kidding, Mr. Janeway, where's your sense of humor? Of course he's too old for me, I'm not going to marry the man . . . unless . . ."

"What?" I snapped. "Unless what?"

"I might consider it if he'd be willing to do one of those convenience things that would let me stay in the country permanently. I might consider anyone who'd do that for me. But Mr. Harkness isn't going to do that. He wants to buy me a supper and I said yes: nothing more to it than that. If you've got something for me to do, though . . ."

I shook my head. "Just don't get in any dark corners."

"I never do, sir, unless they're of my own making. I hope he'll tell me some of the finer points of his specialty."

"I'm sure he will," I said dryly.

"I want to know it all."

"Someday you will," I said, and meant it.

She was learning fast. It'll be a national tragedy if we have to send her back to Scotland, I thought. The enormity of the book business—the fact that most of the books that even a very old dealer sees in a year are books that he's never seen before—simply did not faze her. She was fearless and confident at the edge of the bottomless pit. A genius, confining himself to the narrowest possible specialty, could not begin to know it all. This was the task Pinky Pride had set for herself.

She had learned so much in three months that I had her added to my book fund as a co-signer. She bought from bookscouts and signed away my money as freely as I did. She made mistakes but so did I: she also made at least one sensational buy a week. I knew that someday, in the not-too-distant future, she'd be gone, if not back to Scotland then away to a place of her own. For now, for this short and special time we shared, my job was to keep her happy.

"By the way, I'm giving you a raise," I said.

She considered it for a moment, as if she might turn it down. But she said, "I guess I deserve it."

I heard a laugh from the back room. It had a familiar ring, like something from an old dream. I heard the two guys talking in low voices, and again one of them laughed.

Then they came up front.

It was Jackie Newton, with some gunsel straight out of old Chicago. Jackie wasn't carrying anything, but the enforcer was packing a big gun. You learn to spot things like that. My own gun was on my belt, in the small of my back. I couldn't get it easily, but I'd get it quick enough if something started—probably a lot faster than Jackie would believe.

The gunsel was a bodyguard, a bonecrusher, a cheap hood. They circled the store together and pretended to look at books. I fought down the urge to say something cute ("No coloring books in here, boys" would be a nice touch) and let them do their thing. Miss Pride inched close to the counter and I saw her pluck the scissors out of our supply box.

She was no dummy, Miss Pride.

I looked in her eyes and said, "Why don't you go home now?"

"Uh-uh. Harkness, remember?"

"Go home, Miss Pride."

She didn't move. Jackie turned and looked at her and she stared back at him.

"Wanna go for a ride in a big car?" he said.

She shook her head.

He started coming toward her, looking at me all the time.

"How ya doin', fuckhead?" he said.

It was the opposite of our little meeting the day I had flattened his tire. Now I was playing it mute and Jackie was doing the talking. "I sure wouldn't want to have a place like this . . . all these valuable books . . . such a rough part of town. I hear there're gangs who don't do anything but go around smashing up places like this."

When he was three feet away, he stopped and said, "There's always a scumbag waiting to tear off a piece of your life."

He was doing all the talking.

"Broken window . . . somebody throws a gallon of gas in at midnight. Poof!"

Then he opened his bag and took out the two books he had bought. I knew what was coming and couldn't stop it. He had paid for the books: he had a receipt; the books were his.

He opened the Stephens, ripped out the 140-year-old map and blew his nose in it.

He ripped out two pages of the second volume and did it again.

He tore a page out of the $800 Maxfield Parrish, set it on fire, and lit the cigar the gunsel had been chewing.

"No smoking in here," I said calmly.

"Oh, I'm sorry, I didn't see your sign," Jackie Newton said. He dropped the flickering page on the floor and stepped on it. Then he opened the Parrish and held it out, and the gunsel dropped his soggy cigar inside it. Jackie rolled the book up in his hands and passed it to me over the counter.

"You got a trash can?"

I took the book with two fingers and dropped it into the can.

They headed toward the door.

"Come again," I said.

Jackie laughed as they went out. Miss Pride let out her breath. The scissors slipped out of her fingers and clattered on the floor.

"I recognized him too late," she said. "I didn't know who he was until I remembered his picture just now."

"It's okay."

"Pretty expensive way to show his contempt, wouldn't you say?"

"Depends on your perspective. He can afford it."

"What a terrible way to use your money, though."

I saw Jerry Harkness come to the window. Go away, I thought, I'm not in the mood for this.

But of course he wasn't going away. He opened the door and came in. He had slicked his hair and put on a tie and he wore an electric blue blazer. He looked like the well-dressed man of Greenwich Village, Mr. Cool of 1968.

"You ready?"

Miss Pride got her coat and wrapped her neck in a scarf. Harkness shifted his weight back and forth. His eyes met mine and the cool image melted and flushed. He looked uneasy.

"Okay with you, Janeway?"

"Hey, I'm not her guardian. Just watch your step."

We looked at each other again. What passed between us didn't need words: it was sharp and unmistakable. We were both years away from puberty: we had those years and that experience and a male viewpoint in common. I knew what he wanted and he knew I knew, and I was saying *Don't try it, pal, don't even think about it,* and my voice was as clear as a slap. Only Miss Pride didn't hear it.

I faced a bleak evening alone. Happy Halloween, Janeway. A light snow had begun falling. Tomorrow, I thought, I'd mosey up the block and have a little visit with Mr. Harkness. I shelved that plan at once. Mind your own business, I thought: make her mad and she may just quit and go to work for him. But the night was dark and so was I. Newton had put me on the defensive, Miss Pride had put me on edge, and I didn't know where to go to get a shot of instant light. I didn't want to read, work, go home, or stay where I was. I was at one of those depressed times when nothing seems to help.

It was then that the door popped open and Rita McKinley walked into my life.

24

I knew it was her. I had this vision of her in my head, and she seemed to fit it. Weeks ago I had received a package of photostats from the *AB,* but they contained straight news articles with no pictures; I had read the material through once and passed it on to Hennessey. It wasn't my job anymore, and yet, at odd times of the day or night I'd find myself thinking about her. Somehow she was at the crux of what had happened to Bobby Westfall. We had damn few hard facts, but my gut told me that. Almost everything about her fit the picture I'd had: she was damn good-looking, with dark hair and hazel eyes. I had been told that much by those who knew her, but my mind had filled in the blanks with amazing accuracy until the vision formed that now stood there in the flesh. The only thing I hadn't got right was the wardrobe: I had seen her in furs and jewels and she wore neither. What I could see of her dress under the old and rather plain coat looked common and conservative. She wore a little hat, tilted back on her head. It couldn't've been much protection against the wind.

Her cheeks were rosy from the cold. In her hand she carried a cloth bag (I had pictured her with leather) that
opened and closed by a frayed cord that looped through it.
She was everything, and nothing, that I had imagined her
to be.

"Are you Mr. Janeway?"

I said I was.

"I'm Rita McKinley."

I felt at once what others had felt in her presence—small
and insignificant in the bookseller's cosmos. I'd like to
know how she does that, I thought: I'll bet it's a helluvan
advantage in certain situations. Then I did know. She pro-
jected an aura that was totally real. You could look in her
face and see it: not an ounce of bullshit anywhere. She
came to the counter and said, "That was a blunt message
you left on my machine a while back."

"I tend to get blunt when I don't seem to be having any
effect. Don't you ever return calls?"

"I'm very good about returning calls. This time there
was a mix-up. I've been out of town."

"You've been out of town a long time."

"I've been out of touch almost six months. I'm supposed
to be able to get my messages when I call in, but it didn't
work."

"What'd you do, take a world cruise?"

I didn't expect an answer to that, and I didn't get one.
She went right to the point. "What can I do for you?"

"Nothing, now."

"The phone said something about a murder."

"I thought you didn't get the message."

"My machine recorded it, I just didn't get it when I
called in. Now what's this about a murder?"

"I'm not in the murder business anymore."

"So I see."

She looked around at the store, and again I felt small and insignificant. I felt irritated too, for reasons I only half understood.

"Don't pay any attention to this place," I said. "This is just something to while away my golden years."

"You've done a nice job."

I looked at her for traces of sarcasm, but I couldn't see any. She browsed her way around the room, glancing into the back as she passed the open doors. "You seem to know what you're doing," she said.

"Does that surprise you?"

"Sure. It's not something I'd expect a policeman to know."

"Don't worry, I know how to beat up people too. There's a good deal more to me than pure intellect."

My sense of humor was lost on her. "This is very nice stuff," she said without a hint of a smile.

"Thank you," I said.

"You must've been putting it away for a long time."

I didn't say anything.

"You have very good taste."

"For a cop," I said. I grinned to blunt the mockery and turned my palms up.

"I guess it proves that a good bookman can come from anywhere. Even a librarian has a chance."

"You don't like librarians?"

"I used to be one. They're the world's worst enemies of good books. Other than that, they're fine people."

She fingered a book, opened it, and read something. But her eyes drifted, came up and met mine over the top edge. She had the deadliest eyes. I'd hate to have to lie to this lady with my life at stake, I thought.

"If you don't know it yet, there's an endless war going on between libraries and book dealers," she said. "At best it's an uneasy truce."

"I didn't know that."

"Oh yes; we really hate each other."

"Why is that?"

"For obvious reasons. We're all after the same thing: in some cases, things that are unique. They see us as mercenaries, motivated by greed and excessive profits."

"That's a laugh."

"Sure it is. Try to convince them of that."

"And how do we see them?"

"I know how I see them, having worked with them. I can show you libraries that would make you cry. Priceless, wonderful books given to the library, then put in some moldy basement to rot. Old-timers die and think they're doing the world a favor when they leave their books to the library. They might as well take them out and burn them. Public libraries particularly. They just don't have the staff or knowledge to handle it. And after all, the public's got to have its Judith Krantz and its Janet Dailey. So the library buys fifty copies of that junk and then cries that it has no budget."

"Where'd you work?"

"I started in a library back in Kansas, a good case in point. That library was given a gorgeous collection thirty years ago. It's still right where they put it then, in a basement room. Part of the ceiling came down five years ago and the books are buried under two thousand pounds of plaster. I'd give a lot of money to get that stuff out of there."

"Why don't you try that? Most people respond favorably to money."

"Forget it. There are all kinds of complications when you get into deals like this. Sometimes you win and save some fabulous things. More often you lose. But that's another story. What did you want to ask me?"

"I think you better talk to the man who's handling that case." I wrote Hennessey's name on the back of a bookmark and gave it to her.

"What's it about?"

"I think I should let Hennessey tell you that."

"You said something on the phone about a man named Westfall?"

I nodded. This was tricky water we were navigating. I knew I shouldn't be discussing it with her, but I had been curious for a long time.

"Am I supposed to know him?" she asked.

"Are you telling me you don't know him?"

"Never heard of him before this day."

"What about Stanley Ballard?"

"Him I know. I did an appraisal for him. Nice old man."

"You looked at all his books?"

"Every bloody one. A colossal waste of time."

"You found nothing there?"

"He was in two book clubs, and that's where ninety-nine percent of it came from. You know as well as I do what that stuff's worth."

"The history can be okay."

"But Mr. Ballard wasn't a historian, was he? He was literati, and it was all book club fiction."

Junk, I thought.

She said, "When he called for the appraisal, I told him it wouldn't be a good use of his money unless the books were worthwhile. I don't work cheap, Mr. Janeway. My expertise is every bit as specialized as a lawyer's and just as hard to come by. When I get a call like that, cold, I tend to ask some questions before I jump in the car and go racing down the hill."

"What questions?"

"The same ones you'd ask if you were me. Why they want the appraisal done, for starters. This eliminates most of them right out of the gate. Most of the time they say they just want to know what they're worth. They're just fooling around, wasting their time and mine. When I tell them that the fee for an appraisal starts at sixty dollars an hour, they back off fast. Once in a while you get a real one. He wants to get his books insured and he needs an appraisal before a policy can be written. Maybe he's had a loss, a flood in a basement, and the insurance company doesn't want to pay off. I do a lot of work like that. I don't like insurance companies—they all try to lowball: some of them even claim that the books were never worth what they were insured for. That's where I come in. I'm not shy about telling you, there's nobody better at sticking it to a shyster insurance company. But I'm sure you know all this."

"I don't know any of it. I'm too new at it; I haven't done any appraisals yet."

"It's like money from heaven. Take my advice and the next time you run a Yellow Pages ad, put 'appraisals' in big letters. You go out, look at the stuff, do a little research, write up a report, and collect more money than an auto mechanic makes in a week. These days, that's substantial."

"Do you do mostly insurance claims?"

"No, but I do get a lot of them. I had one just before I left town. It was typical. The guy had lost his whole library in a flood. The pipes broke, the guy was visiting a friend . . . you know the story. There were books in the basement that this man had collected for twenty years. The books had never been appraised, they were supposed to be covered by his homeowner's policy . . . the replacement value, you know the clause. Well, the company wouldn't pay. The guy submitted a bill for two lousy thousand dollars and they rejected it. That's the biggest mistake they ever made. The guy called me and I went over and looked at the stuff. Christ, all he wanted was what he had in them, which was a fraction, believe me, of what it would cost to replace them today. There were some wonderful books; it broke my heart to see them all scummy and ruined. But I went through them and when I was done the guy had a retail valuation of thirty-five thousand dollars."

"And on your say-so, the insurance company rolled over and coughed up."

"They did what they always do, they sent some hot dog up the mountain to challenge my competence. You can imagine how I got along with him. So it looked like we were going to court. That's okay with me if that's how they want to play it. But all of a sudden somebody in that company got his head straightened out. All of a sudden they wanted to settle. They called and asked me to make up a book-by-book manifest, giving retail and wholesale values chapter and verse. I was delighted to do that. Suddenly I'm working on the company's nickel. If I had a cup of coffee while I was putting that list together, it cost the company five dollars. I don't mean to sound crass, but that company could've done what was right and got out of it cheap. When they decided to cheat, the bill went way up. So I gave them a list with references and footnotes and comparatives that they couldn't possibly challenge. It ran sixty pages and took me three days to put together, at eighty-five an hour. They settled with my guy for a little more than a third of the appraised value, eleven-five. What really killed them was having to pay my bill on top of that."

I did the mental arithmetic. "You must've cost them just about what the guy had originally submitted as a total bill."

"Two thousand, forty dollars. And people say there's no justice in the world."

"So what about Ballard?"

"I went through the whole routine with him. Asked him why he wanted the appraisal done, so I could be sure it was a good use of his money. That's what it's all about. If you've got any ethics, this is the first thing you've got to find out."

"What difference does it make, if you find out and you still do the appraisal?"

She recoiled from the question as if a snake were wrapped around it. Her eyes narrowed in anger. "Don't sit there and judge me, sir. It makes a hell of a difference."

"What difference?"

"Are you trying to needle me, or do you really want to know?"

"Like I told you before, it's none of my business anymore."

"Fine. Then I'm wasting my time."

I thought she was going to leave then, but she didn't. She did the store, looking more carefully now at items that had caught her eye earlier. I went back to my bookkeeping and let her browse. It took more than half an hour for her to work her way around the room.

"Look, I'll tell you something and then I've got to go," she said. "I don't care what you think of me or why, but here's what happened. The man told me he'd been in the clubs for fifty years. In all that time, he had bought only the fiction. I told him my bill would be higher than the whole library was worth. He said he didn't care about the money, he just wanted a record left for his heirs so everything would be easy after he was gone. I took it from what he said that the heirs don't get along."

"That's the understatement of the year."

"Well, there you are. He didn't care about the money, he just wanted them to have one less thing to fight about after he'd gone. God damn it, that *is* a good use of his money, if that's how he decides to use it. As long as they know what they're getting into, who am I to tell them they can't do it? I still didn't want to do it. This isn't the kind of work I usually do, and there are plenty of people in Denver who'd be glad for the job and do it well and for a lot less money. If you want to know the truth, I just can't get excited about looking at five million book club books, even if I'm getting paid for it; I don't need the money and I don't do anything anymore unless it excites me. But this old gentleman wanted me. He wanted a document that wouldn't be questioned. It may sound arrogant, Mr. Janeway, but he made it sound like a man's last request."

"It doesn't sound arrogant, it's probably true. He died this summer."

"I'm sorry to hear that. He was a grand old man and I liked him."

"Everybody says that."

She seemed to thaw a little. "He was like . . . my grandfather . . . only his taste in reading was better. There were some fantastic titles in there, but they just won't sell in those cheap editions. What more can I say?"

"You did the appraisal?"

"Yeah; three weeks later I drove down and did it. It didn't take long and I didn't charge him much—just enough to keep it on a professional level."

"How did you do it?"

"What do you mean, how did I do it? I looked at the books and wrote them up. There wasn't anything in there that needed to be itemized individually. They needed to be counted and we did that: rather, he did it before I got there. I told him to do that. There's no sense paying an appraiser for something you can do yourself. All I had to do was look at them. There wasn't a single book that needed to be researched. It took me about four hours to go through it and I was really moving."

"Was there a chance you might have missed something going that fast?"

"There's always a chance with a library that large. All I can tell you is, I looked at every book on those bookshelves. It was just what the man said it was, book club fiction top to bottom. Not worth the paper it was printed on."

"What did your written appraisal say?"

"Just that. No value, except as salvage books. Maybe a decorator might want them, to fill shelves in model homes."

This was her statement and it was now finished. What she had told me so far was harmless: it was what she would tell Hennessey tomorrow or the next day. This was where the questioning began, for a cop. I wasn't a cop anymore and I had to be careful of what I said to her. You don't tell someone what questions the cops are likely to be asking: it sets her on edge, gives her an advantage.

But I couldn't resist this. "Would it surprise you to know that someone bought that library, Miss McKinley? Thought he was getting a helluva deal."

I saw the anger again, but this time she kept it in. "Nothing surprises me," she said. "There's always someone who'll buy something, and there's always someone who'll pay too much. You'll find that out when you've been in it a while."

I gave a little shrug. "This guy knew books," I said, and my alarm went off and that was the last thing I was going to say to Rita McKinley about the Ballard books until she had given her statement to Hennessey.

Her anger simmered to the surface. "Maybe he didn't know them as well as you think. Maybe he lost his mind, Mr. Janeway. Maybe I was in cahoots with someone. What do you want me to say?"

"Nothing."

"Do you think I lowballed the appraisal just so somebody could buy it cheap? Is that what this is all about?"

"It doesn't matter what I think. I'm not the police anymore."

"I've got to go," she said again. "Show me a couple of things in your glass case first."

I took the books out and she looked at them carefully. "Let me see those too, please." She was all business now. I tried to be too. I showed her the books and eventually she put most of them back. What she finally bought were Saul Bellow's two rare novels, perfect copies I had bought from Peter less than a month ago. Ruby had priced them, high retail I had thought at the time: *Dangling Man* at $400; *The Victim* at $250.

She didn't ask for a discount: money seemed to mean nothing to her. I gave her the usual twenty percent and she wrote a check for $520.

And I fell into the pit of aimless chatter. Suddenly the night looked very long and dark, and I hated to see her go.

"I'm surprised you bought those: an old bookman I know said I'd probably die with them. Bellow's supposed to be like Mailer and Roth and Henry Miller. Nobody cares enough to collect them."

"I guess your friend was wrong. At least about these Bellows."

She was heading for the door. I wanted to grab her by the sleeve and show her something. It didn't matter what, as long as it was interesting and she hadn't seen it before.

How would you like to see how a cop really interrogates, Miss McKinley?

What I said, though, was "Look, I didn't mean to imply anything."

She turned at the door and gave me a look. I gave up the fight and made my betrayal of the Denver Police Department complete.

"I knew the books weren't worth anything," I said. "We saw the statements from the club. He kept them all, a complete record, all the way back to the beginning. I could've done that appraisal, just from the records he'd kept."

"Well, then," she said crisply. "I guess I won't go to the electric chair after all."

She had the door open. Now or never, I thought.

"How about dinner some night?"

"I don't think so," she said in the same heartbeat. "Thank you for asking, but no."

The door pulled shut in her wake. I stood again in an empty room on an empty world. A faint trace of her cologne lingered. Her memory lingered a good deal longer.

25

I dreamed about her. We swam together through a sea of books, in my dream. This was wonderful stuff. I hadn't had much to do with love, quote-unquote, in a very long time. Perhaps a bachelor heading into senility doesn't believe in the quote-unquote; maybe it's the one thing he's truly afraid of. But Rita McKinley had lit a fire under me and I knew it. I had gone up like an ember doused with gasoline. This may be normal for an adolescent, but for a man in his thirties who deals in "relationships" rather than "love," the feeling was heady and strange. It wasn't an unpleasant feeling, but with it came the unease of knowing that it would probably turn out to be.

In the morning I called Hennessey to square things away. I was still enough of a cop to do that. I told him about McKinley's after-hours visit, what we'd said, and how much I'd given away. He didn't seem to care much. The mayor wasn't exactly demanding that cops be called in on overtime to solve Bobby Westfall. He would be happy to talk to McKinley, when they made connections, but he wasn't hopeful that anything would come of it.

Two hours later, he called back and said McKinley was coming in around eleven o'clock. After that she was fair game.

Fair but elusive.

I called her number around two. She had the recording on, but she called back less than an hour later.

Her voice was cool and distant. "Well, Mr. Janeway, have you figured it out yet?"

"Figured what out, the murder or the book business?"

"If you ever get the book business figured out, let me know how you did it. What can I do for you?"

"Help me figure it out."

"I told you last night, and I told your Mr. Hennessey again this morning, I don't know anything about it."

"I was talking about the book business. I'd like to come up and see your books."

I felt completely transparent, stripped before the world. I braced for another rebuff and got it.

"There's no margin for you up here," she said. "Everything I've got is very high retail."

"I bet I'll find something."

"I don't think so. You couldn't possibly make any money, and look, I'm very busy now. I just got home, I'm still tired, and I've got a million things to catch up on. Add to that the fact that I'm just not feeling very hospitable. I don't feel like having company."

"Well, that's plain enough."

"I'm sorry. Good-bye."

Strike two on Janeway: bottom of the ninth, two out, and the fans begin to head for the turnstiles. I left the store in Miss Pride's care and made my rounds. I reached the DAV on Montview just as books were being put out. It looked like crap. I looked at it through Rita McKinley's eyes, and all I could see was crap: small-time books eagerly coveted by eternal small-timers. Book club mysteries. Book club science fiction. Dildo books: the *Cosmo Book of Good Sex, How to Make Love to a Man,* screwing seven ways from Sunday, blah blah blah. I hope these aren't the books we're judged by, by archaeologists of the future.

I'd been staring, thinking of Rita McKinley, when my eyes focused on the title *JR* and the name Gaddis. I reached out and plucked it just in time. A shadow loomed over my right shoulder.

"Hiya, Dr. J."

I turned. "Hi, Peter. How's tricks?"

"Could be better. Y' almost missed that one. What's it worth?"

I opened the book, took off the jacket, sniffed for mold. It was a nice enough first: the flyleaf had been creased and some bozo had written his name in it.

"Oh, for this copy, thirty, forty bucks."

Miss McKinley probably wouldn't pick it up, even at $2. But to a guy like Peter, it was a little shot of life.

"Damn," he said. "Another minute and I'da had it."

"You can have it anyway," I said, and I gave it to him.

"Jesus, Dr. J . . ."

"Merry Christmas, two months early."

"Jesus."

We walked out together. In the parking lot we stood and chatted for a moment. I asked if he was finding any books. He said yeah, he had some nice stuff to show me. One or two real honeys. Maybe he'd come in later in the week.

Then he seemed to go stiff. I looked at his face and thought he might be having a heart attack. He tottered and would've fallen if I hadn't grabbed his arm.

"Hey, Pete, you okay?"

"Yeah, sure."

He didn't look okay. He looked like a gaffed fish.

"I gotta go," he said.

"Come on, I'll give you a ride."

"No . . . no ride. Here comes the bus."

He broke away and ran across the street. A car swerved and almost hit him. He spun around and without breaking stride ran full-tilt to the bus stop. He had dropped the copy of *JR* at my feet.

I picked it up and watched the bus roll away. What the hell was that all about? I wondered.

It was about fear. Peter had been so scared of something that his mind had stopped working. Something had scared the hell out of Pete.

I stood where I was and looked around. A busy but harmless intersection: cars raced through on four lanes and people hustled along the sidewalk. Two convenience stores faced each other across the street. On the third corner was a little shopette and a Mexican café. The thrift store took up the fourth corner. I tried to remember what Peter had been doing, where he'd been looking, when it had happened, but I couldn't be sure. I walked across the street and went into one of the convenience stores. I bought some gum. Then I shrugged it off and went back to work.

26

"Rita McKinley called," Miss Pride said when I came in. "About fifteen minutes ago."

I played it cool. Checked the day's receipts. Verified my suspicion that it had been a lousy day. We had barely broken a hundred: cleared expenses was all.

I walked up the street and visited Ruby. He was getting ready to pack it in. Neff had gone home for the day. The firm of Seals & Neff had taken in less than fifty dollars.

It had been a lousy day on Book Row all around.

I didn't go down as far as Jerry Harkness. I could see a light coming from his window, so I knew he was there. I could see a light in Clyde Fix's place as well.

Night had come with a vengeance. I felt alone in the world and I had a hunch that, whatever Rita McKinley had to say to me, it wouldn't make that feeling go away.

But it did. When I called her, she was full of apologies.

"I'm not usually rude to people, Mr. Janeway. Put it down to jet lag."

"I didn't notice at all," I lied.

She spoke into the sudden yawning silence. "If you still want to come up, of course you're welcome."

"Just say when."

"Tomorrow afternoon would be as good a time as any. Make it late afternoon and that'll give me time to wind down from the trip."

I felt light-headed, almost giddy. Janeway's still at bat, folks: as incredible as it is to believe, he's been standing at the plate popping fouls into the bleachers for more than twenty-four hours, and the game's still hanging in the balance.

Miss Pride was watering her plant, which had been repotted twice and was growing into a small tree. I had never seen anything grow like that in just three months.

"What kind of thing is that?" I said.

"I have no idea. Just something I dug up myself."

"If it grows teeth, kill it."

We began to go through the nightly ritual, preparing to close.

"So you didn't tell me," I said. "How was Harkness?"

"A dear. A perfect gentleman."

I sighed.

"I know you'd love an excuse to go up there and tear his head off, but I'm afraid I can't give you one. He was just fine. His manners were beyond reproach."

"Just watch your flank, Miss Pride, just watch the water fore and aft, port and starboard. Now what do you say we lock this baby up and call it a bad day?"

"It *was* pretty dreary. I'll get the lights and put the recording on."

She disappeared into the back room. I locked the front door and began counting the money. I had just got started when I felt my hackles go up. I turned and looked through the glass. Jackie Newton was sitting in a car at the curb, watching me. It was a long black car, not one of his. The gunsel was behind the wheel.

"Uh-huh," I said.

Miss Pride, coming from the back room, said, "Did you say something to me?"

"I said we've got company."

"Oh, God."

"Don't even look at 'em; don't let 'em faze you at all. Just go on about your business and get ready to leave."

I turned the sign around, in case they had any notions of coming in. Miss Pride bustled about gathering her things.

"Are we ready to go?" I said.

"I am."

"Good. I'm driving you home tonight, by way of west Denver. Don't argue with me, let's just go. We'll walk right past the sons of bitches and get in my car and drive away. Got that?"

"I got it."

I flipped the front room lights. The telephone rang.

I heard the machine kick on and then begin recording. I don't like machines that answer telephones, but Miss Pride had talked me into it, so we wouldn't miss anyone with a big library to sell. As usual, she was right: the damned machine had made its cost back, three times over.

"I'm gonna see who that is," I said. "You wait here. Don't look at those guys and don't look worried. I'll be right back."

By the time I got into the office, the recorder had cut off. It was probably Rita McKinley, I thought, cancelling tomorrow. I rewound the tape and played the message.

It was Peter. His voice was tense, strained. "I need to talk to you, right now," he said.

I waited. I knew the line was still open, but he didn't say anything. He was like a man whose attention has suddenly been captured—like the poor scared fool he'd been in the thrift store parking lot.

"Oh, shit," he said, and hung up.

I ran the tape back and replayed it. It didn't make any more sense than anything else he had done that day. I had no idea where he lived or how to reach him. Maybe Ruby knew.

I reset the tape, went up front, killed the last of the lights, and took Miss Pride by the arm. "Let's go."

I locked the door and we walked past the car where Newton and his thug sat waiting. The gunsel started the engine and the car rolled along beside us. I'm gonna put up with this about ten seconds, I thought; then I'm gonna kick some ass. I walked up to Ruby's. The store was closed and locked. I walked past Harkness's, which was also closed. Only Clyde Fix was still open: he sat in the window and watched the street like a vulture.

We went around the corner to the small lot where everyone on Book Row kept their cars. The headlights of the gunsel's car swung behind us in a slow arc. I held the door for Miss Pride, then I walked back to the gunsel's car, which was sitting still with its motor running.

I tapped on the window. Jackie rolled it down a crack.

"That's all for you, Newton. If I see your ass again tonight there's gonna be trouble."

"Izzat so," the gunsel said.

I kept looking at Jackie. "Does this guy speak English? Keep your hands on the wheel, dogbreath; touch that gun and I'll blow you right through the door." There was a long quivering pause. The gunsel's fists clenched around the steering wheel. "Now I'm gonna tell you something,

Newton, and this goes for you too, Anton. If you want to live to celebrate your next birthday, don't fuck with me. You want to put that in Mongolese, Jackie, so the ape can understand it? Don't . . . fuck . . . with me."

"Tough guy," the gunsel said. "I'm gonna walk on you, tough guy."

"You couldn't walk the plank without losing your way. Now get this crate down the street."

Jackie wanted to look amused, but he couldn't sell that. He rolled up his window and motioned with his finger and the car pulled away from the curb. I watched the taillights go and thought again of Vinnie Marranzino. I stood for a long moment after they'd gone, watching the empty street.

Just another day on Book Row.

27

The next day began like every other. How it ended was another matter.

I made my rounds and found nothing of interest. The entire day was colored by my coming meeting with Rita McKinley. I was on edge, nervous and apprehensive and in a very real but strange way, thrilled. I had an early lunch with Hennessey and we talked a little about the Westfall case. Hennessey liked Rita McKinley and was inclined to believe everything she said. The line from the police department now seemed to be that Bobby Westfall had been killed by a petty thief, who was likely to remain unknown until he was caught for another crime and confessed to this as well. "Right, Neal," I said, and he gave me a look over a ten-pound sandwich and decided to say no more about it.

I had time to kill and I didn't want to go into the store. I called in instead, and told Miss Pride I was heading west and probably wouldn't see her till tomorrow. "Well, that's going to be a problem for Peter," she said. "He was here a while ago looking for you. He seemed quite put out when you weren't here. I told him to come back at closing time, you're always here by then."

"Well, tonight I won't be. Did he say what he wanted?"

"No, but he certainly made it sound urgent."

"When he comes in, try to help him. He mentioned to me yesterday that he might have some pretty good books to sell. If he needs some money, give him some. Give him up to a couple of hundred if that's what it takes. Write him a check on the bank up the street and tell him I'll square it with him tomorrow."

"Well, all right, but I don't think that's what it's about. He didn't have any books with him and he didn't say anything about money."

"All right, if worse comes to worst, have him call me up at Rita McKinley's place. Now, one more thing. Call your friend Harkness and let him know you're gonna be alone at closing tonight. Tell Ruby and Neff too."

"I'll be fine, Mr. Janeway."

"Listen to me. Do what I tell you. That's the most dangerous time of day for businesses run by women alone. Just let the others on the block know that you'll be closing up alone tonight. That way they can keep an eye on you."

I heard her sigh with feminist impatience.

"Miss Pride? Are you listening to me?"

"Yes, Mr. Janeway."

"Do it."

"Yes, Mr. Janeway."

I decided to scout west Denver, work my way through Golden and Morrison and let my momentum carry me to McKinley's place by late afternoon. For some reason, west Denver is a bookscout's ghetto. There are a few thrift stores, but nothing to write home about, and Golden is a complete wash. Morrison is an interesting little mountain town, full of antique stores that will sometimes cough up a garnet in the sea of junk. It was, however, less than a blue-ribbon performance: the sum total of the day's work was less than a dozen books, none even on the fringe of greatness. Some days are like that.

It was almost dark when I drove up the road to Rita McKinley's. The clock in my dashboard said 4:53. I was running a little later than I'd planned—a place in Evergreen had caught my eye, and you know how bookscouting is. She had left the gate open and I drove right through. She was working when I arrived: she had a fire going in the yard and huge piles of trash waiting to be fed to it. It was chilly. She wore faded jeans and a red flannel shirt and a heavy coat. The house was perched on top of the mountain, a great stone building with a porch that looked east, toward Denver. You couldn't see the city from there, but that didn't hurt the view. Miss McKinley gave a wave as I came into the yard. I parked beside her car, a plain Dodge about four years old.

From a distance she looked very young, an illusion that dissolved as I came closer. She was one of those women who look better with some age. She'd be a knockout at forty, about six years from now. We said our hellos and I apologized for intruding. She waved that off and led me inside. "My books are all over the house," she said. "It'll take you a long time to see them all. Maybe we should confine ourselves to the big room today."

The house smelled musty, the way a place gets when it's been closed for six months. Her living room was long, with a fireplace and a high ceiling. She had an enormous print of a whale, the picture Rockwell Kent had done for the 1930 edition of *Moby Dick*. There were other whales about—knickknacks on the shelves, pictures on the walls, paintings, photographs. Over the fireplace she had a blown-up photograph of a lone man standing on the bow of a speedboat. A larger boat was in the background, bearing down. I knew what it was: someone from Greenpeace, putting himself between an unseen whale and a boatload of modern whalers.

There weren't many books in the living room, and these she said were junk, "just things I'm reading." The main event was two rooms removed. The whole east wall was made of glass. There were heavy drapes, open now, which she used, probably in the morning, to protect her books against the sun. All the other walls were lined with books.

"Before you get started, there was a call for you about ten minutes ago. It may've been your girl at the store. It sounded pretty confused. Here, I got part of it on the tape machine."

She flipped a small cassette player. The first thing I heard was Peter's voice. He was in the middle of a sentence, as if he'd been talking over the recording. I couldn't make out what he was saying, but his voice sounded almost panicky. He turned away from the phone and there was a jumble of voices. A woman's voice said, "Let me talk to him, Peter. . . . Peter, would you give me that phone . . . give it to me, Peter, right now." There was a click and a bump and Miss Pride came on. "Mr. Janeway, are you there? Hello?" Then I heard her say, lower, as if she'd turned away, "There's nobody on the line, Peter, are you sure you dialed it right?" Then Peter screamed—literally screamed—"It's a fucking tape recorder!" and I heard him shout something but I couldn't make out the words. They were both talking for about ten seconds; then Miss Pride came back on and said in a low voice, "Look, I'm sorry, someone's come in. . . . I'll call you back."

The line went dead.

"You certainly know some strange people, Mr. Janeway," Miss McKinley said.

"I can't imagine what was going on there."

"I think you'd better call her back."

She went out of the room while I called. The phone rang and rang. The clock on the wall said five twenty-five: the store had been closed for twenty-five minutes.

I sat for a moment and stared at the machine. Miss McKinley poked her head in.

"Everything all right?"

"I don't know. Could I hear the tape again?"

But there was nothing on the tape that hadn't been there the first time.

I called Seals & Neff. Ruby answered on the first ring.

"Hey, Rube, this's Janeway. Listen, would you walk up the street and see if everything is okay at my place?"

"Sure. What's wrong?"

"Peter was just in there. I'm afraid he may've been giving Miss Pride some grief."

"Sure . . . gimme your number where you're at. . . . I'll call you right back."

I hung up and sat down to wait.

"How about some coffee?" Miss McKinley said. "I've got some whiskey if you'd like a drink."

"As a matter of fact, it is almost decent time for a bourbon."

"How do you like it?"

"Just like it comes."

She came back with the drink just as Ruby called. She motioned to the phone, that I should answer it, and I did. Ruby said, "Place looks shipshape to me, Dr. J. All locked up tight and the night-light on."

"Did you try the doors?"

"All both of 'em. Walked around, rattled the windows, sang three stanzas of 'The Battle Hymn of the Republic' through the keyhole. Nobody's there, Dr. J. Whatever the bug up Pete's ass was, she must've handled it and got him out of there."

"Okay," I said in a doubtful voice. "Thanks, Ruby."

I looked at Miss McKinley. "What a crazy thing."

"There's probably a simple explanation."

"Yeah . . . but you'd think she'd call back."

"Maybe it slipped her mind. She did say someone had come in. Anyway, there's nothing you can do about it now. Might as well do what you came for."

28

Everything Julian Lambert had said about her books was true, except that even then you weren't prepared for them. You just don't see that many sensational books in one place. It was all literature, published since the mid-1800s, and it was all letter-perfect. You need a bookman's eye to appreciate what a perfect copy of a fifty-year-old book looks like. It does not look like a new book—it looks so wonderfully like an old book that's never been touched. Never been touched by human hands—that's the feeling her books gave you. There were things in that room that I knew hadn't been seen in that condition in half a century. She had a shelf of Jack Londons in crisp dust jackets from before 1910. She had a little poetry piece that had ushered Ernest Hemingway into the book world. She had Mark Twain's copy of *Kim*, signed by Kipling when he and Clemens had met, in 1907. There were so many signed books, variants, unique pieces, books with unusual associations, books from authors' personal libraries, letters, and manuscripts that mere first editions seemed unexciting and trite. She had factory-fresh copies of *Look Homeward Angel,* and Steinbeck's first, awful, but extremely scarce novel, *Cup of Gold.* After a while this becomes meaningless: it degenerates into a simple list of the great, the rare, the wonderful. When I came upon Hawthorne's copy of *Moby Dick,* inscribed by Melville in great friendship and lavishly annotated in Hawthorne's hand, I heard a long deep sigh fill the room. I realized a moment later that it had been my own voice.

The phone rang, and I thought of Miss Pride. I heard the recorder kick on and Rita McKinley's voice repeating the message I had heard so often. At the beep, a man said, "Rita, this is Paul. . . . Call me back when you can." It rang again, almost immediately. The recorder played and beeped and a voice said, "This is George Butler the Third calling from New York. I have decided to buy the four books we discussed yesterday. Would you please ship and bill as soon as possible?" Of course I knew who Butler the Third was. I saw his self-aggrandizing ads in the *AB* all the time. "Mr. George Butler III announces his acquisition of . . ." That kind of thing. George Butler was one of the so-called big boys of the book world. You read his ads and you knew he never put on his pants like a mortal man, he just drifted up and floated down into both legs at once. I wondered what four books George Butler had decided he couldn't live without, and what the tariff would be. Ten thousand? Twenty? Just routine business for Ms. McKinley, who was certainly operating on a high level from her ivory tower in the mountains.

I took a break and called Miss Pride's home number. She wasn't home. I looked through some more books. I had done most of one short wall and still had the long wall and another short one left. I felt light-headed, like a drunk just coming back from a three-week bender. It had been too rich, this feast of her books, and I decided to pack it in for the night. I got up, stretched, and moved to the door. There was no sound in the house, other than the grandfather's clock ticking in the hallway. The clock said it was eight-thirty. I went through the dark hall, drawn by the light at the end. Suddenly I smelled food cooking. When I came into the kitchen, I saw that she had set a table for two.

I didn't see her at first. She was standing by the glass door, perfectly still, lost in thought, looking away into the night. I cleared my throat. She turned. There was a pensive, lonely, almost sad look on her face. I didn't know what else to call it but a window to the soul. It disappeared at once and the mask came up. She looked surprised, as if she'd forgotten I was there.

"Well, Mr. Janeway. You all finished?"

"Give me another week and I might be just getting started."

She didn't say anything.

"I thought I'd buy something," I said. "I guess I wanted to show off. But I've got to tell you, I don't know where to begin."

"It has that effect on people. It can be overwhelming."

"I hope when you go away for months at a time you have some way of protecting it."

"I do lock the gate."

"Don't you even have a burglar alarm?"

She shook her head. "You think I should?"

"Yes, and an armed guard, and spotlights, a siren, and killer dogs. I'd also put a moat around the house and fill it with crocodiles. That's for starters."

"Oh, it's no fun having something if you've got to lock it up . . . if it makes you paranoid."

"There's a difference between paranoia and common sense. You'd hate to come home someday and find all these books gone."

"Yes, but they're only books. I'd just go get some more."

I didn't know what to say to that.

She said, "I love what I do but I'm not very materialistic. If I don't have them, somebody else will. As long as they're not destroyed, the world's no worse off."

"I don't believe you said that. I could spend a week in that room without water, food, or air."

"Speaking of food and water, I'm fixing us something to eat. Hope you don't mind fruit and veggies. I'm trying to stop eating meat."

It was an Eastern dish, very tasty, with nuts and shoots and broccoli under a golden baked crust. She had a good bottle of wine and a little chocolate cake for dessert.

We talked over dinner. She was giving up meat for both main reasons, health and politics. She was an environmentalist, but I had already guessed that. I didn't think the individual could make much difference. She bristled at that and said, "As long as you think that way, you are the enemy. The individual is the only one who can make a difference." I didn't believe that but I didn't want to ruffle her. She was a woman who mattered to me, very suddenly, very keenly, and I wished we could talk without having our conversation sprinkled with land mines. I said, and meant it, that I probably agreed with most of her political views, I just didn't believe some of them could be won that way.

She looked at me with a blank expression. "I can't figure you out, Janeway."

"That makes us even. I can't figure you out."

"I don't know whether you're a poet or a thug."

I laughed at that: couldn't help myself. She shook her head and didn't seem amused.

"What do you do in the summer?" I asked.

"Travel. What do you do?"

"What I do all the time anymore. I look for books. Do you look for books in the summer, in exotic and faraway places?"

"I don't have anything to do with books in the summer. I am, for all practical purposes, closed down between May and September. I don't even read books in the summer."

"What do you do if you get a call on the first of May from some guy in New Mexico, who says he's got ten thousand perfect books and he's selling them all cheap?"

"I tell him he'll have to call someone else. I might refer him to you, if I like you."

"You give me the impression that none of this matters."

"It matters. This collection was put together with tender loving care, so it does matter. It's just not the most important thing."

"What is?"

"I don't think I'll answer that question yet. Maybe I will, if I ever get to know you better. For now, it's none of your business."

We ate in silence for a moment. Then she said, "Tact is not one of my strong points. If you were still a policeman, I guess I'd have to tell you, wouldn't I? You can find out if you want: your friend Mr. Hennessey knows."

"I won't do that."

"Good. And really, it's no big deal. I'm just very . . . very . . . private. I value my privacy more than anything but my freedom."

"Hey." I held up both hands in a gesture of mock surrender.

The phone rang: the recorder kicked on. It was another dealer, in San Francisco, asking if she still had the first edition *Phantom of the Opera.* I knew she had it: I had seen it on my tour of the short wall.

"You've got your phone amplified all over the house?" I said.

She nodded. "That way I can weed out the pests. The answering machine puts a buffer between me and the world; the amplifier lets me know if it's someone I want to talk to now. But I never get calls that can't wait."

"Not even George Butler the Third," I said with false awe.

"George is a very large pain. I don't know why I fool with him."

"You know what I'd like to have?" I said suddenly. "Your Steinbeck, with the penis doodle."

She laughed, the first time I'd seen her do that. " 'Tom Joad on the road.' It's one of my favorite books. Very expensive for that title."

I felt my throat tighten. "How expensive?"

"If you've got to ask, you probably can't afford it. Seriously, you don't have to buy anything. I don't charge admission up here."

I took out my checkbook and tapped it lightly on the table.

Her eyes narrowed and got hard. "Fifteen hundred," she said.

The knot in my throat swelled, but I began to write the check.

"Make it twelve," she said. "I usually don't give or ask for discounts, but I will this time. Make it payable to Greenpeace."

John Dunning

I blinked at her. "Greenpeace?"

"Do you want me to spell it for you?"

"Greenpeace," I said dumbly.

"Greenpeace gives me a reason to get up in the morning."

I handed her the check. "Oh, I'll bet you have at least a thousand very good reasons for getting up in the morning, Miss McKinley."

She blushed when I said that. She really did. I felt a flush in my own cheeks. It had been a long time since I'd tried playing the gallant.

"So," she said, going for more coffee, "you've just bought your first really nice book and paid retail for it. What are you going to do with it?"

"Gonna sell it."

"Good for you. You think there's any margin?"

"For something like this, there's always margin."

"You know, Mr. Janeway, I really do think you're going to turn out to be a good bookman. You already know what sometimes takes people years to learn."

"Which is . . . ?"

"When you buy something unique, and pay twice what it's worth, it's a great bargain. It took me a long time to learn that. Some people never learn it. George Butler never has. Now it's the only way I operate."

"That's fine if your pockets are deep enough."

"That does help. It's hard making it from scratch in the book business."

"Tell me about it."

Please tell me about it, I thought. We were going nowhere fast, on an endless merry-go-round of polite tea talk. I needed a breakthrough, something to batter down the walls she had built around herself. I had a hunch that if

236

I walked out of there without finding that key, she'd never let me come back. There was something at work between us, and it was good but it wasn't all good. I couldn't get a handle on any of it. I knew she was curious about me but she'd never ask: by refusing to talk about herself, she had given up that right. I could see that if there was any opening up to do, I'd be the one to do it. Slowly I turned the talk to my childhood. She listened intently and I was encouraged to go on. It became very personal. Suddenly I was telling her things I had never told anyone.

In the first place, my birth was an accident. My father is a lawyer whose name heads a five-pronged Denver partnership on Seventeenth Street. He makes half a million in a good year and can't remember when his last bad year was. There's no way I'll inherit any of that—my old man and I haven't spoken to each other in fifteen years, and we weren't close even before that. Larry Janeway isn't a man people get close to. He is, however, dignified. He's famous in court for his dignity and composure. Once, as the song went, that composure sorta slipped, and a dalliance with a truly gorgeous woman thirty-seven years ago produced . . . me. Here I sit, brokenhearted. I look at my parents and on one hand I see chilly arrogance and deceit; on the other, frivolous insanity. All the Libertys were crazy, and Jeannie, my mother, was probably certifiable. It was Jeannie, I think, who caused me to distrust beautiful women. I'll take brains, heart, and wit over beauty every time out. What's amazing is how well I survived their best efforts to tear me apart, how, in spite of them, I turned out so well-adjusted and sane. So completely goddamned normal.

"Well, sort of goddamned normal," she said without a smile.

"Oh yeah? How goddamned normal do you think you are?"

"Pretty goddamned normal."

Suddenly she laughed, a schoolgirl giggle that lit her up and made her young again. "Now there's my intelligent conversation of the week," she said, and we both laughed. I wondered if that was the break I was looking for, but it didn't seem to be. She would listen, interested, to anything I wanted to tell her, but still she wouldn't ask. I've never been brilliant at monologue, but I did my best. I told her about life at North High, about growing up in a pool of sharks. "If there's a thug in me, I guess that's where it comes from." Where the poet came from, if there was such a thing, was anybody's guess.

"It's getting late," she said.

Was that strike three? Her tone gave away nothing.

A bold frontal attack, then, seemed to be the last weapon in the old Janeway arsenal.

"Look, give me a break. Why don't you open that door, just a little, and see what's on the other side?"

"I know what's on the other side. I haven't exactly led a monastic life."

"C'mon, let's cut to the chase, Rita. Dinner Friday night and a tour of Denver's hottest hot spots."

"Nope. Not my cup of tea, Mr. Janeway."

"Then I'll rent a tux and we'll go to the Normandy. I don't care."

"I don't think so."

"Oh, take the full thirty seconds and think it over."

She shook her head.

"I know a great restaurant that serves nothing but broccoli. I'll take you there for breakfast. Broccoli pancakes, the best in town. We'll take a ride on the Platte

River bus. Race stickboats down the stream. Walk down Seventeenth Street and stick our tongues out at my old man's law office. Forget about books and crime and everything else for a few hours. Come on, what do you say?"

"No," she said firmly.

"I knew you'd see it my way."

She gave me the long cool stare. "You're pushing, Mr. Janeway. I don't want to be blunt."

"Go ahead, be blunt. I've got a thick skin, I can take it. I'm not gonna fall on my sword. Since we're being blunt, let me ask you something. Are you worried that I'll eat my fish with the salad fork? Or do you big-time book dealers have a rule about not playing with the little guys."

"Don't be nasty, sir."

"I'm just trying to figure you out."

"Then stop trying. It's very simple. I don't want to get involved."

"And you think knowing me will involve you in something?"

"That's exactly what I think."

"How, for God's sake?"

"How do you think? How do men and women always get involved?"

I sat back and looked from afar. "Well, now, that's quite a thing to say."

"A good deal more than I wanted to say."

"So what's wrong with that? It's what makes the world go 'round. If it happens, it happens."

"It's not going to happen, Mr. Janeway, I promise you that."

She had been sitting rigidly in her chair: now she relaxed; sat back and let her breath out slowly. "I didn't want to let you come up here at all. You know that."

"Don't give me that. You called me back, remember?"

"I don't know why I did that."

"You know, all right, you just don't want to say it."

"Doesn't need to be said. You're here, aren't you? Don't be so damned analytical. You're here, I must've wanted to see you again. That doesn't mean I'm going to let you into my life. I'm sorry if that's too blunt, Mr. Janeway, but you can't say you didn't ask for it."

Then a curious thing happened: her hands began to tremble. She groped for words, reached down into a stack of newspapers and came up with THE newspaper. "I never stop my papers when I go away. There's a boy I hire who brings all my mail and newspapers in every day. I guess I should have them stopped but I don't. I like to see what's been happening while I've been gone. Look what I came across this morning."

The story was a little different than the one I had seen. The headline said COP NAMED IN BRUTALITY CHARGE. They had moved my picture out to page 1 for the late edition. It lay on the table, staring up at me, glaring angrily at the angry old world.

"Is this my dessert?"

She just looked at me.

"Miss McKinley, I'm wasting a helluva lot of great one-liners on you. I'm starting to think you've got no sense of humor at all."

She still said nothing. Her eyes burned into my face like tiny suns.

"You want maybe I should comment on this? Is that what you want?"

"I don't know what I want."

"My comment is this. Don't believe everything you read."

"That's it?"

"Tell me what you want and I'll do my best to give it to you. I mean, look, you read that this morning, right? Plenty of time for you to call to cancel. You didn't do that, did you?"

Her eyes never left my face. She gave a shake of her head that was barely a movement.

"Even after I got here, you could've shuffled me in and out. But you didn't do that, either. You gave me a good stiff drink and free run of the place, then you gave me dinner. What am I supposed to make of that?"

She said nothing, did nothing.

"I'm going home," I said.

I stood and paused for just a moment, my hands clasping the back of my chair. We looked at each other. Her face was a solid wall. She said nothing. I went to the door and looked back. What a great exit, I thought: I'll just fade away like some damnfool hero in a bad cowboy movie. In the yard I looked back. She had come to the doorway, a silhouette in the yellow light. I gave her a cheery wave. The hell with you, I thought. Then I thought, Don't walk away, it's too important; don't do this. What you say and do this minute will set the course of your life from this day on, I thought.

I had opened the car door, propped my foot inside, and leaned over the window. When I spoke, my voice carried strong and clear over the mountaintop. "What's in the newspaper is his side of it. Here's my side, in case you're interested. That guy is a killer. I've tried to pin him for more than two years. I guess I finally got sick of it. He raped a woman and beat her silly and was coming back for an encore. He found me there instead. As far as brutality is concerned, forget it—he's plenty big enough to

241

take care of himself. When he says I cuffed him and beat him, he's lying. I took the cuffs off and it was a fair fight. That's the end of it. I'm going home."

I drove down the mountain feeling depressed. But under it was a strange feeling of elation, of joy, making a mix that's almost impossible to describe. I didn't know what was happening but it was big. Oh, was it big! Could I have lived thirty-six years and never once felt this? I stopped at the side of the road about five miles from her house and fought the urge to go back. I won that fight . . . one mark for good judgment.

I'd call her in the morning.

She'd call me.

Somehow we'd get past all the problems of her money and her expertise and my brutal nature.

One way or another, it wasn't over. That was the one sure thing in an unsure world.

29

I got to the store about quarter past midnight. The street was deserted except for an ambulance far away: the overture of another long night on East Colfax. I tucked the Steinbeck under my arm and let myself in. The place had a stale, slightly sour smell at midnight. I locked the door and put the book on the counter, then sat on my stool looking at it. I opened it and looked at the doodle Steinbeck had drawn all those years ago, when fame and glory and money were his, when his talent was at its peak. "May 12, 1940: Tom Joad on the road." A prize, yes, one might even say a small victory, but a hollow one. You can have it back, Miss Rita, you hear that? You can *have* the damn thing. All you've got to do is ask.

I cut a piece of plastic and wrapped the jacket anew. With a light pencil I wrote in the new price, $2,000, and looked in the glass case for the perfect centerpiece spot.

The phone rang.

It can't be, I thought. I watched it ring three times, then I picked it up and said hello.

"I knew you'd be there," she said.

"You're getting pretty smart in your old age."

"It's what I'd've done not so long ago. When you buy your first big piece, you can't wait to see how it looks in its new home. Even if it's midnight."

"For the record, it looks great."

"You're allowed an hour to gloat. After that, it's unbecoming."

There was a long pause, what I was starting to think of as a Ritalike white space. Then she said, "I called to tell you something but I don't know how."

"We could play twenty questions. Is it animal, vegetable, or mineral?"

"Animal," she said. Her voice sounded thick, lusty.

"I kind of thought it would be."

Another pause. I didn't know what to do but fill it with more comic relief.

"Does it walk on two legs, four, or slide on its belly like a reptile?"

"This is difficult," she said. "I know you think I've been manipulating you, but I haven't. I'm just not very consistent sometimes."

"Hey, if I want consistency I'll buy a robot. So you give off mixed signals. That's all part of the human comedy."

"You're angry."

"Just confused, Miss McKinley. First you tell me, in barely couched terms, to break a leg and go blind. Then you call and invite me up. You fix me a dinner but act like I'm the butcher of Auschwitz when I ask you for a date. You'd already read that newspaper, you knew full well that I stomp puppies to death for a hobby, but do I worry? Nah! I'm just glad I got to see your books."

There was white space, of course: a ten-second pause. I

thought of whistling "Time on My Hands," but I didn't do it.

"You are one strange bird, Janeway," she said.

"I'm fascinating as hell, though, you've got to admit that."

"Yes," she said, and I felt that buildup in my throat again, and I hoped I'd be able to get through this conversation without croaking like Henry Aldrich.

"I have a dark secret," she said. "If I tell you what it is, will you promise not to try to see me again?"

"I never bet on a blind. Only fools and bad poker players do that."

"I guess I'll tell you anyway. I don't want you going away thinking I've been playing with you."

"What difference does it make, if I'm going away?"

"I told you before, don't be so goddamned analytical. Take a few things on faith."

"You haven't said anything yet."

"It's very simple. I hate violence, but all my life I've been attracted to violent men."

"That's very interesting," I said, struggling past a pear-sized obstruction in my throat.

"So the reason I didn't want you to come up here today is the same reason I finally did ask you up. The same reason I didn't cancel when I read the paper. The same reason I wouldn't go out with you. Does that make any sense?"

"No, but keep going. I like the sound of it."

"You wear your violence on your sleeve. It goes where you go. You carry it around like other men carry briefcases. It's like a third person in the room. I can't help being appalled by that."

I listened to her breathe. My pear had grown into a grapefruit.

"And yet, I'm always a sucker for a man who can make me believe he'll do anything, if the stakes are big enough."

I gave a wicked laugh.

Gotcha, I thought.

"I don't want to see you again," she said. "I just wanted you to know why."

"I've got a hunch we'll see each other."

"I'm engaged, Mr. Janeway. I'm getting married next month."

"Then it's a good thing I came along when I did."

"Good-bye," she said, and hung up.

God damn it, I thought.

Whoopie! I thought. Yaahoo!

Elation and despair were sisters after all.

I called her back: got the recording. When the beep came, I pictured her sitting in the kitchen listening to my voice. Insanity, the third sister, took over. I got real close and crooned into the phone. "Oh, Riiiiii-ta! This is the mystery voice calling! Guess my name and win a truckload of Judith Krantz first editions. Ooooh, I'm sorry, I'm not George Butler the Third! But that was a fine guess, and wait'll you hear about the grand consolation prize we have in store for you! *Two* truckloads of Judith Krantz first editions! Your home will certainly be a bright one with all those colorful best-sellers lying around. Your friends will gaze in awe—" The tape beeped again, and a good thing, else I might've gone on till dawn. I replaced the phone in the cradle and stared at it for a long moment. Ring, you sonofabitch, I thought, but the bastard just sat there.

Convulsed with laughter, I was sure.

Too weak to call.

Savoring my wit in her solitude.

Damn her.

I worked it off. In a bookstore there's always something to do. I had a small stack of low-end first editions that needed to be priced, so I did that. I watered Miss Pride's plant again, and studied the *AB*. I read for an hour. Sometime after two o'clock I fell asleep in the big deep chair near the front counter.

I opened my eyes to a feeling more desolate than despair. This was not the aching loneliness of new love, it was something far more desperate and immediate. The street was still dark: the world outside was hollow and empty and nothing moved anywhere. The store was like a tomb: still, silent, eerie.

Maybe I'd been dreaming. I hadn't had the Jackie Newton dream in months. Maybe that had come back and I just couldn't remember.

Then it came to me.

It was that sourness I had noticed when I'd first opened the door. It was stronger now, ripe and distinct, almost sweet in a sickening kind of way. When you've been in Homicide as long as I was, that's one thing you never forget.

The smell of death.

I got up and went toward the back. The smell got stronger.

Oh boy, I thought.

I opened the door to the office. I turned on the light. Nothing looked wrong. It was just as Ruby had said: everything shipshape.

But the smell was stronger.

There was one place Ruby couldn't have seen—the bathroom across the hall. That room had no windows, nothing but a skylight, no way for anyone to look in.

I opened the door. Miss Pride stared up at me with glassy eyes. Peter sprawled across her, facedown.

Each had been shot once through the head.

30

The killer had come in just after closing time. Miss Pride had not yet locked the front door.

He had come for a single purpose. No money was missing. No books were missing. He had come to kill. By the time I tried returning Miss Pride's call, at five-twenty-five, she and Peter had probably been dead ten minutes.

He had come through the front door. We keep the back door locked. He had forced Miss Pride to lock up—her keys were still clutched tight in her fingers—and afterward he had used the back door to escape. Unlike the front door, which must be locked with a key, the back door had a latch lock that could be slam-locked from the outside.

The weapon was probably a .38. Ballistics would tell us more.

Miss Pride had been shot first. The shot had hit her in the front of the head, exactly between the eyes: she had fallen over on her back, her head twisted grotesquely against the wall.

Peter had been a more difficult target. In his panic he had done a great deal of scrambling. One slug had missed and gone through the wall. The second one got him.

The killer, of course, had taken the gun away with him.

He had probably worn gloves. There were no fingerprints on the back door latch or on the door itself. There were many prints on the front door, from customers who had come and gone all day long. Most of these would never be identified.

He had come, done his job, and left. The whole thing had probably taken no more than two minutes.

Everything else was speculation. My guess was that Peter had known who killed Bobby Westfall. He had come to the store to tell me about it but the killer got there first. Miss Pride had simply been unlucky, in the wrong place at the wrong time.

As always, there were more questions than answers. If this tied back into the Westfall case, why had Peter waited all these months to tell me about it? How had the killer suddenly learned that Peter was a threat? Why had it happened now, and what had caused it to suddenly come on? Had there been something in the Ballard library so valuable that someone would kill for it, then kill twice more? Was it in the Ballard library at all, and if so, how could Rita have overlooked it? Something small—so small that no one could see it, yet Bobby Westfall had had to take the entire library to be sure of getting it. *Look at the little things, Dr. J.* I heard Ruby's voice telling me that. It's the one lesson that even a good bookman finds hardest to learn. Look at the little stuff—pamphlets, broadsides, tiny books with no lettering on their spines—and remember that one little weatherworn piece could bring more money than an entire library done up in glamour leather.

John Dunning

Something small. Something you know is there but you're not sure where. If you're Bobby Westfall, you have to take every book: tear them apart if necessary, go page by page if necessary, slit the cloth and strip away the bindings if necessary, rip the hinges asunder and shred the pieces through a sieve if necessary. Kill or be killed if necessary. Something small and hidden, it had to be, had to, because if it were small and unhidden it would be too easy to steal. Rita McKinley could easily drop it down her dress while old man Ballard went for coffee; Bobby Westfall could've dropped it in his pocket, the Lord be damned, while he wandered among the stacks and ostensibly tried to make up his mind.

It all came back to money. That's what fueled Bobby and Peter and all the guys like them. Money was the one thing they never had enough of: it was the driving force in their lives. Bobby wanted to be respected as a book dealer, not joked about as a bookscout. It took money to do that. It took other things—knowledge, taste, a keen eye, good juice, a gambler's blood, and a hustler's imagination—but without money you just couldn't get started.

The scene at my place was like a hundred murder scenes I'd been to. Cops. Photographers. Sketchmen. The coroner.

It was the same, only different. This was me on the receiving end. That dead girl was one of mine.

From the moment I found her, I was a cop again.

A cop without a badge.

Hennessey had arrived with his new partner before dawn. Teaming Neal with Lester Cameron had been the final ironic fallout of the Jackie Newton affair, but Boone Steed worked in mysterious ways. Cameron and I had never liked each other: he was too trigger-happy and hot-collared for my taste, though I'd heard it said more than

once that Cameron in action reminded people of me. I
didn't like that much, though I did respect Cameron in a
professional way. I thought he was a good cop, I just didn't
like him as a man. He had a head on his shoulders and a
block of ice where his heart was supposed to be. He had a
take-charge demeanor that was a turnoff, but his record
with DPD was a good one. He and I had been in the same
class at the police academy, long ago. We had never been
bosom buddies, even then. For most of an hour,
Hennessey, Cameron, and I sat in the front room talking.
We were three old pros: I knew what they needed and gave
them what I could. Cameron sat on one of my stools like a
grand high inquisitor and fired off the inevitable questions,
and I answered them like clockwork. I knew the questions
before they were asked. I told him about Miss Pride, where
she'd come from, when and why. I told him about Peter,
and his friendship with Bobby Westfall, who had also been
murdered. Hennessey stood apart as I related this. He
looked out into the dark street, and even when he looked
at me, he avoided my eyes. I guess he knew what I was
thinking, that you can't ever drag your feet on a murder
case, can't ever assume that the victim isn't important
enough to warrant the balls-out effort. You never know
when a killer might come back for an encore.

We talked about Miss Pride. She had no enemies on this
earth, I said, unless she had a dark side that I simply
couldn't imagine. I told them what I thought: that it tied
into Westfall, and Miss Pride was the innocent victim. I
told them how skittish Peter had been the last two days,
how frantic he'd been when he tried to reach me at Rita
McKinley's. I told them about Rita, too, all the facts, all
the rumors. As an afterthought, I told them that Jackie
Newton had been hanging around.

"I don't know," I said. "This doesn't smell like Jackie."

"You sure thought it was before," Hennessey said, looking out the window.

"That was then, this is now."

"What's so different?" Cameron said. "You boys kiss and make up?"

"It doesn't fit Jackie. The first one did: go look up the M.O. yourself if you want to see what I'm talking about. There's a random nature to all of Jackie's old business. This wasn't random. Jackie doesn't come advertising before he kills somebody. That's my opinion."

"Opinions are like assholes," Cameron said. "Everybody's got one."

"That's cute, Lester," I said. "I'll have to remember that one."

By then it was daylight: it was seven-thirty and word of the tragedy had spread up and down the block. People were gathering on the walk and peering in the windows.

"What's the name of the guy who was dating her?" Cameron said.

"You mean Jerry Harkness?"

"If that's the guy who was dating her, that's who I mean."

"I wouldn't say he was dating her. He took her to dinner a couple of nights ago."

"We need to see him. And we need to go up in the hills and see this McKinley woman. See if she's still got that tape, for one thing. Maybe the lab can separate those voices and we can hear what they were saying when they were talking over each other. That should be the first priority. How do I get there?"

"You don't unless you call first. That's the way the lady operates."

"Well, here's the way I operate. You give me her address and let me worry about getting in."

"You could save yourself some grief if you call her. I don't think she did this, do you?"

"I don't know who the hell did it."

"Lester, she was with me at the time."

"Wrong, sport. She was with you when she played you a tape that she said had just been made. Besides, you don't have to pull the trigger to be involved in something."

I nodded slowly. "It's a calculated risk. If she's still got the tape, a phone call might make sure she keeps it."

"Or burns it."

"Or uses it over," Hennessey said. "That's the most likely thing. She'll slip it back in the machine and just use it again. Shucks, even by calling her, we might be erasing it."

"Oh, hell," I said, remembering. "I think I may've already done that."

"What'd you do?" Cameron said meanly.

"I got back here about midnight. She called me almost as soon as I came in the door. We talked for a few minutes, then I called her back. God damn it, she had the recording on. I talked on it for a long time."

"How long?"

"Long enough."

"What'd you talk about?"

"Just stupid bullshit. Dumb, stupid stuff."

"Love talk?" Cameron asked.

"What do you mean by that?"

"I don't think that question requires a translation. Are you involved with this woman, Janeway?"

"Yeah," I said after a moment. "I believe I am."

"Shit," Cameron said.

"Next time I decide to have an affair with a woman, Lester, I'll be sure and come ask your permission first."

"We've got to go get that tape now," Hennessey said, "before she uses it anymore."

"You can't get in there without a warrant," I said.

"You still can't stop playing cop, can you, Janeway?" Cameron said. "I think maybe it's time you remembered who the police are."

"I'm trying to tell you something that might do you some good if you'll just shut up and listen. You don't just walk up to this lady's house and knock on the door. She's got a ten-foot fence and a gate that locks. If you go over that fence without a warrant, anything that comes from that tape is out the window, even if the killer confesses in verse and leaves you his telephone number."

"That's only true if she's involved," Hennessey said. "We couldn't make a case against her with the tape, but we sure as hell could if the killer's somebody else."

"Why not cover your ass?" I said.

"You've always been good at that, haven't you, Janeway?" Cameron said. "Except once."

31

They carried the bodies out in rubber bags strapped to stretchers. The crowd gave a soft collective sigh and moved back from the door. It all seemed to take forever, as if people were trapped in some slow-motion twilight zone. The lab men combed the place, and this is not a hurry-up process. I waited them out. I sat by the door and tried not to think, and when I could see that it was winding down I started working on a new sign for the window. I wrote it on chipboard with a heavy black marking pen. It said, CLOSED UNTIL FURTHER NOTICE.

I began to see familiar faces in the crowd. Clyde Fix. A couple of bookscouts I knew. I saw Ruby standing alone, and Neff a few feet away, also alone. I'd seen it before, how death both repels and attracts, leaving even best friends alone with their darkest fascinations, fears. Jerry Harkness peeked in and asked what had happened. When I told him, he looked sick. He drifted down the street without another word.

Any violent death is bad, but this one was worse than bad. I felt like I'd just been mauled by a tiger.

Then, suddenly, they were all gone. The lab boys rolled up their tents and packed away their gear and the crowd outside began to dissolve. Fifteen minutes later the place was empty. A wave of loneliness washed over me, deep and cutting, almost unbearable. How little we know about people, I thought. Can you ever really know anyone? Already I saw Pinky Pride as a one-dimensional figure. I liked her but I knew in years to come I'd have trouble remembering her face. How little time I had actually spent with her. Never mind, Pinky, I'll spend the time now. I'll spend it now.

I went from room to room turning off the lights. The bathroom was the worst. The blood was still there and the room was puffed with fingerprint dust and there was still the smell of death, but fading now. I'm not much of a crier: I hate to admit that these days, when *macho* is a dirty word and people use it to trap and unmask insensitive bastards like myself, but I did shed a few quiet, private tears for Pinky Pride. Then I dropped my new sign into the front window, locked the front door, and started on the trail of her killer.

32

"I can't believe this," Ruby said. "God damn, that poor kid. That poor sweet kid."

Neff looked truly shaken. He sat in his usual spot behind the counter, but his usually busy hands were idle.

"What were you boys doing last night?" I asked.

"We were right here, Dr. J. You called me here, you know where we were."

"Did you see anything, hear anything, or see anybody unusual?"

I was looking at Neff, who had gone pale. His hands had begun to tremble. "I . . . I think I . . . may've seen him," he said.

"We been sittin' here waiting for the cops to come down, but they never did," Ruby said. "We didn't know what to do."

"They had to chase down something urgent, but they'll be back," I said. "What did you see, Neff?"

But Neff couldn't speak. He put his hand over his face and sat there shivering.

"Give 'im a minute," Ruby said. "This's been one helluva shock."

"For all of us, Ruby," I said. "What were you doing between five and six?"

"Lookin' at books."

"What books?"

"We'd just gotten in some wonderful stuff. I was humped over here at the door, lookin' at the books. I didn't see a thing."

"That's what you were doing when I called?"

"Yeah. Em was here with me, sittin' right where he is now. He didn't feel good. . . ."

"I've had a touch of stomach flu," Neff said. "Had the runs all day long. I thought maybe if I got out a while, if I went on a buy, I'd stop thinking about how lousy I felt. I shoulda gone home and went to bed. But I went out and bought these books instead. I'd just gotten back. I had to hit the can so bad I thought I'd bust. You know how we're set up back there, real cramped, with the toilet right on the alley. I sat down and did my duty, then opened the back door to air the place out. There was a guy . . . coming up from your way . . . Christ, I looked right in his face."

"What'd he look like?"

"Like a man I wouldn't want to run into, in a dark alley at night."

"Give me some color, Neff. Give me a size, a shape. How old was this dude?"

"I don't know. Forty . . . maybe older. I wasn't paying that much attention then. I know he was white, and big."

"How big? Two hundred? Six feet? You tell me, Neff, I'm a lousy mind reader."

"Yeah . . . big. Two hundred . . . at least that. Six feet . . . I don't know. But heavy through here. God, he saw me watching him."

"What did he do when he saw you watching him?"

"Turned his head away . . . like this . . . then went on by."

"Did that strike you as suspicious?"

"Why should it? I didn't know anybody'd been killed. I'm used to seeing weird characters around here; why should I think anything about it? Jesus, the guy looked straight at me. What am I gonna do?"

"Tell the cops what happened, just like you're telling me."

"Well, where the hell are they? And what if that guy comes back before they do?"

"I'm not telling you not to worry about it: somebody's killed three book people in this town and maybe we all better worry a little. If I were you I'd leave the store closed today. Stay together. Go downtown and wait for Hennessey, then tell him what you told me. Could you describe this guy for a police artist?"

"Maybe . . . I'm not sure. I didn't stare at him. When he looked away, so did I."

"How was he dressed?"

"Black. Black slacks, black sport coat open at the neck, pale gray shirt . . . no tie. Jesus, he might've had the gun right there under his coat. He could've shot me."

"Or he could've been some neighborhood bum who had nothing to do with it. I take it you've never seen him around here."

"Never seen him anywhere. He didn't look like a bum to me."

"Did you watch him at all after he went on by?"

"No. I came . . . right back up front."

I let out a long breath. "Okay, let me get a feel.for the time frame. You say you went out on a buy and got back here when . . . about quarter to five?"

"It wasn't much later than that. I didn't look at the clock, but I'm sure I was here by five."

"It was right at closing time, Dr. J," Ruby said. "I remember I was thinking I'd be closing up in a minute, then Em came back."

"Then it was closer to five than quarter to," I said.

"I don't know," Neff said. "I thought it was earlier than that, but you may be right."

"It was a few minutes before five," Ruby said.

"What'd you drive?" I asked.

"My car, same's I always drive. Same one's out back."

"And you came up Colfax, right past all the stores?"

"Yeah."

"When you passed my place, did you happen to look in?"

"I gave it a glance, I always do. I like to see if there's any business on the block. I look in all the stores when I come by."

"Was the store open or closed?"

"I don't remember, I didn't look at the sign. There was nobody in the front, though, I do know that."

"Did you look in at Harkness and Fix?"

"Yeah, sure. Fix was sitting in that chair by his window like he always does. Harkness was gone somewhere—he had that clock on the door that said, you know, be back at such-and-such a time. I didn't notice what time it said. I need some water. This shit's got me shook."

I waited for him to come back. Then I started in again. "So you drove past the stores and pulled up here and unloaded the books. How long did that take?"

260

"No more'n a minute," Ruby said. "There wasn't all that much, quantity-wise. Just three boxes. Didn't take but a second to bring it all in."

I kept looking at Neff. "Then what did you do?"

"Like I told you, headed straight for the can. I thought I'd bust before I got back there."

"How long were you on the pot?"

"No more than a minute. You know how it is when you've got the runs, it's all water."

"Then you opened the back door and saw the guy."

He took a shivery breath, nodded, and let it out.

"So you were back there what . . . two minutes? And this would all have taken place by a few minutes after five? And you didn't see the guy get in any car and drive away, either of you?"

"I didn't see anything," Ruby said.

Neff looked ill. We were all silent for a moment.

"I don't mind telling you, Mr. Janeway, this thing's made a mess of my nerves. I'm not gonna sleep till they catch this bastard."

I gave him an encouraging little nod. "Tell me anything else that comes to you. Hair . . . scars . . ."

"I didn't notice any scars. He had thick black hair with deep recesses. It went way back, made the front of his head look like a big letter M, but the hair was still real thick where it did grow. He had a face like a . . . turtle . . . just a flat line for a mouth. I can't tell you about his eyes: he turned away before I got a look, and I probably wouldn't remember anyway."

"And he didn't say anything?"

"Hell no. The whole thing didn't take more than a few seconds. But that was enough."

"All right," I said. "Stay away from here today. Get

downtown and tell Hennessey what you've told me. Get the artist involved. Do the best you can."

"Sure . . . you bet."

"A couple more questions, then I've got to go," I said. "I talked to Miss Pride in the middle of the day. Told her to call and tell you she'd be there alone at closing. . . ." I looked searchingly at both faces.

Ruby shook his head. "She never called me."

"No," Neff said.

Damn you, Pinky, I thought. Next time do what I tell you.

I felt the shivers in my own spine, and hoped I wasn't coming down with Neff's flu.

"What about Peter?" I said. "I asked you before if you knew where he lived."

"Didn't know then, don't know now," Ruby said.

"What was Peter's last name?"

"Uh, wait a minute . . . yeah, I know it, I just can't call it. Hell, Em, help me out, you know what it is."

"I don't remember."

"Come on, we've written enough hot checks to the old fart. I don't mean that the way it sounds, Dr. J . . . don't want to speak ill of the dead . . . I'm just . . . tryin' to . . . call the damn thing up for you and I can't get a handle on it. Haven't you ever written him a check?"

"I always paid him cash," I said.

"Must be nice. It's on the tip of my tongue, that's how close it is. It's Peter, uh . . . uh . . . God damn it! Peter, uh . . . I know the damn thing as well as I know my own."

"Think about something else for a minute," I said. I looked at three boxes of books stacked against the glass case. "Is this the stuff you bought yesterday?"

"Yeah. Damn lovely stuff it is, too. Go ahead, take a look."

I peeked over the edge and saw a fine copy of Ellison's *Invisible Man*. Under it was *A Clockwork Orange,* a beaut. Under that was a nice double stack, about fifteen books. The three boxes would hold forty, maybe fifty pieces.

"It was a hurry-up deal," Ruby said. "Woman was going out of town, she calls us and needs the cash right now. I tell you, Samson, we had to scrounge to get it up. Fifteen hundred we had to pool, and two hours to do it. But we did it."

I didn't go through the box. For once I didn't feel like looking at books.

I started to leave, stopped at the door and said:

"Hey, Rube! What's Peter's name?"

"Bonnema," he said. "Two *n*'s, and one *m*. Peter Bonnema. By God, Dr. J, that's a good trick. That's a damn good trick."

"Sometimes it works, sometimes it doesn't," I said, and left.

33

Harkness too had been out on a major buy late yesterday. His place reeked of fresh Stephen King. There were King books scattered across the counter and stacked on the floor. He had gotten the call two days ago and had closed early yesterday to go look at the stuff. The buy was in Boulder, thirty miles away. He had closed the store around one-thirty. He had walked up to my place and had stood talking with Miss Pride for about ten minutes. She had mentioned in passing that she would be closing alone—Mr. Janeway had made her tell him that, she explained with a frown—but he had told her he'd be gone at closing time so she should call Seals & Neff and let them know. She had rolled her eyes and said, "You men!" and that was the last time he had seen her. He looked to be on the verge of tears.

I asked what time he had come in last night. "It was almost eight," he said. "By the time I got to Boulder it was quarter to three. The buy didn't take long. King stuff never does. You know what it goes for and so do they: the only question is, can you get it from them for any kind of a decent price, or do they want to make all the money? Usually they want full pop, but this one was reasonable. I only had to pay sixty-five percent."

"Man, that sounds high," I said.

Harkness didn't react at all. He said, "It is, for anything but King. I'll put it away and in a year it'll look cheap, what I paid for it. What the hell difference does it make? What difference does anything make?"

"Yeah," I said.

The Kings had been owned by a woman. Her husband was the collector but he had died and she was trying to figure out the rest of her life. King didn't figure in it, but she could get a fair start with the money he would bring her. "It cost me plenty," Harkness said, "every damn dime I had in the bank, but look at what I got." It was all there, the entire King output: the five major Doubleday firsts, variant jackets on the two *Salem's Lot*s, all the signed limiteds. Harkness didn't seem to care.

"I was done with it by four o'clock," he said. "I should've come back. If I had, maybe she'd still be alive. I'd've got back here before five and taken her to dinner and she'd still be here."

"What did you do instead?"

"Went out to eat alone. Some burger joint near the campus. I sat there for an hour thinking about it."

"Thinking about what?"

"Her."

He looked at me with sad eyes that had aged immeasurably since the last time I had seen him. He said, "I know what you think, Janeway, but you're wrong. She was a kid. I knew that. But there was something about her that got me down deep. I couldn't shake her. You know what that feels like?"

I thought of Rita McKinley, but I didn't say anything.

"I knew it was all wrong . . . man my age, screwing around with a girl her age. But what can you do? When they get you they get you. So I ate a cheap supper and walked around killing time, just thinking about it. Then I came back here. Unloaded my stuff. Worked here till ten o'clock. Went home."

"You didn't see anything?"

"What was to see by then?"

Clyde Fix, as usual, was no help. He had not seen Peter in months. He didn't like the son of a bitch. Peter wasn't welcome in his store. I asked Fix if he'd seen anyone resembling the man Emery Neff had described. He hadn't seen anyone and wouldn't tell me if he had. I wasn't a cop anymore: he knew that. He didn't have to tell me anything.

34

I sat in my store and called Motor Vehicles: told them I was Detective Cameron and needed a rundown on a murder victim. Impersonating a cop is against the law and, strictly speaking, it wasn't necessary. Motor vehicle records are open to everybody, but being a cop speeds the process. Current driver's licenses had been issued to two Peter Bonnemas in Denver. One lived in Cherry Hills Village, a posh country club neighborhood, the other in a rooming house on the fringe of Five Points. It wasn't hard to choose: ten minutes later I pulled up at a rambling old brick tenement near Twenty-second and Arapahoe. I took a small pouch of tools out of my trunk, slipped it into my coat, and went inside. It wasn't the Brown Palace: there was no security door and some of the mailboxes in the stale-smelling foyer looked like they had never borne a name. Peter's name had been scrawled in pencil on a small white card and Scotchtaped to the mailbox for apartment 310. There was a letter inside. I took out my pouch and got a tool and picked open the box. It was really no lock at all, just a simple latch. I lifted the slim envelope out and closed the mailbox. It was handwritten and postmarked Portland, Oregon. The return address said "Mrs. Peter Bonnema, 12335 SW 123rd, Portland." I took it without a second thought, slipped it into my coat, and went upstairs.

The lock on Peter's door was almost as simple as the one on the mailbox. It's a real wonder more of these guys don't get murdered, I thought as I went in. I let out a long breath. Bobby Westfall's so-called apartment had been a cradle of luxury compared with this. There was a dank smell about it, like curdled milk. The bed was a rollaway, layered with old dirt that had worn itself slick: there was no sign that the bed had ever worn a sheet. I saw empty cans on the floor, rat droppings in the corner, and everywhere, of course, the inevitable books. There were two small rooms and a toilet, and books were piled in every crack and corner. There were books on the sills of both windows and piled high in the middle of the floor. I knew I had little time; Cameron and Hennessey would be here before the day was done. I pulled on a pair of gloves and went to work. I handled the books carefully, so as not to destroy any prints, and it was the same as before—almost one hundred percent junk. It was so much like Westfall that I wasn't surprised when I found, pushed away in the back of a closet, a two-foot stack of good books.

Very good books.

It was about the equivalent of the stack I had found at Bobby's: great titles, all modern lit, first editions, perfect condition, a healthy mix of mainstream and genre. I didn't bother making a list this time—I knew at once that when I walked out, these were going with me. I looked at the mysteries and actually felt my mouth water, like one of Pavlov's dogs. Early Rex Stout . . . Ross Macdonald . . .

Cornell Woolrich in his real name and both pseudonyms: a nice little stack adding up to at least four grand retail. I didn't know yet how to assess it, didn't know what to do with it, but I wasn't leaving it here. Rats eat books, you know.

There was nothing else of any possible value: I was finished here as a bookman and now I went through the place with the eyes of a cop. The main room was depressingly bare, a bleak testament to the way some people live today. There was no desk where papers might be stored, no cabinet, no table with drawers. There were some trinkets, some Indian turquoise, probably mid-twenties Navajo that Peter had scouted at a flea market. I pushed it aside and left it there. Under the bed I found a bundle of letters held together by a rubber band. They looked like the same cheap stationery as the one from the mailbox. I thumbed through them and noticed the obvious common denominators. All were signed "Mumsy." Each began with the same line: "Your big box of books arrived today." There had been one letter every two weeks for the last three months. Mumsy was a lean, sparse writer: she got right to the point and didn't linger over flowery sunsets. There was no return address inside because Peter would undoubtedly know it. She had put a return address on the envelope in case the letter, for some reason, had to be returned. Mumsy was a practical soul who didn't write extra words and Peter didn't save envelopes. I had probably fished the only Mumsy envelope in existence out of the mailbox. It had probably been delivered only this morning.

I didn't open it till I got home. It was just like all the others. "Your big box of books arrived today and I put it with all the others." Not much chitchat. "Went over to Dadsy's grave today . . . Your friend Junie Sykes is expecting again, this makes six she's had with five different men. I said at the time and I say again, you are well out of that. You can't eat your heart out forever. . . . Why don't you come home?" A sudden image of Peter wafted up, a vision of the bleak and solitary road he had chosen becoming so clear in the half-dark room. A young man then with little verbal ability, crushed by love. Junie Sykes had eaten him alive and sent him on his way, banished to this. Getting by on fifty-cent books and bummed cigarettes, still carrying the faint hope of the Big Score, the $10 million map found in a Salvation Army store for six bucks. In his mind, Peter Bonnema drove home to Portland in a solid gold Cadillac and snatched Junie Sykes from all that. He would come on like Gary Cooper, tall and lean and silent, infinitely ready to forgive. Life was sooooo good, in that dream, and it was only one . . . god . . . damn . . . score . . . away! Just that moment in time when something wonderful was put out by someone stupid, and he was there. He'd go home vindicated, *king* of the bookscouts!

I opened the drapes and read again through all the letters. It never varied. Mumsy acknowledged the books, wrote a line or two about Dadsy or Dadsy's grave or what Dadsy would think of the world today, and slipped in a stinger about Junie Sykes. It was always "your friend Junie Sykes," slapped on the page like an indictment. Mumsy's apron strings snaked across the country, dooming her son to the life he led, sealing him in squalor.

Mumsy probably hadn't been informed yet. The cops would still be in the early stages of investigating Peter's next of kin, and without the Mumsy letters it might be days before they found her. I picked up the phone and called United Air Lines, got the next flight to Portland charged to my credit card. I called Hertz and had a rental car arranged on the other end.

If Jackie Newton wanted my money, he'd have to hurry. If I kept on this way, there wouldn't be much left.

I had five hours to kill and I killed them well.

I had never stopped believing in that U-Haul lead. A two-ton truck doesn't just materialize on Madison Street: someone somewhere rents it, buys it, or builds it from scratch in a back yard. I sat at my telephone with an open Yellow Pages and dialed one number after another. It didn't take nearly as long when you had a name. Peter Bonnema had rented a truck from an East Colfax gas station on the night of June 10: I had found the place on the sixth or seventh try; told the man I was Cameron of DPD and said I'd be over in a while to look at his records. Then I took a shower and lay down to rest. It was the first sleep I'd had in thirty-six hours.

Eighty minutes later my alarm went off. I got up feeling worse than ever, dressed, threw enough clothes together for a short weekend, locked up, and left. I didn't take any dress clothes or neckties—I wasn't flying to Portland to keynote a national conference of Disgraced Ex-Cops of America.

I pulled into the gas station with an hour to spare. The guy who had actually rented the truck to Peter didn't work there anymore. He wouldn't've remembered anyway, the manager assured me. I thought it was also too much to expect that the same truck would still be on the lot, and it was. "That baby's long gone," the man said. "That went out on a one-way to Florida back in early August." The truck had been rented out of this same station no less than eighteen times between Peter Bonnema and Tampa-Saint Pete: any physical evidence, unlikely under the best circumstances, would've disappeared a dozen times over, but

I had to ask. "Do you people keep stuff that's left in the trucks—papers, notes, anything like that?" The guy said yeah, sure, if it looked valuable or important. He showed me a box of junk. That's all it was, junk: I combed through it and found nothing. I asked to see the original contract that Peter had signed. The original had been turned in to the U-Haul people, but the gas station kept a file of duplicates going back a year. "See, this-un went out without the proper paperwork," the guy said. "That's one of the reasons Jerry don't work here no more, the bastard wouldn't do what I told him. All these trucks are supposed to be backed up with credit cards. I don't care if it's Jesus Christ straight from the cross, if he wants to drive one of these babies out of here he's got to have a card. I tell Jerry this fifteen times, and what's he do? He rents the goddamn thing for cash and we got nothing but the guy's driver's license number on file. What good does that do us if he cracks it up?"

I looked at the pink contract dupe. Peter had signed out at 4:18 on the afternoon of June 10. He had returned the truck in good shape at 2:56 P.M. the following day—at least, someone had returned it: there was no mention made as to whether the same guy had brought it in, but even if old Jerry had been on duty, he wouldn't've noticed. Old Jer wasn't real quick on the uptake. The truck had been out twenty-two hours and change. A few blocks from here, Peter had pulled over and stopped. Bobby Westfall had taken the wheel and Peter had faded into the night. These were the things that weren't noted on the dupe. Bobby had taken over and driven the truck into eternity. By five o'clock he had been at Buckley's store, cocky and alone: by seven he had been at Ballard's, again alone. He had worked alone all night and left in the morning. The obvious thing to do would've been to have Peter come along and help, but

Bobby hadn't done that. Bobby would far rather do all the work himself than let Peter in on his secret.

Here was another important thing. On the contract dupe was a space for mileage. The truck had checked out with 39,523 miles on the odometer. It had come back with 39,597. Seventy-four miles. A guy could play with that in many ways, and none of it was certain. Bobby might've gone to Buckley's and then straight to his real destination. Or he might've spent the entire early evening just cruising, full of restless energy. The whole seventy miles might be accounted for in drifting, waiting for the allotted hour for his appointment. Somehow I didn't think so. Bobby had no driver's license, and that meant that every minute he spent driving was a risk. If a cop pulled him for anything, he'd be in the soup. So he went to Buckley's and killed time, and when Buckley closed the store he went to a café and sat over coffee to wait it out. That was my guess, and that meant he had taken Stanley Ballard's books to some point that could be roughly calculated. Twenty-five to thirty-five miles, fifty to seventy there and back.

Rita McKinley's place, for instance, was just about thirty miles from where I stood.

35

My flight into Portland arrived at seven forty-six, Pacific time. I slept the whole way. Hertz didn't tie me up too badly, and by eight-thirty I was driving south on Interstate 5 through subdivisions called Raleigh Hills, Metzger, and so on. Mumsy Bonnema wasn't easy to find, even with an address. I had to backtrack a couple of times through sprawling suburbs, and it was nine o'clock before I found her. She lived on a rural stretch, far away from neighbors. A mailbox on a post said BONNEMA in faded, worn letters. One of the *n*'s had peeled away, leaving its outline.

I pulled into the driveway. Brace yourself, Mumsy. It wouldn't be the first time I had broken bad news.

The place was weedy and rough, full of untrimmed trees. In a sad way it reminded me of the Liberty place, where I had lived with my crazy mother for the first six years of my life. There were huge piles of junk about, and the house was in pretty shabby shape. I killed the lights, killed the engine, took a deep breath, and got out. A pale yellow light shone through the drawn shades. Somewhere deep in the house, a dog barked. I knocked and the dog went into a frenzy. I heard a voice, a woman shouting at the dog, which, amazingly, shut up. Steps came and the door opened a crack. An eye peeped out.

"Mrs. Bonnema?"

She just watched me: didn't say a thing.

"My name is Janeway. I'm a sergeant with the Denver Police Department. I have some bad news for you."

The door opened wider. I got a glimpse of cheek, of brittle hair and a wrinkled cheek. Her face was old and haggard, as pale as a vampire's. She had deep red lipstick on. It smeared on her teeth and reminded me of Gloria Swanson in *Sunset Boulevard*.

My hopes for a safe and sane trip tottered precariously.

"Where're you from?" The voice was brittle, like the hair.

"Denver."

"A policeman."

I didn't deny it and she didn't ask for ID. In a small brassy voice that had begun to quake, she said, "Is this about Petesey?"

"Yes ma'am."

"Has Petesey been hurt?"

"He's dead, ma'am."

For almost a full minute she stood there, motionless and silent. Then a wail came up, a hideous inhuman cry that finally found its true pitch, somewhere around the scale of an air raid siren. The dog started howling and they blended flawlessly into two-part harmony. She disappeared from the doorway and the door creaked open. I could see her, collapsed in a chair. The wailing never stopped: she had unbelievable lung capacity and that dog, wherever he was,

was pretty amazing too. It might have been comical if it hadn't been about death.

Eventually she had to stop. What she did then was equally enchanting: she began to destroy the room. She had done this on a regular basis, if the state of the house was any evidence. She began by hurling a heavy cut-glass ashtray through the front window. She ripped down the curtains and stomped them into the floor. She smashed and ripped and tore, and all the while the dog howled and howled and occasionally barked when Mumsy got winded and had to rest. She smashed a lamp and finished off a table that looked like it had somehow survived an earlier attack. This too had to pass. She sat on the floor, breathing heavily, muttering what sounded like medieval curses.

I stepped in, but without much enthusiasm. The hospitality of crazy people has always left me cold.

"That selfish little monster," Mumsy said. "That ungrateful, spiteful, rotten child!"

I didn't know whether to sit down, help her up, or stand still and wait for Act Three. She looked up at me and in a voice that had no emotion whatever said, "Did you know Petesey?"

"Yes ma'am."

"He was a selfish child, all his life. Didn't you think so?"

"I didn't know him that well."

"A selfish child. Cared for no one but himself. I knew someday he'd go away and leave me alone. What am I supposed to do now? Who's going to care for me? *You*, young man?"

She leveled her eyes on me and I thought, I'd rather be with Peter. I managed to hold her gaze till she looked away. She grunted and got to her feet. Lit a long black cigarette: filled the place with smoke. Bustled around, picking things up, putting them down, muttering, talking to herself.

"Hope he burns in hell for what he's done to me," she said. "Hope he burns, the selfish boy. It's Dadsy he'll have to answer to now, and we'll see how he likes that. Dadsy knows how to handle errant little boys."

Yes, I had broken a lot of bad news as a cop, but it had never happened quite this way.

You go to the scene, you break the news, you wait through the initial shock waves, the absolute heartbreak, and if you're lucky and the survivors don't collapse you might get to ask a few questions. Usually they had questions too: *Did he suffer? Did he go easily?* I realized suddenly that I was waiting for those questions that would never come. Mumsy Bonnema had no thoughts for Peter. Her world was herself. She was the center of the universe, and even her son was a prop for her amusement, convenience, or comfort. All I wanted at that moment was to put distance between myself and this clutching old bat.

But there was business to do.

"He sent you some books." I said this as a matter of fact, my voice heavy with authority.

"Books!" she shouted. "I'm going to burn those books!"

"I'm afraid not."

"Like to see you stop me. Just you try it. Those books are the reason I'm alone here. *They* took him away from me. If it hadn't been for *books,* Petesey would still be here."

"Let me try to explain something to you, Mrs. Bonnema—"

"Get a job, I said. Go out and find work and take care of your mother like any self-respecting boy should do. But no, would he do that? All his life, all he cared about was books!"

"Where are the books, Mrs. Bonnema?"

She gave a wicked little smile. "That's for me to know."

"You can't destroy them. They're not your property."

"Who says they're not? Didn't Petesey send them to me?"

"They weren't Petesey's to send. Those books are evidence in a murder case. If you try to keep them, or if you destroy them, you can be prosecuted."

"I don't care," she said, but she did care. The key to Mumsy was simple: hit her where she lives.

"You could go to jail, Mrs. Bonnema."

"I don't care. My life is over anyway. Everyone I loved has left me. I hope Dadsy punishes that boy."

I walked around and looked in her face. What the hell, I thought.

"Mrs. Bonnema," I said. "I'd hate to have to arrest you."

"You *dare* talk to me like that. Take them. Take the dirty things and get them out of my house. I never wanted them anyway."

"Where are the books?"

"In the garage, where do you think?"

I started through the house toward the back door.

"It's all junk," she cried. "I'm telling you that right now, there's nothing there but junk." I heard her footsteps: she was following me through the dark house. "Petesey was always off chasing silly dreams," she said. "Always scavenging, pawing through what other people threw out. It was shameful, my son picking through people's trash. I cringe when I think of it, how that must've reflected on *me!* He looked all his life and never found anything but junk. The world called it junk, but—oh no!—not him! He knew it all! Everybody else was wrong and he was right, that's the way he saw it. Everything he found was worth its weight in gold. Hah! He goes all the way to Denver, and what does he send me back? More junk! Can you beat that, Mr. Policeman? Can you beat that? Are you listening to me?"

I groped through the kitchen. The dog growled, very near, and I skirted the sound and felt for the door. I could still hear her yelling: her voice followed me through the yard and into the underbrush. She had turned into a book expert. "A book's gotta be old to be worth anything, everybody knows that. Gotta be old, but does he find *old* books? No, he picks up junk that anyone could find and then tries to tell *me* it's valuable. Same silly thing he's said all his life. . . ." At last she faded: her screeching blended with the crickets and the breeze and maybe she finally gave up. I saw the garage: it was forty yards from the house along a dark path. I pushed open the door and blundered along the wall in search of a light. The light I found was dim, but it was enough. Stacked against the far wall were eight cartons of books, most unopened, all with Denver postmarks. I cut open the tops and looked inside. There were twenty books, give or take, in each box. I took a quick inventory.

One hundred sixty-four titles. Flawless first editions from the period 1927 to 1955.

Retail value? My guess was as good as any.

I called it twenty grand, and started putting the boxes together again.

36

The earliest flight I could get back to Denver was the 6:47. I checked in an hour early and fought the ticket people at the Portland airport. There was a luggage limit and I was over it: even by paying excess freight charges, I couldn't get more than five boxes on board without special permission. I battled my way up the bureaucratic chain, telling them I was a Denver detective working undercover on a case involving a major book theft ring. I didn't have any identification, I said, because undercover cops never carry any, but my story could be verified by Detective Hennessey at DPD. Of course, before they could reach Hennessey, my plane would be gone, I said with the proper degree of helplessness. The man in charge at five-thirty in the morning was a suspicious bird: damned if he didn't call Denver.

"They do verify that a Detective Hennessey is employed with the Denver police," he said to the ticket people. He looked at me severely. "What did you say your name was?"

"Cameron."

He looked at my ticket. "It says Janeway here."

I rolled my eyes. "I'm traveling undercover," I said with just the right edge of strained patience.

"Is there a Detective Cameron on the Denver police force?" he asked the telephone. He nodded and hung up. "Let him through," he said to the ticket people.

God bless United Air Lines.

I slept all the way home.

At Stapleton, the chores of the day arranged themselves in my mind. The first order of business was to secure the books.

I drove to a storage locker I knew, rented a small unit, stacked the boxes two high on pallets off the floor, locked the unit, and went home.

I took a shower, shaved, and ate breakfast. A pot of coffee, double strength, brought me almost back to life, and I sat at the phone and lined up the day's work.

Hennessey. The Ballards. Rita McKinley.

I wanted to know what the cops had found when they had gone into Rita's place yesterday. I wanted to see the artist's sketch, if they had made one, from the description Neff had supplied. Hennessey was the best avenue to that information. But then I looked at the calendar and saw that my entire afternoon was blocked out: today I was scheduled to give my deposition on the Jackie Newton lawsuit. "Son of a bitch," I said. I said a few other things, fought back a temptation to throw my coffee cup through the wall, then settled down and called my lawyer.

Robert Moses wasn't handling my case gratis, but he might as well've been. A long time ago, when I was in uniform, I saved his child from a pervert—strictly my good luck, and the little girl's, that I was four blocks away when the stupid ass snatched the kid in broad daylight. A neighbor had seen it all, had called the cops, and a vehicle description was on the radio in less than two minutes. The dispatcher was still reading it when the car came speeding past the little greasy spoon where I sometimes stopped for coffee. I nailed the guy, and though I was only doing my job, Mose had been in my debt ever since. So he thought, and those are the only kinds of debts that matter. You couldn't put the man off: he owed me a big one, and when Jackie Newton went after my hide, Mose offered his legal services free. We argued over money and finally resolved it this way: he would give me his best shot and I would pay him what I could, when I could pay it. I wondered how he liked making janitor's wages.

"Where the hell've you been?" he said. "I've been trying to get you ever since I saw the paper this morning."

"Been up in Oregon communing with nature. What's the story this afternoon?"

"I dunno, what do you want it to be? I can get it put off, given what happened in your store yesterday. What the hell was that all about?"

"That's what I'm trying to find out. I could sure use the time this afternoon. How long is this likely to take?"

"They're gonna try to sweat you. Levin's a mean little prick; if he thinks you're in a hurry, you'd better pack your supper and bring your toothbrush. That's all this is, you know: he's just trying to run up your legal fees."

"Little does he know," I said.

"This is just the opening salvo, my friend. My guess is they'll try to bring you in again in a few weeks. Levin'll conveniently forget to ask a fairly crucial question, and he'll ask the court for a new deposition. Then there'll be a flood of interrogatories and if we're lucky we might get to trial sometime in 1994. My advice is this. Give 'em a stiff upper lip. Don't let the bastards rattle you. Be there today, right on time if you can. Let him take all night if he wants to. I'll be with you, pal."

"I know you will."

"Our turn comes next week. I can't wait to get that Crowell dame up here. I'm gonna nip this baby right in the bud. See, she's never been deposed before, she don't know what it's all about. If she thinks Jackie Newton frightens her, I'm gonna scare what's left of her into an early grave."

I gave a dry little laugh. "That poor kid."

"Save your sympathy. That poor kid is gonna put you under, if I let her. Which, given the handsome fee you're paying me, I don't intend to do."

"I can't help feeling sorry for her. None of this is her fault."

"It's all her fault. Don't even think of asking me to go easy on her."

"No," I said. "Do what you have to."

"I always do, Clifford. Now, what do you want to do about this afternoon?"

"You've probably rearranged your whole life for this."

"I have made a few minor adjustments, yes. But don't let that worry you; I can always take off and go fishing with my kids."

"No, let's do it. I'd sure like to be out of there by three o'clock if I can. It'd be nice to have some of the day left."

"Don't count on it," Mose said.

I called the mortuary and made arrangements for Miss Pride. I called the cemetery and arranged for a burial plot.

I called Hennessey downtown.

"Where the hell have you been?" It was starting to sound like a catchphrase, something people automatically said when they heard my voice.

We decided to meet for lunch in a place not far from City Hall: from there I could walk over to Levin's office and be there in plenty of time. It was already eleven-fifteen, so I went right over. All I wanted was a beer and a raw egg: Hennessey ate half a horse, with french fries. "Jesus, Neal, you'll be lucky if you live another year," I said, and knocked wood. I hoped he'd live forever, the sweet old son of a bitch. Hennessey had his stern look on. "Let's get down to cases, buddy," he said, and though I somehow guessed that he didn't mean it, I managed to give him my rapt attention.

"I been trying to get you for twelve hours," he said.

"I went for a walk in the mountains."

"What'd ya do there?"

"Walk. Think. Look at butterflies."

"It snowed in the mountains last night. There ain't no butterflies."

"The pretty kind, Neal, that ski and walk on two legs."

There was a long silence. Hennessey had been my partner forever, it seemed: he had deliberately taken a more or less subordinate role because we did our best work that way. But he knew me inside out: he knew when I began to bend the rules because he had seen me do it often enough. He said, "Y'know, my bullshit detector's going crazy here. The needle's knocking the roof off."

I ignored that. "What did you get from McKinley?"

He ignored that. "Cliff, what the hell are you up to?"

I said, "Actually, that elephant sandwich you're eating doesn't look half bad. Maybe I'll have one."

"C'mon, Cliff, stop screwing around. Look, I'll ask you point-blank: are you messing around in this case? If you are, Cameron's got a big package of trouble all wrapped and ready to dump right on your ass."

"When I came back from the hills this morning, I sat

down and made up a list of all the things that bother me. My psychiatrist told me to do that. It's better than scream therapy, Neal, but you know what? I couldn't find Cameron's name anywhere on it."

"God damn it, he'd better be on it."

"Are you gonna eat that pickle?"

"Sure I am. Listen, do you want to talk to me or not?"

"I might, if you'll pull the cork out of your ass and stop being a cop for thirty seconds."

He took a long breath and held it. As he let it out, he said, "I'd just hate to see you take a fall."

I gave a little shrug. "Are we all finished with the dance now? If we are, I'll tell you something: the real truth, forty-carat, government-inspected stuff. You can take it to the bank, Neal. You ready? Here it is. This boy is dead meat. I don't know who he is or where he's hiding, but his ass is mine. He can't go far enough and he can't dig himself a deep enough hole. That's on the record, and frankly I don't give a fuck what Lester thinks."

I picked up his pickle and bit the end off. "Does that answer your question?"

"Yeah," he said grimly. "It's also what I was afraid of."

He ate the rest of the pickle fast.

"This is now my full-time job," I said. "You want to talk turkey, fine. How much time do you have in a day? Did you guys ever get through checking out that U-Haul lead? Well I did, because I've got nothing else going with my time. My business is closed for the duration and I'm on this guy full-time. I can't wait for you guys, Neal, because you've probably got ten other cases on your desk right this minute. Hey, I know how it goes. I also know you've got to get on something like this right now, because evidence tends to dry up. I've already found something that would be ashes now if I'd waited for you. No offense."

"What evidence? What the hell've you found?"

"Only something that puts a whole new slant on things. Don't ask for specifics if you're not willing to punt the football. It's a two-way street. That's simple manners, and I know Mrs. Hennessey didn't raise anything but polite little walruses."

"You're out of your mind. Cameron'd have a hematoma of the left nut if he thought I was sharing information with you."

"It'll give him something to play with. Look, I've got to go, I can't sit here and bullshit all day. You've gotta make up your mind."

He sat perfectly still, struggling with the forces of good and evil.

"Don't hurry on my account," I said. I looked at my watch. "I'm due at an appointment, where I'm getting my ass sued off, in thirty minutes."

"One time and one time only," Hennessey said. "What do you want to know?"

"All the good poop. What happened at McKinley's. You can put in a lot of color. Tell me if her cheeks were rosy or pale when Lester broke her door open and wrestled her down just as she was about to throw the tape into the fire."

"You should do stand-up comedy." He fished in his pocket for a small notebook and leafed through the pages. "At eleven forty-eight yesterday morning, your police department, accompanied by officers from Jefferson County and acting on a warrant signed by District Court Judge Harlan Blakeley, scaled the fence at the mountaintop residence at the end of Road twelve, otherwise known as Crestview Street. . . ."

"I think I've seen this one. In a minute it snows and turns into *Bambi*. I really don't have time for this much color."

He put his notebook away and looked at me long and hard. He was a cop who went by the book, and it broke his heart when he had to go the other way.

"She gave us the tape."

"No kidding. Was it all there?"

"Seemed to be."

"How about the part I erased?"

"Entirely different tape. You remember she had taken the tape out so she could play it for you when you arrived. She had already put another one in the recorder. The tape we wanted was still in the player when we got there."

"Did you listen to it? Stupid question. What was on it?"

"Same thing you heard."

"What'd you make of it?"

"We think it was the killer who came in at the end. Almost had to be, the way it goes. The time's about perfect, and the guy—Peter, right?—seems to fall apart right at that moment."

"Could you make anything out of the section where they're talking together?"

"It was pretty much of a mess. I've listened to one of the copies maybe two dozen times and I can't get it. The lab boys have the original; maybe they'll do some good with it. They've got the equipment: they can do some amazing stuff, separating voices. They might have something for me later today."

"Would it be too much to ask . . . you know, for old time's sake . . . could you tell me what they say?"

"I'm already a dead man. What's one more shot in the head?"

"What was McKinley like while all this was going on?"

"Couldn't've been more cooperative. Went right to the tape player and handed over the tape and we were out of there in ten minutes. Even Lester liked her."

I sat quietly, lost in thought.

"Your turn," Hennessey said.

I started with the U-Haul rental: told him how Peter had rented the truck and gave him the gas station's address. I told him about Portland, and the lovely Mumsy Bonnema. I told him about Peter's books: where I had found them, what I thought they were worth, where I had put them. He kept his eyes closed, a suffering man, all the time I was telling it. At the end, he said, "I don't wanna know how you found out all this, do I?"

"Probably not."

"So what the hell d'you expect me to do with it?"

"I'll try to find a way to get it to you. For now, let's say there's a gray point of law involved."

"Let's say your ass is gray. Come on, Cliff, what am I supposed to do? Just how the hell am I supposed to have gotten those books from Oregon to Denver, let alone found out where they were in the first place?"

"I guess you'll have to follow the evidence, like a good cop always does."

"Right through you. I'll send you postcards in Canon City."

"Yeah, I thought of that. Maybe I will have to do some jail time before it's over. I just know I couldn't leave those books in Portland. By now they'd be ashes in Mumsy's back yard."

"You wouldn't be so particular if the evidence was pornography or dope."

"You may be right."

"You know I'm right." He finished off his beer. "You're crazy, Cliff, you really are." He got up and put on his coat. "You're crazy," he said again. "God dang, you were a good cop, though. You sure were a good cop."

37

"This is getting us nowhere," Levin said. "You admit you hated Mr. Newton. You admit you harassed and persecuted him for more than two years prior to the incident in question. You admit you kidnapped—threatened and beat and illegally handcuffed and detained—Mr. Newton, not in the legal performance of your duty as a Denver police officer, but out of sheer malicious hatred. Then you took Mr. Newton, against his will, for a little ride. Sounds like something out of *The Untouchables,* Mr. Janeway, but this is what, by your own admission, seems to have happened that night. All these things you have admitted for the record, and now, when we come to that little clearing by the river, you would expect us to believe that you removed the handcuffs from Mr. Newton's wrists and not only allowed him an even break but actually let him strike the first blow?"

Mose leaned across the table and in a very weary voice said, "Counselor, if you keep asking questions like that, we'll all be old men before this thing ends. The golden age of oratory is over."

"Mr. Moses, this is a deposition, not a trial. I believe the rules allow me to obtain information in my own way."

"As long as you don't actually expect him to answer that."

Levin puffed on his cigar. He was a little man with a New York accent, a tough Jewish lawyer as someone, I forget who, had said. He turned and looked at me down the length of the table. "Let me ask you this. Are you seriously asking us to believe that you removed those handcuffs and inflicted the severe body and facial damage"—he opened the package of photographs and threw them across the table—"to Mr. Newton that we see in this evidence?"

"That's what happened."

"Now Mr. Newton is a big man, would you agree with that?"

"No."

"Nevertheless, he's bigger than you are, by quite a bit."

"He's got more beef, if that's what you mean."

"How would you describe Mr. Newton, Mr. Janeway? Just his physical appearance, please."

"He's a white male, approximately six feet four inches, two hundred thirty pounds, muscular, brown hair, brown eyes, sometimes wears a mustache."

"And yourself? Describe yourself in the same terms."

"White male, five-eleven, one ninety, dark hair, dark eyes. . . ."

"Mr. Newton outweighs you by some forty pounds, by your own description."

"About that."

"His reach is longer. . . ."

"Yeah."

"And would you say that Mr. Newton carries much fat on him?"

"Not much."

"How much?"

"None that's evident."

"In fact, Mr. Newton is a bodybuilder, isn't that right?"

"That's what I hear."

"He boxes, lifts weights . . . all in all, for his age, a prime specimen of manhood, wouldn't you say?"

"Look," I said, "if you want to ask me questions, go ahead and ask. Don't make statements and try to get me to agree with them."

"Here's a question for you, then. Do you expect us to believe that you took on this man on equal footing—*in spite of the fact that his wrists still bore chafe marks from the shackles that you bound him with*—that you released him and defeated him so overwhelmingly in a fair fight?"

"Is that the end of it?"

"Answer the question, please."

"The answer is yes."

"How did you do it, Mr. Janeway? Frankly, I find it a little hard to believe. How did you conduct this fight and bring it to such a successful conclusion, from your viewpoint?"

"I beat the hell out of him. He tried to beat the hell out of me, but he lost."

"And you expect me to believe that."

"I don't particularly expect anything from you, sir."

"I should apologize for belaboring the point, but I find it very hard to believe—"

"You've said that," Mose said. "Get on with it."

"I'm trying to find out how he managed it," Levin said.

"It wasn't by the Marquis of Queensberry rules," Mose said. "They were two guys brawling in the country. You ever been involved in a fight like that, Levin? One guy throws a punch, then the other. The guy with the most heart usually wins."

"I don't know anything about this so-called heart, Mr. Moses. What I do know is what I see in evidence before me. This is a small man, compared with my client. My client is a man supremely conditioned to such physical combat, yet he was the only one who was physically battered. I'm trying to find out, if the handcuffs really were off, how that happened."

"It's simple," I said.

"If it's so simple, please explain it to me."

"Bring your client in here, clear away the furniture, and I'll show you how it happened."

38

"I don't think he'll ask that question again," Mose said. "I might have to do it for him."

"Why would you do that?" I said.

"Are you kidding? You couldn't have a more perfect answer to the most damaging question we'll get in the whole trial."

"How can it hurt us if nobody asks it?"

"Because it's there, Clifford, whether anybody asks it or not. They'll look at you, they'll look at him; then they'll look at those pictures and they'll ask it themselves. So I'll bring it out. You'll say the same thing all over again. Clear the court, bring him on down here, I'll show you how I did it. Jesus, I love it. You don't say it in any flip or arrogant way. Whatever you do, you don't act disrespectful to the court. You just say it, like you have no doubt whatsoever that it'll turn out the same way again. I'm even flirting with the idea of asking the court's permission to stage a fight between the two of you just for the benefit of the jury. That kinda shit's a little risky and it smacks

293

of an old Perry Mason rerun. The court would never allow it, but it sure makes points. Once you say it, and mean it, the jury never forgets, no matter what that old man on the bench tells them."

We were sitting in a little café across from Levin's office, doing the postmortem on my deposition. Levin had eaten up the afternoon: it was four-thirty and already the streetlights were on. Hard to believe I had been in Oregon just this morning. I felt depressed, as if I had lost a week instead of one afternoon.

"Next time don't look so fierce," Mose said. "Lighten up a little. Think of this as a popularity contest, which it often turns out to be. I know that's distasteful to a purist like you, but a smile at the right time—if it's not forced—can sometimes pay big dividends."

I gave a big stupid grin.

"There you go," Mose said. "Now you've got it. Nobody'll find against a retard." He signaled for more coffee. "Come home with me for dinner."

It sounded good. They were all good people, Mose and his wife, Patty, and their two kids. The daughter I had saved was now nineteen. She was a forest ranger, a child of the earth, a lovely young woman. I hadn't seen her in a long time.

But not tonight. "Think I'm gonna work awhile," I said. "I've gotta make something out of this day."

"You're a real type A, Clifford," Mose said over his coffee. "You better learn to relax, pal, or what happens to you won't be so funny."

I was looking through the front window when the Lamborghini pulled up and stopped in front of Levin's office. Jackie Newton and Barbara Crowell got out just as Levin began to close shop for the day. It was cold in

Denver. They huddled for a moment at the front door, then Levin pointed at the café and they started across the street. Mose must've seen me tighten up. He looked where I was looking, but we didn't say anything. A little bell rang when they came in. The place was crowded: the only open tables were against the far wall, and they had to walk past us to get there. Levin saw me and hesitated. He said something to Jackie and they all looked. Jackie smiled and said something: he pointed to one of the tables and they came toward us. Barbara passed two feet from where I sat. I hadn't seen her in all these weeks: she looked haggard, worn out, drained of life.

"Hello, Barbara," I said.

She couldn't look at me. Her mouth quivered, and Jackie took her arm and propelled her past our table. They sat in a far corner, as far away as possible.

Mose was looking at me over the sugar bowl. "That was Crowell?"

"That was the lady."

"She looks like a nervous breakdown waiting to happen."

"When Jackie gets his hooks in you, he doesn't leave much."

"He'll need more than a hook when I get hold of her. I really think you can stop worrying about this, Clifford. They are in very deep doodoo if that's their main witness."

This was good to hear even if I didn't quite believe it. Mose didn't know how strong Barbara's fear of Jackie Newton could be. I knew it was stronger than any threat of perjury or the risk of public ridicule: I thought it might even be running neck-and-neck with the will to survive. If the fear is intense enough, if it goes on forever and there's still no end in sight, death might begin to look almost appealing.

"You don't look convinced," Mose said. "I promise you, Cliff, I know how to get to people like her."

"Yeah, but what happens to her afterward?"

"Not your concern."

"That's where you're wrong. Her only crime, you know, is being too scared to think."

"Her real crime is that she's a self-centered lying bitch. She'll destroy you or anybody else to get the pressure off herself. I can't work up much sympathy for people like her."

Poor Barbara, I thought, and I looked at her across the room.

"Want some more coffee?" Mose said. "I was gonna go home, but I hate to have those bastards think they ran us off. Let's have another cup."

I took a piece of apple pie with mine. We lingered over small talk far removed from our case. Mose had taken up fishing in his middle age: he was engaged in a herculean effort to master the fly rod. He asked, out of politeness, how the book business was, and I told him it was a lot like urban fishing. On any weekend morning, the fisherman and the bookscout went through the same motions and emotions. A nice catch for both was a dozen good ones. The hunt was the main thing, the chase was its own reward.

I glanced at the table where Levin and Newton sat hunched over papers and briefs. Barbara was wedged between them, her eyes cast into the bottomless gulf of her coffee cup. Any minute now, if she looked deep enough and hard enough, the Loch Ness monster might surface and show her its face. Jackie said something to her and she nodded: he said something else and she looked at him, looked into the face of the monster. Then she looked at me. I could feel her pain half a room away. I tried to smile and then—I couldn't help myself—I winked at her.

She excused herself and went back to the narrow hallway where the rest rooms were.

All I could think in that moment was that line from Shakespeare, how cowards die a dozen times before their deaths.

Death was on my mind.

And I was suddenly very uneasy.

Mose was talking about the summer's best fishing trip. I should take up fishing, he was saying: it was good therapy for us type A types. Scouting for books might bear some superficial resemblances to fishing, if you had a good imagination and wanted to stretch a point, but it was too intense. I needed something to help me relax, Mose said.

Jackie Newton gave me a long look from the far wall. I stared back at him. Levin was talking and shuffling papers. Mose was rattling on about a new lure he had found: fish were supposed to be able to smell it. A waitress brought Mr. Newton's order, putting plates in front of each gentleman and another in front of the empty space where, a few minutes earlier, Barbara Crowell had been sitting.

"She sure is taking her time in there," I said.

"Who?"

"Crowell."

I got up and started back toward the rest rooms. Behind me, Mose called my name. "Hey, Clifford, what the hell do you think you're doing?" There was a note of worry in his voice that almost matched what I suddenly felt in my heart. I went past Jackie's table. Both Jackie and Levin looked at me as I went into the dark hall.

I called Barbara's name.

John Dunning

Doors on opposite sides were designated by gender: pants and skirts. I knocked on the skirts and listened. I pushed the door open and peeped in.

"Barbara?"

I was staring at the outer wall of a toilet stall. I called her name again and got nothing. "Hey, I'm coming in," I said, and did. I looked around the row of johns and there she was, sitting on the floor. She held a small gun in her hand, and she was staring at it the way you imagine a medical student might look at a scalpel before his first operation. Tears were running down her face. She lifted the gun and looked at it, business end first.

"Hey," I said, holding out my hands. "Don't do that."

It was a little .22 revolver. You can buy them cheap all over Denver without permits or hassles: a little gun, made for ladies and kids, but more than enough to do what she had in mind.

"Hey, Barb," I said. I tried to smile and wondered if it looked real. It was real: a smile of fear. Softly, I said, "You know what they say about suicide, honey. Permanent solution to temporary problem. This gets you nothing."

It gets me peace, she seemed to say. I came a little closer and tried to figure my chances. If I rushed her suddenly, without warning, I had about a dead-even chance of getting to her before she could cock the pistol and pull the trigger. She probably didn't know much about guns—a point for my side. But I was still ten feet away—a big point for her.

"Listen, I've got a great idea," I said. "You put that back in your purse and let me take you out of here. We'll go to a place I know and we'll talk it over. Okay? Okay, Barb? We'll talk it over, and if I can't give you at least ten reasons for living we'll both kill ourselves. Now what

298

could be fairer than that? C'mon, Barb. I'll buy you a great dinner and we'll work it out. I know you don't want to do this."

I stopped talking. She had cocked the pistol, taking away my only real chance. I felt a tightness in my chest, almost like hyperventilation.

"Barb, please . . . listen to me . . . Here, look at me."

She did. Again, her misery was like a beacon, filling the room.

"I swear to God there's a way out of this," I said. "I swear there is. I promise you, but only if you do the smart thing."

I could see it in her eyes: she was on the brink, right at the edge. I've seen three people commit suicide, and at the end there's no doubt that it's coming. They all look the same, drained of all hope.

I was going to lose her.

She spoke. Her voice was raw, the words ragged and broken. "I've left a note . . . It clears you . . . backs up everything you said . . ."

"It won't mean anything if you do this. Are you hearing me? Barbara, are you listening to what I'm saying?"

"No."

"Just give me one chance. One chance, Barbara, to prove what I'm telling you. I won't even take the gun away from you, that's how sure I am that you'll see things different. Let me tell you something. Newton can't do anything to me, and I won't let him do anything more to you, either. I've got ways of fixing that bastard that he can't even imagine yet. Just put the gun away and I'll tell you about it."

It was pointing at her right temple: her finger was on the trigger. She was going to do it. I couldn't stop her. Janeway, if you've got any good quotes, you'd better get 'em up now, because there isn't going to be any tomorrow.

"I know a guy who can make Newton hate the day he first saw you. I'm not kidding. I wasn't just yanking your chain that day when I told you that. Just put the gun down a little and let me say this. Just let me say this much, Barbara. Newton's a master at playing the system for his own advantage. He's got it all going his way—money, a sharp lawyer—he knows his rights, old Jackie does. The system's all greased up for scumbags like Jackie Newton. So we'll go outside the system. I couldn't do that when I was a cop, but I damn sure can now. We'll play Jackie's game Jackie's way, and I promise you we'll make him hate it. And he'll never be able to lay a hand on you again. That's the main thing. When we get through with Jackie, he'll never want to see your face again."

"You don't know him," she said. "Don't know what he's capable of."

"Oh yes I do. But I also know what he's not capable of."

She opened her mouth. Nothing came out. I heard a woman come in behind me, stopping suddenly at the end of the toilet partition.

"What's going on?" the woman said.

"Get out of here," I said.

She didn't move: I could feel her behind me; I could hear her breathing.

"Lady, you better do what I tell you. Just turn around and walk out of here."

She went, quickly now. I heard the door swish shut.

"People will be coming now," Barbara said.

"Don't worry about it. I'll keep them away from you."

"Cops . . . cops'll come."

"I'll walk you through that, too. The way it stands now, it's no big deal."

We looked at each other. I hoped to hell I looked sincere. In the distance I heard noises: a woman shouting; someone running; sharp, excited voices. In the dimmer distance, somewhere far outside, a siren.

"They come fast," Barbara said.

"They're just a phone call away, hon. They've got cars all over town."

"Janeway . . ." Her voice broke.

"I'm right here."

"I don't want to live anymore."

"Sure you do. You can't make that decision now . . . you don't know what the alternative is . . . you haven't given me a chance yet."

Now her voice was bitter. "You had plenty of chances. You couldn't do anything. . . ."

The siren got louder. I knew if the cops came in, she would do it. I had maybe two minutes to talk her out of it.

She put the gun in her mouth and my time was up.

One last plea. Desperately, I shouted: "Barbara, for Christ's sake, don't do this to me!"

She blinked.

"Don't do it," I said. "Please."

And I watched her . . . slowly . . . come back from the brink.

She wavered. The gun came out of her mouth.

I reached out my hands. She didn't do anything. The gun was still cocked but she held it limply in her lap.

I touched her: ruffled her hair with my knuckles, touched her cheeks where the tears still ran. Kneeled and looked in her eyes.

Outside, the sirens were very close.

I put an arm around her shoulder and helped her up. "We'll go meet them together," I said. "Give me the gun now and I'll take you outside."

Then the door opened. Jackie Newton was standing in front of us, blocking the way.

"Get out of the way, Newton," I said.

He just stood and looked. His face was full of contempt.

"Move," I said.

He gave a little laugh. "Stupid bitch."

And before I could stop her, Barbara brought up the gun and shot him.

39

They put her in a police car and segregated the witnesses: mainly me. It was getting to be habit-forming. For the second time in two days I told a uniform the bare facts and was told to wait over here, away from the crowd, until a coat-and-tie arrived from downtown. Barbara sat in the car, huddled into herself while a cop leaned across the seat and tried to talk to her. Reading her rights, I imagined: it was amazing how fast your sympathies passed from the cops to the accused, once you knew something about it and were no longer part of that world where the gathering of information must be just so. A plainclothes cop arrived and took charge. He was a burly guy named O'Hara: I had known him for years, though not well. I thought he was probably pretty good. I heard him tell the uniforms not to ask her anything until she could comprehend what she was being asked and what she was saying. She seemed to be in shock, one of the uniforms said. "Okay, let's get her downtown right away and have a doctor check her out," O'Hara said.

All this happened in a few minutes, while the medics were still working on Jackie Newton on the women's room floor.

"Good grief," O'Hara said when he saw me. "Can't you stay out of trouble?"

He went back into the women's room and came out again a few seconds later.

"Well, I guess you finally got the bastard."

"Hey, all I was was the cheering section, O'Hara. If I'd had anything to do with this, she'd've used a real gun."

"Lucky for her she didn't."

The shot had hit Newton in the throat and had gone through his neck. The exit wound was at the base of the skull. It was messy, O'Hara said, but probably not fatal.

Whatever it was, the medics were taking their time.

"You wanna tell me about it?"

I told him the story, omitting nothing about why and how long Newton had been asking for it. Even at that it didn't take long: my main statement would come later, downtown, in a smoky room with a stenographer.

"What do you think my chances are of seeing her?" I said.

O'Hara gave a loud laugh. "What a guy. You know better than to ask a question like that, Janeway."

"I told her I'd help her through it, if I could."

"Well, you shouldn't've told her that."

"I believe she is entitled to see a lawyer. That's the way it works, isn't it, O'Hara? Or have they changed the rules since I went away?"

"Where's your law degree?"

"Standing over there with its thumb in its ear."

I called Mose and he came over.

"How about going down and talking to Crowell?" I said.

He blinked and looked at me as if I had suddenly started talking Arabic.

"I'm serious," I said.

"You're out of your mind, Clifford. You want me to represent that dame?"

"I want you to go talk to her, let her know she's not alone. Come on, Mose, nobody does that better than you. Tell her about your last fishing trip. While you're at it, you might slip in some free advice."

"Cliff, listen to me. There's no way I could properly do something like that. You understand what I'm saying? You know what conflict of interest is, I believe."

"Look, I don't want her facing these dinosaurs alone."

O'Hara let out a bellow. "What a guy!"

They were bringing Newton out now. He lay on a stretcher, his head immobilized by a brace, tubes dangling from his nose and arm. His eyes were open, lovely blue eyes, wet and terrified. He saw me and his terror doubled.

"Merry Christmas, Jackie," I said.

They packed him into the ambulance and slammed the doors. The siren came up and they drove away.

"She's damn lucky she didn't kill him," O'Hara said.

"Oh yeah, she's real lucky. Two months from now she'll have all her old problems back and a whole shopping cart full of legal problems as well. When she finally does get out of jail she'll probably find Jackie Newton waiting at the gate."

If she does, I thought, I'll be there too.

40

It was still on the right side of seven o'clock when I finished up at headquarters. I was wired to the gills and ready to make something happen. I drove out to Stan Ballard's house, more on a whim than anything else. A sign on the door said OFFERED BY JOHN BAILEY ASSOC., and under that was a phone number for an agent named Douglas Barton. There was a lockbox on the door: the place had a sad look about it, as if it had just lost its best friend. It was one of those fine old houses, vintage World War I, that still had a lot of life in it. They built houses to last then, not the prefab cardboard they use today. There was a time in Denver, not so long ago, when a house like this wouldn't last a day on the open market. The oil business was booming and shale was the coming thing, and there was an economic excitement in the Rocky Mountains that hasn't been here since. But the bottom fell out of the oil bucket, they never did figure how to suck the shale dry, and then HUD got into the real estate business and started giving houses away. The Ballard place lay fallow. There were simply more houses than people.

I walked up the steps and peeped through the window. Light fell in from old Mr. Greenwald's place next door and I could see most of the front room. It looked different with everything stripped away. The Ballards had left nothing but the walls and the carpet and, yes, the bookshelves. It was a house made to order for a bookscout, big and solid and already shelved. I wondered what they were asking for it. I went around back and tried to peep in, but visibility was poor: I could see just enough to know that the shelves back there were still intact. I walked across the lawn and tried the garage. It was locked, but I could see that it was a big one, made for two cars and a small workshop. A man could park his car and still have room for five thousand books out here.

I saw a shadow pass the window next door: Mr. Greenwald was watching. There wasn't anything to watch, but old habits die hard. I gave him a wave and walked into his yard. His porch light came on and he stood for a moment watching me through the door glass. He didn't seem to recognize me, but he opened the door anyway.

"I'm surprised it's still available," I said, gesturing to the house.

"If they don't sell it soon it'll start falling apart," he said.

"Are they not taking care of it?"

He made a sour face and waved me away with his hand. "They take care of nothing. They care about nothing. All they want is money. And to play their silly games."

"What games?"

"The game of hating each other. Of beating each other. You never saw anything like it. They act like a pair of dogs with a scrap of meat thrown between them. It's the worst case of jealousy I've ever seen. They don't care anything about the house: they just want to make sure that if there's one dollar left over, the other one doesn't get it."

"Do you know what they're asking for it?"

"Are you interested?"

"I don't know, I might be."

"Come on inside; it's too cold to stand talking like this."

Inside, he offered me coffee, which I was happy to accept. We sat in friendly territory—in his kitchen, surrounded by books—and talked.

"They started at eighty," he said. "That's very reasonable for this place, even in these times, don't you think?"

I did think, and I said so.

"When it didn't sell, they came way down. I hear it's sixty-five now and still no takers. I can't understand that. I'd buy it myself if I had money to burn. I don't know real estate but I know sixty-five for a place like this is nothing. Ten years ago Stan turned down an offer of a hundred and ten. But those were better times."

"There are people who think better times are coming back."

"Then those people could find worse things to do with their money. It's what I'd do, if I were a young man like yourself. I'd buy it strictly as an investment. I'd make them an offer of forty-eight five."

"They'd never take it."

"They'll take it. They just want to get rid of it. They've sold everything but the house and it's hanging around their necks like a millstone. Those two never want to lay eyes on each other again, and this house is the only thing that ties them together. They'll take it, Mr. Janeway. In fact, I think they'll take less than that."

"I didn't think you remembered me."

"I've got a good set of eyes and a good memory for a face."

"If they'd take fifty I'd buy it in a heartbeat."

"Try it on them. They'll fall all over themselves taking it. You see if I'm not right. I've never seen anything like it. Such hate . . . such pure venom. So much energy wasted, just burnt up, on hate."

"Where'd it get started?"

We looked at each other and I knew what I had begun to suspect: this old man had secrets that he hadn't yet told anyone.

"Where'd it get started, Mr. Greenwald?"

"There are things I can't talk about . . . matters of honor."

"There are also three dead people. I understand about honor, sir, but somebody out there is killing people and I'm trying to stop them. It's pretty hard if I'm only playing with half a deck."

He seemed lost in thought. Then his eyes locked on mine and he said, "They are not actually brother and sister." He got up, poured us more coffee, and returned the pot to the stove.

"How do you figure that?"

"It's not something I figured; Stan told me. Val Ballard was an adopted child."

"Well, that explains a few things."

He nodded. "Stan's brother Charles married a delicate woman. Physically delicate . . . you know, frail. It was thought she couldn't have children, so they adopted the boy. Years later she became pregnant with Judith . . . a midlife baby, a great surprise."

"I'll bet."

"There didn't have to be any great conflict with that. Sometimes those things work out fine, and Stan told me they really did try. Charles and his wife did everything possible to raise them equally, to play no favorites. But from the beginning there was anger, resentment, extreme jealousy."

"A modern-day Cathy and Heathcliff," I said.

"Except that love was at the bottom of it all in that story, and here you have just hate."

"I thought something was out of whack when I questioned them. Judith said something—it didn't make sense at the time and I let it get past me. Something like, 'If you're looking for all the living Ballards, I'm it.' "

"Yes. I don't know what good it'll do you. . . ."

"It could be a motive for murder."

"If they were going to murder anyone, it would be each other."

"Maybe. Or maybe they enjoy the hate."

"Now you're talking in riddles."

"You've got to allow for the quirks of human nature," I said. "Maybe they like what's going on between them. You know what I mean. The sweet sorrow, the hate that's really love, the pull of opposites in a single emotion. Maybe they'd be lost without each other. This is the stuff Shakespeare wrote about, isn't it? If you kill off a hate object, it's over. So much better to do him in in other ways . . . to get the better of him in business, to rook him out of his eyeteeth. . . . That you can savor all your life."

"I don't believe it," he said, but I had a feeling he might believe it, deep in his gut.

"You still know something you're not telling me," I said.

"It's nothing . . . harmless."

"I think I'll have to ask you to let me be the judge of that."

He shook his head. "It's just something Stan told me. It couldn't have any bearing on this."

"I think if Mr. Ballard were here, from what I know of him, he'd want you to tell me."

"That may be, but he's not here, and I can't go back on him."

"There are things that make no sense at all about this deal. The man had ten thousand books. I know he got them from the clubs; I've been through every statement going back almost fifty years. They're legitimate, they're in his name, they're annotated in his hand. He writes in the margin when he received a book and when he read it. The books were appraised and the appraiser, who is a helluva respected authority, found nothing of value. And yet, in the last two days, two hundred books have turned up. They did not come from the clubs. They were fine first editions . . . very desirable, very valuable, worth maybe twenty-five thousand dollars. I don't know where they could've come from but here in this house."

"Unbelievable," he said. "People really pay that much, just to own a first edition?"

"Sometimes more than that. Are you telling me, Mr. Greenwald, that neither you nor Mr. Ballard knew what first editions can be worth?"

"We never discussed money. In our generation money was a man's private business. Besides, it's so uninteresting. We didn't care about money."

"Somebody did. Were you here when the woman came to look at the books?"

"I was minding my own business. Stan told me how it had gone, after it was over."

"He told you the woman had appraised the library as worthless."

"That's what he said, yes."

"You never met the lady?"

"No."

"Is there any way I can persuade you to talk to me?"

"That's what I've been doing."

"You have nothing else to say to me?"

"Not at this time."

I got up to leave.

He rose with me, his eyes linked to mine. He won't let me walk out of here, I thought: it's bothering him too much. But when he spoke, it was only about the house. "I think you should buy Stan's house, Mr. Janeway. I really do."

"I'm thinking about it."

"A man would be foolish if he could get a house like that for fifty thousand and he didn't snap it up. You could rent it for more than the payments. In a few years . . . who knows?"

I tried to penetrate that wall. A vast enigmatic gulf lay open between us.

"Sometimes, I've heard, houses talk," he said. "Sometimes they give up secrets. This one may be like that. Sometimes I feel Stan's presence . . . sometimes it seems like he's still there, sitting in the library reading. That's a solid house, Mr. Janeway: more than that, a kind house. I'd buy it myself, if I were younger and had the money."

41

It was just a matter of geography. Val Ballard lived in Littleton, south of town; Judith Ballard Davis was in Park Hill, a few minutes' drive from Madison Street. I went there first.

She peered at me through the screen door and struggled to put a name with my face.

"Detective Janeway," I said. "Remember?"

"Ah," she said, and let me in.

If she knew anything about my recent history, she didn't let on. To her my life began and ended and began again when I walked into, out of, and now back into hers. "You ever catch that guy?" she asked, leading me to the living room. I said no, I was still working on it. She motioned me to the big stuffed chair and asked if I wanted a drink. I said you betcha and she made me a double. She watched me take off the top third in one gulp. She never stopped watching me. I knew I didn't look much like a cop anymore, and I sure didn't feel like one, but she never asked any of the obvious questions—where was my tie, why weren't my shoes shined, how come I was drinking on the job. She just looked at me and waited.

"I went by your house a while ago," I said.

She looked momentarily confused. "Oh, you mean Stan's house."

"It's a nice place. I'm surprised you haven't sold it yet."

"It's a white elephant. You couldn't give it away, the way the Denver market is."

"Maybe you've got the wrong realtor. I think that house should sell."

"Put your money where your mouth is, Detective. You could have my part of it damned cheap. I mean *damned* cheap."

"I'm listening."

"Is this why you came here?"

"No, but I'm listening anyway."

"Make me an offer."

"I'm not really in the market. I wouldn't want to insult you with what I could pay."

"Insult me, please. I've got thick skin and I want to get out of this."

"I'm almost embarrassed to offer it . . . fifty?"

"Give me twenty-five and you could walk out of here with my part right now."

"What do you think your brother would say?"

"Do you mind if we don't call him that? Just hearing it makes my stomach turn."

"What do you want to call him, then?"

"What I call him wouldn't be allowed on the radio. Let's keep it on a high plane. Let's not call him anything. That matches his personality."

"Okay. What do you think *he* would say?"

"He needs the dough worse than I do." She grinned

maliciously. "Alimony. I hope she takes the little pissant for everything he's got or ever will have."

"Well, let's put it this way," I said. "At that price, I'd definitely buy it."

"Detective, you've made my day. Let me freshen up that drink for you."

I put my hand over the top. "I'd better not. I've got a lot to do yet tonight."

"Going to see him?"

"I'll have to, won't I?"

"Call me later, let me know what he says. I know he'll say yes. He'll cough and sputter and blow smoke out of his ass, but in the end he'll be as delighted to be out of it as I am. We can have the papers drawn up over the weekend and I'll never have to see that idiot again." She lit a cigarette. "So what's the real reason you came over here?"

"I've been thinking about those books. I even found some of them."

"So?"

"They weren't exactly the kind of books everyone thought."

"I don't mean to be short, but why should I care? They're gone now. Ancient history. None of my business anymore."

"You might decide to change your mind about that."

"You're talking in riddles, Detective."

"I think you people screwed up. Or maybe just one of you screwed up."

"You'll have to make it plainer than that."

I watched her eyes particularly. Liars usually look away unless they're very accomplished. She was meeting me head-on.

"I think somebody pulled a scam," I said. "I think those

books were worth a helluva lot more than anybody ever knew."

"Who pulled a scam? Are you talking about that little man that got killed?"

"He was just a tool. Somebody else was the main guy."

"And you think it was one of us?"

"Coulda been. The question is, which one?"

"I don't even know what was supposed to've been done."

"I think you're brighter than that, Mrs. Davis."

"Ms. Davis, please. There is no Mr. Davis: never was, never will be. It's my mother's maiden name."

I didn't say anything. I could see by the color in her cheeks that she was getting a glimmer.

"That son of a bitch," she said in a voice that was almost a whisper.

"Somebody's a son of a bitch," I said.

She got up, walked to the window, and came back.

"Let me get this straight. You think one of us found out what the books were really worth, hired somebody to buy them, and . . . is that what's going through your head? Is that what he did to me?"

I shrugged.

"So tell me, how much did the bastard take me for?"

I wasn't sure I wanted to tell her that yet.

"How much?" she pressed.

I finished off my drink.

She lit another cigarette. "Can we get a straight answer here? Christ, you men are all alike."

"If I had a straight answer I'd give it to you. Like I told you, I've only seen two hundred books."

"Then let's start with that. How much would those two hundred books be worth?"

"There's no guarantee they even came from here. It's just my hunch."

"*What's* your hunch? Talk straight, please. How much are those two hundred books worth?"

"In a bookstore, at retail . . . twenty grand. Maybe as much as thirty."

Her nostrils flared, blowing smoke. She looked ready to erupt.

Then she did erupt.

"Thirty thousand dollars! *Thirty thousand dollars for two hundred books!*" She leaped up and spilled her drink. "Son of a fucking bitch!" she screamed. "Do you have any idea how many books there were in that goddamn house?"

"Books are funny things," I said calmly. "Just because one's worth a lot, that doesn't necessarily mean anything as far as the others are concerned."

She was trembling now as she faced me. "What it means, Detective, is that old Stan wasn't quite the klutz that everybody thought. What it means is that Stan knew exactly what he was doing. And what that means, Mr. Janeway, is that there's an excellent possibility that all those books were worth money. Christ, we could be talking a million dollars here! Even the house is nothing compared with that!"

I didn't say anything.

"I will kill that bastard with my own bare hands," she said.

"I wouldn't try that."

"Get away from me! Don't you dare try to stop me."

"I will stop you if you take another step."

"Don't you threaten me. . . ."

"I'm trying to reason with you. Do you want to listen or do you want to fly off half-cocked and screw everything up?"

She sat and folded her hands primly. She made no effort

to blot her spilled drink, which was seeping into the carpet at her feet.

"First of all," I said, "we still don't know for a fact that it happened that way. Two, I still don't know if it was him: it could be you. Three, whoever it is has killed three people. I'm not talking metaphorically here, Ms. Davis. Have you ever seen anyone who's been shot in the face?"

She looked at her hands, which were trembling uncontrollably.

"It's one thing to say you're gonna kill somebody. This boy, whoever he is, is the one with the track record. He bashed the bookscout's brains out and shot two people in the head not two days ago. Do you think you want to get involved in something like that?"

She spoke through clenched teeth. "What do you want?"

"I want you to do nothing . . . understand? Don't make any phone calls, don't go ripping over there. Just sit tight and wait for me."

"God!" she cried. "How can I sit back and let that flaming asshole get away with this!"

"Nobody's getting away with anything. You can't hide eight thousand books in your hip pocket. I'm gonna find them, if I can get you to stay out of the way."

She didn't say anything. I said, "Can I get a couple of straight answers out of you?"

"About what?"

"You and him."

"There is no me and him. Never was. He has nothing to do with me."

"You were raised together."

"That's not my fault."

"Come on, Ms. Davis, what happened between you two?"

"Nothing. It was just a case of hate at first sight."

"Were you jealous of each other?"

"He always was." She lit another smoke; didn't realize that she had one going in the ashtray. "He was an adopted child. He always hated that. Hated me. I never had a chance with him, not from the first."

"Did he ever show any signs of violence, either as a child or later?"

"He never had the guts. He was always sneaky."

"Sneaky how?"

"I caught him looking in the window once . . . I was thirteen . . . that kinda stuff."

"Do you think he's capable of murder?"

She seemed to melt suddenly, and for a long, strange moment, I thought she might cry. She pulled herself out of it just as quickly.

"No," she said.

"That took a lot of effort."

"Damn right. I'd like to say yes, but I just don't think he could ever find the nerve to shoot someone. No, he'd be more the type to hire it done."

I thought of Neff's turtle-faced man.

"A hit man," I said.

"Sure. He'd do that, all right. I wouldn't put that past him at all"

42

I drove south, into the coming snowstorm. I thought about the U-Haul truck and the mileage that Bobby Westfall had racked up. I thought about Greenwald and the screwed-up Ballards and the turtle-faced man. Snow began to crust around the edges of my windshield. The road was getting slick. I had an odd feeling of some omniscient demon riding with me, a malignant force waiting to spring. The strange thing was, I couldn't remember Val Ballard's face: I could hear his voice and see his hands working as he sifted through his uncle's stuff; I could see his red tongue flicking as he licked and stuck labels on this item and that, but his face remained a blank. I could see Bobby Westfall easily enough, and we had only met a few times, months ago. I could see Peter and Pinky: silent passengers with the demon curled up between them. *C'mon, people, talk to me.* "Talk," I said out loud. Tell me something I don't already know. Who's the turtle-faced man, and where are the books, and how-oh-how had Rita McKinley's appraisal been so far off the mark?

In the old days, Littleton was a prime horse-racing town. Centennial was never a big-time track, but it wasn't the bush league either. Carol and I used to come down two or three times a summer to watch the horses run and lose a little of our hard-earned dough. Now when I come, all I feel is loneliness, and an aching sense of my own mortality. They're tearing everything down, and someday soon they'll come up behind me and tear me down too. Something as big as a racetrack ought to have a little bit of immortality attached to it. But they tore old Centennial down and plowed her under. Right out there where the grandstand stood are high-rise offices and apartment buildings. Oh, sacrilege. All that's left of the old days is the ever-flowing Platte: it snakes its way down from the mountains and winds past expensive subdivisions and subdivided farms and modern shopping centers built on the land of old ranches. In one of those houses, just south of the racetrack, Val Ballard lived.

I checked the address. The house sat back from the street in a grove of trees. It was very dark: the trees blotted out all light from the road. A wind had risen and the snow had blown in drifts over the driveway. I came in boldly, with my lights on, and sat for a moment with my lights playing across the front of the house. Nobody home, it looked to me. I turned off the lights, then the motor. The darkness was oppressive. I got out and followed my pen-light up the walk to the front door. I rang the bell, then knocked. Nothing. I walked around the house, into the teeth of the gale, and fought my way across the yard to the garage. He had gone somewhere and he had gone in a hurry. He had left the door up and there were rubber marks on the cement. I could still see the ruts he had left in the yard, only half buried under the snow.

I went back to the car and got my tools. I knew I was a sitting duck for anyone who drove up—my car was there in the open yard, so there'd be no running away from it. When I decide to commit suicide, I don't brood over it. I did think once of consequences. I could get three to five for this. Then I held the penlight in my teeth and picked open the front door lock.

The first thing to do was find an escape hatch. The back door. I crossed the main room and went through a dark corridor and found it. I checked it to make sure it could be opened easily. Fine. Well, not fine, but it wouldn't get any finer. This was it. I had come looking for Ballard, I would tell my executioners. The house was dark but I had noticed the garage door up and had gone around to check. That's how they happened to catch me walking around from the back yard. I would slip out the back way and walk non-chalantly around the house, and this was what I would tell them. I had stopped behind the house to take a leak, a nice touch, I thought, that gave some credibility to a shaggy-dog tale like that.

With that settled, I went through the house, looking for . . . what? I had a half-baked hunch I might even find Stan Ballard's books. The place to start was in the basement. I found it with no trouble, a set of dark stairs that led down from the kitchen. If he came home now, I was sunk. Forget the back door, I'd never make it. I took a long breath and started down. The little light led me to a finished room. There were no books: just a water bed, a chest of drawers, a big-screen TV, a VCR, and a wall of pornographic tapes. I could see at a glance the kind of entertainment he liked, with titles like *Love in Chains* and *Ginger's Fantasy* throbbing on the shelf. It didn't mean anything. There was a room off the main room and I went there and opened the door. No books: not much of anything. The room was unfinished, and there were a few boxes inside, but a peek in them revealed nothing but junk.

I left it all as I had found it. The next likely place was an attic. Ballard didn't have a walk-up attic, but I found a tiny trapdoor in the ceiling. I pushed it open with a broom, which I found in the kitchen. I gripped the rim and chinned myself up into the hole. With my little light in my teeth, I turned my head from one direction to another, dropped, chinned, and did it again from the other side. Nothing. It looked like he had never been up there: the place was two inches deep in dust and had never been disturbed.

I went through his living room. There wasn't even a Reader's Digest condensed book for the criminally brainless. In fact, Ballard didn't have a single book in his entire house that I could see. I looked through the kitchen cupboards, remembering that twice before I had found in closets and cupboards small stacks of very good books. No luck this time. So . . . the hell with the books: maybe I could find a gun. A lot of cases are broken that way, through the almost unbelievable incompetence and stupidity of the killer. I went into the bedroom and looked in all the normal places where a man might keep a gun, and found nothing.

I came at last to his den. He didn't even have a law book. I had never been in a lawyer's house that had not even one book around, and it felt almost empty. He had a filing cabinet and a rolltop desk, neither of which was locked. I opened the cabinet and found his dead files, duplicates of old cases long disposed. I flipped through the folders double-time, looking for high spots. There weren't any.

The bottom drawer was full of pornography. Another waste of time.

The desk had pigeonholes and compartments and many sliding drawers. The pigeonholes were empty, the compartments were full of dust, and the drawers were stuffed with pornography. I didn't go through the whole boring inventory: it just didn't look like the den of a guy who practiced much law.

I found what I found in the last possible place. On top of the desk, pushed far back where it lay in dark shadow, was a yellow pad. The top sheet was filled with doodles and notes. There was a name at the top—Rubicoff—and under it a figure, $1,235. There was a phone number. I recognized the exchange as east Denver, not far from my store. Rubicoff. It sounded familiar, but I couldn't remember from where. At the bottom of the paper he had done some multiplying: the figure 8,500 multiplied by various numbers from 10 to 150. Each time the writing got darker, more slashing, angrier. I didn't know what it meant but I had some guesses. The figure 8,500 might correspond roughly to the number of books in old Stan Ballard's library. The figures were guesswork—somebody's idea of what the library might be worth if the books averaged $10, $50, $75, and so on. He didn't know books very well: it's unheard of to get a high average on that big a library. On the other hand, I hadn't seen a book yet that was worth less than $100.

And what about Rubicoff? I'd lay odds he was the turtle-faced man. I was getting close to cracking it, I thought.

I wrote the number in my notebook. I put everything back exactly as it was. Then I got the hell out of there.

43

I sat in the car and listened to the wind. A cold fear was blowing across the Platte.

At a gas station about half a mile from Val Ballard's, I called Hennessey at home.

"Me, sweetheart," I said when he answered.

"Oh, lucky day."

"What'd you find out on that McKinley tape?"

"I don't want to talk about this on the phone."

"What's Lester doing, running a tap on you now?"

"You're puttin' my ass in one big crack, Cliffie."

"Hey, one big crack deserves another. Come on, Neal, give."

I let the line hiss for a moment.

"What do you expect me to say?" he said.

"I expect you to say yes, Virginia, there is a Santa Claus. I imagine you'll break into song, with the chorus of 'Over the River and Through the Woods.' I'm hoping somewhere along the line you'll tell me something about the McKinley tape."

He sighed. "Why don't you come on over here?"

" 'Cause I'm two thousand miles away and heading in the opposite direction."

"Then I guess I can't help you. I can't talk about it on the phone."

"They separated the voices, didn't they?"

"I don't want to talk about this. . . ."

"They separated the voices."

"I told you before, they can do wonders with modern equipment. You want to talk about that, fine, I can talk all night. I've become a regular scientist since I saw you at lunch, a real electronics wizard. Did you know they can take fifteen people and put 'em to talking all at once, then take machines and separate every voice? Did you know that, Cliffie? Got something to do with timber and pitch. And all I always thought timber was was something loggers yell when they're chopping trees down."

"What did Peter say?"

"I think he yelled timber. Maybe he was an old logger up in Oregon."

"You're a pain in the ass, Hennessey," I said, and meant it.

"Oh yeah? Fine. Someday I'll sit down with you and compare notes and we'll see who the real pain in the ass is."

"It's you, Neal. You're becoming one of them."

"I got news for you. I always was."

"Hang up, then, if that's how it is."

We listened to each other's silence for ten seconds. Then, with an anger in his voice that I'd never heard, he said, "Cliff, you're abusing our friendship. It's bad enough when you put your own neck in a noose, but you want me to stick mine in too and call it for old time's sake. Dammit, you're gonna cost me my badge before this is over."

"I'm sorry you feel that way," I said, but I hung in there, knowing that my silence was working on him.

"God damn it," he said. "This isn't right, Cliff."

I didn't say anything.

"The bastard said nothing, all right? Not one damn thing you or anybody else can use. You want his exact words? I ought to know 'em, I been sitting here listening to the damn thing all afternoon. He said, 'Get away, get away.' He said that twice. Then he said, 'There's nothing you can do to me, people already know.' "

"What people?" I said—aloud, but to myself.

"I should've asked him that," Hennessey said.

"What people?" I said again.

The line was quiet for a moment.

"What about Miss Pride? Did she say anything?"

"She said, 'Oh, hi, everything's fine.' "

I blinked. "She said what?"

"She said, 'Everything's fine, I'll call you back.' "

The silence stretched.

"If you're waiting for an encore, there isn't any," Hennessey said. "That was it, short and sweet: we busted our humps over nothing. I hope you're satisfied."

"Yeah, Neal, I'm satisfied."

"I want you to be happy, old pal. If you're not happy, I'm not happy. Is there anything else I can do for you, buddy?"

"I don't think so."

"Good. Don't ever do that to me again."

"Look, I'm sorry about—"

But he had already hung up.

44

I called Rita McKinley, a futile gesture, I knew.

But, wonder of wonders, she answered the phone. Scooped it up on the first ring.

"Rita McKinley," she said. I love women who answer the phone that way, crisp and cool and professional. "Go to hell you slob" might have been okay too, when the best I expected was a monotone from the damned answering machine.

"Not the real McKinley! Not the genuine article, in the flesh?"

"Janeway!"

"Was that sound I heard you falling off your chair with pleasure at hearing my voice?"

"Where the hell have you been?"

"So far today, everybody I've called has asked me that. I was hoping to get some variation on the main theme from you."

"I've been trying to call you all day. What happened?"

"It's all in the newspaper, Miss Sunshine. I know how you like the crime news, so I assume you've read all about it."

"I want to see you."

"Now this is a definite step in the right direction. After you banished me to the National Leprosarium in Carville, Louisiana, I thought the only way I'd get back up there was to practice pole-vaulting."

"Can you come up? It's snowing pretty hard."

"Be just as hard for you to come down. You got anything to eat up there?"

"Two steaks in the fridge."

"What happened to the diet?"

"Don't ask."

"I'll be up in a while. Better give me at least an hour and a half."

"I'll leave the gate open."

It came again, that chill. "Don't do that," I said. "Look, it's nine-thirty now, I'll meet you at the gate at eleven. Drive your car down. If I'm not there, come back at half past."

"Why don't you want me to leave it open? What's the problem?"

"Tell you when I get there."

I headed west, into the stormy mountains.

45

It was truly a miserable drive. I sloshed along the deserted freeway and slipped into the canyon. By eleven o'clock I still hadn't reached Evergreen. I stopped at another gas station and called her, but she had the recording on. I left a cheery message and pressed on. The canyon too was deserted, leading to the inescapable conclusion that I was the only damn-fool in the state on the highways tonight. The headlights threw up a glare that was blinding, and I couldn't use my brights. Back and forth went the car, left and right in the twisted contour of the canyon road: it reminded me of a pendulum, or a hypnotist's watch. Visions floated on the periphery of my sight. I saw Peter walking beside the car: nervous, furtive. He turned slightly and opened a door and there, yawning back into the dark, was my bookstore. It was empty, except for Miss Pride. Peter was upset. He was so upset that Miss Pride was trying to call me at Rita's house. Then I lost the picture. I knew it was still playing out there but I couldn't see anything. It was like a TV show with the

330

picture turned off. I could hear voices but I couldn't see them.

Miss Pride: *Let me talk to him, Peter. Give me the phone.*

Extrapolate, Janeway, figure it out. Figure it out and maybe the lights will come on again.

Someone had come to the front street window. Peter Bonnema locked eyes with death through a quarter inch of clear plate glass.

Miss Pride: *There's nobody on the line.*

Peter, his voice rising to a panic pitch: *It's a fucking tape recorder!*

And death walked in.

Miss Pride: *Someone's come in, I'll have to call you back.*

That's what I had heard. Hennessey had heard something else.

Peter knew. He knew exactly what was happening.

Get away! Get away! There's nothing you can do to me! People already know!

What people?

There was the source of that cold fear I had felt.

If Peter had bartered names for a few final seconds, those people were in trouble. Whether they knew anything or not, he had signed their death warrants.

My lights picked out her road. It looked like a tunnel, slick and steep and dangerous.

I shoved the car into four-wheel drive and started up.

I wasn't sure how far it was: a couple of miles, I thought, to the gate, maybe another hundred yards after that. I passed a car that had slipped off the road: clattered past it, kept going. You don't stop on a drive like that: you keep the wheels turning, keep the traction, try to slug your way up the hill. I had reached the steepest part of the incline, a place that shot up suddenly and gained hundreds of feet in no time—simple enough in dry weather with the sun shining, not so simple now. I bumped over ruts and kept going. The canyon yawned mistily to my right. The wind was just vicious.

I passed the last of the side roads. There were no lights anywhere, or perhaps it was just that I couldn't see them in the storm. The snow got deeper as I went higher. Not gonna make it, I thought: I could feel the car losing ground with every foot. The road had taken a hairpin curve and now the canyon lay off to my left. I couldn't see anything but snow. I began to look for a place to park and found it a few minutes later: a simple widening of the road at a place where it curved again and began climbing. I pushed my front wheels into a snowbank and stopped.

This was dangerous stuff. I had no coat—only the jacket I had worn to Levin's office. It was adequate for a late-autumn Denver afternoon but wouldn't do for a trek to the Pole. The only hat I had was a silly knitted thing in the trunk. This is how people die in Denver: they start out thinking they're going for a walk; one thing leads to another and it turns into something else. I shimmied the gun around on my belt and zipped the jacket. I got the hat from the trunk and got some bullets for the gun; put the hat on my head and the bullets in my pockets and away I went. The snow was deep, but I was fit and I made good time. I slipped and fell a couple of times but did no harm. I wasn't yet cold—that's another deceptive thing about Rocky Mountain weather, how it sneaks up on you. On the coast, when it gets down to freezing, you freeze: here, I've gone out in short sleeves when the temperature was in the thirties and never felt the need for even a sweater. Then, half an hour later, you notice your fingers are turning blue. Oh, well, it couldn't be much farther. The road was leveling off now: I remembered that from the other day. I'd be there in no time at all, a piece of cake. McKinley and I would spend Christmas together and live happily ever after. Trees were on both sides now: it was very dark. I kept my little light in my teeth and kept my head down, tried to keep my spirits up, and most of all I kept going.

At last I saw the gate, a silvery vision wavering like a mirage. I didn't see her, though, and that bothered me. I looked at my watch: it was quarter to midnight. Could she be sitting up there in the trees with her lights off? My own light was so puny it barely reached to the gate, yet it must seem like a beacon from the 1939 New York World's Fair in this dark. Suddenly the whole world lit up. Flash! She turned on her headlights and it was like a nuclear bomb going off: it froze me stiff and actually drove me back a step. She had her brights on. She flicked them down and I heard the car start. I could see it now, a gaunt outline behind the fence. I saw her pass in front of the headlights and heard the jingle of keys. A moment later the gate swung open.

"Are you crazy?" Her voice was disembodied, floating on the storm.

"Good evening to you, too. How've you been?"

"Don't you know you can die in this weather dressed like that?"

"I was just thinking the same thing. Don't scold me, now, it's been a hard day."

I walked through the gate and got in her car. The heater felt great.

She was certainly dressed for it: she wore heavy pants and a coat that buttoned under her chin. Her hat was

333

pulled down over the coat and only a small square of her face could be seen: eyes, nose, and mouth. Enough.

God, I loved her then.

We went up the hill. The house looked mellow and warm. It was. I stood in the hall watching her take off her gloves, and I thought it again. Jeez, I love her. Never thought that before, about anybody.

What a shock.

"You believe in love at first sight?" I asked.

She turned and looked at me directly. "What a silly question."

"What's your silly answer?"

She took a long time answering, of course . . . a long, endearing moment.

"I think I do," she said. "Yeah."

She blushed.

"I am so tired of being alone," she said.

"Don't be, then."

"Damn you," she said. "Damn you, damn you, Janeway. Of all the things I didn't need in my life, the list begins and ends with you."

"I bet you've been thinking about me constantly."

"You're a thug. My God, a policeman! Me with a cop."

"I'm a refined, wizened dealer in rare books."

"You wouldn't know a rare book if it fell on your head."

"But I learn fast. I soak up knowledge like mere mortals eat soup. I'm witty, I'm bright; I'm a bundle of goddamn laughs in case you hadn't noticed." I stopped, realizing suddenly, sadly, that I had lifted the pitch somewhere. It was almost the same half-joking plea that Miss Pride had used the night she'd come begging for a job.

Rita was looking at me intently.

"Here's the best part," I said. "I don't mind taking orders from a woman."

"How kind of you. How generous."

"Can't you just see it, lighting up the night sky? Janeway and McKinley. What a wow, huh?"

"Six days ago I'd never heard of you. I was five thousand miles away, lying in the sun. Now you're not only taking me over, you're getting top billing."

"That doesn't mean anything. It's like in vaudeville: the straight man always gets top billing."

"Shut up," she said, coming close. She took off her coat and threw it somewhere. The air seemed electric between us: the fine hair was standing up on her arms and neck. I knew if we touched, the static would fry us both.

She threw her arms around me and kissed me hard. The world went pop.

"This is insane," she breathed into my neck.

I kissed her too. Her hand was on my gun. I could feel her heart; I could hear it, like a distant drumbeat.

"You never cared about books," she said. "It's all just a ruse to get in my pants."

"I can't keep anything from you."

"Well," she said. "I guess it worked."

46

I remembered something Ruby had said: *It's the most hypnotic business a man can do.* He was talking about the book business, equating it to making love. I still had the gun in my hand: I don't even remember now how that happened, but somehow the three of us wound up in bed together. I clutched the gun and held on for dear life. That piece of cold blue steel was my last link with sanity. I shuddered my way inside her and she jerked, pulling me all the way down. I held on to the gun and went all the way. This was so right. I closed my eyes and lost it. Oh, I lost it all. Anyone could've come through the front door and killed us both: I wouldn't've known, much less cared. They could've come through with a battering ram and six regiments of cavalry. I think maybe they did. They ripped the door out of the frame and stormed through on the way to the Little Bighorn, and the last man through picked up the door, gave it a paint job, hung it back, closed and locked it good as new. Brushed himself off, saluted, and called me sir: then left us there, before I knew they had come.

"Janeway," she said.

"Mmmm."

"Tell me that isn't your gun mashed against my head."

I took the gun in my other hand and propped myself up.

She began to laugh. "Now that's one for the books. I've just been screwed by a man with a gun and it wasn't even rape."

"That's what you think," I said. "I never had a chance."

47

It was two o'clock in the morning and we were just getting around to the steaks. "This is my day for decadence," Rita said. "Lose my virginity. Go back on meat. I seem to be a wanton, savage creature at heart."

"Jeez, were *you* a virgin too?" I said.

She tousled my hair. I liked that. It showed affection, not just lust. I opened two beers. The steaks were almost done.

We ate. The food was wonderful, the company superb. We didn't talk at all.

It wasn't till much later, sitting by the fire, when she started to unwind. "I called Paul right after I talked to you the other night," she said. "The night . . . it happened."

"Paul is . . . ?"

"The guy I was gonna marry."

"I love the past tense. Go on."

"It was three o'clock in the morning back there. I got him out of bed. Guess I could've waited, but somehow it seemed too important. God, it seemed earthshaking. I felt like my whole world had tilted off its axis."

I kissed the side of her head.

"I called him to say good-bye," she said.

Suddenly there was no more white space, no eternity between the lines. "I met him in Greenpeace a couple of years ago. That's where I go every summer, to work in the field. I saved a whale this year, can you imagine that? Got in a wet suit, put myself between him and the killers, and harassed them till they went away. I didn't know I'd have the courage to do it till the time came: then there was no thought of not doing it, it was what I'd come for. We lost a volunteer this year, did you know that? We had a young man killed in a protest over a nuclear test. I knew him slightly, but his death made everything very suddenly real. I knew I could die too, and I didn't want to. I expected to be blown into nothing every minute. Have you ever seen what a modern harpoon gun can do? It's frightening, and here you are, taunting them, daring them to shoot you with it, knowing they'd like to do just that if they could find a way to call it an accident. They had me on NBC that night. Paul got me a videotape of the broadcast and I never looked at it: it diminishes the real experience too much. It's what Hemingway meant when he wrote about hunting and war. Everything's ruined when you talk too much. I used to read that and think, What macho garbage, but god damn it, he's right. They show a twenty-second clip on Tom Brokaw and what it really was was a two-hour test of wills. Hemingway was right, the old fool. You do something that people call heroic and you can't talk about it, you can't sit in front of a tube and gloat over a tape, all you can do is carry it in your heart. Even talking about it this much fucks it up."

She pointed to the picture on the wall: the guy in the wet suit.

"That's Paul. I'll take his picture down if you want."

"Leave it," I said. I could afford to be generous. I knew Paul would be glad to let me be the picture on the wall and him be here on the sofa.

"He's a good man. I don't know why things never really . . . what's the word?"

"Ignited."

"Yeah, that's the word. He really is a fine man. Doesn't deserve a bitch like me. You, on the other hand . . ."

"I think I can handle you."

"I'm sure you do. So handle me, Janeway: tell me what you want to know."

"Anything you want to tell."

"Oh, please. Don't go soft on me now. You've been pushing me since the moment I first saw you. Long before that, if you count that snotty phone message."

"Then tell me all of it."

It took her a while to get started. We loosened up with brandy and put some logs on the fire.

"I was working in a bookstore in Dallas. We had a customer named William J. Malone. You know the name?"

"Uh-uh."

"You would, if you'd been in the business longer. William J. Malone was a collector of books. You didn't see his name much in the *AB*. He was one of those guys who didn't like limelight. A lot like me that way. Very private. No friends. Distant. I guess to people who didn't know him, full of mystery. But all the so-called big boys of the book world knew him. He had no credit limit with anyone. A thug from your side of the tracks would say he had deep pockets. And the ruling passion of his life was books. Modern lit, that was his thing. He was the last of his line and he never married, but God—what a bookman! Malone knew everything. He had a wall of reference books but he didn't need them. He had it all in his head. The joy of his life was to go into a bookstore and find wonderful things. He didn't care about the money, it was all a game. He paid what they asked and never wanted a discount, didn't matter whether he spent ten dollars or ten thousand. If he wanted something, he got it.

"Malone knew more about books than any ten dealers I ever met. In Dallas, where he lived then, he was a major celebrity in the bookstores, though he tried not to be. I don't know what first attracted him to me—maybe the fact that I didn't scrape and bow whenever he walked in the door. All I know is, suddenly he was in my life. What kept drawing him back to that one bookstore turned out to be . . . am I vain enough to say it? . . . me. We had something going from the start, long before we ever talked of such things. It's like something in the air that only the two of you can see. You know how that can be, Janeway, I know you know."

"I know now."

"Yes. That's exactly right. And when it happens, you don't care who the other person is, how old he is, how much money he's got. People who let stuff like that matter to them are fools. Things like race, religion, politics—none of it matters. So one day Malone came in and asked if I wanted to be his assistant. I quit my job on the spot. The guy I was working for was a jerk: I'd've quit in another week anyway. I didn't even ask Malone what kind of assistant I would be. I didn't care. I had been bouncing around the book business for a few years—libraries, bookstores— and I was tired of it. I was ready for something different. Well, I got it.

"For the next four years we went everywhere. We went all over the world looking for books. Everything I know that's worth knowing I learned in that time. We lived in Paris for six months, went to England every summer. One of the most interesting Jack London collections—part of it's still here, in the big room—we bought in Tokyo, of all places. You get the idea: there isn't much more to tell. Malone never went back to Texas and neither did I. He bought this place. He liked the solitude. He liked the fact that it came with that big fence already up. You can't put up a fence like that anymore—too many zoning restrictions—but they won't let you tear it down either. Malone had always liked Colorado, not in the summer when tourists come swarming in, but in the dead of winter. He liked being snowed in. He was always different than everybody else. I'd still be with him, if he'd lived. I don't think of it as a mad love affair, it wasn't like that. But I know I'd still be with him."

"He died, though."

"You don't have to ask that. I'm sure you've heard the stories. What's the version you heard? Was I supposed to've killed him for his money or his books?"

"It was just talk."

"Yeah, right. Well, I did kill him in a way. He was fifty years old. He smoked too much and couldn't quit, he had always smoked and he was dying from it. I guess there comes a time when it doesn't matter anymore. One day he said to me, 'Rita, I'm not going to die in a hospital.' I knew then what I was in for. During the next couple of days he tended to business. Had a lawyer come up, dictated what amounted to his last will. I knew he was leaving it all to me. It was never discussed between us, but I knew him so well, and you might not believe this . . . I didn't care. We were so businesslike. That's even how he wanted to die, according to a schedule of his own making. He'd had a lethal injection made up—I knew where it was and what it was there for, and when the time came I went to the cabinet and got the stuff and helped him as best I could. God, I was such a coward. I couldn't keep from crying and trembling. . . . I had never seen anyone actually die, and I know he wanted to go with me keeping a stiff upper lip but I just couldn't. I held his head on my lap while he gave himself the shot. That should've been all there was to it, only . . . he wouldn't die. People tell you that stuff always works: it's supposed to be painless and you're gone like the snap of a finger, only it didn't work that way. The man would . . . not . . . die. I thought he just didn't get enough. It knocked him out before . . . you know. And he was in such pain! He writhed and twitched . . . and still he wouldn't die! So I loaded that needle and I gave him another shot, enough to kill a dinosaur . . . and still he lived. It was like some nightmare. Then I remembered his gun.

"I knew it was in the bedroom, but it took me a while to find the shells. I don't know much about guns but I thought I could figure it out. I came into the room and sat beside him. His breathing was heavy and labored. He was struggling, fighting, and I took the gun and put it to his head and cocked it. I remember thinking, 'How can I do this, how can I possibly find the strength?' Then he seemed to relax and I knew he was gone. He just . . . slipped away . . . just in time. Another ten seconds and I might've been in real trouble. I didn't even know how to uncock the stupid gun. I pulled the trigger and blew a hole in the wall. You can still see the mark. I think the sheriff suspects me of something even to this day. When they read the will, I just sat there and didn't say anything, but it was an absolutely grand motive for murder. I knew Malone was well-off, but I was shocked at how much there really was. He never told me how much he had: it was

343

his business and I never particularly wanted to know. I guess I was lucky: I might've had some real explaining to do if Malone hadn't had the foresight to tell his lawyer what he intended. Even now there's a lot of suspicion. To the people on this mountain, and to some in the book trade, I'm the woman who killed her boyfriend and got away with it. So I keep to myself, don't have much to do with anyone, and that's the story. That's how I became rich and famous. It's also why I've been giving it away in buckets. It never really felt like mine."

The day dawned cold and wet and miserable, one of those days in the Rockies when it's too warm to snow and too cold to rain. We had slept for a few hours, and I came awake with her head nestled under my chin and my hand cradling her breast. I lay still, reluctant to wake her. But there was a killer to catch, and today was the day, and the day wasn't getting any younger. I thought I had narrowed it down to an either-or. Everything about it had begun to make sense, except her part in it, and that made no sense at all.

She turned over and opened her eyes. She touched my face and said, "Love me again," and I couldn't, couldn't, say no. Then, spent, we lay under the covers and locked eyes and touched. At some point I said we had to get up. She said, "We don't have to do anything, not ever again." She did get up, though, and for a moment she stood by the bed, naked and lovely. She walked away and I heard the shower start. I stared up at the darkest part of the house and thought about it. And I thought: God bless America, I hope you're not mixed up in this. I tell you it'll break my heart if you are.

48

Either-or: six of one, half a dozen of the other. We came down from the mountain and I did a mental crapshoot. It came up Littleton. We rolled in on Hampden and turned south on Santa Fe Drive. The streets were still slick but it was daylight now and I had made the drive down in less than forty minutes.

I pulled into a Denny's and stopped.

"This's where you get out."

"I told you before, Janeway, I have a constitutional problem with fast food."

"You'll live through it. Have a cup of coffee. Read the paper. And just wait here for me."

"How long am I supposed to wait?"

"Till I come back."

She gave me her long-suffering look. "I hope this isn't the kind of treatment I can expect from you."

She got out and came around to my side. I rolled down the window and she stood for a moment looking at me, her coppery hair wafting around her head. This is how I'll

John Dunning

remember her twenty years from now, I thought: her price-less face framed in the car window on a lousy gray day. She leaned in and kissed me. "Don't get killed," she said in a tiny voice. "You too," I said. She had already turned away and was walking toward the restaurant. "Be back before you know it," I called, but she didn't do anything at that. Strange girl, I thought: strange woman, still full of secrets.

Our discussion that morning had been brief and to the point.

"I'd like you to stay with me today," I had said.

"Sounds lovely. What'll we do? Wanna fly to New York?"

"I'm going out to get the guy who killed those three people."

"And for this you need me?"

"I need to know you're safe," I had said. "I think there's a possibility he may try to kill you next."

A few minutes later I pulled up at Val Ballard's house. I could see the house in the misty morning. If I walked along the road, as I now did, I could soon see the garage. It was closed: the doctor was in. The road told me nothing: it was so full of puddles and melting snow that there was just no reading it. But the furrow he had plowed across the back yard was gone, washed away completely in the night, and there were no fresh tracks to take its place.

He had been home, then, for some time.

I didn't know what to expect: I just hoped I was ready for it. I had my gun in my hand with my jacket folded over it. Now I had to walk across thirty yards of open space to reach the house. The windows were dark: any of them were perfect hiding places for a sniper. I took a breath and went: walked up to the front door just like the Fuller brush man.

There, I flattened against the wall and listened. The house sounded exactly like it had the last time I had been here, nine hours ago: in other words, there was no sound at all. I started around it, stopping at every window. I peered down the hall and saw nothing. Moved on to the next window. Kitchen. No help. A ray of sunshine was starting to peek through the clouds. It cast a beam almost like a rainbow through the kitchen window. I eased my way to the back of the house. Turned the corner. The next window looked into his den, and there he was, sitting at the desk, his back to the window. He wasn't doing anything. I thought maybe he was asleep: that's how still he was. But suddenly he moved: dropped his feet, fumbled, lit a cigarette. He sat there smoking and I stood outside, not two feet from the back of his head, wondering what to do next.

There were really only two choices. I decided to play it straight. I walked around the house, went to the front door, and rang the bell.

I heard him coming immediately.

He jerked open the door and started to say, "It's about fuckin' time." He got most of it out before he realized that it wasn't about time at all.

"Who the hell're you?"

"Detective Janeway. I talked to you at your uncle's house, remember?"

"Yeah, sure. What're you doing here? Hell, it's only eight o'clock."

"Let me in and I'll tell you."

"Look, I'm expecting somebody. I don't have much time."

"That's okay, I won't take much."

Reluctantly he moved away from the door. I went in, keeping the gun handy under the jacket. You never knew what might happen with people.

We went into the living room. It looked vaguely like a place I'd seen before. He asked if I wanted some coffee. I wanted some badly, but I said no. One of my rules is to never eat or drink with people who might want to kill me.

He didn't look the part somehow: he was dressed well, in dry clothes: his hair was combed, and in fact he looked bushy-brained and sharp, like a lawyer about to go into court for a big case. He must've been sizing me up too. "You look like you've been through a war," he said.

"I have."

"I'll bet it's interesting as hell, but like I said, I'm expecting company. What can I do for you?"

"You can tell me what you know about your uncle's books."

He was a lousy liar. He looked away and tried to shrug it off. "What's there to tell? We went all through this."

"We went through something but it wasn't this. Look, you've got things to do and so do I. D'you want to tell me about it, or shall we wait till Mr. Rubicoff gets here and we can all go through it together?"

It was a sucker punch and he almost fell off his chair from the force of it.

"Why don't you get the hell outta here right now?"

"Fine. It's your house. But I'll be back, and I'll tell you something, Ballard. You're gonna have to be a lot better lawyer than I think you are to get yourself out of this mess."

I got up to leave.

"What mess? What're you talking about?"

"Oh, I think you know. Let's not waste time with this."

"Wait a minute. There's no sense being mean about it. We can get along. I mean, can't we get along?"

"I can."

"Sit down."

I eased myself down into the chair.

"How'd you know about Rubicoff?" he said.

"I've got ways. Sometimes they're slow and ponderous but I usually find out in the end. For instance, I know about Rubicoff but I don't know everything. Why don't you tell me?"

"Tell you what?"

We were fencing. This could go on forever. I groped for the words to break us out of it.

"Let's pretend I don't know anything; I'll like it better that way. You tell me who Rubicoff is and how you got mixed up with him."

"He's a dick I hired."

"Keep going. What's it got to do with the books?"

"I hired him to help me find the sons of bitches."

"Let me get this straight. First you all but give the books away. Now you hire a guy to help you get 'em back."

"I didn't know then what I know now."

"Which is what?"

"They're worth a fortune, that's what. And they're still mine, pal, make no mistake about that."

"You sold 'em. You signed a bill of sale."

"Doesn't matter what the hell I signed: that deal was done on a fraudulent premise. The guy knew something I couldn't be expected to know. You just let me find those babies, we'll see who winds up owning them in a court of law."

"How'd you find out about them?"

"About three weeks ago, a guy came and told me."

"Uh-huh. A guy named Peter Bonnema."

"I didn't know his name then; didn't know anything about him. I got a call out of the blue. The guy said I'd given away a fortune and he knew where the stuff was. He had some of it himself, and if I wanted it all back I'd meet him in a café on East Colfax at nine that night."

"Then what happened?"

"He didn't show up. I waited till ten. I don't know what there was about it . . . something told me it was for real. Then when he didn't show I said screw it, some silly bastard wasting my time. But he called me back the next day. I started to hang up on him, but there was something about it . . . I don't know which end is up when it comes to books, and I couldn't care less, but I knew there was something to it. Sometimes you just have a hunch."

I nodded.

"So at nine o'clock that night I'm in the same skuzzy café, and this time the guy comes in and sits down at my table. He was a goddamn bum, a tramp, for Christ's sake. I almost got up and walked out. Then he opens this box and takes out a book. It looks like any other book to me. Who gives a damn about a stupid book? But the guy says, 'Look at this,' and he takes out a little booklet, a catalog from some book dealer in Boston. 'Look at this,' he says, and he shows me in the catalog what the asking price is for a copy of the book he's holding. Six hundred mazumas, buddy! I damn near lost my supper. One fuckin' book, six hundred big ones. Then he takes out another book and another catalog. Three-fifty. Do I need to tell you that by now he's got my attention?"

"What did you do?"

"Asked what he wanted. He wanted one-third, a three-way split. I guess he'd done his homework. Anyway, he knew there was that third party involved."

"Your sister."

He waved that off with an impatient grimace. "Let's just

say that the guy knew what was involved. Before he'd tell
me what happened to the books, I'd have to draw up an
agreement and have it signed by . . . you know. Then I'd
have to sign it myself and we'd have to have it notarized. I
didn't care. The damn thing wouldn't be worth the paper
it's written on. Anybody could break a document like that
when it's based on blackmail or fraud. So I said sure, I'd
have it all drawn up, nice and goddamn legal. He's playing
in my ballpark now. You don't sheist the shysters, Janeway,
and I'm not nearly as bad a lawyer as you think I am. You
bet I'd sign it. We'd see what happened later, in court."

"But then the guy got killed."

"Yeah. I knew I was onto something then."

"So you hired the gumshoe."

"That's right, and a lot of good it's done me so far."

"What's he been doing?"

"Nothing exciting, you can bet on that. He can't find his
ass with both hands, if you want my opinion."

"Where'd you go last night, Ballard?" I said suddenly.

"How'd you know I went anywhere?"

"Tried calling you a couple of times."

"I went driving around. I couldn't get ahold of Rubicoff.
I called his office, called his house—I did everything but go
through City Hall, and I couldn't get anything but that
friggin' answering service. I'm paying this guy more money
than a lawyer makes, and I can't get him on the phone.
Then I finally did get him and he couldn't see me. I
couldn't believe it. He's got another case he's working on,
and that pissed me off. He's gonna be out of town all day
today, can you beat that? A whole goddamn day I'm losing
while this keyhole-peeper is chasing down another guy's
wife in Santa Fe. He says all he can do for me is see me for
a few minutes this morning on his way to the airport. Can

you believe that? Eight hundred dollars I've paid that clown, and maybe he can squeeze me in at eight o'clock on his way to catch a plane for somebody else."

"So you went driving around . . ."

"Yeah. No place special, just workin' off steam. What's the big deal?"

"Maybe nothing. I wanted to talk to you about your uncle's house."

"What about it?"

"I may be interested in buying it."

"You're kidding." Suddenly he was a pussycat.

"I'm not kidding, but I don't have a helluva lot of money to throw around."

"You won't need a lot for my half."

"That's what Ms. Davis said. It may be the only thing you two have ever agreed on."

"What's your offer?"

I shrugged an apology. "Fifty."

"I'll get the papers drawn up this weekend. I want to be done with it."

"That's fine," I said pleasantly. I asked if the house had had a recent appraisal done, if it had been inspected for termites, if there'd been any plumbing problems. I chatted and blabbed, went through all the stalling tactics I could muster, and a few minutes later Rubicoff arrived. We heard his car pull into the yard and the door slam. Ballard's kettle boiled over again. "Just watch what the son of a bitch says!" he shouted. "He won't have time to talk, he'll be in a hurry now 'cause he's late for his flight. Eight hundred I pay this jerk and this is what I get."

He went to the door and threw it open. Footsteps came up the walk. I moved slowly forward, the gun still under my jacket. I saw a shadow pass the window.

Their voices blended. Rubicoff was saying he was sorry, he'd get back on the case in a day or two but right now all he had was a few minutes. Ballard shouted him down. "As far as I'm concerned, pal, you can fuckin' stay in Santa Fe! Gimme my money back, you goddamn crook!"

There was a scuffle: Ballard had thrown a punch. It couldn't have been much of one because two seconds later he was flat on the floor. The guy had decked him without breaking stride. I walked around Ballard, who was struggling to sit up, and I stared into the face of the dick known as Rubicoff.

No turtle face. No flaring nostrils. He was short and bald. He looked like anything but a private detective who had just put his client down for the count.

"You want some too?"

"Not me, bud," I said. "I'm just the lady from the welcome wagon."

I eased my way past, went down the road, and got in my car.

49

Rita came out of the restaurant carrying a newspaper and a steaming bag of goodies. "Well," she said, "I don't see any murderer shackled in the back seat."

"Don't push me, McKinley. Get in."

I headed north toward Denver, up Santa Fe Drive into the heart of the rush hour. She had brought me a king-size cup of coffee and a sweet roll loaded with cinnamon and sugar. She fed it to me while I drove, in tiny morsels between sips of coffee.

"This stuff will kill you," she said. "It's probably half and half, cholesterol and cancer-causing preservatives. You can have mine too if you want it."

"Thanks but no thanks. One dose of death's enough for a morning."

She ate the second roll herself.

We were in heavy traffic, halfway to Denver, when she opened the newspaper. "Interesting item this morning. Your friend Mr. Newton got himself chopped up. I see you were the main witness, as usual. How come you don't tell me the interesting stuff in your life?"

"You get too excited. Read it to me while I drive."

"Sure." She folded the paper over and read.

Nothing I didn't know, except that Crowell still hadn't talked to police and Newton was listed as serious but expected to make it. Jackie's altercations with police, including his continuing troubles with me, were summarized at the end.

I thought of Barbara with a flash of guilt.

"I guess it proves something," I said. "You can drive anybody to murder."

"It proves something else," Rita said. "Murphy's law."

"Which one?"

"Time wounds all heels."

Ruby lived on Capitol Hill, in the 1300 block of Humboldt. I parked out front on the street, and told Rita to stay put.

The apartment was on the third floor. Ruby's face was still full of sleep as he opened the door. "Who the hell's this? Dr. J?" He was in that early-morning fog common to nighthawks, trying valiantly to jump-start his heart with a third cup of coffee. He waved me to a chair, handed me a coffee cup, nodded to the pot simmering on the stove, and disappeared into the john. I heard water splashing and a moment later the toilet flushed. I poured myself a cup, looked around, and sat in the chair. It was a neat place, which surprised me. I could see back into the bedroom, which was also neat except for the unmade bed. It was a plain apartment, almost stark, with high ceilings and old-fashioned radiator steam heating. There were framed nudes on the walls, four lovely Weston prints that added to the bare landscape. I liked it: could've lived there myself.

Ruby came out, fastening his shirt. He still looked foggy, disjointed. He sat and sipped his coffee and only gradually seemed to remember that he had company.

"What's goin' on? What're you doin' out here this time o' day?"

"How long's it take you to wake up?"

"Hour . . . two. I don't get started till the day's half gone. Gotta open the damn store this week. Neff's supposed to be opening, but he still don't feel good. I think he wants to stay away from there, if you ask me. This thing's got him scared plenty. Want some coffee?"

"Got some."

"Oh."

I leaned toward him, the cup clasped in my hands, warming them. "I want to ask you a few more questions."

At that point I had only one essential question. But an idea had begun forming in my mind.

"Tell me about those books again, Ruby."

"What books?"

"The ones Neff bought in Broomfield the day Peter and Pinky were killed."

"Like what more do you want to know?"

"It was a woman, wasn't it?"

"Yeah. Lady moving out of town."

"Did you talk to this woman?"

"On the phone, sure."

"Recognize her voice?"

"Why should I? I never met the lady."

"Did her voice sound like anybody you might know?"

"Jeez, I can't remember. I wasn't thinking in that context. She was just a voice on the phone."

"How much did the buy cost you?"

"Fifteen hundred. And if you think that wasn't a bitch to get up on the spur of the moment . . ."

"How did you get it up?"

"Well, there's still a guy or two who'll loan me money. We wholesaled a few items. Neff borrowed the rest."

"How much did each of you borrow?"

"All's I could get was a couple of bills. We wholesaled a couple of books for three. Neff had to come up with a grand."

"Where'd he get the grand?"

"Hell, he's got his friends, I've got mine."

"How'd you hear about this woman in the first place?"

"She called us cold. Saw our name in the phone book."

"When was this?"

"That same morning."

"So you must've put the deal together in an hour or two."

"We had to, else the books be gone. You know how it is when you get a crack at this kinda stuff. You gotta move now."

"How'd you know the stuff was good?"

"Sometimes you can just tell, Dr. J. What do we have to lose driving up there? The lady seemed to know her books. I mean, she knew 'em inside, outside, six ways from Sunday. None of this chickenshit 'what'll you give me' stuff. She reads off the titles and says what she wants, and she gives us plenty of room to make out on the deal. She knew exactly what she was doing. When you get somebody who talks to you like that, you've got to assume she's got what she says. If she don't, you bring your money back home."

"So you had the deal done by when?"

"We had the money together by, oh . . . two o'clock."

"Then what happened? Did you call her back?"

"She wouldn't give us a number: said she'd already turned off her phone and she'd have to call us."

"Which she did."

"Yeah, just a few minutes after we got the dough together. She calls up and says she'll meet us in Broomfield at three."

"That's when she talked to you?"

"Yeah, just for a minute. I answered the phone. But most of her dealing was with Neff."

"When you answered the phone, she asked to speak to him?"

"Yeah."

"And they agreed to meet . . . and Neff went right after that."

"That's right."

"He left around what . . . two-thirty?"

"I guess it was around then."

"And got back around five."

"Yeah. The deal took no time at all. The woman had just what she said, and it was all top-grade primo stuff. All Neff had to do was look at the stuff and hand her the dough, then drive back here."

"Then he went to the can and you started going through the books."

"Yeah. What's all this about, Dr. J?"

"This woman you talked to. You sure you never heard her voice before?"

"Hell, that's a tough question, Dr. J. I only talked to her a couple of seconds."

I picked up his telephone and dialed Rita's number. When her recording came on, I held it to Ruby's ear.

"I guess that *could* be her. Come to think of it, she did sound like somebody . . ." He squinted, listening. "Who the hell is that—Rita McKinley?"

I didn't say anything.

"That could be her, I guess," Ruby said.

"Did Neff and Rita McKinley ever meet before that day?"

"Well, I told you she's been in our store a couple of times. He might've seen her. I do remember when she was in last year, Neff wasn't here. He had taken off and gone back east, if I remember right. Bookscouting trip. I do remember that the whole time McKinley was in the store there was nobody else but her and me. I felt funny, like a kid just getting started. Nobody's been able to make me feel like that in a long time."

"But Neff wasn't there then."

He shook his head. "What're you gettin' at, Dr. J?"

"I don't know, Ruby." I looked at my watch: it was eight forty-two. "Tell me about the books again. I only saw a couple of titles when I peeked in the box."

Now he came to life. He was fully awake, his motor running on something much stronger than coffee.

"Best batch of stuff we've gotten in years. You sometimes get these kinda books onesy-twosy, never fifty at once. Never three boxes and every one an absolute cherry. Let me see, there was a fine run of Tony Hillerman stuff. All the early ones. *Blessing Way. Dance Hall of the Dead. Fly on the Wall.* All in the two, three-hundred range. It's like pickin' hundred-dollar bills out of the box when those babies come up. You just sit there and add it up, like money in the bank. Hell, it's *better* than money in the bank, 'cause this stuff just keeps gettin' better and better. Hillerman's the hottest writer going, especially in these parts. There were a couple of Rex Stouts from the forties, just *so* salable, so damn good. And Ellery Queen's first book . . . I know you hear me say this all the time, Dr. J, but this was truly the world's best copy by far. Bunch of early Micheners that you don't see much anymore. *Bridges at Toko Ri,* and his first book, *South Pacific.* And some other stuff . . . uh . . ."

"*Clockwork Orange,*" I prompted. "I saw that one myself."

"Yeah, and that lovely Eastlake thing, *Go in Beauty.* What a goddamn book, Dr. J, what a total and complete killer. You ever read that?"

I shook my head.

"A killer book. And let's see, there was some black stuff, a Richard Wright, a Ralph Ellison, and half a dozen horror titles. Just a super *Hell House,* by Matheson . . . that's two and a half now for one this nice . . . and a couple of Lovecrafts, and, oh yeah, another great Matheson title, *I Am Legend.* Now there's a real vampire book, scared the living bejesus out of me one night when I had nothing else to do. So much better than *Salem's Lot,* even King says so, but King's such a nice guy he always puffs everybody else's books and pooh-poohs his own. He's right this time, though. And listen, speaking of black stuff, we got Toni Morrison's first book, *The Bluest Eye* . . . hell, even I never saw that book before. Killer copy, I bet we get five bills for it. Let's see what else . . . great *Crazy in Berlin,* a couple of bills on that, and some Van Guliks with that chink detective, you can get two-fifty easy for those, and a great Chesterton Father Brown with a jacket that'll knock your damn eye out . . ."

I looked at my watch. I had stopped listening. I knew he was lost, drifting through that vast and wonderful world that all true bookmen know. The most hypnotic business a man can do, like making love to a beautiful woman.

"You ever read that novel, Dr. J?"

I shook my head. I didn't know what novel he was talking about.

"My kinda stuff, baby. Just makes my blood go all tingly when I take it out of the box and it looks like it came off the press an hour ago. Yeah, we'll do great on this buy, even if we have to wholesale a few items to keep the wolf at bay. It's like a shot of new blood, you know what I mean? It puts joy back in your heart, makes the world right again for a little while. Wait a minute, there was more. . . ."

"That's enough, Ruby."

"Oh wait, I haven't given you much more than half of it, yet."

"It's enough anyway. I think I've got what I need."

"I don't understand you. What the hell're you lookin' for?"

I looked at my watch. "How's your sense of time, Ruby?"

"I don't understand."

"How long do you think we've been sitting here talking—just since I asked you what was in those boxes? How long do you think it's been?"

"Couldn't be much more than a minute. Two minutes at the outside. Couldn't be any longer than that."

"How about seven minutes and twenty seconds."

Surprise flicked across his face.

Then a flash of horror.

50

I juggled the pieces on the drive north. It gave me a sick, hollow feeling that deepened as we drove.

Rita knew that something had changed between us. She was very sharp that way.

"What's the matter?"

I shook my head and shrugged it off.

"What's wrong with you?" she insisted.

"Nothing." I looked at her and raised my voice to emphasize the point.

I saw her back stiffen. You couldn't bully her or force your will. You could mandate silence by being silent, but you couldn't make the mistake of believing that her own silence meant she was putting up with it.

We went at least ten miles before she spoke again.

"Where're we going? You mind telling me that?"

"Going to see a fella."

"What fella?"

I looked at her again. "You ever hear of Emery Neff?"

"I don't know . . . I guess I've heard that name. He owns one of the bookstores, doesn't he?"

"You never met him?"

"I don't think so."

"You never had occasion to sell him any books?"

"How do I know? Do you remember everybody you ever sold books to? I'll tell you something, I don't much like the way you're acting."

"I'm not acting."

She watched me for a moment, then turned away and lapsed into a curious wooden silence that matched my own. We couldn't talk and we couldn't be quiet: it was so deadly I had to turn on the radio, something I never do when I have people in the car. A couple of educated idiots were screaming at each other on KOA, giving a bad impression of what passes today for talk radio. I couldn't stand it. Eventually I found KEZW, a nostalgia station. They were playing "Sam's Song," a vocal banter by Bing and Gary Crosby that I had heard four thousand times by actual count. At least I could stand that.

Ruby had answered my one essential question by drawing me a map. He had only been here once, almost a year ago, but he remembered it well enough to get me here. I spread the map on the seat as we rolled up the back highway, the mountains sprawling whitely to the left. I caught Rita glancing at the map. Our eyes met again. I stopped at a light and we just looked at each other for a moment. On the radio they were playing "I Hadn't Anyone Till You." Tommy Dorsey. Jack Leonard was singing the vocal refrain.

"Light's green," she said, and I started off again.

Then, without looking my way, she began to take me apart. She did it like a surgeon, without a tremor in her voice to betray her.

"It would seem that I've become a suspect again. I don't like that, not from you."

I didn't say anything.

"Trust is a precious thing to me," she said. "If I didn't think you understood that, I promise you last night wouldn't've happened."

"I know that."

"Then talk to me, you bastard."

Even when the words were loaded, her voice remained calm, icy.

"There may be a woman involved in it," I said. "I don't know what she did or why."

"But you think it was me."

"I don't think anything."

"Wrong answer, Janeway, and a lie to boot."

I nodded.

"This is turning ugly," she said.

"It's always been ugly."

"That's funny, I thought it was something else. What happened to love at first sight?"

"Alive and well. It's got nothing to do with this."

"Then it can't be much good."

"Not true," I said. "I'm just doing what a cop always does. Following my nose."

"Is that what you were doing last night? You may've been following something, but it sure wasn't your nose. You know what I think?"

"I'm afraid to ask."

"You should be. It doesn't put you in a good light."

We were getting close to Longmont. My eyes scanned the road for the turnoff.

I knew the question was coming before she asked it: knew and dreaded.

"How long have you been thinking these things?"

I took a deep breath. "You want an honest answer?"

"You bet."

"It's always been there. I push it back in my head and try to smother it, but it won't ever go away."

"Then it was in bed with us last night."

"It's that goddamn appraisal. I just can't square it."

She gave a dry little laugh. "You're pretty good, though, I'll have to say that. You have a way of saying I love you that makes a girl believe it."

"It's true," I said. "It is, Rita."

"Ah," she said in a small voice.

I thought that might be the end of it, but she said, "What I can't figure out is why I'm supposed to have done this. It couldn't be for money. You want to see my bankbook?" She flipped open her checkbook from First Federal Savings. It made me dizzy, trying to drive and look. What really made me dizzy were all those digits, and not a decimal anywhere in sight. It was like standing on the edge of a deep cliff, looking straight down.

"This is my traveling money. My book account is about four times this big. I have another account that I use for business not related to books. I have another account for investments: my accountant talked me into doing that last year. I seem to take in more money than I can decently spend now; I can't even give it away fast enough. I make money while I'm lying in bed. Would you like to know how much I made last night while you were, ah, following your nose? I can calculate it, give or take a little. I'm making money this minute, for Christ's sake. I don't ever have to lift another finger. What work I do, I do because I've got to do something or go out of my mind. I was never made to be gracefully rich; I'm too restless to be idle. I don't want any more money, don't even want what I've got. So please tell me why I would lie and steal and kill for more stupid money."

I shrugged sadly. Maybe for kicks, I thought: maybe for love. Who can ever know what people will do, or why?

"I've got one other account," she said. "You could call it my fuck you account."

I knew what she meant. I know all about fuck you money, mainly because I've never had any.

In that same flat voice, she said, "You are the most exciting man. All I have to do is think of you and I just tingle. Even that first night. I walked out of your bookstore and it was so powerful I had to stop and lean against something. I thought, there's my guy. It was absolutely terrifying, the most thrilling moment of my life. Couldn't wait to see you again. But you've got no faith, Janeway. I don't think we're going to make it."

"I need to know. You've got to understand that."

"You need to believe. I know it's not quite fair. A just God wouldn't try us like this, before we even know each other. I'm not blaming you, but don't blame me either. This is what I am. At this particular point in my life, I need faith more than love. An equal moment of each would be nice."

"I guess I was a cop too long."

She sighed. "And there isn't any God, and life's not fair."

51

The road snaked away to the left, a narrow blacktop five miles south of Longmont. Houses were sprinkled on both sides. The pavement ended with a bump and the houses fell away and we clattered along a dusty washboard road. Trees appeared on the rolling edge of the prairie.

There was a rutted side road, just where Ruby's map showed it: then the house, peeping through the seams of a wooded arroyo. I turned in and stopped. My odometer showed that we had come twenty-six miles from downtown Denver.

"Looks like nobody's home," Rita said.

"We'll see."

I left her there with the motor running and walked the hundred yards to the house. It was an old country house, American gothic. The windows were dark and in the mid-morning light it looked deserted. A rambling front porch flitted in and out of view through a blowing hedge. The wind was strong, whipping down the front range. Some of the windows had been boarded up: the front railing was down in places and the steps looked rickety and dangerous. On the east end some scaffolding had been erected and there was evidence of recent work. There were no cars in the yard. I watched for a while but saw nothing that mattered.

I moved to the edge of the house, then around to the front. The place was like a crypt: not even a bird to break the monotony, only that steady beating wind. I eased up the steps to the porch, flattened myself beside the door and listened.

Nothing.

How many times have I done this, I thought: how many times when I was a cop did I jack up my courage and walk into trouble with this same gun pointing the way? It never loses its charm: the prospect of sudden death, maybe your own, always comes with a clutching at the throat and a rush of adrenaline. I tried the door. It creaked open and I looked in at a picture of frontier America. Broken old furniture. Antique pictures. Farm relics from another time. A kerosene lamp stood on a table, its glass charred black. An old wooden yoke had been thrown in a corner.

I took one step inside. The floor creaked and in the silence it sounded like a gunshot. I flattened against the door and caught my breath. I waited, listening. I waited so long a mouse scurried across the room.

It didn't look promising. The dust in the parlor was half an inch deep. No one had been through here in at least six months.

Doesn't seem to be Janeway's year for hunches.

If it didn't pan out I was back to zero. Square one. Lookin' for a turtle-faced man and a whole new gambit.

I left deep black prints in the dust. I crossed the scurry marks left by the mouse. It's going to be a wash, I thought, another dead end. I had reached a long dark hallway and still nothing had happened. A thick ribbon of dust, undisturbed since time began, stretched out toward the back of the house.

I lowered the gun. My forces were still on alert, but the condition was downgraded from red to yellow.

There were two rooms on each side of the hall. At the end was another hall that went into the east wing. There was a door, which was closed.

But it opened without creaking when I tried it.

On the other side was a different world. A world of paint and glass and fresh-hung wallboard. A bright world where music played and people lived.

I went back on red alert, following my gun to whatever lay ahead.

A skeleton key was stuck in the door. The radio was playing so softly it could barely be heard a room away. The floor was shiny and new. I saw a kitchen off to the left: well lit, papered yellow, with shiny new appliances. There was a half-finished den and, across from that, a bedroom. A radio sent soft tones down the hall from the kitchen: elevator music from KOSI. The scaffold's shadow leaped across the room.

I peeped into the bedroom.

He was on the bed, fully dressed, lying on top of a bright blue bedspread. He seemed to be sleeping, but his face was to the wall so I couldn't be sure. I had a vision of him lying there, eyes wide, waiting. I went in cautiously and he didn't stir. His breathing was deep and rhythmic, as if he'd been asleep for some time. I eased my way to the side of the bed. I still couldn't see his face. He lay with one arm under him, his hand out of sight. I didn't like that, but I was as ready as a guy ever gets. I leaned over and shook him lightly.

"Get up, Neff," I said, "and bring that hand out very slowly."

He was awake at once: too quickly, I thought, but a man standing over your bed with a gun will bring you up fast. He drew himself up till he was sitting. It was when he tried to look surprised that I knew I had him. He wasn't enough of an actor to pull it off.

"Stand up real easy," I said. "Just like that. Good boy. Now. I want you to go to that wall and put your hands against it, just like you see on TV."

I patted him down. He didn't have anything.

"Sit down over there," I said. "Not there . . . over in the plain wooden chair. Just sit there and face me."

He sat and watched while I did what a good cop always does: checked the obvious, easy places for weapons and found none.

He moved.

"Sit still," I said.

"I was gonna scratch my leg."

"Don't scratch anything. Don't even look at me funny. This gun of mine gets nervous."

"You wouldn't shoot me."

"I sure as hell would."

"So what's going on?"

That was his total and token attempt at denial. He knew he couldn't act and now I knew it too. Ruby had said he had been a magician and maybe that was true, but he'd never win an Oscar for bluffing his way out of a tight one. I had known a few others like that, guys who could lie as long as you didn't suspect them. Look them in the eye, though, and accuse, and they'd fall apart.

Neff was trying to avoid my eyes. He looked at the ceiling, at the window—anywhere but at me. "You like my place, Mr. Janeway? My uncle left it to me; I've been working on it a year. Sealed off this part and I just do a little at a time. Eventually I'll do it all. This isn't really my thing . . . carpentry . . . painting . . . but I do like the way it's coming together. I just do a little here and there. I don't like to sweat much."

"That's what Ruby tells me."

He gave a little laugh: wry, affectionate, almost tender. "Ruby," he said. "What a swell guy. Do anything for anybody. Great guy."

"Would you like to tell me where you put the books?"

He shrugged. Jerked his head to one side. Couldn't seem to find the words.

He looked through the window. He had a clear view of the road from here. "I saw you coming. I knew the way you were coming, cautiously like that . . . well, I just knew. I could've shot you."

"Why didn't you?"

"Gun's in the barn. You'd've seen me run for it. And wasn't sure how much you really knew. I thought maybe I could . . . talk you out of it. Shoulda known better. How'd you find out? What'd I do wrong?"

You were born, I thought.

"Tell me," he said. "I need to know."

"Maybe I'll make you a deal. I might tell you if you tell me where the books are."

"Sure . . . I'll tell you. . . . What've I got to lose?"

I thought about it, and wavered. The evidence was slippery, fragmentary. I feared for its life in a court of law. I had proceeded without regard for its welfare and now I had a strange, almost chilly reaction, talking about it calmly with the killer. Neff gave a little smile and the chill settled in. I didn't need him, I thought: I'd find the books anyway, sooner or later.

But I was a bookman, not a cop, and I wanted to see

them now. I had the fever, the bookseller's madness, and I wanted to see what had driven an otherwise sane man to murder.

How do you figure it out? You think about it all the time. How does a sculptor carve an elephant out of a block of wood? Takes a block of wood and carves away everything that doesn't look like an elephant. When you're sleeping your mind's working on it. When you drive through a snowstorm, dead people whisper in your ear. You even think about it when you're making love and it's then, in fact, that the first glimmer comes working through the haze. Writers and sculptors work that way, why can't cops? Books have been written about the creative process: tens of thousands of words from dusty academics about the writer's vision. The funny thing is, I've always worked that way as a cop, but nobody writes books about that.

You get a vision—not necessarily what is, but what might be.

I was making love with Rita and suddenly I heard Ruby's voice. *It's the most hypnotic business,* he said, and just like that I had broken Neff's alibi. Try to use that in a courtroom. You couldn't, but baby, I saw the vision. At last I put it into words. "I just kept digging, kept after it. It's a process of elimination as much as anything. Judith didn't do it. Ballard didn't do it. There wasn't any turtle-faced man, Neff: it was just a cover you made up on the spot. Once I saw that it might've happened that way, I started remembering things. They all added up to you.

"Here's what happened. Stop me if I go wrong. You walked in a minute or two before five. You threw a bunch of cream puffs down in front of Ruby, knowing he'd go into an instant trance. Then you went back to the crapper, only you didn't stop there. You went on out into the back yard, around the building, and up the street. Your timing had to be perfect. Any little thing could've messed you up: any glitch between one place and the other. A customer who lingered past closing time . . . somebody who saw you go into my store just after five . . . any one of a dozen things, and all of them broke your way. You must've been desperate, Neff, to've tried something like that, and it damn near worked."

He shook his head. "You don't know what desperation is . . ."

"But it all worked. It was already dark: there was nobody on the street; luck was riding on your wagon all the way. It took you what . . . thirty seconds to cover the ground from your back door to my place. You forced Miss Pride to lock the door, then you herded them into the back room and shot them. You were back in your own place in no time, surely less than five minutes. You came through the back and stashed the gun—it was probably still there, somewhere behind the shelves, when I talked to you the next day—and when you came up front, Ruby was right where you'd left him, thinking no time at all had passed. You couldn't've done a better job on him if you'd hypnotized him. In a way it was better than hypnosis.

"The flu was also a fake, a cover for the shakes you had after killing three people. Once I realized that, I started seeing other pieces everywhere. I remembered Ruby once telling me how you protect your privacy. I remembered him talking about the farm you'd inherited. Longmont's just thirty miles from Denver: the truck Bobby used had seventy-four miles on the odometer when he brought it back. I thought how strange it was that you gave your phone number to no one. Even your partner didn't have it. Ruby had laughed about that one night when we were working late in my store—how you didn't want to be called at home no matter what. There was something wrong with that, Neff; it bothered me and I couldn't figure out why. Then I remembered. Hell, *I* had seen your phone number: I'd seen it written down somewhere. Then I remembered where. It was in Bobby Westfall's little address book."

He laughed sadly and shook his head. He looked like he wanted to say something, but he didn't.

"It's there in his book," I said. "We can dig it out of the evidence room and I can show it to you. I'm surprised it took me so long to remember it. So why would you give your number to a bookscout, Neff? There is no bigger pest on this earth than a hungry bookscout, yet you give him your private number when even your partner can't get it. That doesn't make sense . . . unless you and Bobby have something going together. Then it makes all the sense in the world. And that's what happened. You had something going with Bobby. Something more important than your partner or your business or anything else in your life.

"Then there was the matter of the driver's license. Bobby didn't have one but you didn't know that. Ruby knew it, but not you. You still didn't know it, even after you killed Bobby. You never understood how Peter Bonnema got involved in it, because you always assumed that you and Bobby were in it alone. The one thing I never could figure was how you found out about old man Ballard and his books."

"I've known about them for years. Known about . . . thought about them . . ."

"How'd you know?"

"I had a little bookstore on Eighth Avenue. This was long ago, before Ruby and I even knew each other. It was on Eighth near Ogden. That's not far, you know, from where Mr. Ballard lived. One day he came in. We got to talking. He said he had a lot of books. One thing led to another, and I said I'd like to come see them. He was very cordial. So I went to his house . . . I went to his house. The man was . . . simply incredible. He had the best eye for books . . . I can't imagine how he so consistently managed to pick up these things and save them . . . things that appreciated—I don't know how else to say it—beyond belief. And he'd been doing this for forty years. In some cases he had two or three copies of a single title, untouched copies pushed back behind the ones you could see on the shelf. They were all first editions, every one . . . the most immaculate collection I have ever seen, and, Mr. Janeway, I have looked at a lot of books. And the damnedest thing . . . the rarest thing . . . he didn't care about them at all for that purpose. It was like he had no idea or interest in how much they might be worth. Here was the big score everybody dreams about, and there was no way I could buy them, I could just never get the money together. But the old man . . . God, he was so naive. I thought maybe if I threw some money at him—not too much but enough, I could get them away from him. If I was lucky, he wouldn't check any further and for a few grand I'd pull off the heist of a lifetime. I was actually . . . trembling . . . as I tried to assess it. Started to throw out a figure and called it back. Didn't know what to do. Couldn't make it too high or low. You know how it is—go too low and he figures, hell, he might as well keep them; go too high and he begins to suspect what they're really worth. You know how it goes—you play people in this business as much as books. I looked around. He didn't live in luxury, didn't look rich. Five thousand dollars, I thought: that'd really make a difference to this old man. So that's what I said, and he smiled like a gentleman and said that was most generous but he wasn't interested in selling them at that point. Maybe someday, he said. That was ten, twelve years ago, and I want to tell you something, there hasn't been a day that I haven't thought about that stuff. I've dreamed about it . . . it comes to me a dozen times a day, when I look out the window or see the shit the scouts bring in . . . when I realize how hopelessly I've mired myself in the workaday crap."

"And then he died."

"Yeah. The first thing I thought was, now it'll get out. Somebody'll go in there and find it and it'll make a major story. The *AB*'ll carry it, it's that big. Imagine my surprise when nothing happened. I couldn't believe it when those two idiots started to put it in an estate sale. I actually stood outside in the rain one night and watched them through the window. And I went wild with hope. My God, I went crazy. I had to get it, but it had to be done in such a way that it would never be tied to me. I knew there'd be trouble if it became known later that I had bought it. The courts are very consistent on this. They always return valuables to an original owner if someone with specialized knowledge buys it too cheap. And Christ, we were talking less than pennies on the dollar. We were talking nothing!"

"So you hired Bobby to do it."

"The books needed to simply disappear. I needed for them to be swallowed up by someone anonymous. I thought he could keep his mouth shut . . . he seemed perfect."

"Except for one thing. He had no driver's license."

"Two things," Neff said. "I didn't count on him getting so bitter about it. I thought he'd be happy with a few hundred for a hard night's work. But right from the beginning we were bickering, and after a while there was a threat implied in everything he said to me. That one night he just pushed it too far. I picked up the crowbar and before I knew it he was on the floor at my feet. I couldn't believe what I'd done. I wrapped him in an old blanket and dumped him downtown. Then I burned the blanket. And of course, you're right, the son of a bitch never did tell me he had no license."

"Of course not. Why would he want to screw things for himself? By then Bobby smelled a big score too. He went to a friend of his, Peter, and got him to rent the truck. By then Peter smelled a score. He followed Bobby to Ballard's house and waited up the block while Bobby carried out the books. In the morning he followed Bobby again, and Bobby led him straight here. Then Bobby was killed and Peter put two and two together and started bleeding you for the books. He sucked your blood out, first book by book, then by the box."

"It took me months to find out who he was. He was so careful—made me box them up and leave them at a place in the country, and he'd go pick them up later, when he knew I wasn't watching. I might never've found out, but he got too cocky. He sold you a book from Ballard's and I saw it in your store and knew where it had come from . . ."

". . . and you started following him."

"I was in the gas station across from the DAV. Didn't think he could see me there but the bastard had eyes like a hawk. I thought then it was all over; I thought he'd tell you right there on the street."

"He was too scared—too scared to think."

"Yeah, but that wouldn't last. Once he had time to think, I knew he'd be back. I had to get him before that happened."

"He tried to call me that night, in fact, but luck was still breaking your way. He got my recording. He tried the next day too, but I was up in the mountains, at McKinley's place. Finally he had to make a choice: hole up, leave town, or come to me. He knew I was always there at closing time. If he arrived exactly at five, got off the bus right at the store and came straight inside, he'd be fine. He figured I'd protect him. So he called Pinky and told her he was coming in. A few minutes later I called Pinky and told her I wouldn't be there. At that point we didn't know what he wanted or how to reach him: I just assumed he needed money, and I told Pinky to give it to him. I also told her to let you boys know she'd be closing alone, so you could watch out for her. She followed my orders after all, and got herself killed for it. She told you, didn't she? Didn't she, Neff?"

He stared at his hands and said nothing.

"She told you her silly boss was worried about her, but it would probably be okay because Peter was coming in. Peter would be there at five. That's when you knew you had to do it: that's when the whole bloody mess got planned. Peter got there at five, and instead of finding me waiting for him, he found you. You came in right on his heels. What you didn't know was that Pinky was talking to Rita McKinley's recorder. And what she said puts it all on you, as clearly as if she'd told us your name. She said, 'Hi, everything's okay.' I thought about that for a long time after the lab boys got it out of the recording. Why would she say that? It didn't make any sense. She was in the middle of saying good-bye: she was telling me someone had just come in and she'd have to call me back. Why would she suddenly say, 'Hi, everything's okay,' in the middle of hanging up? The only thing that makes sense is that she was talking to the guy who had just walked in. Couldn't be anybody but Harkness, Ruby, or you.

378

Pinky still thought she was talking to a friend, the nice man from the store up the street who had come in to check on her at closing. It's okay, she was saying, Peter's here, I'm not alone. But Peter was already screaming. He knew what was happening. A minute later, so did she."

There didn't seem to be anything else to say: nothing except, for me, the most important thing.

"I've actually come to hate those books," Neff said.

"Don't worry, I'll take 'em off your hands."

"Yeah."

I held my breath, afraid to ask, scared silly of what the answer would bring.

"Who was the woman, Neff?"

He looked at me and didn't answer.

"I need to know that. Was it Rita?"

His lip curled up in a sneer. "Rita," he said. "The big-time book dealer. The biggest thief of all."

"What're you talking about? What's that supposed to mean?"

He smiled and reached into his shirt pocket. I cocked the gun but he only laughed in that faint, sad way. When he opened his fist, he had two tiny capsules in his hand.

"What's that stuff?"

"Guess."

We looked at each other: a long, searching moment. Barbara Crowell flitted through my mind, along with a hundred suicides and suicide attempts I had known over the years.

"Don't do that," I said.

But he popped them into his mouth and swallowed.

"I knew you'd get me," he said. "Knew it that first day, when they put you on Bobby's case. So I had these ready. . . ."

He doubled up and fell out of the chair.

"Neff," I said weakly.

I looked for the phone, but you can't do much with cyanide. It works in a minute.

He went into the shakes and groaned, a long cry of agony.

His pulse slowed, and I could almost see his heart giving up.

I got down beside him and opened his shirt.

Biggest mistake I ever made.

He moved like a snake. I didn't know what had hit me. Suddenly I was down and he was up and through the haze I knew he had kicked me in the head. He had caught me in the temple with the point of his shoe: the hardest kick he could muster. I spun around and he was on my back. He had a rope: I don't know where it came from, but he was a magician and there it was, twisted around my neck. He cut my windpipe, and the next twenty seconds were so desperate that I couldn't think of anything but my heaving lungs. I know the gun fell: it skittered across the floor and slammed into the wall. I was up on one knee with this thing on my back, and I couldn't shake it and if I didn't shake it I was going to die.

I tried to buck him and couldn't. We slammed into the wall. He held on, stuck to me like we'd been born that way, grotesque Siamese twins bent on killing each other. The world turned red. I was losing consciousness. . . .

I heard a scream, then a shot, and the rope went slack.

God, I could breathe again!

But I still had to struggle for it, and for at least a minute I had the heaves.

When the world cleared, I saw Rita standing over Neff's body. She was staring at the mess she'd made, clutching my gun with both hands.

52

I found the key to the storage locker in Neff's hip pocket. It was the only lock-it-yourself place in Longmont.

We drove the four miles from Neff's house in what seemed like total silence. Only when we reached the storage yard did I realize that the radio was still playing.

Benny Goodman. "It Had to Be You."

I drove to unit 254, opened the door, and walked in. It was like walking into King Solomon's Mines.

He had shelved the locker and some of the books were out on open display. Yes, they were wonderful things.

But I was tired of looking. If you get too much new blood, you begin to drown in it.

Rita had lingered but now she came in. She didn't touch anything, just walked along and looked at the spines.

"Well, this is it," I said wearily. "This is what people kill for."

John Dunning

She was just standing, staring at nothing. She looked older in the dim light.

On a worktable in a corner, I found some papers. The name Rita McKinley caught my eye and I leafed through them.

"Looks like a copy of your appraisal," I said. "You want to tell me about this?"

She shook her head and said, "I have no idea."

And that's how the case ended: with a stalemate, a stand-off between someone I loved and everything I believed in. With a dead man and a treasure, a lack of faith, a beautiful girl, and the big question still unanswered.

53

But no:

It really ended on another day six weeks later. Emery
Neff was in his grave and the Ballard heirs were embroiled
in a battle of books that seemed certain to end up in court.
Ruby was in business alone. Rita McKinley had been set
free by the Boulder County DA, who had pronounced the
shooting justified: she had gone somewhere and had left
nothing, not even the damned recording, to tell people
where she'd gone or when she might come home.

I saw Barbara Crowell every couple of weeks. Mose had
found a way to handle her case, as a favor to me. They had
me billed as her star witness, and things weren't looking too
bad for her when all the mitigating factors were taken into
account.

Jackie, after all, hadn't died. He couldn't feed himself or
talk quite right: he'd have to be carried to the potty from
now on, but he was alive. Doctors think he might live that
way for another thirty years. It doesn't sound like much,
but the alternative is nothing at all.

As for me, I was going through the old familiar symptoms of acute burnout. The book business, which had been so fresh and exciting just three months ago, was suddenly old, and I was growing old with it. I dreaded opening the store: I let it slide as long as I could; then I went in and painted the bathroom and opened for business. I had been off for a month: I had spent a lot of money and my rent was due, and it was time to get going again.

But in the end I was back where I'd been in the police department. The days were long and uneventful: the nights were worse. I didn't know where I was going, but I've never been one to languish. I knew I was in some vast personal transition, but only the past was spread out, clear and ugly. The future was still a void.

I closed on the Ballard house. The paperwork was done by the first of December and I was ready to move in. I had planned to be out of the store for three days during the move, and Ruby had promised to bring me someone reliable to run it. That morning, when he came in, the woman with him looked vaguely like someone I had once known. It took me a long moment to recognize her.

I pointed to her face and snapped my fingers. "Millie Farmer, the teaching bookscout."

"Just bookscout, dad. I'm out of teaching forever. If I'm not going to make any money anyway, I might as well have fun doing it."

"You've come to the right place," I said.

I broke her in: walked her through the store and showed her what was what and how to find it. I gave her Miss Pride's key to the front door and said I'd be in each day at four o'clock to be with her when she closed. There seemed to be nothing more to discuss, yet we all knew better. Painful, unfinished business lay between us. There had been a strain between Ruby and me, and now it extended to her. We had never talked about Neff. It made Ruby squirm, as if somehow he had shared the blame for what had happened. Emery Neff had touched us all in some basic, primal way, and none of us had been able to throw off his ghost.

Even now, getting into it wasn't easy.

"Wonder what's gonna happen to those books," I said.

Ruby gave a fidgety shrug and looked out into the street.

"We'll never see another collection like that."

"Probably not," he said.

I looked from one to the other. They said nothing.

"Hey, you want a job full-time?" I said to Millie.

"Hell yes."

"You're hired. Doesn't pay much. Six an hour and all your books at twenty percent off."

"Dad, I just died and went to heaven," she said to Ruby.

I made another try at knocking down some walls. "The thing that beats me is how those books changed from club books to firsts. If I could get the answer to that, I'd die a happy man."

"They never were club books," Ruby said.

"It's not that easy, Ruby. If it were just McKinley's appraisal it would be simple. But I saw all the invoices, all the club flyers. On most of them he had written what he'd ordered and the date. Those damn books are there, the same books he ordered, only they're first editions, not club copies. He was the most compulsive record-keeper you ever saw. When the books came in from the club, he wrote down the dates. Then he wrote what he thought of them after he'd read them. It's all there, in Ballard's own handwriting. Only somehow between now and then a genie got in his house and waved a wand and turned those books into gold."

I could see Ruby wanted to leave but he couldn't find an exit cue.

"What's your answer?" I asked.

"Ain't got no answer. Hell, Dr. J, I don't know. I don't even think it's very interesting. Where the old man got his eye for books—that's where the real mystery is. If we knew that we'd all be rich in no time. How do guys like old man Ballard start from scratch and build a library that just knocks people for a loop? I don't know. Somehow they're plugged into the universe in this queer kinda way. They know what'll be valued, not just now but years from now."

"And they don't even think of value in terms of money," I said. "They have a totally different agenda. And I guess it was a lot easier to build a library then, when the average cost of a book was two bucks."

"It's all relative. You of all people ought to know that. A book has always cost about what a meal in a good restaurant costs. Did then, still does. I get sick of hearing how expensive books are. Which would you rather have, a good book or a tender steak? I know what I'd take, seven days a week."

He moved to the door: he was about to leave.

"That was a good move, hiring this lady," he said. "She'll be good for your business, just like the other one. She's got a sassy mouth but you can handle her. Just give her the back of your hand two or three times a day."

Millie stuck out her tongue.

"You need to unshackle your legs, get free again," Ruby said. "You're going through something, I can see it written all over you. It's a growth spurt. All of a sudden you're tired of retail. You're starting to see where the real fun is in the book business. Usually it takes five years: you've gone through it all in three months. You came into this business almost whole, and now you're ready to move on. The Zen Buddhists have a word for it. *Satori.* It means sudden enlightenment."

"I don't feel suddenly enlightened. I feel as dense as ever. I don't think I'll be able to rest till I know the answers to those two questions."

"What questions?" Millie said.

"How did those books change into fine firsts . . . and who was the woman?"

"What woman?"

"The day Peter and Miss Pride were killed, a woman called and asked for Neff. Ruby talked to her."

Millie Farmer blinked.

"Hell," she said, "I believe that was me."

54

I was out of my apartment in two hours.

I was surprised at how little I had. I wanted few things from that old life: my furniture, such as it was, was old and worn; the Salvation Army had been glad to come for it, and I was having new stuff delivered that afternoon. There had been some doubt about the bed arriving today, and I was prepared to bag it tonight on the floor. I arrived on Madison Street before noon. It was a warm day for December, but Denver is like that: it can have rain, snow, and a heat wave all in the same week.

Greenwald was sitting in a rocker reading a book when I drove up. He greeted me with a wave. I began to move my things in, arranging as I went. I gloried in the bookshelves: how many book dealers have room for ten thousand books at home? I looked through the front window and saw that Greenwald had fallen asleep with the book spread open across his chest. When I looked again, some minutes later, he was gone. But he was back again, wearing a sweater, when I made my last trip to the trailer.

"It's going to snow tonight," he said. "I just saw it on the weather. You can feel it coming already; there's a chill in the air."

He had made us some lunch. "Just come over when you're ready," he said. I went into my bathroom to wash. The floor had two small smooth spots where Stanley Ballard had stood every morning. Untold numbers of shaves he had had, standing at this same glass. Scraping his face with an old-fashioned straight razor (the hook for the strop was still there, fastened to the wall). Looking in his own eyes and seeing no mystery there. Knowing himself thoroughly.

Satori, I thought.

Maybe I'll become a Buddhist.

I knew things I hadn't known before. I could see Emery Neff sitting in his store that day. Ruby had walked up the street for a cup of coffee. Pinky had just called to say that she'd be closing up alone. But Peter was coming in, so everything would be fine.

He knew then what he was going to do. He picked up the phone and dialed a number he had called often in the past few months.

I want to see you . . . today, this afternoon . . . I need you.

And Millie, who thought she'd come to love him, could never say no.

The problem is, I've been gone from the store a lot. Ruby's starting to think I'm not pulling my weight. So here's what we'll do. You call back in ten minutes. I'll see that he answers the phone. Don't tell him who you are, just ask for me. Be formal . . . cool and distant. Call me Mr. Neff. He'll think I'm coming over on a buy, and we'll spend the afternoon together.

But he never came. Millie sat by the phone and it rang an hour later.

389

John Dunning

*Sorry, hon, it's not gonna work . . . not feeling well . . . think
I've got the flu. Going home to lie down . . . no, don't come up,
you'll just get what I've got. I'll make it up to you. . . .*

An illusion, like one of his old magic tricks. Now you
see him, now you don't.

Like that illusion of death he had performed for me
alone: two cold capsules popped into his mouth, and you
were ready to believe anything.

So simple, so easy, once you knew how it was done.

I tried to call Rita, without much hope. There had been
no answer up there for weeks, and there was none now.

Then I remembered that other number. Bobby Westfall
had written it down and dropped the paper when he'd been
in talking to Harkness. It took me a few minutes to find it,
and another few minutes to figure it out.

An out-of-state exchange.

I tried it with a Los Angeles area code and got the intercept operator.

San Francisco.

Intercept.

It rang through to New York. A woman answered.

"Greenpeace Action."

"Is this Greenpeace . . . International?"

"We're part of it."

"Uh . . . is Rita McKinley there?"

"She was here yesterday."

Now what the hell was this about? What had Bobby
been doing with a number for Greenpeace?

"Do you know if she's coming back?"

"I don't know, sir. I believe she was going to Europe."

He had been trying to reach Rita, just before he was
killed. About the time she was off saving whales.

She had been on NBC. Was it not possible that he had seen her Brokaw interview?

Which would mean . . . what?

Could it be Bobby's Christian conscience at work? He and Neff had just pulled off the literary heist of the decade, and you could bet that something was at work.

The woman on the phone was talking.

"Is there a message, sir . . . in case we do hear from her?"

"Just tell her Janeway called."

And please, please call back.

55

Now I sit with old Mr. Greenwald and I know the end is coming. I think I may even know what it is. Satori is working overtime, and my enlightenment is both sudden and overwhelming. It comes in waves, like a tide pushed up by a hurricane.

"So the house is finally yours—the deal, as they say these days, is truly finished."

"It's truly finished, Mr. Greenwald."

"Have some more coffee."

This is how it is in Greenwald's world: civilized society comes first and business is done in its own good time.

Being among the newly enlightened, I don't push him.

And eventually he does get to it. "Things have been preying on my mind since Stan died. I only wanted to do right by him, to do what he wanted done."

"I think you've done that, sir."

He gives me a little smile, gratitude and appreciation, but laced with doubt. Four people, after all, have died. It's hard to know what to do when you don't come equipped with a crystal ball.

"Oscar Wilde once said that a cynic is a man who knows the price of everything and the value of nothing. Judith and Val have become cynics in just that definition of the word."

"I'd agree with that."

"They have not turned out to be good people."

"No one's responsible for that but them."

"Stan felt responsible. He was also horrified. He had a dream one night, not long before he died. They were fighting over his books, tearing them apart. The next morning he told me about it. He said, 'I don't care about the house, don't care about any of it . . . I just don't want them to have my books. Give them away, throw them away, I don't care, but I won't rest easy unless I know they won't get them.' "

"He had no idea what they were worth, did he?"

"I think he knew, toward the end, that they were worth some money. Enough, at least, that there would be a squabble over them. But you're right—he had no real idea. He'd be mortified if he knew."

"He could've saved a lot of trouble and just left them to you."

"Where would I put them? I have my own books, my house is full of books, most of them the same titles he had. Where would I put them?"

"So he figured it the way he always figured—that his library would do the most good by being broken up and given away."

"Sure: give them to the people. Stan gave away books by the carload. He used the book club as his first line of reading, and gave those books away. Gave them to nursing homes, hospitals, people he knew and people he barely knew. He was especially interested in helping young people discover the world of books. So he gave them away, but the ones he liked he kept for himself. Gave away the club books and bought his own copies in the stores downtown."

"And the easiest way to break up the library . . ."

". . . was to leave a document proving that the books had no money value. Done by an expert no one would challenge. Only Stan and I knew, and he asked me to keep that secret until the last of his estate was disposed of. The house was the last of it."

And now we all know. Ballard left the appraisal among his papers but tucked a copy for good measure among his books. Emery Neff found that appraisal, scanned it, and jumped to the logical conclusion: that McKinley was a crook, lowballing so she could buy the books for a song. But Bobby had taken the time to actually read the appraisal. He alone knew the truth, that McKinley had been duped. That's why he was trying to reach McKinley when the deal between Neff and himself had begun to go sour. Maybe a better deal could be struck with McKinley.

Greenwald offers more coffee, served with a sad little smile.

"Stan got the appraisal he wanted. We traded houses the night the appraiser came out. The books she looked at were mine."

SCRIBNER
PROUDLY PRESENTS

THE SIGN OF THE BOOK

JOHN DUNNING

Available in hardcover March 2005
from Scribner

Turn the page for a preview of
The Sign of the Book. . . .

Chapter One

Two years had passed and I knew Erin well. I knew her moods. I knew what she liked and didn't like, what would bore her to tears or light up her face with mischief. I knew what would send her into fits of helpless laughter, what would make her angry, thoughtful, witty, playful, or loving. It takes time to learn someone, but after two years I could say with some real confidence, I know this woman well.

I knew before she said a word that something had messed up her day. She arrived at our bookstore wearing her casual autumn garb, jeans and an untucked flannel shirt.

"What's wrong with you?"

"I am riding on the horns of a dilemma."

I knew she would tell me when she had thought about it. I would add my two cents' worth, she would toss in some wherefores, to which I would add a few interrogatories and lots of footnotes. I am good with footnotes. And after two years I was very good at leaving her alone when all the signs said let her be.

She picked up the duster and disappeared into the back room. That was another bad sign: in troubled times, Erin liked to dust. So I let her ponder her dilemma and dust her way through it in peace. Since she now owned part of my store, she had unlimited dusting privileges. She could dust all day long if she wanted to.

Two customers came and went and one of them made my week, picking up a $1,500 Edward Abbey and a *Crusade in Europe* that Eisenhower had signed and dated here in Denver during his 1955 heart-attack convalescence. Suddenly I was in high cotton: the day, which had begun so modestly ($14 to the good till then), had now dropped five grand in my pocket. I called The Broker and made reservations for two at seven.

At five o'clock I locked the place up and sidled back to check on Erin. She was sitting on a stool with the duster in her hand, staring at the wall. I pulled up the other stool and put an arm over her shoulder. "This is turning into some dilemma, kid."

"Oh, wow. What time is it?"

"Ten after five. I thought you'd have half the world dusted off by now."

"How's the day been?"

I told her and she brightened. I told her about The Broker and she brightened another notch.

We went up front and I waved to the neighborhood hooker as she trolled up East Colfax in the first sortie of her worknight. "Honestly," Erin said, "we've got to get out of here. How do you ever expect to get any business with that going on?"

"She's just a working professional, plying her trade. A gal's gotta do something."

"Hey, I'm a gal," she said testily. "I don't gotta do that."

"Maybe that lady hasn't had your advantages."

The unsavory truth was, I liked it on East Colfax. Since Larimer Street went all respectable and touristy in the early seventies, this had become one of the most entertaining streets in America. City officials, accepting millions in federal urban renewal money, had promised a crackdown on vice, but it took the heart of a cop to know exactly what would happen. The hookers and bums from that part of town had simply migrated to this part of town, and nothing had changed at all. City officials said wow, look what we did, now people can walk up Larimer Street without stumbling over drunks and whores, but here they still were. I could sit on my stool and watch the passing parade through my storefront window all day long: humanity of all kinds walked, drove, skateboarded, and sometimes ran past like bats out of hell. In the few years since I had opened shop on this corner, I had seen a runaway car, a gunfight, half a dozen fistfights, and this lone whore, who had a haunting smile and the world's saddest eyes.

"You are the managing partner," Erin said. "That was our deal and I'm sticking to it. But if my vote meant anything, we would move out of this place tomorrow."

"Of course your vote means something, but you just don't up and move a bookstore. First you've got to have a precise location in mind. Not just Cherry Creek in general or some empty hole in West Denver, but an actual place with traffic and pizzazz. A block or two in any direction can make all the difference."

She looked around. "So this has pizzazz? This has traffic?"

"No, but I've got tenure. I've been here long

enough, people two thousand miles away know where I am. And not to gloat, but I did take in almost two thousand bucks today."

"Yes, you did. I stand completely defeated in the face of such an argument."

I went on, unfazed by her defeat. "There's also the matter of help. If I moved to Cherry Creek, I'd need staff. My overhead would quadruple before I ever got my shingle out, so I'd better not guess wrong. Here I can run it with one employee, who makes herself available around the clock if I need her. What more could a bookseller want? But you know all this, we've had this discussion how many times before?"

"Admit it, you'll never move." Erin sat on the stool and looked at me across the counter. "Would it bother you if we didn't do The Broker tonight? I don't feel like dressing up."

"Say no more."

I called and canceled.

"So where do you want to eat?"

"Oh, next door's fine."

I shivered. Next door was a Mexican restaurant, the third eatery to occupy that spot since I had turned the space on the corner into my version of an east Denver fine books emporium. In fact, half a dozen restaurants had opened and closed there in the past ten years, and I knew that because I had been a young cop when this block had been known as hooker heaven. Gradually the vice squad had turned up the heat, the topless places and the hustlers had kept moving east, and a series of restaurants had come and gone next door. Various chefs had tried Moroccan, Indian, Chinese, and

American cuisine, but none had been able to overcome the street's reputation for harlots and occasional violence. Some people with money just didn't want to come out here, no matter how good the books were.

We settled into a table in the little side room and I ordered from a speckled menu: two Roadrunner burritos, which seemed like pleasant alternatives to the infamous East Colfax dogburger. "What's in this thing we're about to eat?" Erin asked.

"You'll like it better if you don't know."

The waitress brought our Mexican beers and drifted away. Erin reached across the table and squeezed my hand. "Hi," she said.

"Hey. Was that an endearment?"

"Yeah, it was."

I still didn't ask about her trouble. I gave her a friendly squeeze in return and she said, "How're you doing, old man? You still like the book life?"

It was a question she asked periodically. "Some days better than others," I said. "Today was a really good one on both ends of it. Sold two, bought one—a nice ratio."

"What did you buy?" she said, putting things in their proper importance.

"The nicest copy you'll ever see of *Phantom Lady*— Cornell Woolrich in his William Irish motif. Very pricey, very scarce in this condition. I may put two grand on it. That wartime paper just didn't hold up for the long haul, so you never see it this nice."

"You're getting pretty good at this, aren't you?"

"It doesn't take much skill to recognize that baby as a good one."

"But even after all this time you still miss police work."

"Oh, sure. Everything has its high spots. When I was a cop, I loved those high spots like crazy, I guess because I was good at it. You get a certain rush when suddenly you know exactly what happened. Then you go out and prove it. I can point out half a dozen cases that never would've been solved except for me and my squirrelly logic. There may be dozens of others."

"I'd have guessed thousands."

"That might be stretching it by one or two hundred. A dozen I could dredge up with no effort at all." I took a sip of my beer. "Why do you ask, lovely one? Is this leading somewhere? It's getting fairly egotistical on my part."

"I know, but I asked for it. Please continue, for I am fascinated."

"I was really good at it," I said with no apologies. "You never want to give up something you have that much juice for. When I lost it, I missed the hell out of it. You know all this, there's no use lying, I really missed it, I always will."

I thought of my police career and the whole story played in my head in an instant, from that idealistic cherry-faced beginning to the end, when I had taken on a brute, used his face for a punching bag, and lost my job in the process. "But I was lucky, wasn't I? The book trade came along and it was just what I needed: very different, lots of room to grow, interesting work, good people. I figured I'd be in it forever."

"And indeed, you may well be. But nothing's perfect."

I mustered as much sadness as I could dredge up on a $2,000 day. "Alas, no."

"If you had to give this up, how would you feel about it?"

"Devastated. You mean I get lucky enough to find two true callings in one lifetime and then I lose them both? Might as well lie down in front of a bus. What else would I do? Be a PI? It's not the same after you've been the real thing."

"How would you know? You've never done it— not for any kind of a living."

"I know as a shamus you've got no authority. You don't have the weight of the department behind you, and where's the fun in that? You're just another great pretender."

The moment came. I looked at her and said, "So why are you here on a workday? How come you're not in your lawyer's uniform? What's going on with your case? And after all is said and done, am I finally allowed to ask what this problem is all about?"

"The judge adjourned for the afternoon so he could do some research. I think we're gonna win, but of course you never know. Right now it's just a hunch. So I've got the rest of the day off. And let's see, what was that other question? What's this all about? I need your help."

"Say no more."

"Something's come up. I want you to go to Paradise for me."

"You mean the town in western Colorado or just some blissful state of mind?"

"The town. Maybe the other thing too, if you can be civilized."

"Tough assignment. But speaking of the town, why me?"

"You're still the best cop I know. I trust your instincts. Maybe I'm just showing you that if you did want to do cases, you'd have more work than you've got time for."

"The great if. Listen, being a dealer in so-called rare books leaves me no time for anything else anyway. Why do you keep trying to get me out of the book business?"

"I'm not! Why would I do that? You could do both, as you have already so nimbly demonstrated."

Our food came. The waitress asked if there was anything else and went away. Erin took a small bite, then looked up and smiled almost virginly.

"Let's say I want you to go to Paradise and look at some books. You should be able to do that. Look at some books and see if they might be worth anything. Because if they're not, the defendant may lose her house paying for her defense."

"It would be damned unusual for any collection of books to pay for the exorbitant fees you lawyers charge. Is there any reason to think these might be anything special? What did she say when she called you?"

"She didn't call, her attorney did. Fine time to be calling, her preliminary hearing's set for tomorrow."

She didn't have to elaborate. The most critical hours in any investigation are always the ones immediately after the crime's been committed. "Her attorney says she mentioned selling her husband's book collection," she said. "But she's afraid they aren't worth much."

"Trust her, they aren't. I can smell them from here, I don't even have to look. I can't tell you how many of these things I've gone out on. They never pan out."

"I'm sure you're right. Do this for me anyway."

I looked dubious. "Do I actually get to touch these books?"

"Take your surgical gloves along and maybe. You did keep some rubber gloves from your police days?"

"No, but they're cheap and easy to get."

"Kinda like the women you used to run with, before me."

"That's it, I'm outta here."

She touched my hand and squeezed gently. "Poor Cliff."

She took another bite of the Roadrunner. "This really isn't half-bad, is it?"

I shook my head and slugged some beer. "Oh, Erin, you've got to get out more. You're working too hard, your taste buds are dying from neglect. I'll volunteer for the restaurant detail. I promise I'll find us a place that'll thrill your innards."

"When you get back from Paradise."

I ate, putty in her hands, but at some point I had to ask the salient question. "So do you ever plan to tell me about this thing?"

She didn't want to, by now that was almost painfully clear. "Take your time," I said soothingly. "I've got nothing on my plate, we could sit here for days."

"The defendant's name . . ." She swallowed hard, as if the name alone could hurt. "Laura Marshall. Her name is Laura. She's accused of killing her husband. She wants me to defend her, but I've got two cases coming up back-to-back. Even if I took her on, which is far from certain anyway, I couldn't get out there till the middle of next month. That's it in a nutshell."

"I thought you said she had an attorney."

"He's her attorney of the moment. He sounds very competent, but he's never done a case like this."

She gave me a look that said That's it, Janeway, that's all there is.

"Well," I said cautiously, "can we break open that nutshell just a little?"

I waited and finally I gave her my stupid look. "What is it you want me to do, Erin? This isn't just an appraisal job. I get the feeling it's something else."

"Maybe you could talk to her while you're there. Take a look at her case."

"I could do that. I'm sure you don't want me to advise her. The last time I looked, my law degree was damned near nonexistent."

"Go down, talk to her, report back to me. You don't need a law degree for that. Just lots of attitude."

"That I can muster. In fact I'm getting some right now. So tell me more."

"I'd rather have you discover it as you go along."

A long ripe moment followed that declaration.

"She'll tell you the details," Erin said. "And by the way, I pay top rates."

"So now you're bribing me. Is this what we've come to?" I gave her a small headshake. "Something's going on here. This isn't just some yahoo case that dropped on your head. It's more than that."

She stonewalled me across the table.

"Isn't it?" I said.

"She was my best friend in college. In fact, we go back to childhood."

"And . . . ?"

"We haven't seen each other in years . . ."

"Because . . . ?"

"That's irrelevant."

"No, Counselor, what that is is bad-lawyer bafflegab. Tommyrot, bushwa, ca-ca, bunkum, and a cheap oil change. Not to mention piffle and baloney."

She stared.

"Old oil sludge," I said. "Remember those ads? Dirty sludge, gummy rings, sticky valves, blackie carbon. And a bad Roadrunner burrito."

She laughed. "Are you all through?"

"Hell no I'm not through. Help me out just a little here. Make at least some sorry stab at giving me a straight answer."

"Marshall was the first great love of my life. Is that straight enough for you?"

"Ah," I said, mildly crushed. My pain was slightly mitigated by the word first.

"He can't compare to you," she said. "Never could've, never would've, though I had no way of knowing that back then. Remember two years ago just after we met? I told you then I had known another guy long ago who collected books. I guess I've always been attracted to book people. I couldn't imagine I'd wind up with Tarzan of the Bookmen, swinging from one bookstore to another on vines attached to telephone poles."

"It was written in the stars."

"I'm not complaining. But that was then, this is

now. He was my first real love and she was my best friend. More than that. She was closer than a sister to me, we marched to the same heartbeat. I would have trusted either of them with my life. And they had an affair behind my back."

I said, "Ah," again and I squeezed her hand. "Jesus, why would anybody do that to you?"

She shrugged. "It was a long time ago."

"And people do things," I ventured.

"Not things like that."

"So how'd you find out about it? He break down and tell you?"

"She did. Her conscience was killing her and she had to get it right between us."

I took another guess. "So when did you find it in your heart to forgive her?"

"You're assuming facts not in evidence, Janeway." She looked at me across the table, and out of that superserious moment came the steely voice I knew so well. "I'll never forgive her."

"Then why . . ."

"Why doesn't matter. Look, will you do this for me or not?"

I really didn't need to think about it. The answer would have been the same with or without the particulars. All I needed to know was that it was important to her.

"Sure," I said.